AF469491

Uncle Tom's Cabin

Life among the Lowly

By
Harriet Beecher Stowe

Volume 1 of 2

EasyRead

RHYW
ReadHowYouWant Classics Library

Published in 2008 in the US and world markets by ReadHowYouWant.

Copyright © 2007

The text in this edition has been formatted and typeset to make reading easier and more enjoyable for ALL kinds of readers. In addition the text has been formatted to the specifications indicated on the title page. The formatting of this edition is the copyright of Objective Systems Pty Ltd.

Set in 11 pt. Verdana

ReadHowYouWant partners with publishers to provide books for ALL Kinds of Readers. For more information about the Becoming A RHYW Registered Reader and to find more titles in your preferred format visit:
www.readhowyouwant.com

Read How You Want
YOUR CUSTOMIZED BOOK SOURCE

ReadHowYouWant provides access to great literature for all readers. We are committed to bringing you the largest library of classic literature and to making reading as effortless as possible.

We offer high-quality editions of the complete works of all the major literary authors, plus critical books about each author's life and works. Various editions of many titles are available, and for texts not written in English, we are often able to offer a choice of translations.

Our goal is to make reading easier, more enjoyable, and accessible to all readers. And for readers who need alternate format books, we provide the same selection in DAISY, MP3, eBook, and Braille.

ReadHowYouWant also allows readers to customize the books they choose — see ReadHowYouWant.com/customize

For more information please visit ReadHowYouWant.com/format

Other books by Harriet Beecher Stowe

UNCLE TOM'S CABIN

UNCLE TOM'S CABIN

UNCLE TOM'S CABIN

UNCLE TOM'S CABIN

UNCLE TOM'S CABIN

TABLE OF CONTENTS

Chapter 1

In Which the Reader Is Introduced to a Man of Humanity

Late in the afternoon of a chilly day in February, two gentlemen were sitting alone over their wine, in a well-furnished dining parlor, in the town of P–, in Kentucky. There were no servants present, and the gentlemen, with chairs closely approaching, seemed to be discussing some subject with great earnestness.

For convenience sake, we have said, hitherto, two *gentlemen.* One of the parties, however, when critically examined, did not seem, strictly speaking, to come under the species. He was a short, thick-set man, with coarse, commonplace features, and that swaggering air of pretension which marks a low man who is trying to elbow his way upward in the world. He was much over-dressed, in a gaudy vest of many colors, a blue neckerchief, bedropped gayly with yellow spots, and arranged with a flaunting tie, quite in keeping with the general air of the man. His hands, large and coarse, were plentifully bedecked with rings; and he wore a heavy gold watch-chain, with a bundle of seals of portentous size, and a great variety of colors, attached to it, – which, in the ardor of conversation, he was in the habit of flourishing and jingling with evident satisfaction. His conversation was in free and easy defiance of Murray's Grammar,[1] and was garnished at convenient intervals with various profane expressions, which not even the desire to be graphic in our account shall induce us to transcribe.

His companion, Mr. Shelby, had the appearance of a gentleman; and the arrangements of the house, and the general air of the housekeeping, indicated easy, and even opulent circumstances. As we before stated, the two were in the midst of an earnest conversation.

"That is the way I should arrange the matter," said Mr. Shelby.

"I can't make trade that way - I positively can't, Mr. Shelby," said the other, holding up a glass of wine between his eye and the light.

"Why, the fact is, Haley, Tom is an uncommon fellow; he is certainly worth that sum anywhere, - steady, honest, capable, manages my whole farm like a clock."

"You mean honest, as niggers go," said Haley, helping himself to a glass of brandy.

"No; I mean, really, Tom is a good, steady, sensible, pious fellow. He got religion at a camp-meeting, four years ago; and I believe he really *did* get it. I've trusted him, since then, with everything I have, - money, house, horses, - and let him come and go

---

1 English Grammar (1795), by Lindley Murray (1745-1826), the most authoritative American grammarian of his day.

round the country; and I always found him true and square in everything."

"Some folks don't believe there is pious niggers Shelby," said Haley, with a candid flourish of his hand, "but *I do.* I had a fellow, now, in this yer last lot I took to Orleans – 't was as good as a meetin, now, really, to hear that critter pray; and he was quite gentle and quiet like. He fetched me a good sum, too, for I bought him cheap of a man that was 'bliged to sell out; so I realized six hundred on him. Yes, I consider religion a valeyable thing in a nigger, when it's the genuine article, and no mistake."

"Well, Tom's got the real article, if ever a fellow had," rejoined the other. "Why, last fall, I let him go to Cincinnati alone, to do business for me, and bring home five hundred dollars. 'Tom,' says I to him, 'I trust you, because I think you're a Christian – I know you wouldn't cheat.' Tom comes back, sure enough; I knew he would. Some low fellows, they say, said to him – 'Tom, why don't you make tracks for Canada?' 'Ah, master trusted me, and I couldn't,' – they told me about it. I am sorry to part with Tom, I must say. You ought to let him cover the whole balance of the debt; and you would, Haley, if you had any conscience."

"Well, I've got just as much conscience as any man in business can afford to keep, – just a little, you know, to swear by, as 't were," said the trader, jocularly; "and, then, I'm ready to do anything in reason to 'blige friends; but this yer, you see, is a leetle too hard on a fellow – a leetle too hard." The trader sighed contemplatively, and poured out some more brandy.

"Well, then, Haley, how will you trade?" said Mr. Shelby, after an uneasy interval of silence.

"Well, haven't you a boy or gal that you could throw in with Tom?"

"Hum! – none that I could well spare; to tell the truth, it's only hard necessity makes me willing to sell at all. I don't like parting with any of my hands, that's a fact."

Here the door opened, and a small quadroon boy, between four and five years of age, entered the room. There was something in his appearance remarkably beautiful and engaging. His black hair, fine as floss silk, hung in glossy curls about his round, dimpled face, while a pair of large dark eyes, full of fire and softness, looked out from beneath the rich, long lashes, as he peered curiously into the apartment. A gay robe of scarlet and yellow plaid, carefully made and neatly fitted, set off to advantage the dark and rich style of his beauty; and a certain comic air of assurance, blended with bashfulness, showed that he had been not unused to being petted and noticed by his master.

"Hulloa, Jim Crow!" said Mr. Shelby, whistling, and snapping a bunch of raisins towards him, "pick that up, now!"

The child scampered, with all his little strength, after the prize, while his master laughed.

"Come here, Jim Crow," said he. The child came up, and the master patted the curly head, and chucked him under the chin.

"Now, Jim, show this gentleman how you can dance and sing." The boy commenced one of those wild, grotesque songs common among the negroes, in a rich, clear voice, accompanying his singing with many comic evolutions of the hands, feet, and whole body, all in perfect time to the music.

"Bravo!" said Haley, throwing him a quarter of an orange.

"Now, Jim, walk like old Uncle Cudjoe, when he has the rheumatism," said his master.

Instantly the flexible limbs of the child assumed the appearance of deformity and distortion, as, with his back humped up, and his master's stick in his hand, he hobbled about the room, his childish face drawn into a doleful pucker, and spitting from right to left, in imitation of an old man.

Both gentlemen laughed uproariously.

"Now, Jim," said his master, "show us how old Elder Robbins leads the psalm." The boy drew his chubby face down to a formidable length, and commenced toning a psalm tune through his nose, with imperturbable gravity.

"Hurrah! bravo! what a young 'un!" said Haley; "that chap's a case, I'll promise. Tell you what," said he, suddenly clapping his hand on Mr. Shelby's shoulder, "fling in that chap, and I'll settle the business – I will. Come, now, if that ain't doing the thing up about the rightest!"

At this moment, the door was pushed gently open, and a young quadroon woman, apparently about twenty-five, entered the room.

There needed only a glance from the child to her, to identify her as its mother. There was the same rich, full, dark eye, with its long lashes; the same ripples of silky black hair. The brown of her complexion gave way on the cheek to a perceptible flush, which deepened as she saw the gaze of the strange man fixed upon her in bold and undisguised admiration. Her dress was of the neatest possible fit, and set off to advantage her finely moulded shape; – a delicately formed hand and a trim foot and ankle were items of appearance that did not escape the quick eye of the trader, well used to run up at a glance the points of a fine female article.

"Well, Eliza?" said her master, as she stopped and looked hesitatingly at him.

"I was looking for Harry, please, sir;" and the boy bounded toward her, showing his spoils, which he had gathered in the skirt of his robe.

"Well, take him away then," said Mr. Shelby; and hastily she withdrew, carrying the child on her arm.

"By Jupiter," said the trader, turning to him in admiration, "there's an article, now! You might make your fortune on that ar gal in Orleans, any day. I've seen over a thousand, in my day, paid down for gals not a bit handsomer."

"I don't want to make my fortune on her," said Mr. Shelby, dryly; and, seeking to turn the conversation, he uncorked a bottle of fresh wine, and asked his companion's opinion of it.

"Capital, sir, – first chop!" said the trader; then turning, and slapping his hand familiarly on Shelby's shoulder, he added–

"Come, how will you trade about the gal? – what shall I say for her – what'll you take?"

"Mr. Haley, she is not to be sold," said Shelby. "My wife would not part with her for her weight in gold."

"Ay, ay! women always say such things, cause they ha'nt no sort of calculation. Just show 'em how many watches, feathers, and trinkets, one's weight in gold would buy, and that alters the case, *I* reckon."

"I tell you, Haley, this must not be spoken of; I say no, and I mean no," said Shelby, decidedly.

"Well, you'll let me have the boy, though," said the trader; "you must own I've come down pretty handsomely for him."

"What on earth can you want with the child?" said Shelby.

"Why, I've got a friend that's going into this yer branch of the business – wants to buy up handsome boys to raise for the market. Fancy articles entirely – sell for waiters, and so on, to rich 'uns, that can pay for handsome 'uns. It sets off one of yer great places – a real handsome boy to open door, wait, and tend. They fetch a good sum; and this little devil is such a comical, musical concern, he's just the article!"

"I would rather not sell him," said Mr. Shelby, thoughtfully; "the fact is, sir, I'm a humane man, and I hate to take the boy from his mother, sir."

"O, you do? – La! yes – something of that ar natur. I understand, perfectly. It is *mighty* onpleasant getting on with women, sometimes, I al'ays hates these yer screechin,' screamin' times. They are mighty onpleasant; but, as I manages business, I generally avoids 'em, sir. Now, what if you get the girl off for a day, or a week, or so; then the thing's done quietly, – all over before she comes home. Your wife might get her some ear-rings, or a new gown, or some such truck, to make up with her."

"I'm afraid not."

"Lor bless ye, yes! These critters ain't like white folks, you know; they gets over things, only manage right. Now, they say," said Haley, assuming a candid and confidential air, "that this kind o' trade is hardening to the feelings; but I never found it so. Fact is, I never could do things up the way some fellers manage the business. I've seen 'em as would pull a woman's child out of her arms, and set him up to sell, and she screechin' like mad all the time; – very bad policy – damages the article – makes 'em quite unfit for service sometimes. I knew a real handsome gal once, in Orleans, as was entirely ruined by this sort o' handling.

The fellow that was trading for her didn't want her baby; and she was one of your real high sort, when her blood was up. I tell you, she squeezed up her child in her arms, and talked, and went on real awful. It kinder makes my blood run cold to think of 't; and when they carried off the child, and locked her up, she jest went ravin' mad, and died in a week. Clear waste, sir, of a thousand dollars, just for want of management, – there's where 't is. It's always best to do the humane thing, sir; that's been *my* experience." And the trader leaned back in his chair, and folded his arm, with an air of virtuous decision, apparently considering himself a second Wilberforce.

The subject appeared to interest the gentleman deeply; for while Mr. Shelby was thoughtfully peeling an orange, Haley broke out afresh, with becoming diffidence, but as if actually driven by the force of truth to say a few words more.

"It don't look well, now, for a feller to be praisin' himself; but I say it jest because it's the truth. I believe I'm reckoned to bring in about the finest droves of niggers that is brought in, – at least, I've been told so; if I have once, I reckon I have a hundred times, – all in good case, – fat and likely, and I lose as few as any man in the business. And I lays it all to my management, sir; and humanity, sir, I may say, is the great pillar of *my* management."

Mr. Shelby did not know what to say, and so he said, "Indeed!"

"Now, I've been laughed at for my notions, sir, and I've been talked to. They an't pop'lar, and they an't common; but I stuck to 'em, sir; I've stuck to 'em, and realized well on 'em; yes, sir, they have paid their passage, I may say," and the trader laughed at his joke.

There was something so piquant and original in these elucidations of humanity, that Mr. Shelby could not help laughing in company. Perhaps you laugh too, dear reader; but you know humanity comes out in a variety of strange forms now-a-days, and there is no end to the odd things that humane people will say and do.

Mr. Shelby's laugh encouraged the trader to proceed.

"It's strange, now, but I never could beat this into people's heads. Now, there was Tom Loker, my old partner, down in Natchez; he was a clever fellow, Tom was, only the very devil with niggers, – on principle 't was, you see, for a better hearted feller never broke bread; 't was his *system*, sir. I used to talk to Tom. 'Why, Tom,' I used to say, 'when your gals takes on and cry, what's the use o' crackin on 'em over the head, and knockin' on 'em round? It's ridiculous,' says I, 'and don't do no sort o' good. Why, I don't see no harm in their cryin',' says I; 'it's natur,' says I, 'and if natur can't blow off one way, it will another. Besides, Tom,' says I, 'it jest spiles your gals; they get sickly, and down in the mouth; and sometimes they gets ugly, – particular yallow gals do, – and it's the devil and all gettin' on 'em broke in. Now,' says I, 'why can't you kinder coax 'em up, and speak 'em fair? Depend on it, Tom, a little humanity, thrown in along, goes a heap further than all your jawin' and crackin'; and it pays better,' says I, 'depend on 't.'

But Tom couldn't get the hang on 't; and he spiled so many for me, that I had to break off with him, though he was a good-hearted fellow, and as fair a business hand as is goin'."

"And do you find your ways of managing do the business better than Tom's?" said Mr. Shelby.

"Why, yes, sir, I may say so. You see, when I any ways can, I takes a leetle care about the onpleasant parts, like selling young uns and that, - get the gals out of the way - out of sight, out of mind, you know, - and when it's clean done, and can't be helped, they naturally gets used to it. 'Tan't, you know, as if it was white folks, that's brought up in the way of 'spectin' to keep their children and wives, and all that. Niggers, you know, that's fetched up properly, ha'n't no kind of 'spectations of no kind; so all these things comes easier."

"I'm afraid mine are not properly brought up, then," said Mr. Shelby.

"S'pose not; you Kentucky folks spile your niggers. You mean well by 'em, but 'tan't no real kindness, arter all. Now, a nigger, you see, what's got to be hacked and tumbled round the world, and sold to Tom, and Dick, and the Lord knows who, 'tan't no kindness to be givin' on him notions and expectations, and bringin' on him up too well, for the rough and tumble comes all the harder on him arter. Now, I venture to say, your niggers would be quite chop-fallen in a place where some of your plantation niggers would be singing and whooping like all possessed. Every man, you know, Mr. Shelby, naturally thinks well of his own ways; and I think I treat niggers just about as well as it's ever worth while to treat 'em."

"It's a happy thing to be satisfied," said Mr. Shelby, with a slight shrug, and some perceptible feelings of a disagreeable nature.

"Well," said Haley, after they had both silently picked their nuts for a season, "what do you say?"

"I'll think the matter over, and talk with my wife," said Mr. Shelby. "Meantime, Haley, if you want the matter carried on in the quiet way you speak of, you'd best not let your business in this neighborhood be known. It will get out among my boys, and it will not be a particularly quiet business getting away any of my fellows, if they know it, I'll promise you."

"O! certainly, by all means, mum! of course. But I'll tell you. I'm in a devil of a hurry, and shall want to know, as soon as possible, what I may depend on," said he, rising and putting on his overcoat.

"Well, call up this evening, between six and seven, and you shall have my answer," said Mr. Shelby, and the trader bowed himself out of the apartment.

"I'd like to have been able to kick the fellow down the steps," said he to himself, as he saw the door fairly closed, "with his impudent assurance; but he knows how much he has me at advantage. If anybody had ever said to me that I should sell Tom down south to one of those rascally traders, I should have said, 'Is thy servant a dog, that he should do this thing?' And now it must come, for aught I see. And Eliza's child, too! I know that I shall have some fuss with wife about that; and, for that matter, about Tom, too. So much for being in debt, - heigho! The fellow sees his advantage, and means to push it."

Perhaps the mildest form of the system of slavery is to be seen in the State of Kentucky. The general prevalence of agricultural pursuits of a quiet and gradual nature, not requiring those periodic seasons of hurry and pressure that are called for in the business of more southern districts, makes the task of the negro a more healthful and reasonable one; while the master, content with a more gradual style of acquisition, has not those temptations to hardheartedness which always overcome frail human nature when the prospect of sudden and rapid gain is weighed in the balance, with no heavier counterpoise than the interests of the helpless and unprotected.

Whoever visits some estates there, and witnesses the good-humored indulgence of some masters and mistresses, and the affectionate loyalty of some slaves, might be tempted to dream the oft-fabled poetic legend of a patriarchal institution, and all that; but over and above the scene there broods a portentous shadow - the shadow of *law*. So long as the law considers all these human beings, with beating hearts and living affections, only as so many *things* belonging to a master, - so long as the failure, or misfortune, or imprudence, or death of the kindest owner, may cause them any day to exchange a life of kind protection and indulgence for one of hopeless misery and toil, - so long it is impossible to make anything beautiful or desirable in the best regulated administration of slavery.

Mr. Shelby was a fair average kind of man, good-natured and kindly, and disposed to easy indulgence of those around him, and there had never been a lack of anything which might contribute to the physical comfort of the negroes on his estate. He had, however, speculated largely and quite loosely; had involved himself deeply, and his notes to a large amount had come into the hands of Haley; and this small piece of information is the key to the preceding conversation.

Now, it had so happened that, in approaching the door, Eliza had caught enough of the conversation to know that a trader was making offers to her master for somebody.

She would gladly have stopped at the door to listen, as she came out; but her mistress just then calling, she was obliged to hasten away.

Still she thought she heard the trader make an offer for her boy; – could she be mistaken? Her heart swelled and throbbed, and she involuntarily strained him so tight that the little fellow looked up into her face in astonishment.

"Eliza, girl, what ails you today?" said her mistress, when Eliza had upset the wash-pitcher, knocked down the workstand, and finally was abstractedly offering her mistress a long nightgown in place of the silk dress she had ordered her to bring from the wardrobe.

Eliza started. "O, missis!" she said, raising her eyes; then, bursting into tears, she sat down in a chair, and began sobbing.

"Why, Eliza child, what ails you?" said her mistress.

"O! missis, missis," said Eliza, "there's been a trader talking with master in the parlor! I heard him."

"Well, silly child, suppose there has."

"O, missis, *do* you suppose mas'r would sell my Harry?" And the poor creature threw herself into a chair, and sobbed convulsively.

"Sell him! No, you foolish girl! You know your master never deals with those southern traders, and never means to sell any of his servants, as long as they behave well. Why, you silly child, who do you think would want to buy your Harry? Do you think all the world are set on him as you are, you goosie? Come, cheer up, and hook my dress. There now, put my back hair up in that pretty braid you learnt the other day, and don't go listening at doors any more."

"Well, but, missis, *you* never would give your consent – to – to–"

"Nonsense, child! to be sure, I shouldn't. What do you talk so for? I would as soon have one of my own children sold. But really, Eliza, you are getting altogether too proud of that little fellow. A man can't put his nose into the door, but you think he must be coming to buy him."

Reassured by her mistress' confident tone, Eliza proceeded nimbly and adroitly with her toilet, laughing at her own fears, as she proceeded.

Mrs. Shelby was a woman of high class, both intellectually and morally. To that natural magnanimity and generosity of mind which one often marks as characteristic of the women of Kentucky, she added high moral and religious sensibility and principle, carried out with great energy and ability into practical results. Her husband, who made no professions to any particular religious character, nevertheless reverenced and respected the consistency of hers, and stood, perhaps, a little in awe of her opinion. Certain it was that he gave her unlimited scope in all her benevolent efforts for the comfort, instruction, and improvement of her servants, though he never took any decided part in them himself. In fact, if not exactly a believer in the doctrine of the efficiency of the extra good works of saints, he really seemed somehow or other to fancy that his wife had piety and benevolence enough for two – to indulge a shadowy expectation of getting into heaven through her superabundance of qualities to which he made no particular pretension.

The heaviest load on his mind, after his conversation with the trader, lay in the foreseen necessity of breaking to his wife the arrangement contemplated, – meeting the importunities and opposition which he knew he should have reason to encounter.

Mrs. Shelby, being entirely ignorant of her husband's embarrassments, and knowing only the general kindliness of his temper, had been quite sincere in the entire incredulity with which she had met Eliza's suspicions. In fact, she dismissed the matter from her mind, without a second thought; and being occupied in preparations for an evening visit, it passed out of her thoughts entirely.

Chapter 2

The Mother

Eliza had been brought up by her mistress, from girlhood, as a petted and indulged favorite.

The traveller in the south must often have remarked that peculiar air of refinement, that softness of voice and manner, which seems in many cases to be a particular gift to the quadroon and mulatto women. These natural graces in the quadroon are often united with beauty of the most dazzling kind, and in almost every case with a personal appearance prepossessing and agreeable. Eliza, such as we have described her, is not a fancy sketch, but taken from remembrance, as we saw her, years ago, in Kentucky. Safe under the protecting care of her mistress, Eliza had reached maturity without those temptations which make beauty so fatal an inheritance to a slave. She had been married to a bright and talented young mulatto man, who was a slave on a neighboring estate, and bore the name of George Harris.

This young man had been hired out by his master to work in a bagging factory, where his adroitness and ingenuity caused him to be considered the first hand in the place. He had invented a machine for the cleaning of the hemp, which, considering the education and circumstances of the inventor, displayed quite as much mechanical genius as Whitney's cotton-gin.[2]

He was possessed of a handsome person and pleasing manners, and was a general favorite in the factory. Nevertheless, as this young man was in the eye of the law not a man, but a thing, all these superior qualifications were subject to the control of a vulgar, narrow-minded, tyrannical master. This same gentleman, having heard of the fame of George's invention, took a ride over to the factory, to see what this intelligent chattel had been about. He was received with great enthusiasm by the employer, who congratulated him on possessing so valuable a slave.

He was waited upon over the factory, shown the machinery by George, who, in high spirits, talked so fluently, held himself so erect, looked so handsome and manly, that his master began to feel an uneasy consciousness of inferiority. What business had his slave to be marching round the country, inventing machines, and holding up his head among gentlemen? He'd soon put a stop to it. He'd take him back, and put him to hoeing and digging, and "see if he'd step about so smart." Accordingly, the manufacturer and all hands concerned were astounded when he suddenly demanded George's wages, and announced his intention of taking him home.

"But, Mr. Harris," remonstrated the manufacturer, "isn't this rather sudden?"

---

2 A machine of this description was really the invention of a young colored man in Kentucky.

"What if it is? – isn't the man *mine*?"

"We would be willing, sir, to increase the rate of compensation."

"No object at all, sir. I don't need to hire any of my hands out, unless I've a mind to."

"But, sir, he seems peculiarly adapted to this business."

"Dare say he may be; never was much adapted to anything that I set him about, I'll be bound."

"But only think of his inventing this machine," interposed one of the workmen, rather unluckily.

"O yes! a machine for saving work, is it? He'd invent that, I'll be bound; let a nigger alone for that, any time. They are all labor-saving machines themselves, every one of 'em. No, he shall tramp!"

George had stood like one transfixed, at hearing his doom thus suddenly pronounced by a power that he knew was irresistible. He folded his arms, tightly pressed in his lips, but a whole volcano of bitter feelings burned in his bosom, and sent streams of fire through his veins. He breathed short, and his large dark eyes flashed like live coals; and he might have broken out into some dangerous ebullition, had not the kindly manufacturer touched him on the arm, and said, in a low tone,

"Give way, George; go with him for the present. We'll try to help you, yet."

The tyrant observed the whisper, and conjectured its import, though he could not hear what was said; and he inwardly strengthened himself in his determination to keep the power he possessed over his victim.

George was taken home, and put to the meanest drudgery of the farm. He had been able to repress every disrespectful word; but the flashing eye, the gloomy and troubled brow, were part of a natural language that could not be repressed, - indubitable signs, which showed too plainly that the man could not become a thing.

It was during the happy period of his employment in the factory that George had seen and married his wife. During that period, - being much trusted and favored by his employer, - he had free liberty to come and go at discretion. The marriage was highly approved of by Mrs. Shelby, who, with a little womanly complacency in match-making, felt pleased to unite her handsome favorite with one of her own class who seemed in every way suited to her; and so they were married in her mistress' great parlor, and her mistress herself adorned the bride's beautiful hair with orange-blossoms, and threw over it the bridal veil, which certainly could scarce have rested on a fairer head; and there was no lack of white gloves, and cake and wine, - of admiring guests to praise the bride's beauty, and her mistress' indulgence and liberality. For a year or two Eliza saw her husband frequently, and there was nothing to interrupt their happiness, except the loss of two infant children, to whom she was passionately attached, and whom she mourned with a grief so intense as to call for gentle remonstrance from her mistress, who sought, with maternal anxiety, to direct her naturally passionate feelings within the bounds of reason and religion.

After the birth of little Harry, however, she had gradually become tranquillized and settled; and every bleeding tie and throbbing nerve, once more entwined with that little life, seemed to become sound and healthful, and Eliza was a happy woman up to the time that her husband was rudely torn from his kind employer, and brought under the iron sway of his legal owner.

The manufacturer, true to his word, visited Mr. Harris a week or two after George had been taken away, when, as he hoped, the heat of the occasion had passed away, and tried every possible inducement to lead him to restore him to his former employment.

"You needn't trouble yourself to talk any longer," said he, doggedly; "I know my own business, sir."

"I did not presume to interfere with it, sir. I only thought that you might think it for your interest to let your man to us on the terms proposed."

"O, I understand the matter well enough. I saw your winking and whispering, the day I took him out of the factory; but you don't come it over me that way. It's a free country, sir; the man's *mine*, and I do what I please with him, – that's it!"

And so fell George's last hope; – nothing before him but a life of toil and drudgery, rendered more bitter by every little smarting vexation and indignity which tyrannical ingenuity could devise.

A very humane jurist once said, The worst use you can put a man to is to hang him. No; there is another use that a man can be put to that is WORSE!

Chapter 3

The Husband and Father

Mrs. Shelby had gone on her visit, and Eliza stood in the verandah, rather dejectedly looking after the retreating carriage, when a hand was laid on her shoulder. She turned, and a bright smile lighted up her fine eyes.

"George, is it you? How you frightened me! Well; I am so glad you 's come! Missis is gone to spend the afternoon; so come into my little room, and we'll have the time all to ourselves."

Saying this, she drew him into a neat little apartment opening on the verandah, where she generally sat at her sewing, within call of her mistress.

"How glad I am! – why don't you smile? – and look at Harry – how he grows." The boy stood shyly regarding his father through his curls, holding close to the skirts of his mother's dress. "Isn't he beautiful?" said Eliza, lifting his long curls and kissing him.

"I wish he'd never been born!" said George, bitterly. "I wish I'd never been born myself!"

Surprised and frightened, Eliza sat down, leaned her head on her husband's shoulder, and burst into tears.

"There now, Eliza, it's too bad for me to make you feel so, poor girl!" said he, fondly; "it's too bad: O, how I wish you never had seen me – you might have been happy!"

"George! George! how can you talk so? What dreadful thing has happened, or is going to happen? I'm sure we've been very happy, till lately."

"So we have, dear," said George. Then drawing his child on his knee, he gazed intently on his glorious dark eyes, and passed his hands through his long curls.

"Just like you, Eliza; and you are the handsomest woman I ever saw, and the best one I ever wish to see; but, oh, I wish I'd never seen you, nor you me!"

"O, George, how can you!"

"Yes, Eliza, it's all misery, misery, misery! My life is bitter as wormwood; the very life is burning out of me. I'm a poor, miserable, forlorn drudge; I shall only drag you down with me, that's all. What's the use of our trying to do anything, trying to know anything, trying to be anything? What's the use of living? I wish I was dead!"

"O, now, dear George, that is really wicked! I know how you feel about losing your place in the factory, and you have a hard master; but pray be patient, and perhaps something–"

"Patient!" said he, interrupting her; "haven't I been patient? Did I say a word when he came and took me away, for no earthly reason, from the place where everybody was kind to me? I'd paid him truly every cent of my earnings, – and they all say I worked well."

"Well, it *is* dreadful," said Eliza; "but, after all, he is your master, you know."

"My master! and who made him my master? That's what I think of – what right has he to me? I'm a man as much as he is. I'm a better man than he is. I know more about business than he does; I am a better manager than he is; I can read better than he can; I can write a better hand, – and I've learned it all myself, and no thanks to him, – I've learned it in spite of him; and now what right has he to make a dray-horse of me? – to take me from things I can do, and do better than he can, and put me to work that any horse can do? He tries to do it; he says he'll bring me down and humble me, and he puts me to just the hardest, meanest and dirtiest work, on purpose!"

"O, George! George! you frighten me! Why, I never heard you talk so; I'm afraid you'll do something dreadful. I don't wonder at your feelings, at all; but oh, do be careful – do, do – for my sake – for Harry's!"

"I have been careful, and I have been patient, but it's growing worse and worse; flesh and blood can't bear it any longer; – every chance he can get to insult and torment me, he takes. I thought I could do my work well, and keep on quiet, and have some time to read and learn out of work hours; but the more he see I can do, the more he loads on. He says that though I don't say anything, he sees I've got the devil in me, and he means to bring it out; and one of these days it will come out in a way that he won't like, or I'm mistaken!"

"O dear! what shall we do?" said Eliza, mournfully.

"It was only yesterday," said George, "as I was busy loading stones into a cart, that young Mas'r Tom stood there, slashing his whip so near the horse that the creature was frightened. I asked him to stop, as pleasant as I could, – he just kept right on. I begged him again, and then he turned on me, and began striking me. I held his hand, and then he screamed and kicked and ran to his father, and told him that I was fighting him. He came in a rage, and said he'd teach me who was my master; and he tied me to a tree, and cut switches for young master, and told him that he might whip me till he was tired; – and he did do it! If I don't make him remember it, some time!" and the brow of the young man grew dark, and his eyes burned with an expression that made his young wife tremble. "Who made this man my master? That's what I want to know!" he said.

"Well," said Eliza, mournfully, "I always thought that I must obey my master and mistress, or I couldn't be a Christian."

"There is some sense in it, in your case; they have brought you up like a child, fed you, clothed you, indulged you, and taught you, so that you have a good education; that is some reason why they should claim you. But I have been kicked and cuffed and sworn at, and at the best only let alone; and what do I owe? I've paid for all my keeping a hundred times over. I *won't* bear it. No, I *won't!*" he said, clenching his hand with a fierce frown.

Eliza trembled, and was silent. She had never seen her husband in this mood before; and her gentle system of ethics seemed to bend like a reed in the surges of such passions.

"You know poor little Carlo, that you gave me," added George; "the creature has been about all the comfort that I've had. He has slept with me nights, and followed me around days, and kind o' looked at me as if he understood how I felt. Well, the other day I was just feeding him with a few old scraps I picked up by the kitchen door, and Mas'r came along, and said I was feeding him up at his expense, and that he couldn't afford to have every nigger keeping his dog, and ordered me to tie a stone to his neck and throw him in the pond."

"O, George, you didn't do it!"

"Do it? not I! – but he did. Mas'r and Tom pelted the poor drowning creature with stones. Poor thing! he looked at me so mournful, as if he wondered why I didn't save him. I had to take a flogging because I wouldn't do it myself. I don't care. Mas'r will find out that I'm one that whipping won't tame. My day will come yet, if he don't look out."

"What are you going to do? O, George, don't do anything wicked; if you only trust in God, and try to do right, he'll deliver you."

"I an't a Christian like you, Eliza; my heart's full of bitterness; I can't trust in God. Why does he let things be so?"

"O, George, we must have faith. Mistress says that when all things go wrong to us, we must believe that God is doing the very best."

"That's easy to say for people that are sitting on their sofas and riding in their carriages; but let 'em be where I am, I guess it would come some harder. I wish I could be good; but my heart burns, and can't be reconciled, anyhow. You couldn't in my place, – you can't now, if I tell you all I've got to say. You don't know the whole yet."

"What can be coming now?"

"Well, lately Mas'r has been saying that he was a fool to let me marry off the place; that he hates Mr. Shelby and all his tribe, because they are proud, and hold their heads up above him, and that I've got proud notions from you; and he says he won't let me come here any more, and that I shall take a wife and settle down on his place. At first he only scolded and grumbled these things; but yesterday he told me that I should take Mina for a wife, and settle down in a cabin with her, or he would sell me down river."

"Why – but you were married to *me*, by the minister, as much as if you'd been a white man!" said Eliza, simply.

"Don't you know a slave can't be married? There is no law in this country for that; I can't hold you for my wife, if he chooses to part us. That's why I wish I'd never seen you, – why I wish I'd never been born; it would have been better for us both, – it would have been better for this poor child if he had never been born. All this may happen to him yet!"

"O, but master is so kind!"

"Yes, but who knows? – he may die – and then he may be sold to nobody knows who. What pleasure is it that he is handsome, and smart, and bright? I tell you, Eliza, that a sword will pierce through your soul for every good and pleasant thing your child is or has; it will make him worth too much for you to keep."

The words smote heavily on Eliza's heart; the vision of the trader came before her eyes, and, as if some one had struck her a deadly blow, she turned pale and gasped for breath. She looked nervously out on the verandah, where the boy, tired of the grave conversation, had retired, and where he was riding triumphantly up and down on Mr. Shelby's walking-stick. She would have spoken to tell her husband her fears, but checked herself.

"No, no, – he has enough to bear, poor fellow!" she thought. "No, I won't tell him; besides, it an't true; Missis never deceives us."

"So, Eliza, my girl," said the husband, mournfully, "bear up, now; and good-by, for I'm going."

"Going, George! Going where?"

"To Canada," said he, straightening himself up; "and when I'm there, I'll buy you; that's all the hope that's left us. You have a kind master, that won't refuse to sell you. I'll buy you and the boy; - God helping me, I will!"

"O, dreadful! if you should be taken?"

"I won't be taken, Eliza; I'll *die* first! I'll be free, or I'll die!"

"You won't kill yourself!"

"No need of that. They will kill me, fast enough; they never will get me down the river alive!"

"O, George, for my sake, do be careful! Don't do anything wicked; don't lay hands on yourself, or anybody else! You are tempted too much - too much; but don't - go you must - but go carefully, prudently; pray God to help you."

"Well, then, Eliza, hear my plan. Mas'r took it into his head to send me right by here, with a note to Mr. Symmes, that lives a mile past. I believe he expected I should come here to tell you what I have. It would please him, if he thought it would aggravate 'Shelby's folks,' as he calls 'em. I'm going home quite resigned, you understand, as if all was over. I've got some preparations made, - and there are those that will help me; and, in the course of a week or so, I shall be among the missing, some day. Pray for me, Eliza; perhaps the good Lord will hear *you*."

"O, pray yourself, George, and go trusting in him; then you won't do anything wicked."

"Well, now, *good-by*," said George, holding Eliza's hands, and gazing into her eyes, without moving. They stood silent; then there were last words, and sobs, and bitter weeping, - such parting as those may make whose hope to meet again is as the spider's web, - and the husband and wife were parted.

Chapter 4

An Evening in Uncle Tom's Cabin

The cabin of Uncle Tom was a small log building, close adjoining to "the house," as the negro *par excellence* designates his master's dwelling. In front it had a neat garden-patch, where, every summer, strawberries, raspberries, and a variety of fruits and vegetables, flourished under careful tending. The whole front of it was covered by a large scarlet bignonia and a native multiflora rose, which, entwisting and interlacing, left scarce a vestige of the rough logs to be seen. Here, also, in summer, various brilliant annuals, such as marigolds, petunias, four-o'clocks, found an indulgent corner in which to unfold their splendors, and were the delight and pride of Aunt Chloe's heart.

Let us enter the dwelling. The evening meal at the house is over, and Aunt Chloe, who presided over its preparation as head cook, has left to inferior officers in the kitchen the business of clearing away and washing dishes, and come out into her own snug territories, to "get her ole man's supper"; therefore, doubt not that it is her you see by the fire, presiding with anxious interest over certain frizzling items in a stew-pan, and anon with grave consideration lifting the cover of a bake-kettle, from whence steam forth indubitable intimations of "something good." A round, black, shining face is hers, so glossy as to suggest the idea that she might have been washed over with white of eggs, like one of her own tea rusks. Her whole plump countenance beams with satisfaction and contentment from under her well-starched checked turban, bearing on it, however, if we must confess it, a little of that tinge of self-consciousness which becomes the first cook of the neighborhood, as Aunt Chloe was universally held and acknowledged to be.

A cook she certainly was, in the very bone and centre of her soul. Not a chicken or turkey or duck in the barn-yard but looked grave when they saw her approaching, and seemed evidently to be reflecting on their latter end; and certain it was that she was always meditating on trussing, stuffing and roasting, to a degree that was calculated to inspire terror in any reflecting fowl living. Her corn-cake, in all its varieties of hoe-cake, dodgers, muffins, and other species too numerous to mention, was a sublime mystery to all less practised compounders; and she would shake her fat sides with honest pride and merriment, as she would narrate the fruitless efforts that one and another of her compeers had made to attain to her elevation.

The arrival of company at the house, the arranging of dinners and suppers "in style," awoke all the energies of her soul; and no sight was more welcome to her than a pile of travelling trunks launched on the verandah, for then she foresaw fresh efforts and fresh triumphs.

Just at present, however, Aunt Chloe is looking into the bake-pan; in which congenial operation we shall leave her till we finish our picture of the cottage.

In one corner of it stood a bed, covered neatly with a snowy spread; and by the side of it was a piece of carpeting, of some considerable size. On this piece of carpeting Aunt Chloe took her stand, as being decidedly in the upper walks of life; and it and the bed by which it lay, and the whole corner, in fact, were treated with distinguished consideration, and made, so far as possible, sacred from the marauding inroads and desecrations of little folks. In fact, that corner was the *drawing-room* of the establishment. In the other corner was a bed of much humbler pretensions, and evidently designed for *use*. The wall over the fireplace was adorned with some very brilliant scriptural prints, and a portrait of General Washington, drawn and colored in a manner which would certainly have astonished that hero, if ever he happened to meet with its like.

On a rough bench in the corner, a couple of woolly-headed boys, with glistening black eyes and fat shining cheeks, were busy in superintending the first walking operations of the baby, which, as is usually the case, consisted in getting up on its feet, balancing a moment, and then tumbling down, - each successive failure being violently cheered, as something decidedly clever.

A table, somewhat rheumatic in its limbs, was drawn out in front of the fire, and covered with a cloth, displaying cups and saucers of a decidedly brilliant pattern, with other symptoms of an approaching meal. At this table was seated Uncle Tom, Mr. Shelby's best hand, who, as he is to be the hero of our story, we must daguerreotype for our readers. He was a large, broad-chested, powerfully-made man, of a full glossy black, and a face whose truly African features were characterized by an expression of grave and steady good sense, united with much kindliness and benevolence. There was something about his whole air self-respecting and dignified, yet united with a confiding and humble simplicity.

He was very busily intent at this moment on a slate lying before him, on which he was carefully and slowly endeavoring to accomplish a copy of some letters, in which operation he was overlooked by young Mas'r George, a smart, bright boy of thirteen, who appeared fully to realize the dignity of his position as instructor.

"Not that way, Uncle Tom, – not that way," said he, briskly, as Uncle Tom laboriously brought up the tail of his *g* the wrong side out; "that makes a *q*, you see."

"La sakes, now, does it?" said Uncle Tom, looking with a respectful, admiring air, as his young teacher flourishingly scrawled *q*'s and *g*'s innumerable for his edification; and then, taking the pencil in his big, heavy fingers, he patiently recommenced.

"How easy white folks al'us does things!" said Aunt Chloe, pausing while she was greasing a griddle with a scrap of bacon on her fork, and regarding young Master George with pride. "The way he can write, now! and read, too! and then to come out here evenings and read his lessons to us, – it's mighty interestin'!"

"But, Aunt Chloe, I'm getting mighty hungry," said George. "Isn't that cake in the skillet almost done?"

"Mose done, Mas'r George," said Aunt Chloe, lifting the lid and peeping in, – "browning beautiful – a real lovely brown. Ah! let me alone for dat. Missis let Sally try to make some cake, t' other day, jes to *larn* her, she said. 'O, go way, Missis,' said I; 'it really hurts my feelin's, now, to see good vittles spilt dat ar way! Cake ris all to one side - no shape at all; no more than my shoe; go way!'"

And with this final expression of contempt for Sally's greenness, Aunt Chloe whipped the cover off the bake-kettle, and disclosed to view a neatly-baked pound-cake, of which no city confectioner need to have been ashamed. This being evidently the central point of the entertainment, Aunt Chloe began now to bustle about earnestly in the supper department.

"Here you, Mose and Pete! get out de way, you niggers! Get away, Mericky, honey, - mammy'll give her baby some fin, by and by. Now, Mas'r George, you jest take off dem books, and set down now with my old man, and I'll take up de sausages, and have de first griddle full of cakes on your plates in less dan no time."

"They wanted me to come to supper in the house," said George; "but I knew what was what too well for that, Aunt Chloe."

"So you did - so you did, honey," said Aunt Chloe, heaping the smoking batter-cakes on his plate; "you know'd your old aunty'd keep the best for you. O, let you alone for dat! Go way!" And, with that, aunty gave George a nudge with her finger, designed to be immensely facetious, and turned again to her griddle with great briskness.

"Now for the cake," said Mas'r George, when the activity of the griddle department had somewhat subsided; and, with that, the youngster flourished a large knife over the article in question.

"La bless you, Mas'r George!" said Aunt Chloe, with earnestness, catching his arm, "you wouldn't be for cuttin' it wid dat ar great heavy knife! Smash all down – spile all de pretty rise of it. Here, I've got a thin old knife, I keeps sharp a purpose. Dar now, see! comes apart light as a feather! Now eat away – you won't get anything to beat dat ar."

"Tom Lincon says," said George, speaking with his mouth full, "that their Jinny is a better cook than you."

"Dem Lincons an't much count, no way!" said Aunt Chloe, contemptuously; "I mean, set along side *our* folks. They 's 'spectable folks enough in a kinder plain way; but, as to gettin' up anything in style, they don't begin to have a notion on 't. Set Mas'r Lincon, now, alongside Mas'r Shelby! Good Lor! and Missis Lincon, – can she kinder sweep it into a room like my missis, – so kinder splendid, yer know! O, go way! don't tell me nothin' of dem Lincons!" – and Aunt Chloe tossed her head as one who hoped she did know something of the world.

"Well, though, I've heard you say," said George, "that Jinny was a pretty fair cook."

"So I did," said Aunt Chloe, – "I may say dat. Good, plain, common cookin', Jinny'll do; – make a good pone o' bread, – bile her taters *far*, – her corn cakes isn't extra, not extra now, Jinny's corn cakes isn't, but then they's far, – but, Lor, come to de higher branches, and what *can* she do? Why, she makes pies – sartin she does; but what kinder crust? Can she make your real flecky paste, as melts in your mouth, and lies all up like a puff? Now, I went over thar when Miss Mary was gwine to be married, and Jinny she jest showed me de weddin' pies. Jinny and I is good friends, ye know. I never said nothin'; but go 'long, Mas'r George! Why, I shouldn't sleep a wink for a week, if I had a batch of pies like dem ar. Why, dey wan't no 'count 't all."

"I suppose Jinny thought they were ever so nice," said George.

"Thought so! – didn't she? Thar she was, showing em, as innocent – ye see, it's jest here, Jinny *don't know*. Lor, the family an't nothing! She can't be spected to know! 'Ta'nt no fault o' hem. Ah, Mas'r George, you doesn't know half your privileges in yer family and bringin' up!" Here Aunt Chloe sighed, and rolled up her eyes with emotion.

"I'm sure, Aunt Chloe, I understand I my pie and pudding privileges," said George. "Ask Tom Lincon if I don't crow over him, every time I meet him."

Aunt Chloe sat back in her chair, and indulged in a hearty guffaw of laughter, at this witticism of young Mas'r's, laughing till the tears rolled down her black, shining cheeks, and varying the exercise with playfully slapping and poking Mas'r Georgey, and telling him to go way, and that he was a case – that he was fit to kill her, and that he sartin would kill her, one of these days; and, between each of these sanguinary predictions, going off into a laugh, each longer and stronger than the other, till George really began to think that he was a very dangerously witty fellow, and that it became him to be careful how he talked "as funny as he could."

"And so ye telled Tom, did ye? O, Lor! what young uns will be up ter! Ye crowed over Tom? O, Lor! Mas'r George, if ye wouldn't make a hornbug laugh!"

"Yes," said George, "I says to him, 'Tom, you ought to see some of Aunt Chloe's pies; they're the right sort,' says I."

"Pity, now, Tom couldn't," said Aunt Chloe, on whose benevolent heart the idea of Tom's benighted condition seemed to make a strong impression. "Ye oughter just ask him here to dinner, some o' these times, Mas'r George," she added; "it would look quite pretty of ye. Ye know, Mas'r George, ye oughtenter feel 'bove nobody, on 'count yer privileges, 'cause all our privileges is gi'n to us; we ought al'ays to 'member that," said Aunt Chloe, looking quite serious.

"Well, I mean to ask Tom here, some day next week," said George; "and you do your prettiest, Aunt Chloe, and we'll make him stare. Won't we make him eat so he won't get over it for a fortnight?"

"Yes, yes – sartin," said Aunt Chloe, delighted "you'll see. Lor! to think of some of our dinners! Yer mind dat ar great chicken pie I made when we guv de dinner to General Knox? I and Missis, we come pretty near quarrelling about dat ar crust. What does get into ladies sometimes, I don't know; but, sometimes, when a body has de heaviest kind o' 'sponsibility on 'em, as ye may say, and is all kinder *'seris'* and taken up, dey takes dat ar time to be hangin' round and kinder interferin'! Now, Missis, she wanted me to do dis way, and she wanted me to do dat way; and, finally, I got kinder sarcy, and, says I, 'Now, Missis, do jist look at dem beautiful white hands o' yourn with long fingers, and all a sparkling with rings, like my white lilies when de dew 's on 'em; and look at my great black stumpin hands. Now, don't ye think dat de Lord must have meant *me* to make de pie-crust, and you to stay in de parlor'? Dar! I was jist so sarcy, Mas'r George."

"And what did mother say?" said George.

"Say? – why, she kinder larfed in her eyes – dem great handsome eyes o' hern; and, says she, 'Well, Aunt Chloe, I think you are about in the right on 't,' says she; and she went off in de parlor. She oughter cracked me over de head for bein' so sarcy; but dar's whar 't is – I can't do nothin' with ladies in de kitchen!"

"Well, you made out well with that dinner, – I remember everybody said so," said George.

"Didn't I? And wan't I behind de dinin'-room door dat bery day? and didn't I see de General pass his plate three times for some more dat bery pie? – and, says he, 'You must have an uncommon cook, Mrs. Shelby.' Lor! I was fit to split myself.

"And de Gineral, he knows what cookin' is," said Aunt Chloe, drawing herself up with an air. "Bery nice man, de Gineral! He comes of one of de bery *fustest* families in Old Virginny! He knows what's what, now, as well as I do – de Gineral. Ye see, there's pints in all pies, Mas'r George; but tan't everybody knows what they is, or as orter be. But the Gineral, he knows; I knew by his 'marks he made. Yes, he knows what de *pints* is!"

By this time, Master George had arrived at that pass to which even a boy can come (under uncommon circumstances, when he really could not eat another morsel), and, therefore, he was at leisure to notice the pile of woolly heads and glistening eyes which were regarding their operations hungrily from the opposite corner.

"Here, you Mose, Pete," he said, breaking off liberal bits, and throwing it at them; "you want some, don't you? Come, Aunt Chloe, bake them some cakes."

And George and Tom moved to a comfortable seat in the chimney-corner, while Aunte Chloe, after baking a goodly pile of cakes, took her baby on her lap, and began alternately filling its mouth and her own, and distributing to Mose and Pete, who seemed rather to prefer eating theirs as they rolled about on the floor under the table, tickling each other, and occasionally pulling the baby's toes.

"O! go long, will ye?" said the mother, giving now and then a kick, in a kind of general way, under the table, when the movement became too obstreperous. "Can't ye be decent when white folks comes to see ye? Stop dat ar, now, will ye? Better mind yerselves, or I'll take ye down a button-hole lower, when Mas'r George is gone!"

What meaning was couched under this terrible threat, it is difficult to say; but certain it is that its awful indistinctness seemed to produce very little impression on the young sinners addressed.

"La, now!" said Uncle Tom, "they are so full of tickle all the while, they can't behave theirselves."

Here the boys emerged from under the table, and, with hands and faces well plastered with molasses, began a vigorous kissing of the baby.

"Get along wid ye!" said the mother, pushing away their woolly heads. "Ye'll all stick together, and never get clar, if ye do dat fashion. Go long to de spring and wash yerselves!" she said, seconding her exhortations by a slap, which resounded very formidably, but which seemed only to knock out so much more laugh from the young ones, as they tumbled precipitately over each other out of doors, where they fairly screamed with merriment.

"Did ye ever see such aggravating young uns?" said Aunt Chloe, rather complacently, as, producing an old towel, kept for such emergencies, she poured a little water out of the cracked tea-pot on it, and began rubbing off the molasses from the baby's face and hands; and, having polished her till she shone, she set her down in Tom's lap, while she busied herself in clearing away supper. The baby employed the intervals in pulling Tom's nose, scratching his face, and burying her fat hands in his woolly hair, which last operation seemed to afford her special content.

"Aint she a peart young un?" said Tom, holding her from him to take a full-length view; then, getting up, he set her on his broad shoulder, and began capering and dancing with her, while Mas'r George snapped at her with his pocket-handkerchief, and Mose and Pete, now returned again, roared after her like bears, till Aunt Chloe declared that they "fairly took her head off" with their noise. As, according to her own statement, this surgical operation was a matter of daily occurrence in the cabin, the declaration no whit abated the merriment, till every one had roared and tumbled and danced themselves down to a state of composure.

"Well, now, I hopes you're done," said Aunt Chloe, who had been busy in pulling out a rude box of a trundle-bed; "and now, you Mose and you Pete, get into thar; for we 's goin' to have the meetin'."

"O mother, we don't wanter. We wants to sit up to meetin', – meetin's is so curis. We likes 'em."

"La, Aunt Chloe, shove it under, and let 'em sit up," said Mas'r George, decisively, giving a push to the rude machine.

Aunt Chloe, having thus saved appearances, seemed highly delighted to push the thing under, saying, as she did so, "Well, mebbe 't will do 'em some good."

The house now resolved itself into a committee of the whole, to consider the accommodations and arrangements for the meeting.

"What we 's to do for cheers, now, *I* declar I don't know," said Aunt Chloe. As the meeting had been held at Uncle Tom's weekly, for an indefinite length of time, without any more "cheers," there seemed some encouragement to hope that a way would be discovered at present.

"Old Uncle Peter sung both de legs out of dat oldest cheer, last week," suggested Mose.

"You go long! I'll boun' you pulled 'em out; some o' your shines," said Aunt Chloe.

"Well, it'll stand, if it only keeps jam up agin de wall!" said Mose.

"Den Uncle Peter mus'n't sit in it, cause he al'ays hitches when he gets a singing. He hitched pretty nigh across de room, t' other night," said Pete.

"Good Lor! get him in it, then," said Mose, "and den he'd begin, 'Come saints – and sinners, hear me tell,' and den down he'd go," – and Mose imitated precisely the nasal tones of the old man, tumbling on the floor, to illustrate the supposed catastrophe.

"Come now, be decent, can't ye?" said Aunt Chloe; "an't yer shamed?"

Mas'r George, however, joined the offender in the laugh, and declared decidedly that Mose was a "buster." So the maternal admonition seemed rather to fail of effect.

"Well, ole man," said Aunt Chloe, "you'll have to tote in them ar bar'ls."

"Mother's bar'ls is like dat ar widder's, Mas'r George was reading 'bout, in de good book, – dey never fails," said Mose, aside to Peter.

"I'm sure one on 'em caved in last week," said Pete, "and let 'em all down in de middle of de singin'; dat ar was failin', warnt it?"

During this aside between Mose and Pete, two empty casks had been rolled into the cabin, and being secured from rolling, by stones on each side, boards were laid across them, which arrangement, together with the turning down of certain tubs and pails, and the disposing of the rickety chairs, at last completed the preparation.

"Mas'r George is such a beautiful reader, now, I know he'll stay to read for us," said Aunt Chloe; "'pears like 't will be so much more interestin'."

George very readily consented, for your boy is always ready for anything that makes him of importance.

The room was soon filled with a motley assemblage, from the old gray-headed patriarch of eighty, to the young girl and lad of fifteen. A little harmless gossip ensued on various themes, such as where old Aunt Sally got her new red headkerchief, and how "Missis was a going to give Lizzy that spotted muslin gown, when she'd got her new berage made up;" and how Mas'r Shelby was thinking of buying a new sorrel colt, that was going to prove an addition to the glories of the place. A few of the worshippers belonged to families hard by, who had got permission to attend, and who brought in various choice scraps of information, about the sayings and doings at the house and on the place, which circulated as freely as the same sort of small change does in higher circles.

After a while the singing commenced, to the evident delight of all present. Not even all the disadvantage of nasal intonation could prevent the effect of the naturally fine voices, in airs at once wild and spirited. The words were sometimes the well-known and common hymns sung in the churches about, and sometimes of a wilder, more indefinite character, picked up at camp-meetings.

The chorus of one of them, which ran as follows, was sung with great energy and unction:

> "Die on the field of battle,
> Die on the field of battle,
> Glory in my soul."

Another special favorite had oft repeated the words–

> "O, I'm going to glory, - won't you come along with me?
> Don't you see the angels beck'ning, and a calling me away?
> Don't you see the golden city and the everlasting day?"

There were others, which made incessant mention of "Jordan's banks," and "Canaan's fields," and the "New Jerusalem;" for the negro mind, impassioned and imaginative, always attaches itself to hymns and expressions of a vivid and pictorial nature; and, as they sung, some laughed, and some cried, and some clapped hands, or shook hands rejoicingly with each other, as if they had fairly gained the other side of the river.

Various exhortations, or relations of experience, followed, and intermingled with the singing. One old gray-headed woman, long past work, but much revered as a sort of chronicle of the past, rose, and leaning on her staff, said – "Well, chil'en! Well, I'm mighty glad to hear ye all and see ye all once more, 'cause I don't know when I'll be gone to glory; but I've done got ready, chil'en; 'pears like I'd got my little bundle all tied up, and my bonnet on, jest a waitin' for the stage to come along and take me home; sometimes, in the night, I think I hear the wheels a rattlin', and I'm lookin' out all the time; now, you jest be ready too, for I tell ye all, chil'en," she said striking her staff hard on the floor, "dat ar *glory* is a mighty thing! It's a mighty thing, chil'en, – you don'no nothing about it, – it's *wonderful*." And the old creature sat down, with streaming tears, as wholly overcome, while the whole circle struck up–

"O Canaan, bright Canaan
I'm bound for the land of Canaan."

Mas'r George, by request, read the last chapters of Revelation, often interrupted by such exclamations as "The *sakes* now!" "Only hear that!" "Jest think on 't!" "Is all that a comin' sure enough?"

George, who was a bright boy, and well trained in religious things by his mother, finding himself an object of general admiration, threw in expositions of his own, from time to time, with a commendable seriousness and gravity, for which he was admired by the young and blessed by the old; and it was agreed, on all hands, that "a minister couldn't lay it off better than he did; that 't was reely 'mazin'!"

Uncle Tom was a sort of patriarch in religious matters, in the neighborhood. Having, naturally, an organization in which the *morale* was strongly predominant, together with a greater breadth and cultivation of mind than obtained among his companions, he was looked up to with great respect, as a sort of minister among them; and the simple, hearty, sincere style of his exhortations might have edified even better educated persons. But it was in prayer that he especially excelled. Nothing could exceed the touching simplicity, the childlike earnestness, of his prayer, enriched with the language of Scripture, which seemed so entirely to have wrought itself into his being, as to have become a part of himself, and to drop from his lips unconsciously; in the language of a pious old negro, he "prayed right up." And so much did his prayer always work on the devotional feelings of his audiences, that there seemed often a danger that it would be lost altogether in the abundance of the responses which broke out everywhere around him.

While this scene was passing in the cabin of the man, one quite otherwise passed in the halls of the master.

The trader and Mr. Shelby were seated together in the dining room afore-named, at a table covered with papers and writing utensils.

Mr. Shelby was busy in counting some bundles of bills, which, as they were counted, he pushed over to the trader, who counted them likewise.

"All fair," said the trader; "and now for signing these yer."

Mr. Shelby hastily drew the bills of sale towards him, and signed them, like a man that hurries over some disagreeable business, and then pushed them over with the money. Haley produced, from a well-worn valise, a parchment, which, after looking over it a moment, he handed to Mr. Shelby, who took it with a gesture of suppressed eagerness.

"Wal, now, the thing's *done*!" said the trader, getting up.

"It's *done*!" said Mr. Shelby, in a musing tone; and, fetching a long breath, he repeated, *"It's done!"*

"Yer don't seem to feel much pleased with it, 'pears to me," said the trader.

"Haley," said Mr. Shelby, "I hope you'll remember that you promised, on your honor, you wouldn't sell Tom, without knowing what sort of hands he's going into."

"Why, you've just done it sir," said the trader.

"Circumstances, you well know, *obliged* me," said Shelby, haughtily.

"Wal, you know, they may 'blige *me*, too," said the trader. "Howsomever, I'll do the very best I can in gettin' Tom a good berth; as to my treatin' on him bad, you needn't be a grain afeard. If there's anything that I thank the Lord for, it is that I'm never noways cruel."

After the expositions which the trader had previously given of his humane principles, Mr. Shelby did not feel particularly reassured by these declarations; but, as they were the best comfort the case admitted of, he allowed the trader to depart in silence, and betook himself to a solitary cigar.

Chapter 5

Showing the Feelings of Living Property on Changing Owners

Mr. and Mrs. Shelby had retired to their apartment for the night. He was lounging in a large easy-chair, looking over some letters that had come in the afternoon mail, and she was standing before her mirror, brushing out the complicated braids and curls in which Eliza had arranged her hair; for, noticing her pale cheeks and haggard eyes, she had excused her attendance that night, and ordered her to bed. The employment, naturally enough, suggested her conversation with the girl in the morning; and turning to her husband, she said, carelessly,

"By the by, Arthur, who was that low-bred fellow that you lugged in to our dinner-table today?"

"Haley is his name," said Shelby, turning himself rather uneasily in his chair, and continuing with his eyes fixed on a letter.

"Haley! Who is he, and what may be his business here, pray?"

"Well, he's a man that I transacted some business with, last time I was at Natchez," said Mr. Shelby.

"And he presumed on it to make himself quite at home, and call and dine here, ay?"

"Why, I invited him; I had some accounts with him," said Shelby.

"Is he a negro-trader?" said Mrs. Shelby, noticing a certain embarrassment in her husband's manner.

"Why, my dear, what put that into your head?" said Shelby, looking up.

"Nothing, - only Eliza came in here, after dinner, in a great worry, crying and taking on, and said you were talking with a trader, and that she heard him make an offer for her boy - the ridiculous little goose!"

"She did, hey?" said Mr. Shelby, returning to his paper, which he seemed for a few moments quite intent upon, not perceiving that he was holding it bottom upwards.

"It will have to come out," said he, mentally; "as well now as ever."

"I told Eliza," said Mrs. Shelby, as she continued brushing her hair, "that she was a little fool for her pains, and that you never had anything to do with that sort of persons. Of course, I knew you never meant to sell any of our people, - least of all, to such a fellow."

"Well, Emily," said her husband, "so I have always felt and said; but the fact is that my business lies so that I cannot get on without. I shall have to sell some of my hands."

"To that creature? Impossible! Mr. Shelby, you cannot be serious."

"I'm sorry to say that I am," said Mr. Shelby. "I've agreed to sell Tom."

"What! our Tom? – that good, faithful creature! – been your faithful servant from a boy! O, Mr. Shelby! – and you have promised him his freedom, too, – you and I have spoken to him a hundred times of it. Well, I can believe anything now, – I can believe *now* that you could sell little Harry, poor Eliza's only child!" said Mrs. Shelby, in a tone between grief and indignation.

"Well, since you must know all, it is so. I have agreed to sell Tom and Harry both; and I don't know why I am to be rated, as if I were a monster, for doing what every one does every day."

"But why, of all others, choose these?" said Mrs. Shelby. "Why sell them, of all on the place, if you must sell at all?"

"Because they will bring the highest sum of any, – that's why. I could choose another, if you say so. The fellow made me a high bid on Eliza, if that would suit you any better," said Mr. Shelby.

"The wretch!" said Mrs. Shelby, vehemently.

"Well, I didn't listen to it, a moment, – out of regard to your feelings, I wouldn't; – so give me some credit."

"My dear," said Mrs. Shelby, recollecting herself, "forgive me. I have been hasty. I was surprised, and entirely unprepared for this; – but surely you will allow me to intercede for these poor creatures. Tom is a noble-hearted, faithful fellow, if he is black. I do believe, Mr. Shelby, that if he were put to it, he would lay down his life for you."

"I know it, – I dare say; – but what's the use of all this? – I can't help myself."

"Why not make a pecuniary sacrifice? I'm willing to bear my part of the inconvenience. O, Mr. Shelby, I have tried – tried most faithfully, as a Christian woman should – to do my duty to these poor, simple, dependent creatures. I have cared for them, instructed them, watched over them, and know all their little cares and joys, for years; and how can I ever hold up my head again among them, if, for the sake of a little paltry gain, we sell such a faithful, excellent, confiding creature as poor Tom, and tear from him in a moment all we have taught him to love and value? I have taught them the duties of the family, of parent and child, and husband and wife; and how can I bear to have this open acknowledgment that we care for no tie, no duty, no relation, however sacred, compared with money? I have talked with Eliza about her boy – her duty to him as a Christian mother, to watch over him, pray for him, and bring him up in a Christian way; and now what can I say, if you tear him away, and sell him, soul and body, to a profane, unprincipled man, just to save a little money? I have told her that one soul is worth more than all the money in the world; and how will she believe me when she sees us turn round and sell her child? – sell him, perhaps, to certain ruin of body and soul!"

"I'm sorry you feel so about it, – indeed I am," said Mr. Shelby; "and I respect your feelings, too, though I don't pretend to share them to their full extent; but

I tell you now, solemnly, it's of no use – I can't help myself. I didn't mean to tell you this Emily; but, in plain words, there is no choice between selling these two and selling everything. Either they must go, or *all* must. Haley has come into possession of a mortgage, which, if I don't clear off with him directly, will take everything before it. I've raked, and scraped, and borrowed, and all but begged, – and the price of these two was needed to make up the balance, and I had to give them up. Haley fancied the child; he agreed to settle the matter that way, and no other. I was in his power, and *had* to do it. If you feel so to have them sold, would it be any better to have *all* sold?"

Mrs. Shelby stood like one stricken. Finally, turning to her toilet, she rested her face in her hands, and gave a sort of groan.

"This is God's curse on slavery! – a bitter, bitter, most accursed thing! – a curse to the master and a curse to the slave! I was a fool to think I could make anything good out of such a deadly evil. It is a sin to hold a slave under laws like ours, – I always felt it was, – I always thought so when I was a girl, – I thought so still more after I joined the church; but I thought I could gild it over, – I thought, by kindness, and care, and instruction, I could make the condition of mine better than freedom – fool that I was!"

"Why, wife, you are getting to be an abolitionist, quite."

"Abolitionist! if they knew all I know about slavery, they *might* talk! We don't need them to tell us; you know I never thought that slavery was right – never felt willing to own slaves."

"Well, therein you differ from many wise and pious men," said Mr. Shelby. "You remember Mr. B.'s sermon, the other Sunday?"

"I don't want to hear such sermons; I never wish to hear Mr. B. in our church again. Ministers can't help the evil, perhaps, - can't cure it, any more than we can, - but defend it! - it always went against my common sense. And I think you didn't think much of that sermon, either."

"Well," said Shelby, "I must say these ministers sometimes carry matters further than we poor sinners would exactly dare to do. We men of the world must wink pretty hard at various things, and get used to a deal that isn't the exact thing. But we don't quite fancy, when women and ministers come out broad and square, and go beyond us in matters of either modesty or morals, that's a fact. But now, my dear, I trust you see the necessity of the thing, and you see that I have done the very best that circumstances would allow."

"O yes, yes!" said Mrs. Shelby, hurriedly and abstractedly fingering her gold watch, - "I haven't any jewelry of any amount," she added, thoughtfully; "but would not this watch do something? - it was an expensive one, when it was bought. If I could only at least save Eliza's child, I would sacrifice anything I have."

"I'm sorry, very sorry, Emily," said Mr. Shelby, "I'm sorry this takes hold of you so; but it will do no good. The fact is, Emily, the thing's done; the bills of sale are already signed, and in Haley's hands;

and you must be thankful it is no worse. That man has had it in his power to ruin us all, – and now he is fairly off. If you knew the man as I do, you'd think that we had had a narrow escape."

"Is he so hard, then?"

"Why, not a cruel man, exactly, but a man of leather, – a man alive to nothing but trade and profit, – cool, and unhesitating, and unrelenting, as death and the grave. He'd sell his own mother at a good percentage – not wishing the old woman any harm, either."

"And this wretch owns that good, faithful Tom, and Eliza's child!"

"Well, my dear, the fact is that this goes rather hard with me; it's a thing I hate to think of. Haley wants to drive matters, and take possession tomorrow. I'm going to get out my horse bright and early, and be off. I can't see Tom, that's a fact; and you had better arrange a drive somewhere, and carry Eliza off. Let the thing be done when she is out of sight."

"No, no," said Mrs. Shelby; "I'll be in no sense accomplice or help in this cruel business. I'll go and see poor old Tom, God help him, in his distress! They shall see, at any rate, that their mistress can feel for and with them. As to Eliza, I dare not think about it. The Lord forgive us! What have we done, that this cruel necessity should come on us?"

There was one listener to this conversation whom Mr. and Mrs. Shelby little suspected.

Communicating with their apartment was a large closet, opening by a door into the outer passage. When Mrs. Shelby had dismissed Eliza for the night, her feverish and excited mind had suggested the idea of this closet; and she had hidden herself there, and, with her ear pressed close against the crack of the door, had lost not a word of the conversation.

When the voices died into silence, she rose and crept stealthily away. Pale, shivering, with rigid features and compressed lips, she looked an entirely altered being from the soft and timid creature she had been hitherto. She moved cautiously along the entry, paused one moment at her mistress' door, and raised her hands in mute appeal to Heaven, and then turned and glided into her own room. It was a quiet, neat apartment, on the same floor with her mistress. There was a pleasant sunny window, where she had often sat singing at her sewing; there a little case of books, and various little fancy articles, ranged by them, the gifts of Christmas holidays; there was her simple wardrobe in the closet and in the drawers:- here was, in short, her home; and, on the whole, a happy one it had been to her. But there, on the bed, lay her slumbering boy, his long curls falling negligently around his unconscious face, his rosy mouth half open, his little fat hands thrown out over the bedclothes, and a smile spread like a sunbeam over his whole face.

"Poor boy! poor fellow!" said Eliza; "they have sold you! but your mother will save you yet!"

No tear dropped over that pillow; in such straits as these, the heart has no tears to give, - it drops only blood, bleeding itself away in silence. She took a piece of paper and a pencil, and wrote, hastily,

"O, Missis! dear Missis! don't think me ungrateful, – don't think hard of me, any way, – I heard all you and master said tonight. I am going to try to save my boy – you will not blame me! God bless and reward you for all your kindness!"

Hastily folding and directing this, she went to a drawer and made up a little package of clothing for her boy, which she tied with a handkerchief firmly round her waist; and, so fond is a mother's remembrance, that, even in the terrors of that hour, she did not forget to put in the little package one or two of his favorite toys, reserving a gayly painted parrot to amuse him, when she should be called on to awaken him. It was some trouble to arouse the little sleeper; but, after some effort, he sat up, and was playing with his bird, while his mother was putting on her bonnet and shawl.

"Where are you going, mother?" said he, as she drew near the bed, with his little coat and cap.

His mother drew near, and looked so earnestly into his eyes, that he at once divined that something unusual was the matter.

"Hush, Harry," she said; "mustn't speak loud, or they will hear us. A wicked man was coming to take little Harry away from his mother, and carry him 'way off in the dark; but mother won't let him – she's going to put on her little boy's cap and coat, and run off with him, so the ugly man can't catch him."

Saying these words, she had tied and buttoned on the child's simple outfit, and, taking him in her arms, she whispered to him to be very still; and, opening a door in her room which led into the outer verandah, she glided noiselessly out.

It was a sparkling, frosty, starlight night, and the mother wrapped the shawl close round her child, as, perfectly quiet with vague terror, he clung round her neck.

Old Bruno, a great Newfoundland, who slept at the end of the porch, rose, with a low growl, as she came near. She gently spoke his name, and the animal, an old pet and playmate of hers, instantly, wagging his tail, prepared to follow her, though apparently revolving much, in this simple dog's head, what such an indiscreet midnight promenade might mean. Some dim ideas of imprudence or impropriety in the measure seemed to embarrass him considerably; for he often stopped, as Eliza glided forward, and looked wistfully, first at her and then at the house, and then, as if reassured by reflection, he pattered along after her again. A few minutes brought them to the window of Uncle Tom's cottage, and Eliza stopping, tapped lightly on the window-pane.

The prayer-meeting at Uncle Tom's had, in the order of hymn-singing, been protracted to a very late hour; and, as Uncle Tom had indulged himself in a few lengthy solos afterwards, the consequence was, that, although it was now between twelve and one o'clock, he and his worthy helpmeet were not yet asleep.

"Good Lord! what's that?" said Aunt Chloe, starting up and hastily drawing the curtain. "My sakes alive, if it an't Lizy! Get on your clothes, old man, quick! – there's old Bruno, too, a pawin round; what on airth! I'm gwine to open the door."

And suiting the action to the word, the door flew open, and the light of the tallow candle, which Tom had hastily lighted, fell on the haggard face and dark, wild eyes of the fugitive.

"Lord bless you! – I'm skeered to look at ye, Lizy! Are ye tuck sick, or what's come over ye?"

"I'm running away – Uncle Tom and Aunt Chloe – carrying off my child – Master sold him!"

"Sold him?" echoed both, lifting up their hands in dismay.

"Yes, sold him!" said Eliza, firmly; "I crept into the closet by Mistress' door tonight, and I heard Master tell Missis that he had sold my Harry, and you, Uncle Tom, both, to a trader; and that he was going off this morning on his horse, and that the man was to take possession today."

Tom had stood, during this speech, with his hands raised, and his eyes dilated, like a man in a dream. Slowly and gradually, as its meaning came over him, he collapsed, rather than seated himself, on his old chair, and sunk his head down upon his knees.

"The good Lord have pity on us!" said Aunt Chloe. "O! it don't seem as if it was true! What has he done, that Mas'r should sell *him*?"

"He hasn't done anything, – it isn't for that. Master don't want to sell, and Missis she's always good. I heard her plead and beg for us; but he told her 't was no use; that he was in this man's debt, and that this man had got the power over him; and that if he didn't pay him off clear, it would end in his having to sell the place and all the people, and move off. Yes, I heard him say there was no choice between selling these two and selling all, the man was driving him so hard. Master said he was sorry; but oh, Missis – you ought to have heard her talk! If she an't a Christian and an angel, there never was one. I'm a wicked girl to leave her so; but, then, I can't help it. She said, herself, one soul was worth more than the world; and this boy has a soul, and if I let him be carried off, who knows what'll become of it? It must be right: but, if it an't right, the Lord forgive me, for I can't help doing it!"

"Well, old man!" said Aunt Chloe, "why don't you go, too? Will you wait to be toted down river, where they kill niggers with hard work and starving? I'd a heap rather die than go there, any day! There's time for ye, – be off with Lizy, – you've got a pass to come and go any time. Come, bustle up, and I'll get your things together."

Tom slowly raised his head, and looked sorrowfully but quietly around, and said,

"No, no – I an't going. Let Eliza go – it's her right! I wouldn't be the one to say no – 'tan't in *natur* for her to stay; but you heard what she said! If I must be sold, or all the people on the place, and everything go to rack, why, let me be sold. I s'pose I can bar it as well as any on 'em," he added, while something like a sob and a sigh shook his broad, rough chest convulsively. "Mas'r always found me on the spot - he always will. I never have broke trust, nor used my pass no ways contrary to my word, and I never will. It's better for me alone to go, than to break up the place and sell all. Mas'r an't to blame, Chloe, and he'll take care of you and the poor–"

Here he turned to the rough trundle bed full of little woolly heads, and broke fairly down. He leaned over the back of the chair, and covered his face with his large hands. Sobs, heavy, hoarse and loud, shook the chair, and great tears fell through his fingers on the floor; just such tears, sir, as you dropped into the coffin where lay your first-born son; such tears, woman, as you shed when you heard the cries of your dying babe. For, sir, he was a man, - and you are but another man. And, woman, though dressed in silk and jewels, you are but a woman, and, in life's great straits and mighty griefs, ye feel but one sorrow!

"And now," said Eliza, as she stood in the door, "I saw my husband only this afternoon, and I little knew then what was to come. They have pushed him to the very last standing place, and he told me, today, that he was going to run away. Do try, if you can, to get word to him. Tell him how I went, and why I went; and tell him I'm going to try and find Canada. You must give my love to him, and tell him, if I never see him again," she turned away, and stood with her back to them for a moment, and then added, in a husky voice, "tell him to be as good as he can, and try and meet me in the kingdom of heaven."

"Call Bruno in there," she added. "Shut the door on him, poor beast! He mustn't go with me!"

A few last words and tears, a few simple adieus and blessings, and clasping her wondering and affrighted child in her arms, she glided noiselessly away.

Chapter 6

Discovery

Mr. and Mrs. Shelby, after their protracted discussion of the night before, did not readily sink to repose, and, in consequence, slept somewhat later than usual, the ensuing morning.

"I wonder what keeps Eliza," said Mrs. Shelby, after giving her bell repeated pulls, to no purpose.

Mr. Shelby was standing before his dressing-glass, sharpening his razor; and just then the door opened, and a colored boy entered, with his shaving-water.

"Andy," said his mistress, "step to Eliza's door, and tell her I have rung for her three times. Poor thing!" she added, to herself, with a sigh.

Andy soon returned, with eyes very wide in astonishment.

"Lor, Missis! Lizy's drawers is all open, and her things all lying every which way; and I believe she's just done clared out!"

The truth flashed upon Mr. Shelby and his wife at the same moment. He exclaimed,

"Then she suspected it, and she's off!"

"The Lord be thanked!" said Mrs. Shelby. "I trust she is."

"Wife, you talk like a fool! Really, it will be something pretty awkward for me, if she is. Haley saw that I hesitated about selling this child, and he'll think I connived at it, to get him out of the way. It touches my honor!" And Mr. Shelby left the room hastily.

There was great running and ejaculating, and opening and shutting of doors, and appearance of faces in all shades of color in different places, for about a quarter of an hour. One person only, who might have shed some light on the matter, was entirely silent, and that was the head cook, Aunt Chloe. Silently, and with a heavy cloud settled down over her once joyous face, she proceeded making out her breakfast biscuits, as if she heard and saw nothing of the excitement around her.

Very soon, about a dozen young imps were roosting, like so many crows, on the verandah railings, each one determined to be the first one to apprize the strange Mas'r of his ill luck.

"He'll be rael mad, I'll be bound," said Andy.

"*Won't* he swar!" said little black Jake.

"Yes, for he *does* swar," said woolly-headed Mandy. "I hearn him yesterday, at dinner. I hearn all about it then, 'cause I got into the closet where Missis keeps the great jugs, and I hearn every word." And Mandy, who had never in her life thought of the meaning of a word she had heard, more than a black cat, now took airs of superior wisdom, and strutted about, forgetting to state that, though actually coiled up among the jugs at the time specified, she had been fast asleep all the time.

When, at last, Haley appeared, booted and spurred, he was saluted with the bad tidings on every hand. The young imps on the verandah were not disappointed in their hope of hearing him "swar," which he did with a fluency and fervency which delighted them all amazingly, as they ducked and dodged hither and thither, to be out of the reach of his riding-whip; and, all whooping off together, they tumbled, in a pile of immeasurable giggle, on the withered turf under the verandah, where they kicked up their heels and shouted to their full satisfaction.

"If I had the little devils!" muttered Haley, between his teeth.

"But you ha'nt got 'em, though!" said Andy, with a triumphant flourish, and making a string of indescribable mouths at the unfortunate trader's back, when he was fairly beyond hearing.

"I say now, Shelby, this yer 's a most extro'rnary business!" said Haley, as he abruptly entered the parlor. "It seems that gal 's off, with her young un."

"Mr. Haley, Mrs. Shelby is present," said Mr. Shelby.

"I beg pardon, ma'am," said Haley, bowing slightly, with a still lowering brow; "but still I say, as I said before, this yer's a sing'lar report. Is it true, sir?"

"Sir," said Mr. Shelby, "if you wish to communicate with me, you must observe something of the decorum of a gentleman. Andy, take Mr. Haley's hat and riding-whip. Take a seat, sir. Yes, sir; I regret to say that the young woman, excited by overhearing, or having reported to her, something of this business, has taken her child in the night, and made off."

"I did expect fair dealing in this matter, I confess," said Haley.

"Well, sir," said Mr. Shelby, turning sharply round upon him, "what am I to understand by that remark? If any man calls my honor in question, I have but one answer for him."

The trader cowered at this, and in a somewhat lower tone said that "it was plaguy hard on a fellow, that had made a fair bargain, to be gulled that way."

"Mr. Haley," said Mr. Shelby, "if I did not think you had some cause for disappointment, I should not have borne from you the rude and unceremonious style of your entrance into my parlor this morning. I say thus much, however, since appearances call for it, that I shall allow of no insinuations cast upon me, as if I were at all partner to any unfairness in this matter. Moreover, I shall feel bound to give you every assistance, in the use of horses, servants, &c., in the recovery of your property. So, in short, Haley," said he, suddenly dropping from the tone of dignified coolness to his ordinary one of easy frankness, "the best way for you is to keep good-natured and eat some breakfast, and we will then see what is to be done."

Mrs. Shelby now rose, and said her engagements would prevent her being at the breakfast-table that morning;

and, deputing a very respectable mulatto woman to attend to the gentlemen's coffee at the side-board, she left the room.

"Old lady don't like your humble servant, over and above," said Haley, with an uneasy effort to be very familiar.

"I am not accustomed to hear my wife spoken of with such freedom," said Mr. Shelby, dryly.

"Beg pardon; of course, only a joke, you know," said Haley, forcing a laugh.

"Some jokes are less agreeable than others," rejoined Shelby.

"Devilish free, now I've signed those papers, cuss him!" muttered Haley to himself; "quite grand, since yesterday!"

Never did fall of any prime minister at court occasion wider surges of sensation than the report of Tom's fate among his compeers on the place. It was the topic in every mouth, everywhere; and nothing was done in the house or in the field, but to discuss its probable results. Eliza's flight - an unprecedented event on the place - was also a great accessory in stimulating the general excitement.

Black Sam, as he was commonly called, from his being about three shades blacker than any other son of ebony on the place, was revolving the matter profoundly in all its phases and bearings, with a comprehensiveness of vision and a strict lookout to his own personal well-being, that would have done credit to any white patriot in Washington.

"It's an ill wind dat blow nowhar, – dat ar a fact," said Sam, sententiously, giving an additional hoist to his pantaloons, and adroitly substituting a long nail in place of a missing suspender-button, with which effort of mechanical genius he seemed highly delighted.

"Yes, it's an ill wind blows nowhar," he repeated. "Now, dar, Tom's down – wal, course der's room for some nigger to be up – and why not dis nigger? – dat's de idee. Tom, a ridin' round de country – boots blacked – pass in his pocket – all grand as Cuffee – but who he? Now, why shouldn't Sam? – dat's what I want to know."

"Halloo, Sam – O Sam! Mas'r wants you to cotch Bill and Jerry," said Andy, cutting short Sam's soliloquy.

"High! what's afoot now, young un?"

"Why, you don't know, I s'pose, that Lizy's cut stick, and clared out, with her young un?"

"You teach your granny!" said Sam, with infinite contempt; "knowed it a heap sight sooner than you did; this nigger an't so green, now!"

"Well, anyhow, Mas'r wants Bill and Jerry geared right up; and you and I 's to go with Mas'r Haley, to look arter her."

"Good, now! dat's de time o' day!" said Sam. "It's Sam dat's called for in dese yer times. He's de nigger. See if I don't cotch her, now; Mas'r'll see what Sam can do!"

"Ah! but, Sam," said Andy, "you'd better think twice; for Missis don't want her cotched, and she'll be in yer wool."

"High!" said Sam, opening his eyes. "How you know dat?"

"Heard her say so, my own self, dis blessed mornin', when I bring in Mas'r's shaving-water. She sent me to see why Lizy didn't come to dress her; and when I telled her she was off, she jest ris up, and ses she, 'The Lord be praised;' and Mas'r, he seemed rael mad, and ses he, 'Wife, you talk like a fool.' But Lor! she'll bring him to! I knows well enough how that'll be, – it's allers best to stand Missis' side the fence, now I tell yer."

Black Sam, upon this, scratched his woolly pate, which, if it did not contain very profound wisdom, still contained a great deal of a particular species much in demand among politicians of all complexions and countries, and vulgarly denominated "knowing which side the bread is buttered;" so, stopping with grave consideration, he again gave a hitch to his pantaloons, which was his regularly organized method of assisting his mental perplexities.

"Der an't no sayin' – never – 'bout no kind o' thing in *dis* yer world," he said, at last. Sam spoke like a philosopher, emphasizing *this* – as if he had had a large experience in different sorts of worlds, and therefore had come to his conclusions advisedly.

"Now, sartin I'd a said that Missis would a scoured the varsal world after Lizy," added Sam, thoughtfully.

"So she would," said Andy; "but can't ye see through a ladder, ye black nigger? Missis don't want dis yer Mas'r Haley to get Lizy's boy; dat's de go!"

"High!" said Sam, with an indescribable intonation, known only to those who have heard it among the negroes.

"And I'll tell yer more 'n all," said Andy; "I specs you'd better be making tracks for dem hosses, - mighty sudden, too, - for I hearn Missis 'quirin' arter yer, - so you've stood foolin' long enough."

Sam, upon this, began to bestir himself in real earnest, and after a while appeared, bearing down gloriously towards the house, with Bill and Jerry in a full canter, and adroitly throwing himself off before they had any idea of stopping, he brought them up alongside of the horse-post like a tornado. Haley's horse, which was a skittish young colt, winced, and bounced, and pulled hard at his halter.

"Ho, ho!" said Sam, "skeery, ar ye?" and his black visage lighted up with a curious, mischievous gleam. "I'll fix ye now!" said he.

There was a large beech-tree overshadowing the place, and the small, sharp, triangular beech-nuts lay scattered thickly on the ground. With one of these in his fingers, Sam approached the colt, stroked and patted, and seemed apparently busy in soothing his agitation. On pretence of adjusting the saddle, he adroitly slipped under it the sharp little nut, in such a manner that the least weight brought upon the saddle would annoy the nervous sensibilities of the animal, without leaving any perceptible graze or wound.

"Dar!" he said, rolling his eyes with an approving grin; "me fix 'em!"

At this moment Mrs. Shelby appeared on the balcony, beckoning to him. Sam approached with as good a determination to pay court as did ever suitor after a vacant place at St. James' or Washington.

"Why have you been loitering so, Sam? I sent Andy to tell you to hurry."

"Lord bless you, Missis!" said Sam, "horses won't be cotched all in a minit; they'd done clared out way down to the south pasture, and the Lord knows whar!"

"Sam, how often must I tell you not to say 'Lord bless you, and the Lord knows,' and such things? It's wicked."

"O, Lord bless my soul! I done forgot, Missis! I won't say nothing of de sort no more."

"Why, Sam, you just *have* said it again."

"Did I? O, Lord! I mean – I didn't go fur to say it."

"You must be *careful*, Sam."

"Just let me get my breath, Missis, and I'll start fair. I'll be bery careful."

"Well, Sam, you are to go with Mr. Haley, to show him the road, and help him. Be careful of the horses, Sam; you know Jerry was a little lame last week; *don't ride them too fast*."

Mrs. Shelby spoke the last words with a low voice, and strong emphasis.

"Let dis child alone for dat!" said Sam, rolling up his eyes with a volume of meaning. "Lord knows! High! Didn't say dat!" said he, suddenly catching his breath, with a ludicrous flourish of apprehension, which made his mistress laugh, spite of herself. "Yes, Missis, I'll look out for de hosses!"

"Now, Andy," said Sam, returning to his stand under the beech-trees, "you see I wouldn't be 't all surprised if dat ar gen'lman's crittur should gib a fling, by and by, when he comes to be a gettin' up. You know, Andy, critturs *will* do such things;" and therewith Sam poked Andy in the side, in a highly suggestive manner.

"High!" said Andy, with an air of instant appreciation.

"Yes, you see, Andy, Missis wants to make time, – dat ar's clar to der most or'nary 'bserver. I jis make a little for her. Now, you see, get all dese yer hosses loose, caperin' permiscus round dis yer lot and down to de wood dar, and I spec Mas'r won't be off in a hurry."

Andy grinned.

"Yer see," said Sam, "yer see, Andy, if any such thing should happen as that Mas'r Haley's horse *should* begin to act contrary, and cut up, you and I jist lets go of our'n to help him, and *we'll help him* – oh yes!" And Sam and Andy laid their heads back on their shoulders, and broke into a low, immoderate laugh, snapping their fingers and flourishing their heels with exquisite delight.

At this instant, Haley appeared on the verandah. Somewhat mollified by certain cups of very good coffee, he came out smiling and talking, in tolerably restored humor. Sam and Andy, clawing for certain fragmentary palm-leaves, which they were in the habit of considering as hats, flew to the horseposts, to be ready to "help Mas'r."

Sam's palm-leaf had been ingeniously disentangled from all pretensions to braid, as respects its brim; and the slivers starting apart, and standing upright, gave it a blazing air of freedom and defiance, quite equal to that of any Fejee chief; while the whole brim of Andy's being departed bodily, he rapped the crown on his head with a dexterous thump, and looked about well pleased, as if to say, "Who says I haven't got a hat?"

"Well, boys," said Haley, "look alive now; we must lose no time."

"Not a bit of him, Mas'r!" said Sam, putting Haley's rein in his hand, and holding his stirrup, while Andy was untying the other two horses.

The instant Haley touched the saddle, the mettlesome creature bounded from the earth with a sudden spring, that threw his master sprawling, some feet off, on the soft, dry turf. Sam, with frantic ejaculations, made a dive at the reins, but only succeeded in brushing the blazing palm-leaf afore-named into the horse's eyes, which by no means tended to allay the confusion of his nerves. So, with great vehemence, he overturned Sam, and, giving two or three contemptuous snorts, flourished his heels vigorously in the air, and was soon prancing away towards the lower end of the lawn, followed by Bill and Jerry, whom Andy had not failed to let loose, according to contract, speeding them off with various direful ejaculations. And now ensued a miscellaneous scene of confusion. Sam and Andy ran and shouted, - dogs barked here and there, - and Mike, Mose, Mandy, Fanny, and all the smaller specimens on the place, both male and female, raced, clapped hands, whooped, and shouted, with outrageous officiousness and untiring zeal.

Haley's horse, which was a white one, and very fleet and spirited, appeared to enter into the spirit of the scene with great gusto; and having for his coursing ground a lawn of nearly half a mile in extent, gently sloping down on every side into indefinite woodland, he appeared to take infinite delight in seeing how near he could allow his pursuers to approach him, and then, when within a hand's breadth, whisk off with a start and a snort, like a mischievous beast as he was and career far down into some alley of the wood-lot. Nothing was further from Sam's mind than to have any one of the troop taken until such season as should seem to him most befitting, - and the exertions that he made were certainly most heroic. Like the sword of Coeur De Lion, which always blazed in the front and thickest of the battle, Sam's palm-leaf was to be seen everywhere when there was the least danger that a horse could be caught; there he would bear down full tilt, shouting, "Now for it! cotch him! cotch him!" in a way that would set everything to indiscriminate rout in a moment.

Haley ran up and down, and cursed and swore and stamped miscellaneously. Mr. Shelby in vain tried to shout directions from the balcony, and Mrs. Shelby from her chamber window alternately laughed and wondered, – not without some inkling of what lay at the bottom of all this confusion.

At last, about twelve o'clock, Sam appeared triumphant, mounted on Jerry, with Haley's horse by his side, reeking with sweat, but with flashing eyes and dilated nostrils, showing that the spirit of freedom had not yet entirely subsided.

"He's cotched!" he exclaimed, triumphantly. "If 't hadn't been for me, they might a bust themselves, all on 'em; but I cotched him!"

"You!" growled Haley, in no amiable mood. "If it hadn't been for you, this never would have happened."

"Lord bless us, Mas'r," said Sam, in a tone of the deepest concern, "and me that has been racin' and chasin' till the sweat jest pours off me!"

"Well, well!" said Haley, "you've lost me near three hours, with your cursed nonsense. Now let's be off, and have no more fooling."

"Why, Mas'r," said Sam, in a deprecating tone, "I believe you mean to kill us all clar, horses and all. Here we are all just ready to drop down, and the critters all in a reek of sweat. Why, Mas'r won't think of startin' on now till arter dinner. Mas'rs' hoss wants rubben down; see how he splashed hisself; and Jerry limps too; don't think Missis would be willin' to have us start dis yer way, no how. Lord bless you, Mas'r, we can ketch up, if we do stop. Lizy never was no great of a walker."

Mrs. Shelby, who, greatly to her amusement, had overheard this conversation from the verandah, now resolved to do her part. She came forward, and, courteously expressing her concern for Haley's accident, pressed him to stay to dinner, saying that the cook should bring it on the table immediately.

Thus, all things considered, Haley, with rather an equivocal grace, proceeded to the parlor, while Sam, rolling his eyes after him with unutterable meaning, proceeded gravely with the horses to the stable-yard.

"Did yer see him, Andy? *did* yer see him?" said Sam, when he had got fairly beyond the shelter of the barn, and fastened the horse to a post. "O, Lor, if it warn't as good as a meetin', now, to see him a dancin' and kickin' and swarin' at us. Didn't I hear him? Swar away, ole fellow (says I to myself); will yer have yer hoss now, or wait till you cotch him? (says I). Lor, Andy, I think I can see him now." And Sam and Andy leaned up against the barn and laughed to their hearts' content.

"Yer oughter seen how mad he looked, when I brought the hoss up. Lord, he'd a killed me, if he durs' to; and there I was a standin' as innercent and as humble."

"Lor, I seed you," said Andy; "an't you an old hoss, Sam?"

"Rather specks I am," said Sam; "did yer see Missis up stars at the winder? I seed her laughin'."

"I'm sure, I was racin' so, I didn't see nothing," said Andy.

"Well, yer see," said Sam, proceeding gravely to wash down Haley's pony, "I 'se 'quired what yer may call a habit *o' bobservation*, Andy. It's a very 'portant habit, Andy; and I 'commend yer to be cultivatin' it, now yer young. Hist up that hind foot, Andy. Yer see, Andy, it's *bobservation* makes all de difference in niggers. Didn't I see which way the wind blew dis yer mornin'? Didn't I see what Missis wanted, though she never let on? Dat ar's bobservation, Andy. I 'spects it's what you may call a faculty. Faculties is different in different peoples, but cultivation of 'em goes a great way."

"I guess if I hadn't helped your bobservation dis mornin', yer wouldn't have seen your way so smart," said Andy.

"Andy," said Sam, "you 's a promisin' child, der an't no manner o' doubt. I thinks lots of yer, Andy; and I don't feel no ways ashamed to take idees from you. We oughtenter overlook nobody, Andy, cause the smartest on us gets tripped up sometimes. And so, Andy, let's go up to the house now. I'll be boun' Missis'll give us an uncommon good bite, dis yer time."

Chapter 7

The Mother's Struggle

It is impossible to conceive of a human creature more wholly desolate and forlorn than Eliza, when she turned her footsteps from Uncle Tom's cabin.

Her husband's suffering and dangers, and the danger of her child, all blended in her mind, with a confused and stunning sense of the risk she was running, in leaving the only home she had ever known, and cutting loose from the protection of a friend whom she loved and revered. Then there was the parting from every familiar object, – the place where she had grown up, the trees under which she had played, the groves where she had walked many an evening in happier days, by the side of her young husband, – everything, as it lay in the clear, frosty starlight, seemed to speak reproachfully to her, and ask her whither could she go from a home like that?

But stronger than all was maternal love, wrought into a paroxysm of frenzy by the near approach of a fearful danger. Her boy was old enough to have walked by her side, and, in an indifferent case, she would only have led him by the hand; but now the bare thought of putting him out of her arms made her shudder, and she strained him to her bosom with a convulsive grasp, as she went rapidly forward.

The frosty ground creaked beneath her feet, and she trembled at the sound; every quaking leaf and fluttering shadow sent the blood backward to her heart, and quickened her footsteps. She wondered within herself at the strength that seemed to be come upon her; for she felt the weight of her boy as if it had been a feather, and every flutter of fear seemed to increase the supernatural power that bore her on, while from her pale lips burst forth, in frequent ejaculations, the prayer to a Friend above – "Lord, help! Lord, save me!"

If it were *your* Harry, mother, or your Willie, that were going to be torn from you by a brutal trader, tomorrow morning, – if you had seen the man, and heard that the papers were signed and delivered, and you had only from twelve o'clock till morning to make good your escape, – how fast could *you* walk? How many miles could you make in those few brief hours, with the darling at your bosom, – the little sleepy head on your shoulder, – the small, soft arms trustingly holding on to your neck?

For the child slept. At first, the novelty and alarm kept him waking; but his mother so hurriedly repressed every breath or sound, and so assured him that if he were only still she would certainly save him, that he clung quietly round her neck, only asking, as he found himself sinking to sleep,

"Mother, I don't need to keep awake, do I?"

"No, my darling; sleep, if you want to."

"But, mother, if I do get asleep, you won't let him get me?"

"No! so may God help me!" said his mother, with a paler cheek, and a brighter light in her large dark eyes.

"You're *sure*, an't you, mother?"

"Yes, *sure*!" said the mother, in a voice that startled herself; for it seemed to her to come from a spirit within, that was no part of her; and the boy dropped his little weary head on her shoulder, and was soon asleep. How the touch of those warm arms, the gentle breathings that came in her neck, seemed to add fire and spirit to her movements! It seemed to her as if strength poured into her in electric streams, from every gentle touch and movement of the sleeping, confiding child. Sublime is the dominion of the mind over the body, that, for a time, can make flesh and nerve impregnable, and string the sinews like steel, so that the weak become so mighty.

The boundaries of the farm, the grove, the wood-lot, passed by her dizzily, as she walked on; and still she went, leaving one familiar object after another, slacking not, pausing not, till reddening daylight found her many a long mile from all traces of any familiar objects upon the open highway.

She had often been, with her mistress, to visit some connections, in the little village of T–, not far from the Ohio river, and knew the road well. To go thither, to escape across the Ohio river, were the first hurried outlines of her plan of escape; beyond that, she could only hope in God.

When horses and vehicles began to move along the highway, with that alert perception peculiar to a state of excitement, and which seems to be a sort of inspiration, she became aware that her headlong pace and distracted air might bring on her remark and suspicion. She therefore put the boy on the ground, and, adjusting her dress and bonnet, she walked on at as rapid a pace as she thought consistent with the preservation of appearances. In her little bundle she had provided a store of cakes and apples, which she used as expedients for quickening the speed of the child, rolling the apple some yards before them, when the boy would run with all his might after it; and this ruse, often repeated, carried them over many a half-mile.

After a while, they came to a thick patch of woodland, through which murmured a clear brook. As the child complained of hunger and thirst, she climbed over the fence with him; and, sitting down behind a large rock which concealed them from the road, she gave him a breakfast out of her little package. The boy wondered and grieved that she could not eat; and when, putting his arms round her neck, he tried to wedge some of his cake into her mouth, it seemed to her that the rising in her throat would choke her.

"No, no, Harry darling! mother can't eat till you are safe! We must go on – on – till we come to the river!" And she hurried again into the road, and again constrained herself to walk regularly and composedly forward.

She was many miles past any neighborhood where she was personally known. If she should chance to meet any who knew her, she reflected that the well-known kindness of the family would be of itself a blind to suspicion, as making it an unlikely supposition that she could be a fugitive. As she was also so white as not to be known as of colored lineage, without a critical survey, and her child was white also, it was much easier for her to pass on unsuspected.

On this presumption, she stopped at noon at a neat farmhouse, to rest herself, and buy some dinner for her child and self; for, as the danger decreased with the distance, the supernatural tension of the nervous system lessened, and she found herself both weary and hungry.

The good woman, kindly and gossipping, seemed rather pleased than otherwise with having somebody come in to talk with; and accepted, without examination, Eliza's statement, that she "was going on a little piece, to spend a week with her friends," – all which she hoped in her heart might prove strictly true.

An hour before sunset, she entered the village of T–, by the Ohio river, weary and foot-sore, but still strong in heart. Her first glance was at the river, which lay, like Jordan, between her and the Canaan of liberty on the other side.

It was now early spring, and the river was swollen and turbulent; great cakes of floating ice were swinging heavily to and fro in the turbid waters. Owing to the peculiar form of the shore on the Kentucky side, the land bending far out into the water, the ice had been lodged and detained in great quantities, and the narrow channel which swept round the bend was full of ice, piled one cake over another, thus forming a temporary barrier to the descending ice, which lodged, and formed a great, undulating raft, filling up the whole river, and extending almost to the Kentucky shore.

Eliza stood, for a moment, contemplating this unfavorable aspect of things, which she saw at once must prevent the usual ferry-boat from running, and then turned into a small public house on the bank, to make a few inquiries.

The hostess, who was busy in various fizzing and stewing operations over the fire, preparatory to the evening meal, stopped, with a fork in her hand, as Eliza's sweet and plaintive voice arrested her.

"What is it?" she said.

"Isn't there any ferry or boat, that takes people over to B–, now?" she said.

"No, indeed!" said the woman; "the boats has stopped running."

Eliza's look of dismay and disappointment struck the woman, and she said, inquiringly,

"May be you're wanting to get over? – anybody sick? Ye seem mighty anxious?"

"I've got a child that's very dangerous," said Eliza. "I never heard of it till last night, and I've walked quite a piece today, in hopes to get to the ferry."

"Well, now, that's onlucky," said the woman, whose motherly sympathies were much aroused;

"I'm re'lly consarned for ye. Solomon!" she called, from the window, towards a small back building. A man, in leather apron and very dirty hands, appeared at the door.

"I say, Sol," said the woman, "is that ar man going to tote them bar'ls over tonight?"

"He said he should try, if 't was any way prudent," said the man.

"There's a man a piece down here, that's going over with some truck this evening, if he durs' to; he'll be in here to supper tonight, so you'd better set down and wait. That's a sweet little fellow," added the woman, offering him a cake.

But the child, wholly exhausted, cried with weariness.

"Poor fellow! he isn't used to walking, and I've hurried him on so," said Eliza.

"Well, take him into this room," said the woman, opening into a small bed-room, where stood a comfortable bed. Eliza laid the weary boy upon it, and held his hands in hers till he was fast asleep. For her there was no rest. As a fire in her bones, the thought of the pursuer urged her on; and she gazed with longing eyes on the sullen, surging waters that lay between her and liberty.

Here we must take our leave of her for the present, to follow the course of her pursuers.

Though Mrs. Shelby had promised that the dinner should be hurried on table, yet it was soon seen, as the thing has often been seen before, that it required more than one to make a bargain. So, although the order was fairly given out in Haley's hearing, and carried to Aunt Chloe by at least half a dozen juvenile messengers, that dignitary only gave certain very gruff snorts, and tosses of her head, and went on with every operation in an unusually leisurely and circumstantial manner.

For some singular reason, an impression seemed to reign among the servants generally that Missis would not be particularly disobliged by delay; and it was wonderful what a number of counter accidents occurred constantly, to retard the course of things. One luckless wight contrived to upset the gravy; and then gravy had to be got up *de novo*, with due care and formality, Aunt Chloe watching and stirring with dogged precision, answering shortly, to all suggestions of haste, that she "warn't a going to have raw gravy on the table, to help nobody's catchings." One tumbled down with the water, and had to go to the spring for more; and another precipitated the butter into the path of events; and there was from time to time giggling news brought into the kitchen that "Mas'r Haley was mighty oneasy, and that he couldn't sit in his cheer no ways, but was a walkin' and stalkin' to the winders and through the porch."

"Sarves him right!" said Aunt Chloe, indignantly. "He'll get wus nor oneasy, one of these days, if he don't mend his ways. *His* master'll be sending for him, and then see how he'll look!"

"He'll go to torment, and no mistake," said little Jake.

"He desarves it!" said Aunt Chloe, grimly; "he's broke a many, many, many hearts, – I tell ye all!" she said, stopping, with a fork uplifted in her hands; "it's like what Mas'r George reads in Ravelations, – souls a callin' under the altar! and a callin' on the Lord for vengeance on sich! – and by and by the Lord he'll hear 'em – so he will!"

Aunt Chloe, who was much revered in the kitchen, was listened to with open mouth; and, the dinner being now fairly sent in, the whole kitchen was at leisure to gossip with her, and to listen to her remarks.

"Sich'll be burnt up forever, and no mistake; won't ther?" said Andy.

"I'd be glad to see it, I'll be boun'," said little Jake.

"Chil'en!" said a voice, that made them all start. It was Uncle Tom, who had come in, and stood listening to the conversation at the door.

"Chil'en!" he said, "I'm afeard you don't know what ye're sayin'. Forever is a *dre'ful* word, chil'en; it's awful to think on 't. You oughtenter wish that ar to any human crittur."

"We wouldn't to anybody but the soul-drivers," said Andy; "nobody can help wishing it to them, they 's so awful wicked."

"Don't natur herself kinder cry out on 'em?" said Aunt Chloe. "Don't dey tear der suckin' baby right off his mother's breast, and sell him, and der little children as is crying and holding on by her clothes, – don't dey pull 'em off and sells 'em? Don't dey tear wife and husband apart?" said Aunt Chloe, beginning to cry, "when it's jest takin' the very life on 'em? – and all the while does they feel one bit, don't dey drink and smoke, and take it oncommon easy? Lor, if the devil don't get them, what's he good for?" And Aunt Chloe covered her face with her checked apron, and began to sob in good earnest.

"Pray for them that 'spitefully use you, the good book says," says Tom.

"Pray for 'em!" said Aunt Chloe; "Lor, it's too tough! I can't pray for 'em."

"It's natur, Chloe, and natur 's strong," said Tom, "but the Lord's grace is stronger; besides, you oughter think what an awful state a poor crittur's soul 's in that'll do them ar things, – you oughter thank God that you an't *like* him, Chloe. I'm sure I'd rather be sold, ten thousand times over, than to have all that ar poor crittur's got to answer for."

"So 'd I, a heap," said Jake. "Lor, *shouldn't* we cotch it, Andy?"

Andy shrugged his shoulders, and gave an acquiescent whistle.

"I'm glad Mas'r didn't go off this morning, as he looked to," said Tom; "that ar hurt me more than sellin', it did. Mebbe it might have been natural for him, but 't would have come desp't hard on me, as has known him from a baby; but I've seen Mas'r, and I begin ter feel sort o' reconciled to the Lord's will now. Mas'r couldn't help hisself; he did right, but I'm feared things will be kinder goin' to rack, when I'm gone Mas'r can't be spected to be a pryin' round everywhar, as I've done, a keepin' up all the ends. The boys all means well, but they 's powerful car'less. That ar troubles me."

The bell here rang, and Tom was summoned to the parlor.

"Tom," said his master, kindly, "I want you to notice that I give this gentleman bonds to forfeit a thousand dollars if you are not on the spot when he wants you; he's going today to look after his other business, and you can have the day to yourself. Go anywhere you like, boy."

"Thank you, Mas'r," said Tom.

"And mind yourself," said the trader, "and don't come it over your master with any o' yer nigger tricks; for I'll take every cent out of him, if you an't thar. If he'd hear to me, he wouldn't trust any on ye – slippery as eels!"

"Mas'r," said Tom, – and he stood very straight, – "I was jist eight years old when ole Missis put you into my arms, and you wasn't a year old. 'Thar,' says she, 'Tom, that's to be *your* young Mas'r; take good care on him,' says she. And now I jist ask you, Mas'r, have I ever broke word to you, or gone contrary to you, 'specially since I was a Christian?"

Mr. Shelby was fairly overcome, and the tears rose to his eyes.

"My good boy," said he, "the Lord knows you say but the truth; and if I was able to help it, all the world shouldn't buy you."

"And sure as I am a Christian woman," said Mrs. Shelby, "you shall be redeemed as soon as I can any bring together means. Sir," she said to Haley, "take good account of who you sell him to, and let me know."

"Lor, yes, for that matter," said the trader, "I may bring him up in a year, not much the wuss for wear, and trade him back."

"I'll trade with you then, and make it for your advantage," said Mrs. Shelby.

"Of course," said the trader, "all 's equal with me; li'ves trade 'em up as down, so I does a good business. All I want is a livin', you know, ma'am; that's all any on us wants, I, s'pose."

Mr. and Mrs. Shelby both felt annoyed and degraded by the familiar impudence of the trader, and yet both saw the absolute necessity of putting a constraint on their feelings. The more hopelessly sordid and insensible he appeared, the greater became Mrs. Shelby's dread of his succeeding in recapturing Eliza and her child, and of course the greater her motive for detaining him by every female artifice. She therefore graciously smiled, assented, chatted familiarly, and did all she could to make time pass imperceptibly.

At two o'clock Sam and Andy brought the horses up to the posts, apparently greatly refreshed and invigorated by the scamper of the morning.

Sam was there new oiled from dinner, with an abundance of zealous and ready officiousness. As Haley approached, he was boasting, in flourishing style, to Andy, of the evident and eminent success of the operation, now that he had "farly come to it."

"Your master, I s'pose, don't keep no dogs," said Haley, thoughtfully, as he prepared to mount.

"Heaps on 'em," said Sam, triumphantly; "thar's Bruno – he's a roarer! and, besides that, 'bout every nigger of us keeps a pup of some natur or uther."

"Poh!" said Haley, – and he said something else, too, with regard to the said dogs, at which Sam muttered,

"I don't see no use cussin' on 'em, no way."

"But your master don't keep no dogs (I pretty much know he don't) for trackin' out niggers."

Sam knew exactly what he meant, but he kept on a look of earnest and desperate simplicity.

"Our dogs all smells round considable sharp. I spect they's the kind, though they han't never had no practice. They 's *far* dogs, though, at most anything, if you'd get 'em started. Here, Bruno," he called, whistling to the lumbering Newfoundland, who came pitching tumultuously toward them.

"You go hang!" said Haley, getting up. "Come, tumble up now."

Sam tumbled up accordingly, dexterously contriving to tickle Andy as he did so, which occasioned Andy to split out into a laugh, greatly to Haley's indignation, who made a cut at him with his riding-whip.

"I 's 'stonished at yer, Andy," said Sam, with awful gravity. "This yer's a seris bisness, Andy. Yer mustn't be a makin' game. This yer an't no way to help Mas'r."

"I shall take the straight road to the river," said Haley, decidedly, after they had come to the boundaries of the estate. "I know the way of all of 'em, – they makes tracks for the underground."

"Sartin," said Sam, "dat's de idee. Mas'r Haley hits de thing right in de middle. Now, der's two roads to de river, – de dirt road and der pike, – which Mas'r mean to take?"

Andy looked up innocently at Sam, surprised at hearing this new geographical fact, but instantly confirmed what he said, by a vehement reiteration.

"Cause," said Sam, "I'd rather be 'clined to 'magine that Lizy 'd take de dirt road, bein' it's the least travelled."

Haley, notwithstanding that he was a very old bird, and naturally inclined to be suspicious of chaff, was rather brought up by this view of the case.

"If yer warn't both on yer such cussed liars, now!" he said, contemplatively as he pondered a moment.

The pensive, reflective tone in which this was spoken appeared to amuse Andy prodigiously, and he drew a little behind, and shook so as apparently to run a great risk of failing off his horse, while Sam's face was immovably composed into the most doleful gravity.

"Course," said Sam, "Mas'r can do as he'd ruther, go de straight road, if Mas'r thinks best, – it's all one to us. Now, when I study 'pon it, I think de straight road de best, *deridedly*."

"She would naturally go a lonesome way," said Haley, thinking aloud, and not minding Sam's remark.

"Dar an't no sayin'," said Sam; "gals is pecular; they never does nothin' ye thinks they will; mose gen'lly the contrary. Gals is nat'lly made contrary; and so, if you thinks they've gone one road, it is sartin you'd better go t' other, and then you'll be sure to find 'em. Now, my private 'pinion is, Lizy took der road; so I think we'd better take de straight one."

This profound generic view of the female sex did not seem to dispose Haley particularly to the straight road, and he announced decidedly that he should go the other, and asked Sam when they should come to it.

"A little piece ahead," said Sam, giving a wink to Andy with the eye which was on Andy's side of the head; and he added, gravely, "but I've studded on de matter, and I'm quite clar we ought not to go dat ar way. I nebber been over it no way. It's despit lonesome, and we might lose our way, - whar we'd come to, de Lord only knows."

"Nevertheless," said Haley, "I shall go that way."

"Now I think on 't, I think I hearn 'em tell that dat ar road was all fenced up and down by der creek, and thar, an't it, Andy?"

Andy wasn't certain; he'd only "hearn tell" about that road, but never been over it. In short, he was strictly noncommittal.

Haley, accustomed to strike the balance of probabilities between lies of greater or lesser magnitude, thought that it lay in favor of the dirt road aforesaid. The mention of the thing he thought he perceived was involuntary on Sam's part at first, and his confused attempts to dissuade him he set down to a desperate lying on second thoughts, as being unwilling to implicate Liza.

When, therefore, Sam indicated the road, Haley plunged briskly into it, followed by Sam and Andy.

Now, the road, in fact, was an old one, that had formerly been a thoroughfare to the river, but abandoned for many years after the laying of the new pike. It was open for about an hour's ride, and after that it was cut across by various farms and fences.

Sam knew this fact perfectly well, – indeed, the road had been so long closed up, that Andy had never heard of it. He therefore rode along with an air of dutiful submission, only groaning and vociferating occasionally that 't was "desp't rough, and bad for Jerry's foot."

"Now, I jest give yer warning," said Haley, "I know yer; yer won't get me to turn off this road, with all yer fussin' – so you shet up!"

"Mas'r will go his own way!" said Sam, with rueful submission, at the same time winking most Portentously to Andy, whose delight was now very near the explosive point.

Sam was in wonderful spirits, – professed to keep a very brisk lookout, – at one time exclaiming that he saw "a gal's bonnet" on the top of some distant eminence, or calling to Andy "if that thar wasn't 'Lizy' down in the hollow;" always making these exclamations in some rough or craggy part of the road, where the sudden quickening of speed was a special inconvenience to all parties concerned, and thus keeping Haley in a state of constant commotion.

After riding about an hour in this way, the whole party made a precipitate and tumultuous descent into a barn-yard belonging to a large farming establishment. Not a soul was in sight, all the hands being employed in the fields; but, as the barn stood conspicuously and plainly square across the road, it was evident that their journey in that direction had reached a decided finale.

"Wan't dat ar what I telled Mas'r?" said Sam, with an air of injured innocence. "How does strange gentleman spect to know more about a country dan de natives born and raised?"

"You rascal!" said Haley, "you knew all about this."

"Didn't I tell yer I *knowd*, and yer wouldn't believe me? I telled Mas'r 't was all shet up, and fenced up, and I didn't spect we could get through, – Andy heard me."

It was all too true to be disputed, and the unlucky man had to pocket his wrath with the best grace he was able, and all three faced to the right about, and took up their line of march for the highway.

In consequence of all the various delays, it was about three-quarters of an hour after Eliza had laid her child to sleep in the village tavern that the party came riding into the same place. Eliza was standing by the window, looking out in another direction, when Sam's quick eye caught a glimpse of her. Haley and Andy were two yards behind. At this crisis, Sam contrived to have his hat blown off, and uttered a loud and characteristic ejaculation, which startled her at once; she drew suddenly back; the whole train swept by the window, round to the front door.

A thousand lives seemed to be concentrated in that one moment to Eliza. Her room opened by a side door to the river. She caught her child, and sprang down the steps towards it. The trader caught a full glimpse of her just as she was disappearing down the bank; and throwing himself from his horse, and calling loudly on Sam and Andy, he was after her like a hound after a deer. In that dizzy moment her feet to her scarce seemed to touch the ground, and a moment brought her to the water's edge. Right on behind they came; and, nerved with strength such as God gives only to the desperate, with one wild cry and flying leap, she vaulted sheer over the turbid current by the shore, on to the raft of ice beyond. It was a desperate leap – impossible to anything but madness and despair; and Haley, Sam, and Andy, instinctively cried out, and lifted up their hands, as she did it.

The huge green fragment of ice on which she alighted pitched and creaked as her weight came on it, but she staid there not a moment. With wild cries and desperate energy she leaped to another and still another cake; stumbling – leaping – slipping – springing upwards again! Her shoes are gone – her stockings cut from her feet – while blood marked every step; but she saw nothing, felt nothing, till dimly, as in a dream, she saw the Ohio side, and a man helping her up the bank.

"Yer a brave gal, now, whoever ye ar!" said the man, with an oath.

Eliza recognized the voice and face for a man who owned a farm not far from her old home.

"O, Mr. Symmes! – save me – do save me – do hide me!" said Elia.

"Why, what's this?" said the man. "Why, if 'tan't Shelby's gal!"

"My child! – this boy! – he'd sold him! There is his Mas'r," said she, pointing to the Kentucky shore. "O, Mr. Symmes, you've got a little boy!"

"So I have," said the man, as he roughly, but kindly, drew her up the steep bank. "Besides, you're a right brave gal. I like grit, wherever I see it."

When they had gained the top of the bank, the man paused.

"I'd be glad to do something for ye," said he; "but then there's nowhar I could take ye. The best I can do is to tell ye to go *thar,*" said he, pointing to a large white house which stood by itself, off the main street of the village. "Go thar; they're kind folks. Thar's no kind o' danger but they'll help you, – they're up to all that sort o' thing."

"The Lord bless you!" said Eliza, earnestly.

"No 'casion, no 'casion in the world," said the man. "What I've done's of no 'count."

"And, oh, surely, sir, you won't tell any one!"

"Go to thunder, gal! What do you take a feller for? In course not," said the man. "Come, now, go along like a likely, sensible gal, as you are. You've arnt your liberty, and you shall have it, for all me."

The woman folded her child to her bosom, and walked firmly and swiftly away. The man stood and looked after her.

"Shelby, now, mebbe won't think this yer the most neighborly thing in the world; but what's a feller to do? If he catches one of my gals in the same fix, he's welcome to pay back. Somehow I never could see no kind o' critter a strivin' and pantin', and trying to clar theirselves, with the dogs arter 'em and go agin 'em. Besides, I don't see no kind of 'casion for me to be hunter and catcher for other folks, neither."

So spoke this poor, heathenish Kentuckian, who had not been instructed in his constitutional relations, and consequently was betrayed into acting in a sort of Christianized manner, which, if he had been better situated and more enlightened, he would not have been left to do.

Haley had stood a perfectly amazed spectator of the scene, till Eliza had disappeared up the bank, when he turned a blank, inquiring look on Sam and Andy.

"That ar was a tolable fair stroke of business," said Sam.

"The gal 's got seven devils in her, I believe!" said Haley. "How like a wildcat she jumped!"

"Wal, now," said Sam, scratching his head, "I hope Mas'r'll 'scuse us trying dat ar road. Don't think I feel spry enough for dat ar, no way!" and Sam gave a hoarse chuckle.

"*You* laugh!" said the trader, with a growl.

"Lord bless you, Mas'r, I couldn't help it now," said Sam, giving way to the long pent-up delight of his soul. "She looked so curi's, a leapin' and springin' – ice a crackin' – and only to hear her, – plump! ker chunk! ker splash! Spring! Lord! how she goes it!" and Sam and Andy laughed till the tears rolled down their cheeks.

"I'll make ye laugh t' other side yer mouths!" said the trader, laying about their heads with his riding-whip.

Both ducked, and ran shouting up the bank, and were on their horses before he was up.

"Good-evening, Mas'r!" said Sam, with much gravity. "I berry much spect Missis be anxious 'bout Jerry. Mas'r Haley won't want us no longer. Missis wouldn't hear of our ridin' the critters over Lizy's bridge tonight;" and, with a facetious poke into Andy's ribs, he started off, followed by the latter, at full speed, – their shouts of laughter coming faintly on the wind.

Chapter 8

Eliza's Escape

Eliza made her desperate retreat across the river just in the dusk of twilight. The gray mist of evening, rising slowly from the river, enveloped her as she disappeared up the bank, and the swollen current and floundering masses of ice presented a hopeless barrier between her and her pursuer. Haley therefore slowly and discontentedly returned to the little tavern, to ponder further what was to be done. The woman opened to him the door of a little parlor, covered with a rag carpet, where stood a table with a very shining black oil-cloth, sundry lank, high-backed wood chairs, with some plaster images in resplendent colors on the mantel-shelf, above a very dimly-smoking grate; a long hard-wood settle extended its uneasy length by the chimney, and here Haley sat him down to meditate on the instability of human hopes and happiness in general.

"What did I want with the little cuss, now," he said to himself, "that I should have got myself treed like a coon, as I am, this yer way?" and Haley relieved himself by repeating over a not very select litany of imprecations on himself, which, though there was the best possible reason to consider them as true, we shall, as a matter of taste, omit.

He was startled by the loud and dissonant voice of a man who was apparently dismounting at the door. He hurried to the window.

"By the land! if this yer an't the nearest, now, to what I've heard folks call Providence," said Haley. "I do b'lieve that ar's Tom Loker."

Haley hastened out. Standing by the bar, in the corner of the room, was a brawny, muscular man, full six feet in height, and broad in proportion. He was dressed in a coat of buffalo-skin, made with the hair outward, which gave him a shaggy and fierce appearance, perfectly in keeping with the whole air of his physiognomy. In the head and face every organ and lineament expressive of brutal and unhesitating violence was in a state of the highest possible development. Indeed, could our readers fancy a bull-dog come unto man's estate, and walking about in a hat and coat, they would have no unapt idea of the general style and effect of his physique. He was accompanied by a travelling companion, in many respects an exact contrast to himself. He was short and slender, lithe and catlike in his motions, and had a peering, mousing expression about his keen black eyes, with which every feature of his face seemed sharpened into sympathy; his thin, long nose, ran out as if it was eager to bore into the nature of things in general; his sleek, thin, black hair was stuck eagerly forward, and all his motions and evolutions expressed a dry, cautious acuteness. The great man poured out a big tumbler half full of raw spirits, and gulped it down without a word. The little man stood tiptoe, and putting his head first to one side and then the other, and snuffing considerately in the directions of the various bottles, ordered at last a mint julep, in a thin and quivering voice, and with an air of great circumspection. When poured out, he took it and looked at it with a sharp, complacent air, like a man who thinks he has done about the right thing, and hit the nail on the head, and proceeded to dispose of it in short and well-advised sips.

"Wal, now, who'd a thought this yer luck 'ad come to me? Why, Loker, how are ye?" said Haley, coming forward, and extending his hand to the big man.

"The devil!" was the civil reply. "What brought you here, Haley?"

The mousing man, who bore the name of Marks, instantly stopped his sipping, and, poking his head forward, looked shrewdly on the new acquaintance, as a cat sometimes looks at a moving dry leaf, or some other possible object of pursuit.

"I say, Tom, this yer's the luckiest thing in the world. I'm in a devil of a hobble, and you must help me out."

"Ugh? aw! like enough!" grunted his complacent acquaintance. "A body may be pretty sure of that, when *you're* glad to see 'em; something to be made off of 'em. What's the blow now?"

"You've got a friend here?" said Haley, looking doubtfully at Marks; "partner, perhaps?"

"Yes, I have. Here, Marks! here's that ar feller that I was in with in Natchez."

"Shall be pleased with his acquaintance," said Marks, thrusting out a long, thin hand, like a raven's claw. "Mr. Haley, I believe?"

"The same, sir," said Haley. "And now, gentlemen, seein' as we've met so happily, I think I'll stand up to a small matter of a treat in this here parlor. So, now, old coon," said he to the man at the bar, "get us hot water, and sugar, and cigars, and plenty of the *real stuff* and we'll have a blow-out."

Behold, then, the candles lighted, the fire stimulated to the burning point in the grate, and our three worthies seated round a table, well spread with all the accessories to good fellowship enumerated before.

Haley began a pathetic recital of his peculiar troubles. Loker shut up his mouth, and listened to him with gruff and surly attention. Marks, who was anxiously and with much fidgeting compounding a tumbler of punch to his own peculiar taste, occasionally looked up from his employment, and, poking his sharp nose and chin almost into Haley's face, gave the most earnest heed to the whole narrative. The conclusion of it appeared to amuse him extremely, for he shook his shoulders and sides in silence, and perked up his thin lips with an air of great internal enjoyment.

"So, then, ye'r fairly sewed up, an't ye?" he said; "he! he! he! It's neatly done, too."

"This yer young-un business makes lots of trouble in the trade," said Haley, dolefully.

"If we could get a breed of gals that didn't care, now, for their young uns," said Marks; "tell ye, I think 't would be 'bout the greatest mod'rn improvement I knows on," – and Marks patronized his joke by a quiet introductory sniggle.

"Jes so," said Haley; "I never couldn't see into it; young uns is heaps of trouble to 'em; one would think, now, they'd be glad to get clar on 'em; but they arn't. And the more trouble a young un is, and the more good for nothing, as a gen'l thing, the tighter they sticks to 'em."

"Wal, Mr. Haley," said Marks, "'est pass the hot water. Yes, sir, you say 'est what I feel and all'us have. Now, I bought a gal once, when I was in the trade, – a tight, likely wench she was, too, and quite considerable smart, – and she had a young un that was mis'able sickly; it had a crooked back, or something or other; and I jest gin 't away to a man that thought he'd take his chance raising on 't, being it didn't cost nothin'; – never thought, yer know, of the gal's taking' on about it, – but, Lord, yer oughter seen how she went on. Why, re'lly, she did seem to me to valley the child more 'cause *'t was* sickly and cross, and plagued her; and she warn't making b'lieve, neither, – cried about it, she did, and lopped round, as if she'd lost every friend she had. It re'lly was droll to think on 't. Lord, there ain't no end to women's notions."

"Wal, jest so with me," said Haley. "Last summer, down on Red river, I got a gal traded off on me, with a likely lookin' child enough, and his eyes looked as bright as yourn; but, come to look, I found him stone blind. Fact – he was stone blind. Wal, ye see, I thought there warn't no harm in my jest passing him along, and not sayin' nothin'; and I'd got him nicely swapped off for a keg o' whiskey; but come to get him away from the gal, she was jest like a tiger. So 't was before we started, and I hadn't got my gang chained up; so what should she do but ups on a cotton-bale, like a cat, ketches a knife from one of the deck hands, and, I tell ye, she made all fly for a minit, till she saw 't wan't no use; and she jest turns round, and pitches head first, young un and all, into the river, - went down plump, and never ris."

"Bah!" said Tom Loker, who had listened to these stories with ill-repressed disgust, - "shif'less, both on ye! *my* gals don't cut up no such shines, I tell ye!"

"Indeed! how do you help it?" said Marks, briskly.

"Help it? why, I buys a gal, and if she's got a young un to be sold, I jest walks up and puts my fist to her face, and says, 'Look here, now, if you give me one word out of your head, I'll smash yer face in. I won't hear one word - not the beginning of a word.' I says to 'em, 'This yer young un's mine, and not yourn, and you've no kind o' business with it. I'm going to sell it, first chance; mind, you don't cut up none o' yer shines about it, or I'll make ye wish ye'd never been born.' I tell ye, they sees it an't no play, when I gets hold. I makes 'em as whist as fishes; and if one on 'em begins and gives a yelp, why, -" and Mr. Loker brought down his fist with a thump that fully explained the hiatus.

"That ar's what ye may call *emphasis*," said Marks, poking Haley in the side, and going into another small giggle. "An't Tom peculiar? he! he! I say, Tom, I s'pect you make 'em *understand*, for all niggers' heads is woolly. They don't never have no doubt o' your meaning, Tom. If you an't the devil, Tom, you 's his twin brother, I'll say that for ye!"

Tom received the compliment with becoming modesty, and began to look as affable as was consistent, as John Bunyan says, "with his doggish nature."

Haley, who had been imbibing very freely of the staple of the evening, began to feel a sensible elevation and enlargement of his moral faculties, - a phenomenon not unusual with gentlemen of a serious and reflective turn, under similar circumstances.

"Wal, now, Tom," he said, "ye re'lly is too bad, as I al'ays have told ye; ye know, Tom, you and I used to talk over these yer matters down in Natchez, and I used to prove to ye that we made full as much, and was as well off for this yer world, by treatin' on 'em well, besides keepin' a better chance for comin' in the kingdom at last, when wust comes to wust, and thar an't nothing else left to get, ye know."

"Boh!" said Tom, "*don't* I know? - don't make me too sick with any yer stuff, - my stomach is a leetle riled now;" and Tom drank half a glass of raw brandy.

"I say," said Haley, and leaning back in his chair and gesturing impressively, "I'll say this now, I al'ays meant to drive my trade so as to make money on 't *fust* and *foremost*, as much as any man; but, then, trade an't everything, and money an't everything, 'cause we 's all got souls. I don't care, now, who hears me say it, - and I think a cussed sight on it, - so I may as well come out with it. I b'lieve in religion, and one of these days, when I've got matters tight and snug, I calculates to tend to my soul and them ar matters; and so what's the use of doin' any more wickedness than 's re'lly necessary? – it don't seem to me it's 't all prudent."

"Tend to yer soul!" repeated Tom, contemptuously; "take a bright lookout to find a soul in you, – save yourself any care on that score. If the devil sifts you through a hair sieve, he won't find one."

"Why, Tom, you're cross," said Haley; "why can't ye take it pleasant, now, when a feller's talking for your good?"

"Stop that ar jaw o' yourn, there," said Tom, gruffly. "I can stand most any talk o' yourn but your pious talk, – that kills me right up. After all, what's the odds between me and you? 'Tan't that you care one bit more, or have a bit more feelin' – it's clean, sheer, dog meanness, wanting to cheat the devil and save your own skin; don't I see through it? And your 'gettin' religion,' as you call it, arter all, is too p'isin mean for any crittur; – run up a bill with the devil all your life, and then sneak out when pay time comes! Bob!"

"Come, come, gentlemen, I say; this isn't business," said Marks. "There's different ways, you know, of looking at all subjects. Mr. Haley is a very nice man, no doubt, and has his own conscience; and, Tom, you have your ways, and very good ones, too, Tom; but quarrelling, you know, won't answer no kind of purpose. Let's go to business. Now, Mr. Haley, what is it? – you want us to undertake to catch this yer gal?"

"The gal's no matter of mine, – she's Shelby's; it's only the boy. I was a fool for buying the monkey!"

"You're generally a fool!" said Tom, gruffly.

"Come, now, Loker, none of your huffs," said Marks, licking his lips; "you see, Mr. Haley 's a puttin' us in a way of a good job, I reckon; just hold still - these yer arrangements is my forte. This yer gal, Mr. Haley, how is she? what is she?"

"Wal! white and handsome - well brought up. I'd a gin Shelby eight hundred or a thousand, and then made well on her."

"White and handsome - well brought up!" said Marks, his sharp eyes, nose and mouth, all alive with enterprise. "Look here, now, Loker, a beautiful opening. We'll do a business here on our own account; - we does the catchin'; the boy, of course, goes to Mr. Haley, - we takes the gal to Orleans to speculate on. An't it beautiful?"

Tom, whose great heavy mouth had stood ajar during this communication, now suddenly snapped it together, as a big dog closes on a piece of meat, and seemed to be digesting the idea at his leisure.

"Ye see," said Marks to Haley, stirring his punch as he did so, "ye see, we has justices convenient at all p'ints along shore, that does up any little jobs in our line quite reasonable. Tom, he does the knockin' down and that ar; and I come in all dressed up - shining boots - everything first chop, when the swearin' 's to be done. You oughter see, now," said Marks, in a glow of professional pride, "how I can tone it off. One day, I'm Mr. Twickem, from New Orleans; 'nother day, I'm just come from my plantation on Pearl river, where I works seven hundred niggers; then, again, I come out a distant relation of Henry Clay, or some old cock in Kentuck. Talents is different, you know. Now, Tom's roarer when there's any thumping or fighting to be done; but at lying he an't good, Tom an't, – ye see it don't come natural to him; but, Lord, if thar's a feller in the country that can swear to anything and everything, and put in all the circumstances and flourishes with a long face, and carry 't through better 'n I can, why, I'd like to see him, that's all! I b'lieve my heart, I could get along and snake through, even if justices were more particular than they is. Sometimes I rather wish they was more particular; 't would be a heap more relishin' if they was, – more fun, yer know."

Tom Loker, who, as we have made it appear, was a man of slow thoughts and movements, here interrupted Marks by bringing his heavy fist down on the table, so as to make all ring again, *"It'll do!"* he said.

"Lord bless ye, Tom, ye needn't break all the glasses!" said Marks; "save your fist for time o' need."

"But, gentlemen, an't I to come in for a share of the profits?" said Haley.

"An't it enough we catch the boy for ye?" said Loker. "What do ye want?"

"Wal," said Haley, "if I gives you the job, it's worth something, – say ten per cent. on the profits, expenses paid."

"Now," said Loker, with a tremendous oath, and striking the table with his heavy fist, "don't I know *you*, Dan

Haley? Don't you think to come it over me! Suppose Marks and I have taken up the catchin' trade, jest to 'commodate gentlemen like you, and get nothin' for ourselves? – Not by a long chalk! we'll have the gal out and out, and you keep quiet, or, ye see, we'll have both, – what's to hinder? Han't you show'd us the game? It's as free to us as you, I hope. If you or Shelby wants to chase us, look where the partridges was last year; if you find them or us, you're quite welcome."

"O, wal, certainly, jest let it go at that," said Haley, alarmed; "you catch the boy for the job; – you allers did trade *far* with me, Tom, and was up to yer word."

"Ye know that," said Tom; "I don't pretend none of your snivelling ways, but I won't lie in my 'counts with the devil himself. What I ses I'll do, I will do, – you know *that*, Dan Haley."

"Jes so, jes so, – I said so, Tom," said Haley; "and if you'd only promise to have the boy for me in a week, at any point you'll name, that's all I want."

"But it an't all I want, by a long jump," said Tom. "Ye don't think I did business with you, down in Natchez, for nothing, Haley; I've learned to hold an eel, when I catch him. You've got to fork over fifty dollars, flat down, or this child don't start a peg. I know yer."

"Why, when you have a job in hand that may bring a clean profit of somewhere about a thousand or sixteen hundred, why, Tom, you're onreasonable," said Haley.

"Yes, and hasn't we business booked for five weeks to come, – all we can do? And suppose we leaves all, and goes to bush-whacking round arter yer young uns, and finally doesn't catch the gal, – and gals allers is the devil *to* catch, – what's then? would you pay us a cent – would you? I think I see you a doin' it – ugh! No, no; flap down your fifty. If we get the job, and it pays, I'll hand it back; if we don't, it's for our trouble, – that's *far*, an't it, Marks?"

"Certainly, certainly," said Marks, with a conciliatory tone; "it's only a retaining fee, you see, – he! he! he! – we lawyers, you know. Wal, we must all keep good-natured, – keep easy, yer know. Tom'll have the boy for yer, anywhere ye'll name; won't ye, Tom?"

"If I find the young un, I'll bring him on to Cincinnati, and leave him at Granny Belcher's, on the landing," said Loker.

Marks had got from his pocket a greasy pocket-book, and taking a long paper from thence, he sat down, and fixing his keen black eyes on it, began mumbling over its contents:

> "Barnes – Shelby County – boy Jim, three hundred dollars for him, dead or alive.
>
> "Edwards – Dick and Lucy – man and wife, six hundred dollars; wench Polly and two children – six hundred for her or her head."

"I'm jest a runnin' over our business, to see if we can take up this yer handily. Loker," he said, after a pause, "we must set Adams and Springer on the track of these yer; they've been booked some time."

"They'll charge too much," said Tom.

"I'll manage that ar; they 's young in the business, and must spect to work cheap," said Marks, as he continued to read. "Ther's three on 'em easy cases, 'cause all you've got to do is to shoot 'em, or swear they is shot; they couldn't, of course, charge much for that. Them other cases," he said, folding the paper, "will bear puttin' off a spell. So now let's come to the particulars. Now, Mr. Haley, you saw this yer gal when she landed?"

"To be sure, – plain as I see you."

"And a man helpin' on her up the bank?" said Loker.

"To be sure, I did."

"Most likely," said Marks, "she's took in somewhere; but where, 's a question. Tom, what do you say?"

"We must cross the river tonight, no mistake," said Tom.

"But there's no boat about," said Marks. "The ice is running awfully, Tom; an't it dangerous?"

"Don'no nothing 'bout that, – only it's got to be done," said Tom, decidedly.

"Dear me," said Marks, fidgeting, "it'll be – I say," he said, walking to the window, "it's dark as a wolf's mouth, and, Tom–"

"The long and short is, you're scared, Marks; but I can't help that, – you've got to go. Suppose you want to lie by a day or two, till the gal 's been carried on the underground line up to Sandusky or so, before you start."

"O, no; I an't a grain afraid," said Marks, "only–"

"Only what?" said Tom.

"Well, about the boat. Yer see there an't any boat."

"I heard the woman say there was one coming along this evening, and that a man was going to cross over in it. Neck or nothing, we must go with him," said Tom.

"I s'pose you've got good dogs," said Haley.

"First rate," said Marks. "But what's the use? you han't got nothin' o' hers to smell on."

"Yes, I have," said Haley, triumphantly. "Here's her shawl she left on the bed in her hurry; she left her bonnet, too."

"That ar's lucky," said Loker; "fork over."

"Though the dogs might damage the gal, if they come on her unawars," said Haley.

"That ar's a consideration," said Marks. "Our dogs tore a feller half to pieces, once, down in Mobile, 'fore we could get 'em off."

"Well, ye see, for this sort that's to be sold for their looks, that ar won't answer, ye see," said Haley.

"I do see," said Marks. "Besides, if she's got took in, 'tan't no go, neither. Dogs is no 'count in these yer up states where these critters gets carried; of course, ye can't get on their track. They only does down in plantations, where niggers, when they runs, has to do their own running, and don't get no help."

"Well," said Loker, who had just stepped out to the bar to make some inquiries, "they say the man's come with the boat; so, Marks–"

That worthy cast a rueful look at the comfortable quarters he was leaving, but slowly rose to obey. After exchanging a few words of further arrangement, Haley, with visible reluctance, handed over the fifty dollars to Tom, and the worthy trio separated for the night.

If any of our refined and Christian readers object to the society into which this scene introduces them, let us beg them to begin and conquer their prejudices in time. The catching business, we beg to remind them, is rising to the dignity of a lawful and patriotic profession. If all the broad land between the Mississippi and the Pacific becomes one great market for bodies and souls, and human property retains the locomotive tendencies of this nineteenth century, the trader and catcher may yet be among our aristocracy.

While this scene was going on at the tavern, Sam and Andy, in a state of high felicitation, pursued their way home.

Sam was in the highest possible feather, and expressed his exultation by all sorts of supernatural howls and ejaculations, by divers odd motions and contortions of his whole system. Sometimes he would sit backward, with his face to the horse's tail and sides, and then, with a whoop and a somerset, come right side up in his place again, and, drawing on a grave face, begin to lecture Andy in high-sounding tones for laughing and playing the fool. Anon, slapping his sides with his arms, he would burst forth in peals of laughter, that made the old woods ring as they passed. With all these evolutions, he contrived to keep the horses up to the top of their speed, until, between ten and eleven, their heels resounded on the gravel at the end of the balcony. Mrs. Shelby flew to the railings.

"Is that you, Sam? Where are they?"

"Mas'r Haley 's a-restin' at the tavern; he's drefful fatigued, Missis."

"And Eliza, Sam?"

"Wal, she's clar 'cross Jordan. As a body may say, in the land o' Canaan."

"Why, Sam, what *do* you mean?" said Mrs. Shelby, breathless, and almost faint, as the possible meaning of these words came over her.

"Wal, Missis, de Lord he persarves his own. Lizy's done gone over the river into 'Hio, as 'markably as if de Lord took her over in a charrit of fire and two hosses."

Sam's vein of piety was always uncommonly fervent in his mistress' presence; and he made great capital of scriptural figures and images.

"Come up here, Sam," said Mr. Shelby, who had followed on to the verandah, "and tell your mistress what she wants. Come, come, Emily," said he, passing his arm round her, "you are cold and all in a shiver; you allow yourself to feel too much."

"Feel too much! Am not I a woman, – a mother? Are we not both responsible to God for this poor girl? My God! lay not this sin to our charge."

"What sin, Emily? You see yourself that we have only done what we were obliged to."

"There's an awful feeling of guilt about it, though," said Mrs. Shelby. "I can't reason it away."

"Here, Andy, you nigger, be alive!" called Sam, under the verandah; "take these yer hosses to der barn; don't ye hear Mas'r a callin'?" and Sam soon appeared, palm-leaf in hand, at the parlor door.

"Now, Sam, tell us distinctly how the matter was," said Mr. Shelby. "Where is Eliza, if you know?"

"Wal, Mas'r, I saw her, with my own eyes, a crossin' on the floatin' ice. She crossed most 'markably; it wasn't no less nor a miracle; and I saw a man help her up the 'Hio side, and then she was lost in the dusk."

"Sam, I think this rather apocryphal, – this miracle. Crossing on floating ice isn't so easily done," said Mr. Shelby.

"Easy! couldn't nobody a done it, without de Lord. Why, now," said Sam, "'t was jist dis yer way. Mas'r Haley, and me, and Andy, we comes up to de little tavern by the river, and I rides a leetle ahead, – (I 's so zealous to be a cotchin' Lizy, that I couldn't hold in, no way), – and when I comes by the tavern winder, sure enough there she was, right in plain sight, and dey diggin' on behind. Wal, I loses off my hat, and sings out nuff to raise the dead. Course Lizy she hars, and she dodges back, when Mas'r Haley he goes past the door; and then, I tell ye, she clared out de side door; she went down de river bank; – Mas'r Haley he seed her, and yelled out, and him, and me, and Andy, we took arter. Down she come to the river, and thar was the current running ten feet wide by the shore, and over t' other side ice a sawin' and a jiggling up and down, kinder as 't were a great island. We come right behind her, and I thought my soul he'd got her sure enough, – when she gin sich a screech as I never hearn, and thar she was, clar over t' other side of the current, on the ice, and then on she went, a screech-ing and a jumpin', – the ice went crack! c'wallop! cracking! chunk! and she a boundin' like a buck! Lord, the spring that ar gal's got in her an't common, I'm o' 'pinion."

Mrs. Shelby sat perfectly silent, pale with excitement, while Sam told his story.

"God be praised, she isn't dead!" she said; "but where is the poor child now?"

"De Lord will pervide," said Sam, rolling up his eyes piously. "As I've been a sayin', dis yer 's a providence and no mistake, as Missis has allers been a instructin' on us. Thar's allers instruments ris up to do de Lord's will. Now, if 't hadn't been for me today, she'd a been took a dozen times. Warn't it I started off de hosses, dis yer morning' and kept 'em chasin' till nigh dinner time? And didn't I car Mas'r Haley night five miles out of de road, dis evening, or else he'd a come up with Lizy as easy as a dog arter a coon. These yer 's all providences."

"They are a kind of providences that you'll have to be pretty sparing of, Master Sam. I allow no such practices with gentlemen on my place," said Mr. Shelby, with as much sternness as he could command, under the circumstances.

Now, there is no more use in making believe be angry with a negro than with a child; both instinctively see the true state of the case, through all attempts to affect the contrary; and Sam was in no wise disheartened by this rebuke, though he assumed an air of doleful gravity, and stood with the corners of his mouth lowered in most penitential style.

"Mas'r quite right, – quite; it was ugly on me, – there's no disputin' that ar; and of course Mas'r and Missis wouldn't encourage no such works. I'm sensible of dat ar; but a poor nigger like me 's 'mazin' tempted to act ugly sometimes, when fellers will cut up such shines as dat ar Mas'r Haley; he an't no gen'l'man no way;

anybody's been raised as I've been can't help a seein' dat ar."

"Well, Sam," said Mrs. Shelby, "as you appear to have a proper sense of your errors, you may go now and tell Aunt Chloe she may get you some of that cold ham that was left of dinner today. You and Andy must be hungry."

"Missis is a heap too good for us," said Sam, making his bow with alacrity, and departing.

It will be perceived, as has been before intimated, that Master Sam had a native talent that might, undoubtedly, have raised him to eminence in political life, – a talent of making capital out of everything that turned up, to be invested for his own especial praise and glory; and having done up his piety and humility, as he trusted, to the satisfaction of the parlor, he clapped his palm-leaf on his head, with a sort of rakish, free-and-easy air, and proceeded to the dominions of Aunt Chloe, with the intention of flourishing largely in the kitchen.

"I'll speechify these yer niggers," said Sam to himself, "now I've got a chance. Lord, I'll reel it off to make 'em stare!"

It must be observed that one of Sam's especial delights had been to ride in attendance on his master to all kinds of political gatherings, where, roosted on some rail fence, or perched aloft in some tree, he would sit watching the orators, with the greatest apparent gusto, and then, descending among the various brethren of his own color, assembled on the same errand, he would edify and delight them with the most ludicrous burlesques and imitations, all delivered with the most imperturbable earnestness and solemnity; and though the auditors immediately about him were generally of his own color, it not infrequently happened that they were fringed pretty deeply with those of a fairer complexion, who listened, laughing and winking, to Sam's great self-congratulation. In fact, Sam considered oratory as his vocation, and never let slip an opportunity of magnifying his office.

Now, between Sam and Aunt Chloe there had existed, from ancient times, a sort of chronic feud, or rather a decided coolness; but, as Sam was meditating something in the provision department, as the necessary and obvious foundation of his operations, he determined, on the present occasion, to be eminently conciliatory; for he well knew that although "Missis' orders" would undoubtedly be followed to the letter, yet he should gain a considerable deal by enlisting the spirit also. He therefore appeared before Aunt Chloe with a touchingly subdued, resigned expression, like one who has suffered immeasurable hardships in behalf of a persecuted fellow-creature, - enlarged upon the fact that Missis had directed him to come to Aunt Chloe for whatever might be wanting to make up the balance in his solids and fluids, - and thus unequivocally acknowledged her right and supremacy in the cooking department, and all thereto pertaining.

The thing took accordingly. No poor, simple, virtuous body was ever cajoled by the attentions of an electioneering politician with more ease than Aunt Chloe was won over by Master Sam's suavities; and if he had been the prodigal son himself, he could not have been overwhelmed with more maternal bountifulness; and he soon found himself seated, happy and glorious, over a large tin pan, containing a sort of *olla podrida* of all that had appeared on the table for two or three days past. Savory morsels of ham, golden blocks of corn-cake, fragments of pie of every conceivable mathematical figure, chicken wings, gizzards, and drumsticks, all appeared in picturesque confusion; and Sam, as monarch of all he surveyed, sat with his palm-leaf cocked rejoicingly to one side, and patronizing Andy at his right hand.

The kitchen was full of all his compeers, who had hurried and crowded in, from the various cabins, to hear the termination of the day's exploits. Now was Sam's hour of glory. The story of the day was rehearsed, with all kinds of ornament and varnishing which might be necessary to heighten its effect; for Sam, like some of our fashionable dilettanti, never allowed a story to lose any of its gilding by passing through his hands. Roars of laughter attended the narration, and were taken up and prolonged by all the smaller fry, who were lying, in any quantity, about on the floor, or perched in every corner. In the height of the uproar and laughter, Sam, however, preserved an immovable gravity, only from time to time rolling his eyes up, and giving his auditors divers inexpressibly droll glances, without departing from the sententious elevation of his oratory.

"Yer see, fellow-countrymen," said Sam, elevating a turkey's leg, with energy, "yer see, now what dis yer chile 's up ter, for fendin' yer all, – yes, all on yer. For him as tries to get one o' our people is as good as tryin' to get all; yer see the principle 's de same, –

dat ar's clar. And any one o' these yer drivers that comes smelling round arter any our people, why, he's got *me* in his way; *I'm* the feller he's got to set in with, – I'm the feller for yer all to come to, bredren, – I'll stand up for yer rights, – I'll fend 'em to the last breath!"

"Why, but Sam, yer telled me, only this mornin', that you'd help this yer Mas'r to cotch Lizy; seems to me yer talk don't hang together," said Andy.

"I tell you now, Andy," said Sam, with awful superiority, "don't yer be a talkin' 'bout what yer don't know nothin' on; boys like you, Andy, means well, but they can't be spected to collusitate the great principles of action."

Andy looked rebuked, particularly by the hard word collusitate, which most of the youngerly members of the company seemed to consider as a settler in the case, while Sam proceeded.

"Dat ar was *conscience*, Andy; when I thought of gwine arter Lizy, I railly spected Mas'r was sot dat way. When I found Missis was sot the contrar, dat ar was conscience *more yet*, – cause fellers allers gets more by stickin' to Missis' side, – so yer see I 's persistent either way, and sticks up to conscience, and holds on to principles. Yes, *principles*," said Sam, giving an enthusiastic toss to a chicken's neck, – "what's principles good for, if we isn't persistent, I wanter know? Thar, Andy, you may have dat ar bone, – 'tan't picked quite clean."

Sam's audience hanging on his words with open mouth, he could not but proceed.

"Dis yer matter 'bout persistence, feller-niggers," said Sam, with the air of one entering into an abstruse subject, "dis yer 'sistency 's a thing what an't seed into very clar, by most anybody. Now, yer see, when a feller stands up for a thing one day and night, de contrar de next, folks ses (and nat'rally enough dey ses), why he an't persistent, – hand me dat ar bit o' corn-cake, Andy. But let's look inter it. I hope the gen'lmen and der fair sex will scuse my usin' an or'nary sort o' 'parison. Here! I'm a trying to get top o' der hay. Wal, I puts up my larder dis yer side; 'tan't no go; – den, cause I don't try dere no more, but puts my larder right de contrar side, an't I persistent? I'm persistent in wantin' to get up which ary side my larder is; don't you see, all on yer?"

"It's the only thing ye ever was persistent in, Lord knows!" muttered Aunt Chloe, who was getting rather restive; the merriment of the evening being to her somewhat after the Scripture comparison, – like "vinegar upon nitre."

"Yes, indeed!" said Sam, rising, full of supper and glory, for a closing effort. "Yes, my feller-citizens and ladies of de other sex in general, I has principles, – I'm proud to 'oon 'em, – they 's perquisite to dese yer times, and ter *all* times. I has principles, and I sticks to 'em like forty, – jest anything that I thinks is principle, I goes in to 't; – I wouldn't mind if dey burnt me 'live, – I'd walk right up to de stake, I would, and say, here I comes to shed my last blood fur my principles, fur my country, fur de gen'l interests of society."

"Well," said Aunt Chloe, "one o' yer principles will have to be to get to bed some time tonight, and not be a keepin' everybody up till mornin'; now, every one of you young uns that don't want to be cracked, had better be scase, mighty sudden."

"Niggers! all on yer," said Sam, waving his palm-leaf with benignity, "I give yer my blessin'; go to bed now, and be good boys."

And, with this pathetic benediction, the assembly dispersed.

Chapter 9

In Which It Appears That a Senator Is But a Man

The light of the cheerful fire shone on the rug and carpet of a cosey parlor, and glittered on the sides of the tea-cups and well-brightened tea-pot, as Senator Bird was drawing off his boots, preparatory to inserting his feet in a pair of new handsome slippers, which his wife had been working for him while away on his senatorial tour. Mrs. Bird, looking the very picture of delight, was superintending the arrangements of the table, ever and anon mingling admonitory remarks to a number of frolicsome juveniles, who were effervescing in all those modes of untold gambol and mischief that have astonished mothers ever since the flood.

"Tom, let the door-knob alone, – there's a man! Mary! Mary! don't pull the cat's tail, – poor pussy! Jim, you mustn't climb on that table, – no, no! – You don't know, my dear, what a surprise it is to us all, to see you here tonight!" said she, at last, when she found a space to say something to her husband.

"Yes, yes, I thought I'd just make a run down, spend the night, and have a little comfort at home. I'm tired to death, and my head aches!"

Mrs. Bird cast a glance at a camphor-bottle, which stood in the half-open closet, and appeared to meditate an approach to it, but her husband interposed.

"No, no, Mary, no doctoring! a cup of your good hot tea, and some of our good home living, is what I want. It's a tiresome business, this legislating!"

And the senator smiled, as if he rather liked the idea of considering himself a sacrifice to his country.

"Well," said his wife, after the business of the tea-table was getting rather slack, "and what have they been doing in the Senate?"

Now, it was a very unusual thing for gentle little Mrs. Bird ever to trouble her head with what was going on in the house of the state, very wisely considering that she had enough to do to mind her own. Mr. Bird, therefore, opened his eyes in surprise, and said,

"Not very much of importance."

"Well; but is it true that they have been passing a law forbidding people to give meat and drink to those poor colored folks that come along? I heard they were talking of some such law, but I didn't think any Christian legislature would pass it!"

"Why, Mary, you are getting to be a politician, all at once."

"No, nonsense! I wouldn't give a fip for all your politics, generally, but I think this is something downright cruel and unchristian. I hope, my dear, no such law has been passed."

"There has been a law passed forbidding people to help off the slaves that come over from Kentucky, my dear; so much of that thing has been done by these reckless Abolitionists, that our brethren in Kentucky are very strongly excited, and it seems necessary, and no more than Christian and kind, that something should be done by our state to quiet the excitement."

"And what is the law? It don't forbid us to shelter those poor creatures a night, does it, and to give 'em something comfortable to eat, and a few old clothes, and send them quietly about their business?"

"Why, yes, my dear; that would be aiding and abetting, you know."

Mrs. Bird was a timid, blushing little woman, of about four feet in height, and with mild blue eyes, and a peach-blow complexion, and the gentlest, sweetest voice in the world; – as for courage, a moderate-sized cock-turkey had been known to put her to rout at the very first gobble, and a stout house-dog, of moderate capacity, would bring her into subjection merely by a show of his teeth. Her husband and children were her entire world, and in these she ruled more by entreaty and persuasion than by command or argument. There was only one thing that was capable of arousing her, and that provocation came in on the side of her unusually gentle and sympathetic nature; – anything in the shape of cruelty would throw her into a passion, which was the more alarming and inexplicable in proportion to the general softness of her nature. Generally the most indulgent and easy to be entreated of all mothers, still her boys had a very reverent remembrance of a most vehement chastisement she once bestowed on them, because she found them leagued with several graceless boys of the neighborhood, stoning a defenceless kitten.

"I'll tell you what," Master Bill used to say, "I was scared that time. Mother came at me so that I thought she was crazy, and I was whipped and tumbled off to bed, without any supper, before I could get over wondering what had come about; and, after that, I heard mother crying outside the door, which made me feel worse than all the rest. I'll tell you what," he'd say, "we boys never stoned another kitten!"

On the present occasion, Mrs. Bird rose quickly, with very red cheeks, which quite improved her general appearance, and walked up to her husband, with quite a resolute air, and said, in a determined tone,

"Now, John, I want to know if you think such a law as that is right and Christian?"

"You won't shoot me, now, Mary, if I say I do!"

"I never could have thought it of you, John; you didn't vote for it?"

"Even so, my fair politician."

"You ought to be ashamed, John! Poor, homeless, houseless creatures! It's a shameful, wicked, abominable law, and I'll break it, for one, the first time I get a chance; and I hope I *shall* have a chance, I do! Things have got to a pretty pass, if a woman can't give a warm supper and a bed to poor, starving creatures, just because they are slaves, and have been abused and oppressed all their lives, poor things!"

"But, Mary, just listen to me. Your feelings are all quite right, dear, and interesting, and I love you for them; but, then, dear, we mustn't suffer our feelings to run away with our judgment; you must consider it's a matter of private feeling, – there are great public interests involved, – there is such a state of public agitation rising, that we must put aside our private feelings."

"Now, John, I don't know anything about politics, but I can read my Bible; and there I see that I must feed the hungry, clothe the naked, and comfort the desolate; and that Bible I mean to follow."

"But in cases where your doing so would involve a great public evil–"

"Obeying God never brings on public evils. I know it can't. It's always safest, all round, to *do as He* bids us.

"Now, listen to me, Mary, and I can state to you a very clear argument, to show–"

"O, nonsense, John! you can talk all night, but you wouldn't do it. I put it to you, John, – would *you* now turn away a poor, shivering, hungry creature from your door, because he was a runaway? *Would* you, now?"

Now, if the truth must be told, our senator had the misfortune to be a man who had a particularly humane and accessible nature, and turning away anybody that was in trouble never had been his forte; and what was worse for him in this particular pinch of the argument was, that his wife knew it, and, of course was making an assault on rather an indefensible point. So he had recourse to the usual means of gaining time for such cases made and provided; he said "ahem," and coughed several times, took out his pocket-handkerchief, and began to wipe his glasses. Mrs. Bird, seeing the defenceless condition of the enemy's territory, had no more conscience than to push her advantage.

"I should like to see you doing that, John – I really should! Turning a woman out of doors in a snowstorm, for instance; or may be you'd take her up and put her in jail, wouldn't you? You would make a great hand at that!"

"Of course, it would be a very painful duty," began Mr. Bird, in a moderate tone.

"Duty, John! don't use that word! You know it isn't a duty – it can't be a duty! If folks want to keep their slaves from running away, let 'em treat 'em well, – that's my doctrine. If I had slaves (as I hope I never shall have), I'd risk their wanting to run away from me, or you either, John. I tell you folks don't run away when they are happy; and when they do run, poor creatures! they suffer enough with cold and hunger and fear, without everybody's turning against them; and, law or no law, I never will, so help me God!"

"Mary! Mary! My dear, let me reason with you."

"I hate reasoning, John, – especially reasoning on such subjects. There's a way you political folks have of coming round and round a plain right thing; and you don't believe in it yourselves, when it comes to practice. I know *you* well enough, John. You don't believe it's right any more than I do; and you wouldn't do it any sooner than I."

At this critical juncture, old Cudjoe, the black man-of-all-work, put his head in at the door, and wished "Missis would come into the kitchen;" and our senator, tolerably relieved, looked after his little wife with a whimsical mixture of amusement and vexation, and, seating himself in the arm-chair, began to read the papers.

After a moment, his wife's voice was heard at the door, in a quick, earnest tone, – "John! John! I do wish you'd come here, a moment."

He laid down his paper, and went into the kitchen, and started, quite amazed at the sight that presented itself:– A young and slender woman, with garments torn and frozen, with one shoe gone, and the stocking torn away from the cut and bleeding foot, was laid back in a deadly swoon upon two chairs. There was the impress of the despised race on her face, yet none could help feeling its mournful and pathetic beauty, while its stony sharpness, its cold, fixed, deathly aspect, struck a solemn chill over him. He drew his breath short, and stood in silence. His wife, and their only colored domestic, old Aunt Dinah, were busily engaged in restorative measures; while old Cudjoe had got the boy on his knee, and was busy pulling off his shoes and stockings, and chafing his little cold feet.

"Sure, now, if she an't a sight to behold!" said old Dinah, compassionately; "'pears like 't was the heat that made her faint. She was tol'able peart when she cum in, and asked if she couldn't warm herself here a spell; and I was just a-askin' her where she cum from, and she fainted right down. Never done much hard work, guess, by the looks of her hands."

"Poor creature!" said Mrs. Bird, compassionately, as the woman slowly unclosed her large, dark eyes, and looked vacantly at her. Suddenly an expression of agony crossed her face, and she sprang up, saying, "O, my Harry! Have they got him?"

The boy, at this, jumped from Cudjoe's knee, and running to her side put up his arms. "O, he's here! he's here!" she exclaimed.

"O, ma'am!" said she, wildly, to Mrs. Bird, "do protect us! don't let them get him!"

"Nobody shall hurt you here, poor woman," said Mrs. Bird, encouragingly. "You are safe; don't be afraid."

"God bless you!" said the woman, covering her face and sobbing; while the little boy, seeing her crying, tried to get into her lap.

With many gentle and womanly offices, which none knew better how to render than Mrs. Bird, the poor woman was, in time, rendered more calm. A temporary bed was provided for her on the settle, near the fire; and, after a short time, she fell into a heavy slumber, with the child, who seemed no less weary, soundly sleeping on her arm; for the mother resisted, with nervous anxiety, the kindest attempts to take him from her; and, even in sleep, her arm encircled him with an unrelaxing clasp, as if she could not even then be beguiled of her vigilant hold.

Mr. and Mrs. Bird had gone back to the parlor, where, strange as it may appear, no reference was made, on either side, to the preceding conversation; but Mrs. Bird busied herself with her knitting-work, and Mr. Bird pretended to be reading the paper.

"I wonder who and what she is!" said Mr. Bird, at last, as he laid it down.

"When she wakes up and feels a little rested, we will see," said Mrs. Bird.

"I say, wife!" said Mr. Bird after musing in silence over his newspaper.

"Well, dear!"

"She couldn't wear one of your gowns, could she, by any letting down, or such matter? She seems to be rather larger than you are."

A quite perceptible smile glimmered on Mrs. Bird's face, as she answered, "We'll see."

Another pause, and Mr. Bird again broke out,

"I say, wife!"

"Well! What now?"

"Why, there's that old bombazin cloak, that you keep on purpose to put over me when I take my afternoon's nap; you might as well give her that, – she needs clothes."

At this instant, Dinah looked in to say that the woman was awake, and wanted to see Missis.

Mr. and Mrs. Bird went into the kitchen, followed by the two eldest boys, the smaller fry having, by this time, been safely disposed of in bed.

The woman was now sitting up on the settle, by the fire. She was looking steadily into the blaze, with a calm, heart-broken expression, very different from her former agitated wildness.

"Did you want me?" said Mrs. Bird, in gentle tones. "I hope you feel better now, poor woman!"

A long-drawn, shivering sigh was the only answer; but she lifted her dark eyes, and fixed them on her with such a forlorn and imploring expression, that the tears came into the little woman's eyes.

"You needn't be afraid of anything; we are friends here, poor woman! Tell me where you came from, and what you want," said she.

"I came from Kentucky," said the woman.

"When?" said Mr. Bird, taking up the interogatory.

"Tonight."

"How did you come?"

"I crossed on the ice."

"Crossed on the ice!" said every one present.

"Yes," said the woman, slowly, "I did. God helping me, I crossed on the ice; for they were behind me – right behind – and there was no other way!"

"Law, Missis," said Cudjoe, "the ice is all in broken-up blocks, a swinging and a tetering up and down in the water!"

"I know it was – I know it!" said she, wildly; "but I did it! I wouldn't have thought I could, – I didn't think I should get over, but I didn't care! I could but die, if I didn't. The Lord helped me; nobody knows how much the Lord can help 'em, till they try," said the woman, with a flashing eye.

"Were you a slave?" said Mr. Bird.

"Yes, sir; I belonged to a man in Kentucky."

"Was he unkind to you?"

"No, sir; he was a good master."

"And was your mistress unkind to you?"

"No, sir – no! my mistress was always good to me."

"What could induce you to leave a good home, then, and run away, and go through such dangers?"

The woman looked up at Mrs. Bird, with a keen, scrutinizing glance, and it did not escape her that she was dressed in deep mourning.

"Ma'am," she said, suddenly, "have you ever lost a child?"

The question was unexpected, and it was thrust on a new wound; for it was only a month since a darling child of the family had been laid in the grave.

Mr. Bird turned around and walked to the window, and Mrs. Bird burst into tears; but, recovering her voice, she said,

"Why do you ask that? I have lost a little one."

"Then you will feel for me. I have lost two, one after another, - left 'em buried there when I came away; and I had only this one left. I never slept a night without him; he was all I had. He was my comfort and pride, day and night; and, ma'am, they were going to take him away from me, - to *sell* him, - sell him down south, ma'am, to go all alone, - a baby that had never been away from his mother in his life! I couldn't stand it, ma'am. I knew I never should be good for anything, if they did; and when I knew the papers the papers were signed, and he was sold, I took him and came off in the night; and they chased me, - the man that bought him, and some of Mas'r's folks, - and they were coming down right behind me, and I heard 'em. I jumped right on to the ice; and how I got across, I don't know, – but, first I knew, a man was helping me up the bank."

The woman did not sob nor weep. She had gone to a place where tears are dry; but every one around her was, in some way characteristic of themselves, showing signs of hearty sympathy.

The two little boys, after a desperate rummaging in their pockets, in search of those pocket-handkerchiefs which mothers know are never to be found there, had thrown themselves disconsolately into the skirts of their mother's gown, where they were sobbing, and wiping their eyes and noses, to their hearts' content; – Mrs. Bird had her face fairly hidden in her pocket-handkerchief; and old Dinah, with tears streaming down her black, honest face, was ejaculating, "Lord have mercy on us!" with all the fervor of a camp-meeting; – while old Cudjoe, rubbing his eyes very hard with his cuffs, and making a most uncommon variety of wry faces, occasionally responded in the same key, with great fervor. Our senator was a statesman, and of course could not be expected to cry, like other mortals; and so he turned his back to the company, and looked out of the window, and seemed particularly busy in clearing his throat and wiping his spectacle-glasses, occasionally blowing his nose in a manner that was calculated to excite suspicion, had any one been in a state to observe critically.

"How came you to tell me you had a kind master?" he suddenly exclaimed, gulping down very resolutely some kind of rising in his throat, and turning suddenly round upon the woman.

"Because he *was* a kind master; I'll say that of him, any way; – and my mistress was kind; but they couldn't help themselves. They were owing money; and there was some way, I can't tell how, that a man had a hold on them, and they were obliged to give him his will. I listened, and heard him telling mistress that, and she begging and pleading for me, – and he told her he couldn't help himself, and that the papers were all drawn; – and then it was I took him and left my home, and came away. I knew 't was no use of my trying to live, if they did it; for 't 'pears like this child is all I have."

"Have you no husband?"

"Yes, but he belongs to another man. His master is real hard to him, and won't let him come to see me, hardly ever; and he's grown harder and harder upon us, and he threatens to sell him down south; – it's like I'll never see *him* again!"

The quiet tone in which the woman pronounced these words might have led a superficial observer to think that she was entirely apathetic; but there was a calm, settled depth of anguish in her large, dark eye, that spoke of something far otherwise.

"And where do you mean to go, my poor woman?" said Mrs. Bird.

"To Canada, if I only knew where that was. Is it very far off, is Canada?" said she, looking up, with a simple, confiding air, to Mrs. Bird's face.

"Poor thing!" said Mrs. Bird, involuntarily.

"Is 't a very great way off, think?" said the woman, earnestly.

"Much further than you think, poor child!" said Mrs. Bird; "but we will try to think what can be done for you. Here, Dinah, make her up a bed in your own room, close by the kitchen, and I'll think what to do for her in the morning. Meanwhile, never fear, poor woman; put your trust in God; he will protect you."

Mrs. Bird and her husband reentered the parlor. She sat down in her little rocking-chair before the fire, swaying thoughtfully to and fro. Mr. Bird strode up and down the room, grumbling to himself, "Pish! pshaw! confounded awkward business!" At length, striding up to his wife, he said,

"I say, wife, she'll have to get away from here, this very night. That fellow will be down on the scent bright and early tomorrow morning: if 't was only the woman, she could lie quiet till it was over; but that little chap can't be kept still by a troop of horse and foot, I'll warrant me; he'll bring it all out, popping his head out of some window or door. A pretty kettle of fish it would be for me, too, to be caught with them both here, just now! No; they'll have to be got off tonight."

"Tonight! How is it possible? – where to?"

"Well, I know pretty well where to," said the senator, beginning to put on his boots, with a reflective air; and, stopping when his leg was half in, he embraced his knee with both hands, and seemed to go off in deep meditation.

"It's a confounded awkward, ugly business," said he, at last, beginning to tug at his boot-straps again, "and that's a fact!" After one boot was fairly on, the senator sat with the other in his hand, profoundly studying the figure of the carpet. "It will have to be done, though, for aught I see, – hang it all!" and he drew the other boot anxiously on, and looked out of the window.

Now, little Mrs. Bird was a discreet woman, – a woman who never in her life said, "I told you so!" and, on the present occasion, though pretty well aware of the shape her husband's meditations were taking, she very prudently forbore to meddle with them, only sat very quietly in her chair, and looked quite ready to hear her liege lord's intentions, when he should think proper to utter them.

"You see," he said, "there's my old client, Van Trompe, has come over from Kentucky, and set all his slaves free; and he has bought a place seven miles up the creek, here, back in the woods, where nobody goes, unless they go on purpose; and it's a place that isn't found in a hurry. There she'd be safe enough; but the plague of the thing is, nobody could drive a carriage there tonight, but *me*."

"Why not? Cudjoe is an excellent driver."

"Ay, ay, but here it is. The creek has to be crossed twice; and the second crossing is quite dangerous, unless one knows it as I do. I have crossed it a hundred times on horseback, and know exactly the turns to take. And so, you see, there's no help for it. Cudjoe must put in the horses, as quietly as may be, about twelve o'clock, and I'll take her over; and then, to give color to the matter, he must carry me on to the next tavern to take the stage for Columbus, that comes by about three or four, and so it will look as if I had had the carriage only for that. I shall get into business bright and early in the morning. But I'm thinking I shall feel rather cheap there, after all that's been said and done; but, hang it, I can't help it!"

"Your heart is better than your head, in this case, John," said the wife, laying her little white hand on his. "Could I ever have loved you, had I not known you better than you know yourself?" And the little woman looked so handsome, with the tears sparkling in her eyes, that the senator thought he must be a decidedly clever fellow, to get such a pretty creature into such a passionate admiration of him; and so, what could he do but walk off soberly, to see about the carriage. At the door, however, he stopped a moment, and then coming back, he said, with some hesitation.

"Mary, I don't know how you'd feel about it, but there's that drawer full of things - of - of - poor little Henry's." So saying, he turned quickly on his heel, and shut the door after him.

His wife opened the little bed-room door adjoining her room and, taking the candle, set it down on the top of a bureau there; then from a small recess she took a key, and put it thoughtfully in the lock of a drawer, and made a sudden pause, while two boys, who, boy like, had followed close on her heels, stood looking, with silent, significant glances, at their mother. And oh! mother that reads this, has there never been in your house a drawer, or a closet, the opening of which has been to you like the opening again of a little grave? Ah! happy mother that you are, if it has not been so.

Mrs. Bird slowly opened the drawer. There were little coats of many a form and pattern, piles of aprons, and rows of small stockings; and even a pair of little shoes, worn and rubbed at the toes, were peeping from the folds of a paper. There was a toy horse and wagon, a top, a ball, - memorials gathered with many a tear and many a heart-break! She sat down by the drawer, and, leaning her head on her hands over it, wept till the tears fell through her fingers into the drawer; then suddenly raising her head, she began, with nervous haste, selecting the plainest and most substantial articles, and gathering them into a bundle.

"Mamma," said one of the boys, gently touching her arm, "you going to give away *those* things?"

"My dear boys," she said, softly and earnestly, "if our dear, loving little Henry looks down from heaven, he would be glad to have us do this. I could not find it in my heart to give them away to any common person - to anybody that was happy; but I give them to a mother more heart-broken and sorrowful than I am; and I hope God will send his blessings with them!"

There are in this world blessed souls, whose sorrows all spring up into joys for others; whose earthly hopes, laid in the grave with many tears, are the seed from which spring healing flowers and balm for the desolate and the distressed. Among such was the delicate woman who sits there by the lamp, dropping slow tears, while she prepares the memorials of her own lost one for the outcast wanderer.

After a while, Mrs. Bird opened a wardrobe, and, taking from thence a plain, serviceable dress or two, she sat down busily to her work-table, and, with needle, scissors, and thimble, at hand, quietly commenced the "letting down" process which her husband had recommended, and continued busily at it till the old clock in the corner struck twelve, and she heard the low rattling of wheels at the door.

"Mary," said her husband, coming in, with his overcoat in his hand, "you must wake her up now; we must be off."

Mrs. Bird hastily deposited the various articles she had collected in a small plain trunk, and locking it, desired her husband to see it in the carriage, and then proceeded to call the woman. Soon, arrayed in a cloak, bonnet, and shawl, that had belonged to her benefactress, she appeared at the door with her child in her arms. Mr. Bird hurried her into the carriage, and Mrs. Bird pressed on after her to the carriage steps. Eliza leaned out of the carriage, and put out her hand, - a hand as soft and beautiful as was given in return. She fixed her large, dark eyes, full of earnest meaning, on Mrs. Bird's face, and seemed going to speak. Her lips moved, - she tried once or twice, but there was no sound, - and pointing upward, with a look never to be forgotten, she fell back in the seat, and covered her face. The door was shut, and the carriage drove on.

What a situation, now, for a patriotic senator, that had been all the week before spurring up the legislature of his native state to pass more stringent resolutions against escaping fugitives, their harborers and abettors!

Our good senator in his native state had not been exceeded by any of his brethren at Washington, in the sort of eloquence which has won for them immortal renown! How sublimely he had sat with his hands in his pockets, and scouted all sentimental weakness of those who would put the welfare of a few miserable fugitives before great state interests!

He was as bold as a lion about it, and "mightily convinced" not only himself, but everybody that heard him; – but then his idea of a fugitive was only an idea of the letters that spell the word, – or at the most, the image of a little newspaper picture of a man with a stick and bundle with "Ran away from the subscriber" under it. The magic of the real presence of distress, – the imploring human eye, the frail, trembling human hand, the despairing appeal of helpless agony, – these he had never tried. He had never thought that a fugitive might be a hapless mother, a defenceless child, – like that one which was now wearing his lost boy's little well-known cap; and so, as our poor senator was not stone or steel, – as he was a man, and a downright noble-hearted one, too, – he was, as everybody must see, in a sad case for his patriotism. And you need not exult over him, good brother of the Southern States; for we have some inklings that many of you, under similar circumstances, would not do much better. We have reason to know, in Kentucky, as in Mississippi, are noble and generous hearts, to whom never was tale of suffering told in vain. Ah, good brother! is it fair for you to expect of us services which your own brave, honorable heart would not allow you to render, were you in our place?

Be that as it may, if our good senator was a political sinner, he was in a fair way to expiate it by his night's penance. There had been a long continuous period of rainy weather, and the soft, rich earth of Ohio, as every one knows, is admirably suited to the manufacture of mud – and the road was an Ohio railroad of the good old times.

"And pray, what sort of a road may that be?" says some eastern traveller, who has been accustomed to connect no ideas with a railroad, but those of smoothness or speed.

Know, then, innocent eastern friend, that in benighted regions of the west, where the mud is of unfathomable and sublime depth, roads are made of round rough logs, arranged transversely side by side, and coated over in their pristine freshness with earth, turf, and whatsoever may come to hand, and then the rejoicing native calleth it a road, and straightway essayeth to ride thereupon. In process of time, the rains wash off all the turf and grass aforesaid, move the logs hither and thither, in picturesque positions, up, down and crosswise, with divers chasms and ruts of black mud intervening.

Over such a road as this our senator went stumbling along, making moral reflections as continuously as under the circumstances could be expected, – the carriage proceeding along much as follows, – bump! bump! bump! slush! down in the mud! – the senator, woman and child, reversing their positions so suddenly as to come, without any very accurate adjustment, against the windows of the down-hill side. Carriage sticks fast, while Cudjoe on the outside is heard making a great muster among the horses. After various ineffectual pullings and twitchings, just as the senator is losing all patience, the carriage suddenly rights itself with a bounce, – two front wheels go down into another abyss, and senator, woman, and child, all tumble promiscuously on to the front seat, – senator's hat is jammed over his eyes and nose quite unceremoniously, and he considers himself fairly extinguished; – child cries, and Cudjoe on the outside delivers animated addresses to the horses, who are kicking, and floundering, and straining under repeated cracks of the whip. Carriage springs up, with another bounce, – down go the hind wheels, – senator, woman, and child, fly over on to the back seat, his elbows encountering her bonnet, and both her feet being jammed into his hat, which flies off in the concussion. After a few moments the "slough" is passed, and the horses stop, panting; – the senator finds his hat, the woman straightens her bonnet and hushes her child, and they brace themselves for what is yet to come.

For a while only the continuous bump! bump! intermingled, just by way of variety, with divers side plunges and compound shakes; and they begin to flatter themselves that they are not so badly off, after all. At last, with a square plunge, which puts all on to their feet and then down into their seats with incredible quickness, the carriage stops, – and, after much outside commotion, Cudjoe appears at the door.

"Please, sir, it's powerful bad spot, this yer. I don't know how we 's to get clar out. I'm a thinkin' we'll have to be a gettin' rails."

The senator despairingly steps out, picking gingerly for some firm foothold; down goes one foot an immeasurable depth, - he tries to pull it up, loses his balance, and tumbles over into the mud, and is fished out, in a very despairing condition, by Cudjoe.

But we forbear, out of sympathy to our readers' bones. Western travellers, who have beguiled the midnight hour in the interesting process of pulling down rail fences, to pry their carriages out of mud holes, will have a respectful and mournful sympathy with our unfortunate hero. We beg them to drop a silent tear, and pass on.

It was full late in the night when the carriage emerged, dripping and bespattered, out of the creek, and stood at the door of a large farmhouse.

It took no inconsiderable perseverance to arouse the inmates; but at last the respectable proprietor appeared, and undid the door. He was a great, tall, bristling Orson of a fellow, full six feet and some inches in his stockings, and arrayed in a red flannel hunting-shirt. A very heavy mat of sandy hair, in a decidedly tousled condition, and a beard of some days' growth, gave the worthy man an appearance, to say the least, not particularly prepossessing. He stood for a few minutes holding the candle aloft, and blinking on our travellers with a dismal and mystified expression that was truly ludicrous. It cost some effort of our senator to induce him to comprehend the case fully; and while he is doing his best at that, we shall give him a little introduction to our readers.

Honest old John Van Trompe was once quite a considerable land-owner and slave-owner in the State of Kentucky. Having "nothing of the bear about him but the skin," and being gifted by nature with a great, honest, just heart, quite equal to his gigantic frame, he had been for some years witnessing with repressed uneasiness the workings of a system equally bad for oppressor and oppressed. At last, one day, John's great heart had swelled altogether too big to wear his bonds any longer; so he just took his pocket-book out of his desk, and went over into Ohio, and bought a quarter of a township of good, rich land, made out free papers for all his people, - men, women, and children, - packed them up in wagons, and sent them off to settle down; and then honest John turned his face up the creek, and sat quietly down on a snug, retired farm, to enjoy his conscience and his reflections.

"Are you the man that will shelter a poor woman and child from slave-catchers?" said the senator, explicitly.

"I rather think I am," said honest John, with some considerable emphasis.

"I thought so," said the senator.

"If there's anybody comes," said the good man, stretching his tall, muscular form upward, "why here I'm ready for him: and I've got seven sons, each six foot high, and they'll be ready for 'em. Give our respects to 'em," said John; "tell 'em it's no matter how soon they call, - make no kinder difference to us," said John, running his fingers through the shock of hair that thatched his head, and bursting out into a great laugh.

Weary, jaded, and spiritless, Eliza dragged herself up to the door, with her child lying in a heavy sleep on her arm. The rough man held the candle to her face, and uttering a kind of compassionate grunt, opened the door of a small bed-room adjoining to the large kitchen where they were standing, and motioned her to go in. He took down a candle, and lighting it, set it upon the table, and then addressed himself to Eliza.

"Now, I say, gal, you needn't be a bit afeard, let who will come here. I'm up to all that sort o' thing," said he, pointing to two or three goodly rifles over the mantel-piece; "and most people that know me know that 't wouldn't be healthy to try to get anybody out o' my house when I'm agin it. So *now* you jist go to sleep now, as quiet as if yer mother was a rockin' ye," said he, as he shut the door.

"Why, this is an uncommon handsome un," he said to the senator. "Ah, well; handsome uns has the greatest cause to run, sometimes, if they has any kind o' feelin, such as decent women should. I know all about that."

The senator, in a few words, briefly explained Eliza's history.

"O! ou! aw! now, I want to know?" said the good man, pitifully; "sho! now sho! That's natur now, poor crittur! hunted down now like a deer, – hunted down, jest for havin' natural feelin's, and doin' what no kind o' mother could help a doin'! I tell ye what, these yer things make me come the nighest to swearin', now, o' most anything," said honest John, as he wiped his eyes with the back of a great, freckled, yellow hand. "I tell yer what, stranger, it was years and years before I'd jine the church, 'cause the ministers round in our parts used to preach that the Bible went in for these ere cuttings up, - and I couldn't be up to 'em with their Greek and Hebrew, and so I took up agin 'em, Bible and all. I never jined the church till I found a minister that was up to 'em all in Greek and all that, and he said right the contrary; and then I took right hold, and jined the church, - I did now, fact," said John, who had been all this time uncorking some very frisky bottled cider, which at this juncture he presented.

"Ye'd better jest put up here, now, till daylight," said he, heartily, "and I'll call up the old woman, and have a bed got ready for you in no time."

"Thank you, my good friend," said the senator, "I must be along, to take the night stage for Columbus."

"Ah! well, then, if you must, I'll go a piece with you, and show you a cross road that will take you there better than the road you came on. That road's mighty bad."

John equipped himself, and, with a lantern in hand, was soon seen guiding the senator's carriage towards a road that ran down in a hollow, back of his dwelling. When they parted, the senator put into his hand a ten-dollar bill.

"It's for her," he said, briefly.

"Ay, ay," said John, with equal conciseness.

They shook hands, and parted.

Chapter 10

The Property Is Carried Off

The February morning looked gray and drizzling through the window of Uncle Tom's cabin. It looked on downcast faces, the images of mournful hearts. The little table stood out before the fire, covered with an ironing-cloth; a coarse but clean shirt or two, fresh from the iron, hung on the back of a chair by the fire, and Aunt Chloe had another spread out before her on the table. Carefully she rubbed and ironed every fold and every hem, with the most scrupulous exactness, every now and then raising her hand to her face to wipe off the tears that were coursing down her cheeks.

Tom sat by, with his Testament open on his knee, and his head leaning upon his hand; - but neither spoke. It was yet early, and the children lay all asleep together in their little rude trundle-bed.

Tom, who had, to the full, the gentle, domestic heart, which woe for them! has been a peculiar characteristic of his unhappy race, got up and walked silently to look at his children.

"It's the last time," he said.

Aunt Chloe did not answer, only rubbed away over and over on the coarse shirt, already as smooth as hands could make it; and finally setting her iron suddenly down with a despairing plunge, she sat down to the table, and "lifted up her voice and wept."

"S'pose we must be resigned; but oh Lord! how ken I? If I know'd anything whar you 's goin', or how they'd sarve you! Missis says she'll try and 'deem ye, in a year or two; but Lor! nobody never comes up that goes down thar! They kills 'em! I've hearn 'em tell how dey works 'em up on dem ar plantations."

"There'll be the same God there, Chloe, that there is here."

"Well," said Aunt Chloe, "s'pose dere will; but de Lord lets dreffful things happen, sometimes. I don't seem to get no comfort dat way."

"I'm in the Lord's hands," said Tom; "nothin' can go no furder than he lets it; – and thar's *one* thing I can thank him for. It's *me* that's sold and going down, and not you nur the chil'en. Here you're safe; – what comes will come only on me; and the Lord, he'll help me, – I know he will."

Ah, brave, manly heart, – smothering thine own sorrow, to comfort thy beloved ones! Tom spoke with a thick utterance, and with a bitter choking in his throat, – but he spoke brave and strong.

"Let's think on our marcies!" he added, tremulously, as if he was quite sure he needed to think on them very hard indeed.

"Marcies!" said Aunt Chloe; "don't see no marcy in 't! 'tan't right! 'tan't right it should be so! Mas'r never ought ter left it so that ye *could* be took for his debts. Ye've arnt him all he gets for ye, twice over. He owed ye yer freedom, and ought ter gin 't to yer years ago.

Mebbe he can't help himself now, but I feel it's wrong. Nothing can't beat that ar out o' me. Sich a faithful crittur as ye've been, – and allers sot his business 'fore yer own every way, – and reckoned on him more than yer own wife and chil'en! Them as sells heart's love and heart's blood, to get out thar scrapes, de Lord'll be up to 'em!"

"Chloe! now, if ye love me, ye won't talk so, when perhaps jest the last time we'll ever have together! And I'll tell ye, Chloe, it goes agin me to hear one word agin Mas'r. Wan't he put in my arms a baby? – it's natur I should think a heap of him. And he couldn't be spected to think so much of poor Tom. Mas'rs is used to havin' all these yer things done for 'em, and nat'lly they don't think so much on 't. They can't be spected to, no way. Set him 'longside of other Mas'rs – who's had the treatment and livin' I've had? And he never would have let this yer come on me, if he could have seed it aforehand. I know he wouldn't."

"Wal, any way, thar's wrong about it *somewhar,*" said Aunt Chloe, in whom a stubborn sense of justice was a predominant trait; "I can't jest make out whar 't is, but thar's wrong somewhar, I'm *clar* o' that."

"Yer ought ter look up to the Lord above – he's above all – thar don't a sparrow fall without him."

"It don't seem to comfort me, but I spect it orter," said Aunt Chloe. "But dar's no use talkin'; I'll jes wet up de corn-cake, and get ye one good breakfast, 'cause nobody knows when you'll get another."

In order to appreciate the sufferings of the negroes sold south, it must be remembered that all the instinctive affections of that race are peculiarly strong. Their local attachments are very abiding. They are not naturally daring and enterprising, but home-loving and affectionate. Add to this all the terrors with which ignorance invests the unknown, and add to this, again, that selling to the south is set before the negro from childhood as the last severity of punishment. The threat that terrifies more than whipping or torture of any kind is the threat of being sent down river. We have ourselves heard this feeling expressed by them, and seen the unaffected horror with which they will sit in their gossipping hours, and tell frightful stories of that "down river," which to them is

> "That undiscovered country, from whose bourn
> No traveller returns."[3]

A missionary figure among the fugitives in Canada told us that many of the fugitives confessed themselves to have escaped from comparatively kind masters, and that they were induced to brave the perils of escape, in almost every case, by the desperate horror with which they regarded being sold south, – a doom which was hanging either

---

3 A slightly inaccurate quotation from Hamlet, Act III, scene I, lines 369-370.

over themselves or their husbands, their wives or children. This nerves the African, naturally patient, timid and unenterprising, with heroic courage, and leads him to suffer hunger, cold, pain, the perils of the wilderness, and the more dread penalties of recapture.

The simple morning meal now smoked on the table, for Mrs. Shelby had excused Aunt Chloe's attendance at the great house that morning. The poor soul had expended all her little energies on this farewell feast, – had killed and dressed her choicest chicken, and prepared her corn-cake with scrupulous exactness, just to her husband's taste, and brought out certain mysterious jars on the mantel-piece, some preserves that were never produced except on extreme occasions.

"Lor, Pete," said Mose, triumphantly, "han't we got a buster of a breakfast!" at the same time catching at a fragment of the chicken.

Aunt Chloe gave him a sudden box on the ear. "Thar now! crowing over the last breakfast yer poor daddy's gwine to have to home!"

"O, Chloe!" said Tom, gently.

"Wal, I can't help it," said Aunt Chloe, hiding her face in her apron; "I 's so tossed about it, it makes me act ugly."

The boys stood quite still, looking first at their father and then at their mother, while the baby, climbing up her clothes, began an imperious, commanding cry.

"Thar!" said Aunt Chloe, wiping her eyes and taking up the baby; "now I 's done, I hope, – now do eat something. This yer's my nicest chicken. Thar, boys, ye shall have some, poor critturs! Yer mammy's been cross to yer."

The boys needed no second invitation, and went in with great zeal for the eatables; and it was well they did so, as otherwise there would have been very little performed to any purpose by the party.

"Now," said Aunt Chloe, bustling about after breakfast, "I must put up yer clothes. Jest like as not, he'll take 'em all away. I know thar ways – mean as dirt, they is! Wal, now, yer flannels for rhumatis is in this corner; so be careful, 'cause there won't nobody make ye no more. Then here's yer old shirts, and these yer is new ones. I toed off these yer stockings last night, and put de ball in 'em to mend with. But Lor! who'll ever mend for ye?" and Aunt Chloe, again overcome, laid her head on the box side, and sobbed. "To think on 't! no crittur to do for ye, sick or well! I don't railly think I ought ter be good now!"

The boys, having eaten everything there was on the breakfast-table, began now to take some thought of the case; and, seeing their mother crying, and their father looking very sad, began to whimper and put their hands to their eyes. Uncle Tom had the baby on his knee, and was letting her enjoy herself to the utmost extent, scratching his face and pulling his hair, and occasionally breaking out into clamorous explosions of delight, evidently arising out of her own internal reflections.

"Ay, crow away, poor crittur!" said Aunt Chloe; "ye'll have to come to it, too! ye'll live to see yer husband sold, or mebbe be sold yerself; and these yer boys, they's to be sold, I s'pose, too, jest like as not, when dey gets good for somethin'; an't no use in niggers havin' nothin'!"

Here one of the boys called out, "Thar's Missis a-comin' in!"

"She can't do no good; what's she coming for?" said Aunt Chloe.

Mrs. Shelby entered. Aunt Chloe set a chair for her in a manner decidedly gruff and crusty. She did not seem to notice either the action or the manner. She looked pale and anxious.

"Tom," she said, "I come to –" and stopping suddenly, and regarding the silent group, she sat down in the chair, and, covering her face with her handkerchief, began to sob.

"Lor, now, Missis, don't – don't!" said Aunt Chloe, bursting out in her turn; and for a few moments they all wept in company. And in those tears they all shed together, the high and the lowly, melted away all the heart-burnings and anger of the oppressed. O, ye who visit the distressed, do ye know that everything your money can buy, given with a cold, averted face, is not worth one honest tear shed in real sympathy?

"My good fellow," said Mrs. Shelby, "I can't give you anything to do you any good. If I give you money, it will only be taken from you. But I tell you solemnly, and before God, that I will keep trace of you, and bring you back as soon as I can command the money; – and, till then, trust in God!"

Here the boys called out that Mas'r Haley was coming, and then an unceremonious kick pushed open the door. Haley stood there in very ill humor, having ridden hard the night before, and being not at all pacified by his ill success in recapturing his prey.

"Come," said he, "ye nigger, ye'r ready? Servant, ma'am!" said he, taking off his hat, as he saw Mrs. Shelby.

Aunt Chloe shut and corded the box, and, getting up, looked gruffly on the trader, her tears seeming suddenly turned to sparks of fire.

Tom rose up meekly, to follow his new master, and raised up his heavy box on his shoulder. His wife took the baby in her arms to go with him to the wagon, and the children, still crying, trailed on behind.

Mrs. Shelby, walking up to the trader, detained him for a few moments, talking with him in an earnest manner; and while she was thus talking, the whole family party proceeded to a wagon, that stood ready harnessed at the door. A crowd of all the old and young hands on the place stood gathered around it, to bid farewell to their old associate. Tom had been looked up to, both as a head servant and a Christian teacher, by all the place, and there was much honest sympathy and grief about him, particularly among the women.

"Why, Chloe, you bar it better 'n we do!" said one of the women, who had been weeping freely, noticing the gloomy calmness with which Aunt Chloe stood by the wagon.

"I 's done *my* tears!" she said, looking grimly at the trader, who was coming up. "I does not feel to cry 'fore dat ar old limb, no how!"

"Get in!" said Haley to Tom, as he strode through the crowd of servants, who looked at him with lowering brows.

Tom got in, and Haley, drawing out from under the wagon seat a heavy pair of shackles, made them fast around each ankle.

A smothered groan of indignation ran through the whole circle, and Mrs. Shelby spoke from the verandah, – "Mr. Haley, I assure you that precaution is entirely unnecessary."

"Don' know, ma'am; I've lost one five hundred dollars from this yer place, and I can't afford to run no more risks."

"What else could she spect on him?" said Aunt Chloe, indignantly, while the two boys, who now seemed to comprehend at once their father's destiny, clung to her gown, sobbing and groaning vehemently.

"I'm sorry," said Tom, "that Mas'r George happened to be away."

George had gone to spend two or three days with a companion on a neighboring estate, and having departed early in the morning, before Tom's misfortune had been made public, had left without hearing of it.

"Give my love to Mas'r George," he said, earnestly.

Haley whipped up the horse, and, with a steady, mournful look, fixed to the last on the old place, Tom was whirled away.

Mr. Shelby at this time was not at home. He had sold Tom under the spur of a driving necessity, to get out of the power of a man whom he dreaded, - and his first feeling, after the consummation of the bargain, had been that of relief. But his wife's expostulations awoke his half-slumbering regrets; and Tom's manly disinterestedness increased the unpleasantness of his feelings. It was in vain that he said to himself that he had a *right* to do it, - that everybody did it, - and that some did it without even the excuse of necessity; - he could not satisfy his own feelings; and that he might not witness the unpleasant scenes of the consummation, he had gone on a short business tour up the country, hoping that all would be over before he returned.

Tom and Haley rattled on along the dusty road, whirling past every old familiar spot, until the bounds of the estate were fairly passed, and they found themselves out on the open pike. After they had ridden about a mile, Haley suddenly drew up at the door of a blacksmith's shop, when, taking out with him a pair of handcuffs, he stepped into the shop, to have a little alteration in them.

"These yer 's a little too small for his build," said Haley, showing the fetters, and pointing out to Tom.

"Lor! now, if thar an't Shelby's Tom. He han't sold him, now?" said the smith.

"Yes, he has," said Haley.

"Now, ye don't! well, reely," said the smith, "who'd a thought it! Why, ye needn't go to fetterin' him up this yer way. He's the faithfullest, best crittur–"

"Yes, yes," said Haley; "but your good fellers are just the critturs to want ter run off. Them stupid ones, as doesn't care whar they go, and shifless, drunken ones, as don't care for nothin', they'll stick by, and like as not be rather pleased to be toted round; but these yer prime fellers, they hates it like sin. No way but to fetter 'em; got legs, – they'll use 'em, – no mistake."

"Well," said the smith, feeling among his tools, "them plantations down thar, stranger, an't jest the place a Kentuck nigger wants to go to; they dies thar tol'able fast, don't they?"

"Wal, yes, tol'able fast, ther dying is; what with the 'climating and one thing and another, they dies so as to keep the market up pretty brisk," said Haley.

"Wal, now, a feller can't help thinkin' it's a mighty pity to have a nice, quiet, likely feller, as good un as

Tom is, go down to be fairly ground up on one of them ar sugar plantations."

"Wal, he's got a fa'r chance. I promised to do well by him. I'll get him in house-servant in some good old family, and then, if he stands the fever and 'climating, he'll have a berth good as any nigger ought ter ask for."

"He leaves his wife and chil'en up here, s'pose?"

"Yes; but he'll get another thar. Lord, thar's women enough everywhar," said Haley.

Tom was sitting very mournfully on the outside of the shop while this conversation was going on. Suddenly he heard the quick, short click of a horse's hoof behind him; and, before he could fairly awake from his surprise, young Master George sprang into the wagon, threw his arms tumultuously round his neck, and was sobbing and scolding with energy.

"I declare, it's real mean! I don't care what they say, any of 'em! It's a nasty, mean shame! If I was a man, they shouldn't do it, - they should not, *so*!" said George, with a kind of subdued howl.

"O! Mas'r George! this does me good!" said Tom. "I couldn't bar to go off without seein' ye! It does me real good, ye can't tell!" Here Tom made some movement of his feet, and George's eye fell on the fetters.

"What a shame!" he exclaimed, lifting his hands. "I'll knock that old fellow down - I will!"

"No you won't, Mas'r George; and you must not talk so loud. It won't help me any, to anger him."

"Well, I won't, then, for your sake; but only to think of it – isn't it a shame? They never sent for me, nor sent me any word, and, if it hadn't been for Tom Lincon, I shouldn't have heard it. I tell you, I blew 'em up well, all of 'em, at home!"

"That ar wasn't right, I'm 'feard, Mas'r George."

"Can't help it! I say it's a shame! Look here, Uncle Tom," said he, turning his back to the shop, and speaking in a mysterious tone, *"I've brought you my dollar!"*

"O! I couldn't think o' takin' on 't, Mas'r George, no ways in the world!" said Tom, quite moved.

"But you *shall* take it!" said George; "look here – I told Aunt Chloe I'd do it, and she advised me just to make a hole in it, and put a string through, so you could hang it round your neck, and keep it out of sight; else this mean scamp would take it away. I tell ye, Tom, I want to blow him up! it would do me good!"

"No, don't Mas'r George, for it won't do *me* any good."

"Well, I won't, for your sake," said George, busily tying his dollar round Tom's neck; "but there, now, button your coat tight over it, and keep it, and remember, every time you see it, that I'll come down after you, and bring you back. Aunt Chloe and I have been talking about it. I told her not to fear; I'll see to it, and I'll tease father's life out, if he don't do it."

"O! Mas'r George, ye mustn't talk so 'bout yer father!"

"Lor, Uncle Tom, I don't mean anything bad."

"And now, Mas'r George," said Tom, "ye must be a good boy; 'member how many hearts is sot on ye. Al'ays keep close to yer mother. Don't be gettin' into any of them foolish ways boys has of gettin' too big to mind their mothers. Tell ye what, Mas'r George, the Lord gives good many things twice over; but he don't give ye a mother but once. Ye'll never see sich another woman, Mas'r George, if ye live to be a hundred years old. So, now, you hold on to her, and grow up, and be a comfort to her, thar's my own good boy, - you will now, won't ye?"

"Yes, I will, Uncle Tom," said George seriously.

"And be careful of yer speaking, Mas'r George. Young boys, when they comes to your age, is wilful, sometimes - it is natur they should be. But real gentlemen, such as I hopes you'll be, never lets fall on words that isn't 'spectful to thar parents. Ye an't 'fended, Mas'r George?"

"No, indeed, Uncle Tom; you always did give me good advice."

"I 's older, ye know," said Tom, stroking the boy's fine, curly head with his large, strong hand, but speaking in a voice as tender as a woman's, "and I sees all that's bound up in you. O, Mas'r George, you has everything, - l'arnin', privileges, readin', writin', - and you'll grow up to be a great, learned, good man and all the people on the place and your mother and father'll be so proud on ye! Be a good Mas'r, like yer father; and be a Christian, like yer mother. 'Member yer Creator in the days o' yer youth, Mas'r George."

"I'll be *real* good, Uncle Tom, I tell you," said George. "I'm going to be a *first-rater*; and don't you be discouraged. I'll have you back to the place, yet. As I told Aunt Chloe this morning, I'll build our house all over, and you shall have a room for a parlor with a carpet on it, when I'm a man. O, you'll have good times yet!"

Haley now came to the door, with the handcuffs in his hands.

"Look here, now, Mister," said George, with an air of great superiority, as he got out, "I shall let father and mother know how you treat Uncle Tom!"

"You're welcome," said the trader.

"I should think you'd be ashamed to spend all your life buying men and women, and chaining them, like cattle! I should think you'd feel mean!" said George.

"So long as your grand folks wants to buy men and women, I'm as good as they is," said Haley; "'tan't any meaner sellin' on 'em, that 't is buyin'!"

"I'll never do either, when I'm a man," said George; "I'm ashamed, this day, that I'm a Kentuckian. I always was proud of it before;" and George sat very straight on his horse, and looked round with an air, as if he expected the state would be impressed with his opinion.

"Well, good-by, Uncle Tom; keep a stiff upper lip," said George.

"Good-by, Mas'r George," said Tom, looking fondly and admiringly at him. "God Almighty bless you! Ah! Kentucky han't got many like you!" he said, in the fulness of his heart, as the frank, boyish face was lost to his view. Away he went, and Tom looked, till the clatter of his horse's heels died away, the last sound or sight of his home. But over his heart there seemed to be a warm spot, where those young hands had placed that precious dollar. Tom put up his hand, and held it close to his heart.

"Now, I tell ye what, Tom," said Haley, as he came up to the wagon, and threw in the handcuffs, "I mean to start fa'r with ye, as I gen'ally do with my niggers; and I'll tell ye now, to begin with, you treat me fa'r, and I'll treat you fa'r; I an't never hard on my niggers. Calculates to do the best for 'em I can. Now, ye see, you'd better jest settle down comfortable, and not be tryin' no tricks; because nigger's tricks of all sorts I'm up to, and it's no use. If niggers is quiet, and don't try to get off, they has good times with me; and if they don't, why, it's thar fault, and not mine."

Tom assured Haley that he had no present intentions of running off. In fact, the exhortation seemed rather a superfluous one to a man with a great pair of iron fetters on his feet. But Mr. Haley had got in the habit of commencing his relations with his stock with little exhortations of this nature, calculated, as he deemed, to inspire cheerfulness and confidence, and prevent the necessity of any unpleasant scenes.

And here, for the present, we take our leave of Tom, to pursue the fortunes of other characters in our story.

Chapter 11

In Which Property Gets into an Improper State of Mind

It was late in a drizzly afternoon that a traveler alighted at the door of a small country hotel, in the village of N–, in Kentucky. In the barroom he found assembled quite a miscellaneous company, whom stress of weather had driven to harbor, and the place presented the usual scenery of such reunions. Great, tall, raw-boned Kentuckians, attired in hunting-shirts, and trailing their loose joints over a vast extent of territory, with the easy lounge peculiar to the race, – rifles stacked away in the corner, shot-pouches, game-bags, hunting-dogs, and little negroes, all rolled together in the corners, – were the characteristic features in the picture. At each end of the fireplace sat a long-legged gentleman, with his chair tipped back, his hat on his head, and the heels of his muddy boots reposing sublimely on the mantel-piece, – a position, we will inform our readers, decidedly favorable to the turn of reflection incident to western taverns, where travellers exhibit a decided preference for this particular mode of elevating their understandings.

Mine host, who stood behind the bar, like most of his country men, was great of stature, good-natured and loose-jointed, with an enormous shock of hair on his head, and a great tall hat on the top of that.

In fact, everybody in the room bore on his head this characteristic emblem of man's sovereignty; whether it were felt hat, palm-leaf, greasy beaver, or fine new chapeau, there it reposed with true republican independence. In truth, it appeared to be the characteristic mark of every individual. Some wore them tipped rakishly to one side - these were your men of humor, jolly, free-and-easy dogs; some had them jammed independently down over their noses - these were your hard characters, thorough men, who, when they wore their hats, *wanted* to wear them, and to wear them just as they had a mind to; there were those who had them set far over back - wide-awake men, who wanted a clear prospect; while careless men, who did not know, or care, how their hats sat, had them shaking about in all directions. The various hats, in fact, were quite a Shakespearean study.

Divers negroes, in very free-and-easy pantaloons, and with no redundancy in the shirt line, were scuttling about, hither and thither, without bringing to pass any very particular results, except expressing a generic willingness to turn over everything in creation generally for the benefit of Mas'r and his guests. Add to this picture a jolly, crackling, rollicking fire, going rejoicingly up a great wide chimney, - the outer door and every window being set wide open, and the calico window-curtain flopping and snapping in a good stiff breeze of damp raw air, - and you have an idea of the jollities of a Kentucky tavern.

Your Kentuckian of the present day is a good illustration of the doctrine of transmitted instincts and peculiarities. His fathers were mighty hunters, - men who lived in the woods, and slept under the free, open heavens, with the stars to hold their candles; and their descendant to this day always acts as if the house were his camp, – wears his hat at all hours, tumbles himself about, and puts his heels on the tops of chairs or mantelpieces, just as his father rolled on the green sward, and put his upon trees and logs, – keeps all the windows and doors open, winter and summer, that he may get air enough for his great lungs, – calls everybody "stranger," with nonchalant *bonhommie*, and is altogether the frankest, easiest, most jovial creature living.

Into such an assembly of the free and easy our traveller entered. He was a short, thick-set man, carefully dressed, with a round, good-natured countenance, and something rather fussy and particular in his appearance. He was very careful of his valise and umbrella, bringing them in with his own hands, and resisting, pertinaciously, all offers from the various servants to relieve him of them. He looked round the barroom with rather an anxious air, and, retreating with his valuables to the warmest corner, disposed them under his chair, sat down, and looked rather apprehensively up at the worthy whose heels illustrated the end of the mantel-piece, who was spitting from right to left, with a courage and energy rather alarming to gentlemen of weak nerves and particular habits.

"I say, stranger, how are ye?" said the aforesaid gentleman, firing an honorary salute of tobacco-juice in the direction of the new arrival.

"Well, I reckon," was the reply of the other, as he dodged, with some alarm, the threatening honor.

"Any news?" said the respondent, taking out a strip of tobacco and a large hunting-knife from his pocket.

"Not that I know of," said the man.

"Chaw?" said the first speaker, handing the old gentleman a bit of his tobacco, with a decidedly brotherly air.

"No, thank ye – it don't agree with me," said the little man, edging off.

"Don't, eh?" said the other, easily, and stowing away the morsel in his own mouth, in order to keep up the supply of tobacco-juice, for the general benefit of society.

The old gentleman uniformly gave a little start whenever his long-sided brother fired in his direction; and this being observed by his companion, he very good-naturedly turned his artillery to another quarter, and proceeded to storm one of the fire-irons with a degree of military talent fully sufficient to take a city.

"What's that?" said the old gentleman, observing some of the company formed in a group around a large handbill.

"Nigger advertised!" said one of the company, briefly.

Mr. Wilson, for that was the old gentleman's name, rose up, and, after carefully adjusting his valise and umbrella, proceeded deliberately to take out his spectacles and fix them on his nose; and, this operation being performed, read as follows:

> "Ran away from the subscriber, my mulatto boy, George. Said George six feet in height, a very

> light mulatto, brown curly hair; is very intelligent, speaks handsomely, can read and write, will probably try to pass for a white man, is deeply scarred on his back and shoulders, has been branded in his right hand with the letter H.
>
> "I will give four hundred dollars for him alive, and the same sum for satisfactory proof that he has been killed."

The old gentleman read this advertisement from end to end in a low voice, as if he were studying it.

The long-legged veteran, who had been besieging the fire-iron, as before related, now took down his cumbrous length, and rearing aloft his tall form, walked up to the advertisement and very deliberately spit a full discharge of tobacco-juice on it.

"There's my mind upon that!" said he, briefly, and sat down again.

"Why, now, stranger, what's that for?" said mine host.

"I'd do it all the same to the writer of that ar paper, if he was here," said the long man, coolly resuming his old employment of cutting tobacco. "Any man that owns a boy like that, and can't find any better way o' treating on him, *deserves* to lose him. Such papers as these is a shame to Kentucky; that's my mind right out, if anybody wants to know!"

"Well, now, that's a fact," said mine host, as he made an entry in his book.

"I've got a gang of boys, sir," said the long man, resuming his attack on the fire-irons, "and I jest tells 'em – 'Boys,' says I, – '*run* now! dig! put! jest when ye want to! I never shall come to look after you!' That's the way I keep mine. Let 'em know they are free to run any time, and it jest breaks up their wanting to. More 'n all, I've got free papers for 'em all recorded, in case I gets keeled up any o' these times, and they know it; and I tell ye, stranger, there an't a fellow in our parts gets more out of his niggers than I do. Why, my boys have been to Cincinnati, with five hundred dollars' worth of colts, and brought me back the money, all straight, time and agin. It stands to reason they should. Treat 'em like dogs, and you'll have dogs' works and dogs' actions. Treat 'em like men, and you'll have men's works." And the honest drover, in his warmth, endorsed this moral sentiment by firing a perfect *feu de joi* at the fireplace.

"I think you're altogether right, friend," said Mr. Wilson; "and this boy described here *is* a fine fellow – no mistake about that. He worked for me some half-dozen years in my bagging factory, and he was my best hand, sir. He is an ingenious fellow, too: he invented a machine for the cleaning of hemp – a really valuable affair; it's gone into use in several factories. His master holds the patent of it."

"I'll warrant ye," said the drover, "holds it and makes money out of it, and then turns round and brands the boy in his right hand. If I had a fair chance, I'd mark him, I reckon so that he'd carry it *one* while."

"These yer knowin' boys is allers aggravatin' and sarcy," said a coarse-looking fellow, from the other side of the room; "that's why they gets cut up and marked so. If they behaved themselves, they wouldn't."

"That is to say, the Lord made 'em men, and it's a hard squeeze gettin 'em down into beasts," said the drover, dryly.

"Bright niggers isn't no kind of 'vantage to their masters," continued the other, well entrenched, in a coarse, unconscious obtuseness, from the contempt of his opponent; "what's the use o' talents and them things, if you can't get the use on 'em yourself? Why, all the use they make on 't is to get round you. I've had one or two of these fellers, and I jest sold 'em down river. I knew I'd got to lose 'em, first or last, if I didn't."

"Better send orders up to the Lord, to make you a set, and leave out their souls entirely," said the drover.

Here the conversation was interrupted by the approach of a small one-horse buggy to the inn. It had a genteel appearance, and a well-dressed, gentlemanly man sat on the seat, with a colored servant driving.

The whole party examined the new comer with the interest with which a set of loafers in a rainy day usually examine every newcomer. He was very tall, with a dark, Spanish complexion, fine, expressive black eyes, and close-curling hair, also of a glossy blackness. His well-formed aquiline nose, straight thin lips, and the admirable contour of his finely-formed limbs, impressed the whole company instantly with the idea of something uncommon. He walked easily in among the company, and with a nod indicated to his waiter where to place his trunk, bowed to the company, and, with his hat in his hand, walked up leisurely to the bar, and gave in his name as Henry Butter, Oaklands, Shelby County. Turning, with an indifferent air, he sauntered up to the advertisement, and read it over.

"Jim," he said to his man, "seems to me we met a boy something like this, up at Beman's, didn't we?"

"Yes, Mas'r," said Jim, "only I an't sure about the hand."

"Well, I didn't look, of course," said the stranger with a careless yawn. Then walking up to the landlord, he desired him to furnish him with a private apartment, as he had some writing to do immediately.

The landlord was all obsequious, and a relay of about seven negroes, old and young, male and female, little and big, were soon whizzing about, like a covey of partridges, bustling, hurrying, treading on each other's toes, and tumbling over each other, in their zeal to get Mas'r's room ready, while he seated himself easily on a chair in the middle of the room, and entered into conversation with the man who sat next to him.

The manufacturer, Mr. Wilson, from the time of the entrance of the stranger, had regarded him with an air of disturbed and uneasy curiosity. He seemed to himself to have met and been acquainted with him somewhere, but he could not recollect. Every few moments, when the man spoke, or moved, or smiled, he would start and fix his eyes on him, and then suddenly withdraw them, as the bright, dark eyes met his with such unconcerned coolness. At last, a sudden recollection seemed to flash upon him, for he stared at the stranger with such an air of blank amazement and alarm, that he walked up to him.

"Mr. Wilson, I think," said he, in a tone of recognition, and extending his hand. "I beg your pardon, I didn't recollect you before. I see you remember me, – Mr. Butler, of Oaklands, Shelby County."

"Ye – yes – yes, sir," said Mr. Wilson, like one speaking in a dream.

Just then a negro boy entered, and announced that Mas'r's room was ready.

"Jim, see to the trunks," said the gentleman, negligently; then addressing himself to Mr. Wilson, he added – "I should like to have a few moments' conversation with you on business, in my room, if you please."

Mr. Wilson followed him, as one who walks in his sleep; and they proceeded to a large upper chamber, where a new-made fire was crackling, and various servants flying about, putting finishing touches to the arrangements.

When all was done, and the servants departed, the young man deliberately locked the door, and putting the key in his pocket, faced about, and folding his arms on his bosom, looked Mr. Wilson full in the face.

"George!" said Mr. Wilson.

"Yes, George," said the young man.

"I couldn't have thought it!"

"I am pretty well disguised, I fancy," said the young man, with a smile. "A little walnut bark has made my yellow skin a genteel brown, and I've dyed my hair black; so you see I don't answer to the advertisement at all."

"O, George! but this is a dangerous game you are playing. I could not have advised you to it."

"I can do it on my own responsibility," said George, with the same proud smile.

We remark, *en passant*, that George was, by his father's side, of white descent. His mother was one of those unfortunates of her race, marked out by personal beauty to be the slave of the passions of her possessor, and the mother of children who may never know a father. From one of the proudest families in Kentucky he had inherited a set of fine European features, and a high, indomitable spirit. From his mother he had received only a slight mulatto tinge, amply compensated by its accompanying rich, dark eye. A slight change in the tint of the skin and the color of his hair had metamorphosed him into the Spanish-looking fellow he then appeared; and as gracefulness of movement and gentlemanly manners had always been perfectly natural to him, he found no difficulty in playing the bold part he had adopted – that of a gentleman travelling with his domestic.

Mr. Wilson, a good-natured but extremely fidgety and cautious old gentleman, ambled up and down the room, appearing, as John Bunyan hath it, "much tumbled up and down in his mind," and divided between his wish to help George, and a certain confused notion of maintaining law and order: so, as he shambled about, he delivered himself as follows:

"Well, George, I s'pose you're running away – leaving your lawful master, George – (I don't wonder at it) – at the same time, I'm sorry, George, – yes, decidedly – I think I must say that, George – it's my duty to tell you so."

"Why are you sorry, sir?" said George, calmly.

"Why, to see you, as it were, setting yourself in opposition to the laws of your country."

"*My* country!" said George, with a strong and bitter emphasis; "what country have I, but the grave, – and I wish to God that I was laid there!"

"Why, George, no – no – it won't do; this way of talking is wicked – unscriptural. George, you've got a hard master – in fact, he is – well he conducts himself reprehensibly – I can't pretend to defend him. But you know how the angel commanded Hagar to return to her mistress, and submit herself under the hand;[4] and the apostle sent back Onesimus to his master."[5]

---

4 Gen. 16. The angel bade the pregnant Hagar return to her mistress Sarai, even though Sarai had dealt harshly with her.

5 Phil. 1:10. Onesimus went back to his master to become no longer a servant but a "brother beloved."

"Don't quote Bible at me that way, Mr. Wilson," said George, with a flashing eye, "don't! for my wife is a Christian, and I mean to be, if ever I get to where I can; but to quote Bible to a fellow in my circumstances, is enough to make him give it up altogether. I appeal to God Almighty; – I'm willing to go with the case to Him, and ask Him if I do wrong to seek my freedom."

"These feelings are quite natural, George," said the good-natured man, blowing his nose. "Yes, they're natural, but it is my duty not to encourage 'em in you. Yes, my boy, I'm sorry for you, now; it's a bad case – very bad; but the apostle says, 'Let everyone abide in the condition in which he is called.' We must all submit to the indications of Providence, George, – don't you see?"

George stood with his head drawn back, his arms folded tightly over his broad breast, and a bitter smile curling his lips.

"I wonder, Mr. Wilson, if the Indians should come and take you a prisoner away from your wife and children, and want to keep you all your life hoeing corn for them, if you'd think it your duty to abide in the condition in which you were called. I rather think that you'd think the first stray horse you could find an indication of Providence – shouldn't you?"

The little old gentleman stared with both eyes at this illustration of the case; but, though not much of a reasoner, he had the sense in which some logicians on this particular subject do not excel, – that of saying nothing, where nothing could be said. So, as he stood carefully stroking his umbrella, and folding and patting down all the creases in it, he proceeded on with his exhortations in a general way.

"You see, George, you know, now, I always have stood your friend; and whatever I've said, I've said for your good. Now, here, it seems to me, you're running an awful risk. You can't hope to carry it out. If you're taken, it will be worse with you than ever; they'll only abuse you, and half kill you, and sell you down the river."

"Mr. Wilson, I know all this," said George. "I *do* run a risk, but –" he threw open his overcoat, and showed two pistols and a bowie-knife. "There!" he said, "I'm ready for 'em! Down south I never *will* go. No! if it comes to that, I can earn myself at least six feet of free soil, – the first and last I shall ever own in Kentucky!"

"Why, George, this state of mind is awful; it's getting really desperate George. I'm concerned. Going to break the laws of your country!"

"My country again! Mr. Wilson, *you* have a country; but what country have *I*, or any one like me, born of slave mothers? What laws are there for us? We don't make them, – we don't consent to them, – we have nothing to do with them; all they do for us is to crush us, and keep us down. Haven't I heard your Fourth-of-July speeches? Don't you tell us all, once a year, that governments derive their just power from the consent of the governed? Can't a fellow *think*, that hears such things? Can't he put this and that together, and see what it comes to?"

Mr. Wilson's mind was one of those that may not unaptly be represented by a bale of cotton, - downy, soft, benevolently fuzzy and confused. He really pitied George with all his heart, and had a sort of dim and cloudy perception of the style of feeling that agitated him; but he deemed it his duty to go on talking *good* to him, with infinite pertinacity.

"George, this is bad. I must tell you, you know, as a friend, you'd better not be meddling with such notions; they are bad, George, very bad, for boys in your condition, - very;" and Mr. Wilson sat down to a table, and began nervously chewing the handle of his umbrella.

"See here, now, Mr. Wilson," said George, coming up and sitting himself determinately down in front of him; "look at me, now. Don't I sit before you, every way, just as much a man as you are? Look at my face, - look at my hands, - look at my body," and the young man drew himself up proudly; "why am I *not* a man, as much as anybody? Well, Mr. Wilson, hear what I can tell you. I had a father - one of your Kentucky gentlemen - who didn't think enough of me to keep me from being sold with his dogs and horses, to satisfy the estate, when he died. I saw my mother put up at sheriff's sale, with her seven children. They were sold before her eyes, one by one, all to different masters; and I was the youngest. She came and kneeled down before old Mas'r, and begged him to buy her with me, that she might have at least one child with her; and he kicked her away with his heavy boot. I saw him do it; and the last that I heard was her moans and screams, when I was tied to his horse's neck, to be carried off to his place."

"Well, then?"

"My master traded with one of the men, and bought my oldest sister. She was a pious, good girl, – a member of the Baptist church, – and as handsome as my poor mother had been. She was well brought up, and had good manners. At first, I was glad she was bought, for I had one friend near me. I was soon sorry for it. Sir, I have stood at the door and heard her whipped, when it seemed as if every blow cut into my naked heart, and I couldn't do anything to help her; and she was whipped, sir, for wanting to live a decent Christian life, such as your laws give no slave girl a right to live; and at last I saw her chained with a trader's gang, to be sent to market in Orleans, – sent there for nothing else but that, – and that's the last I know of her. Well, I grew up, – long years and years, – no father, no mother, no sister, not a living soul that cared for me more than a dog; nothing but whipping, scolding, starving. Why, sir, I've been so hungry that I have been glad to take the bones they threw to their dogs; and yet, when I was a little fellow, and laid awake whole nights and cried, it wasn't the hunger, it wasn't the whipping, I cried for. No, sir, it was for *my mother* and *my sisters*, – it was because I hadn't a friend to love me on earth. I never knew what peace or comfort was. I never had a kind word spoken to me till I came to work in your factory. Mr. Wilson, you treated me well; you encouraged me to do well, and to learn to read and write, and to try to make something of myself; and God knows how grateful I am for it. Then, sir, I found my wife; you've seen her, – you know how beautiful she is. When I found she loved me, when I married her, I scarcely could believe I was alive, I was so happy; and, sir, she is as good as she is beautiful. But now what? Why, now comes my master, takes me right away from my work, and my friends, and all I like, and grinds me down into the very dirt! And why? Because, he says, I forgot who I was; he says, to teach me that I am only a nigger! After all, and last of all, he comes between me and my wife, and says I shall give her up, and live with another woman. And all this your laws give him power to do, in spite of God or man. Mr. Wilson, look at it! There isn't *one* of all these things, that have broken the hearts of my mother and my sister, and my wife and myself, but your laws allow, and give every man power to do, in Kentucky, and none can say to him nay! Do you call these the laws of *my* country? Sir, I haven't any country, anymore than I have any father. But I'm going to have one. I don't want anything of *your* country, except to be let alone, – to go peaceably out of it; and when I get to Canada, where the laws will own me and protect me, that *shall* be my country, and its laws I will obey. But if any man tries to stop me, let him take care, for I am desperate. I'll fight for my liberty to the last breath I breathe. You say your fathers did it; if it was right for them, it is right for me!"

This speech, delivered partly while sitting at the table, and partly walking up and down the room, – delivered with tears, and flashing eyes, and despairing gestures, – was altogether too much for the good-natured old body to whom it was addressed, who had pulled out a great yellow silk pocket-handkerchief, and was mopping up his face with great energy.

"Blast 'em all!" he suddenly broke out. "Haven't I always said so – the infernal old cusses! I hope I an't swearing, now. Well! go ahead, George, go ahead; but be careful, my boy; don't shoot anybody, George, unless – well – you'd *better* not shoot, I reckon; at least, I wouldn't *hit* anybody, you know. Where is your wife, George?" he added, as he nervously rose, and began walking the room.

"Gone, sir gone, with her child in her arms, the Lord only knows where; – gone after the north star; and when we ever meet, or whether we meet at all in this world, no creature can tell."

"Is it possible! astonishing! from such a kind family?"

"Kind families get in debt, and the laws of *our* country allow them to sell the child out of its mother's bosom to pay its master's debts," said George, bitterly.

"Well, well," said the honest old man, fumbling in his pocket: "I s'pose, perhaps, I an't following my judgment, – hang it, I *won't* follow my judgment!" he added, suddenly; "so here, George," and, taking out a roll of bills from his pocket-book, he offered them to George.

"No, my kind, good sir!" said George, "you've done a great deal for me, and this might get you into trouble. I have money enough, I hope, to take me as far as I need it."

"No; but you must, George. Money is a great help everywhere; - can't have too much, if you get it honestly. Take it, - *do* take it, *now*, - do, my boy!"

"On condition, sir, that I may repay it at some future time, I will," said George, taking up the money.

"And now, George, how long are you going to travel in this way? - not long or far, I hope. It's well carried on, but too bold. And this black fellow, - who is he?"

"A true fellow, who went to Canada more than a year ago. He heard, after he got there, that his master was so angry at him for going off that he had whipped his poor old mother; and he has come all the way back to comfort her, and get a chance to get her away."

"Has he got her?"

"Not yet; he has been hanging about the place, and found no chance yet. Meanwhile, he is going with me as far as Ohio, to put me among friends that helped him, and then he will come back after her.

"Dangerous, very dangerous!" said the old man.

George drew himself up, and smiled disdainfully.

The old gentleman eyed him from head to foot, with a sort of innocent wonder.

"George, something has brought you out wonderfully. You hold up your head, and speak and move like another man," said Mr. Wilson.

"Because I'm a *freeman*!" said George, proudly. "Yes, sir; I've said Mas'r for the last time to any man. *I'm free!"*

"Take care! You are not sure, – you may be taken."

"All men are free and *equal in the grave*, if it comes to that, Mr. Wilson," said George.

"I'm perfectly dumb-founded with your boldness!" said Mr. Wilson, – "to come right here to the nearest tavern!"

"Mr. Wilson, it is *so* bold, and this tavern is so near, that they will never think of it; they will look for me on ahead, and you yourself wouldn't know me. Jim's master don't live in this county; he isn't known in these parts. Besides, he is given up; nobody is looking after him, and nobody will take me up from the advertisement, I think."

"But the mark in your hand?"

George drew off his glove, and showed a newly-healed scar in his hand.

"That is a parting proof of Mr. Harris' regard," he said, scornfully. "A fortnight ago, he took it into his head to give it to me, because he said he believed I should try to get away one of these days. Looks interesting, doesn't it?" he said, drawing his glove on again.

"I declare, my very blood runs cold when I think of it, – your condition and your risks!" said Mr. Wilson.

"Mine has run cold a good many years, Mr. Wilson; at present, it's about up to the boiling point," said George.

"Well, my good sir," continued George, after a few moments' silence, "I saw you knew me; I thought I'd just have this talk with you, lest your surprised looks should bring me out. I leave early tomorrow morning, before daylight; by tomorrow night I hope to sleep safe in Ohio. I shall travel by daylight, stop at the best hotels, go to the dinner-tables with the lords of the land. So, good-by, sir; if you hear that I'm taken, you may know that I'm dead!"

George stood up like a rock, and put out his hand with the air of a prince. The friendly little old man shook it heartily, and after a little shower of caution, he took his umbrella, and fumbled his way out of the room.

George stood thoughtfully looking at the door, as the old man closed it. A thought seemed to flash across his mind. He hastily stepped to it, and opening it, said,

"Mr. Wilson, one word more."

The old gentleman entered again, and George, as before, locked the door, and then stood for a few moments looking on the floor, irresolutely. At last, raising his head with a sudden effort – "Mr. Wilson, you have shown yourself a Christian in your treatment of me, – I want to ask one last deed of Christian kindness of you."

"Well, George."

"Well, sir, – what you said was true. I *am* running a dreadful risk. There isn't, on earth, a living soul to care if I die," he added, drawing his breath hard, and speaking with a great effort, – "I shall be kicked out and buried like a dog, and nobody'll think of it a day after, – *only my poor wife!* Poor soul! she'll mourn and grieve; and if you'd only contrive, Mr. Wilson, to send this little pin to her. She gave it to me for a Christmas present, poor child! Give it to her, and tell her I loved her to the last. Will you? *Will* you?" he added, earnestly.

"Yes, certainly – poor fellow!" said the old gentleman, taking the pin, with watery eyes, and a melancholy quiver in his voice.

"Tell her one thing," said George; "it's my last wish, if she *can* get to Canada, to go there. No matter how kind her mistress is, – no matter how much she loves her home; beg her not to go back, – for slavery always ends in misery. Tell her to bring up our boy a free man, and then he won't suffer as I have. Tell her this, Mr. Wilson, will you?"

"Yes, George. I'll tell her; but I trust you won't die; take heart, – you're a brave fellow. Trust in the Lord, George. I wish in my heart you were safe through, though, – that's what I do."

"*Is* there a God to trust in?" said George, in such a tone of bitter despair as arrested the old gentleman's words. "O, I've seen things all my life that have made me feel that there can't be a God. You Christians don't know how these things look to us. There's a God for you, but is there any for us?"

"O, now, don't – don't, my boy!" said the old man, almost sobbing as he spoke; "don't feel so! There is – there is; clouds and darkness are around about him, but righteousness and judgment are the habitation of his throne. There's a *God*, George, – believe it; trust in Him, and I'm sure He'll help you. Everything will be set right, – if not in this life, in another."

The real piety and benevolence of the simple old man invested him with a temporary dignity and authority, as he spoke. George stopped his distracted walk up and down the room, stood thoughtfully a moment, and then said, quietly,

"Thank you for saying that, my good friend; I'll *think of that."*

Chapter 12

Select Incident of Lawful Trade

> "In Ramah there was a voice heard, - weeping, and lamentation, and great mourning; Rachel weeping for her children, and would not be comforted."[6]

Mr. Haley and Tom jogged onward in their wagon, each, for a time, absorbed in his own reflections. Now, the reflections of two men sitting side by side are a curious thing, - seated on the same seat, having the same eyes, ears, hands and organs of all sorts, and having pass before their eyes the same objects, - it is wonderful what a variety we shall find in these same reflections!

As, for example, Mr. Haley: he thought first of Tom's length, and breadth, and height, and what he would sell for, if he was kept fat and in good case till he got him into market. He thought of how he should make out his gang; he thought of the respective market value of certain supposititious men and women and children who were to compose it, and other kindred topics of the business; then he thought of himself, and how humane he was, that whereas other men chained their "niggers" hand and foot both, he only put fetters on the feet, and left Tom the use of his hands, as long

---

6 Jer. 31:15.

as he behaved well; and he sighed to think how ungrateful human nature was, so that there was even room to doubt whether Tom appreciated his mercies. He had been taken in so by "niggers" whom he had favored; but still he was astonished to consider how good-natured he yet remained!

As to Tom, he was thinking over some words of an unfashionable old book, which kept running through his head, again and again, as follows: "We have here no continuing city, but we seek one to come; wherefore God himself is not ashamed to be called our God; for he hath prepared for us a city." These words of an ancient volume, got up principally by "ignorant and unlearned men," have, through all time, kept up, somehow, a strange sort of power over the minds of poor, simple fellows, like Tom. They stir up the soul from its depths, and rouse, as with trumpet call, courage, energy, and enthusiasm, where before was only the blackness of despair.

Mr. Haley pulled out of his pocket sundry newspapers, and began looking over their advertisements, with absorbed interest. He was not a remarkably fluent reader, and was in the habit of reading in a sort of recitative half-aloud, by way of calling in his ears to verify the deductions of his eyes. In this tone he slowly recited the following paragraph:

> "EXECUTOR'S SALE, - NEGROES! - Agreeably to order of court, will be sold, on Tuesday, February 20, before the Court-house door, in the town of Washington, Kentucky, the following negroes: Hagar, aged 60; John, aged 30; Ben, aged 21; Saul, aged 25; Albert, aged 14. Sold for the

benefit of the creditors and heirs of the estate of Jesse Blutchford,

"SAMUEL MORRIS, THOMAS FLINT, Executors."

"This yer I must look at," said he to Tom, for want of somebody else to talk to.

"Ye see, I'm going to get up a prime gang to take down with ye, Tom; it'll make it sociable and pleasant like, – good company will, ye know. We must drive right to Washington first and foremost, and then I'll clap you into jail, while I does the business."

Tom received this agreeable intelligence quite meekly; simply wondering, in his own heart, how many of these doomed men had wives and children, and whether they would feel as he did about leaving them. It is to be confessed, too, that the naive, off-hand information that he was to be thrown into jail by no means produced an agreeable impression on a poor fellow who had always prided himself on a strictly honest and upright course of life. Yes, Tom, we must confess it, was rather proud of his honesty, poor fellow, – not having very much else to be proud of; – if he had belonged to some of the higher walks of society, he, perhaps, would never have been reduced to such straits. However, the day wore on, and the evening saw Haley and Tom comfortably accommodated in Washington, – the one in a tavern, and the other in a jail.

About eleven o'clock the next day, a mixed throng was gathered around the court-house steps, – smoking, chewing, spitting, swearing, and conversing, according to their respective tastes and turns, – waiting for the auction to commence. The men and women to be sold sat in a group apart, talking in a low tone to each other. The woman who had been advertised by the name of Hagar was a regular African in feature and figure. She might have been sixty, but was older than that by hard work and disease, was partially blind, and somewhat crippled with rheumatism. By her side stood her only remaining son, Albert, a bright-looking little fellow of fourteen years. The boy was the only survivor of a large family, who had been successively sold away from her to a southern market. The mother held on to him with both her shaking hands, and eyed with intense trepidation every one who walked up to examine him.

"Don't be feard, Aunt Hagar," said the oldest of the men, "I spoke to Mas'r Thomas 'bout it, and he thought he might manage to sell you in a lot both together."

"Dey needn't call me worn out yet," said she, lifting her shaking hands. "I can cook yet, and scrub, and scour, – I'm wuth a buying, if I do come cheap; – tell em dat ar, – you *tell* em," she added, earnestly.

Haley here forced his way into the group, walked up to the old man, pulled his mouth open and looked in, felt of his teeth, made him stand and straighten himself, bend his back, and perform various evolutions to show his muscles; and then passed on to the next, and put him through the same trial. Walking up last to the boy, he felt of his arms, straightened his hands, and looked at his fingers, and made him jump, to show his agility.

"He an't gwine to be sold widout me!" said the old woman, with passionate eagerness; "he and I goes in a lot together; I 's rail strong yet, Mas'r and can do heaps o' work, – heaps on it, Mas'r."

"On plantation?" said Haley, with a contemptuous glance. "Likely story!" and, as if satisfied with his examination, he walked out and looked, and stood with his hands in his pocket, his cigar in his mouth, and his hat cocked on one side, ready for action.

"What think of 'em?" said a man who had been following Haley's examination, as if to make up his own mind from it.

"Wal," said Haley, spitting, "I shall put in, I think, for the youngerly ones and the boy."

"They want to sell the boy and the old woman together," said the man.

"Find it a tight pull; – why, she's an old rack o' bones, – not worth her salt."

"You wouldn't then?" said the man.

"Anybody 'd be a fool 't would. She's half blind, crooked with rheumatis, and foolish to boot."

"Some buys up these yer old critturs, and ses there's a sight more wear in 'em than a body 'd think," said the man, reflectively.

"No go, 't all," said Haley; "wouldn't take her for a present, – fact, – I've *seen*, now."

"Wal, 't is kinder pity, now, not to buy her with her son, – her heart seems so sot on him, – s'pose they fling her in cheap."

"Them that's got money to spend that ar way, it's all well enough. I shall bid off on that ar boy for a plantation-hand; – wouldn't be bothered with her, no way, not if they'd give her to me," said Haley.

"She'll take on desp't," said the man.

"Nat'lly, she will," said the trader, coolly.

The conversation was here interrupted by a busy hum in the audience; and the auctioneer, a short, bustling, important fellow, elbowed his way into the crowd. The old woman drew in her breath, and caught instinctively at her son.

"Keep close to yer mammy, Albert, – close, – dey'll put us up togedder," she said.

"O, mammy, I'm feard they won't," said the boy.

"Dey must, child; I can't live, no ways, if they don't" said the old creature, vehemently.

The stentorian tones of the auctioneer, calling out to clear the way, now announced that the sale was about to commence. A place was cleared, and the bidding began. The different men on the list were soon knocked off at prices which showed a pretty brisk demand in the market; two of them fell to Haley.

"Come, now, young un," said the auctioneer, giving the boy a touch with his hammer, "be up and show your springs, now."

"Put us two up togedder, togedder, – do please, Mas'r," said the old woman, holding fast to her boy.

"Be off," said the man, gruffly, pushing her hands away; "you come last. Now, darkey, spring;" and, with the word, he pushed the boy toward the block, while a deep, heavy groan rose behind him. The boy paused, and looked back; but there was no time to stay, and, dashing the tears from his large, bright eyes, he was up in a moment.

His fine figure, alert limbs, and bright face, raised an instant competition, and half a dozen bids simultaneously met the ear of the auctioneer. Anxious, half-frightened, he looked from side to side, as he heard the clatter of contending bids, – now here, now there, – till the hammer fell. Haley had got him. He was pushed from the block toward his new master, but stopped one moment, and looked back, when his poor old mother, trembling in every limb, held out her shaking hands toward him.

"Buy me too, Mas'r, for de dear Lord's sake! – buy me, – I shall die if you don't!"

"You'll die if I do, that's the kink of it," said Haley, – "no!" And he turned on his heel.

The bidding for the poor old creature was summary. The man who had addressed Haley, and who seemed not destitute of compassion, bought her for a trifle, and the spectators began to disperse.

The poor victims of the sale, who had been brought up in one place together for years, gathered round the despairing old mother, whose agony was pitiful to see.

"Couldn't dey leave me one? Mas'r allers said I should have one, – he did," she repeated over and over, in heart-broken tones.

"Trust in the Lord, Aunt Hagar," said the oldest of the men, sorrowfully.

"What good will it do?" said she, sobbing passionately.

"Mother, mother, – don't! don't!" said the boy. "They say you 's got a good master."

"I don't care, – I don't care. O, Albert! oh, my boy! you 's my last baby. Lord, how ken I?"

"Come, take her off, can't some of ye?" said Haley, dryly; "don't do no good for her to go on that ar way."

The old men of the company, partly by persuasion and partly by force, loosed the poor creature's last despairing hold, and, as they led her off to her new master's wagon, strove to comfort her.

"Now!" said Haley, pushing his three purchases together, and producing a bundle of handcuffs, which he proceeded to put on their wrists; and fastening each handcuff to a long chain, he drove them before him to the jail.

A few days saw Haley, with his possessions, safely deposited on one of the Ohio boats. It was the commencement of his gang, to be augmented, as the boat moved on, by various other merchandise of the same kind, which he, or his agent, had stored for him in various points along shore.

The La Belle Riviere, as brave and beautiful a boat as ever walked the waters of her namesake river, was floating gayly down the stream, under a brilliant sky, the stripes and stars of free America waving and fluttering over head; the guards crowded with well-dressed ladies and gentlemen walking and enjoying the delightful day. All was full of life, buoyant and rejoicing; – all but Haley's gang, who were stored, with other freight, on the lower deck, and who, somehow, did not seem to appreciate their various privileges, as they sat in a knot, talking to each other in low tones.

"Boys," said Haley, coming up, briskly, "I hope you keep up good heart, and are cheerful. Now, no sulks, ye see; keep stiff upper lip, boys; do well by me, and I'll do well by you."

The boys addressed responded the invariable "Yes, Mas'r," for ages the watchword of poor Africa; but it's to be owned they did not look particularly cheerful; they had their various little prejudices in favor of wives, mothers, sisters, and children, seen for the last time, – and though "they that wasted them required of them mirth," it was not instantly forthcoming.

"I've got a wife," spoke out the article enumerated as "John, aged thirty," and he laid his chained hand on

Tom's knee, – "and she don't know a word about this, poor girl!"

"Where does she live?" said Tom.

"In a tavern a piece down here," said John; "I wish, now, I *could* see her once more in this world," he added.

Poor John! It *was* rather natural; and the tears that fell, as he spoke, came as naturally as if he had been a white man. Tom drew a long breath from a sore heart, and tried, in his poor way, to comfort him.

And over head, in the cabin, sat fathers and mothers, husbands and wives; and merry, dancing children moved round among them, like so many little butterflies, and everything was going on quite easy and comfortable.

"O, mamma," said a boy, who had just come up from below, "there's a negro trader on board, and he's brought four or five slaves down there."

"Poor creatures!" said the mother, in a tone between grief and indignation.

"What's that?" said another lady.

"Some poor slaves below," said the mother.

"And they've got chains on," said the boy.

"What a shame to our country that such sights are to be seen!" said another lady.

"O, there's a great deal to be said on both sides of the subject," said a genteel woman, who sat at her state-room door sewing, while her little girl and boy were playing round her. "I've been south, and I must say I think the negroes are better off than they would be to be free."

"In some respects, some of them are well off, I grant," said the lady to whose remark she had answered. "The most dreadful part of slavery, to my mind, is its outrages on the feelings and affections, - the separating of families, for example."

"That *is* a bad thing, certainly," said the other lady, holding up a baby's dress she had just completed, and looking intently on its trimmings; "but then, I fancy, it don't occur often."

"O, it does," said the first lady, eagerly; "I've lived many years in Kentucky and Virginia both, and I've seen enough to make any one's heart sick. Suppose, ma'am, your two children, there, should be taken from you, and sold?"

"We can't reason from our feelings to those of this class of persons," said the other lady, sorting out some worsteds on her lap.

"Indeed, ma'am, you can know nothing of them, if you say so," answered the first lady, warmly. "I was born and brought up among them. I know they *do* feel, just as keenly, - even more so, perhaps, - as we do."

The lady said "Indeed!" yawned, and looked out the cabin window, and finally repeated, for a finale, the remark with which she had begun, – "After all, I think they are better off than they would be to be free."

"It's undoubtedly the intention of Providence that the African race should be servants, – kept in a low condition," said a grave-looking gentleman in black, a clergyman, seated by the cabin door. "'Cursed be Canaan; a servant of servants shall he be,' the scripture says."[7]

"I say, stranger, is that ar what that text means?" said a tall man, standing by.

"Undoubtedly. It pleased Providence, for some inscrutable reason, to doom the race to bondage, ages ago; and we must not set up our opinion against that."

"Well, then, we'll all go ahead and buy up niggers," said the man, "if that's the way of Providence, – won't we, Squire?" said he, turning to Haley, who had been standing, with his hands in his pockets, by the stove and intently listening to the conversation.

"Yes," continued the tall man, "we must all be resigned to the decrees of Providence. Niggers must be sold, and trucked round, and kept under; it's

---

7 Gen. 9:25. This is what Noah says when he wakes out of drunkenness and realizes that his youngest son, Ham, father of Canaan, has seen him naked.

what they's made for. 'Pears like this yer view 's quite refreshing, an't it, stranger?" said he to Haley.

"I never thought on 't," said Haley, "I couldn't have said as much, myself; I ha'nt no larning. I took up the trade just to make a living; if 'tan't right, I calculated to 'pent on 't in time, ye know."

"And now you'll save yerself the trouble, won't ye?" said the tall man. "See what 't is, now, to know scripture. If ye'd only studied yer Bible, like this yer good man, ye might have know'd it before, and saved ye a heap o' trouble. Ye could jist have said, 'Cussed be' – what's his name? – 'and 't would all have come right.'" And the stranger, who was no other than the honest drover whom we introduced to our readers in the Kentucky tavern, sat down, and began smoking, with a curious smile on his long, dry face.

A tall, slender young man, with a face expressive of great feeling and intelligence, here broke in, and repeated the words, "'All things whatsoever ye would that men should do unto you, do ye even so unto them.' I suppose," he added, "*that* is scripture, as much as 'Cursed be Canaan.'"

"Wal, it seems quite *as* plain a text, stranger," said John the drover, "to poor fellows like us, now;" and John smoked on like a volcano.

The young man paused, looked as if he was going to say more, when suddenly the boat stopped, and the company made the usual steamboat rush, to see where they were landing.

"Both them ar chaps parsons?" said John to one of the men, as they were going out.

The man nodded.

As the boat stopped, a black woman came running wildly up the plank, darted into the crowd, flew up to where the slave gang sat, and threw her arms round that unfortunate piece of merchandise before enumerate – "John, aged thirty," and with sobs and tears bemoaned him as her husband.

But what needs tell the story, told too oft, – every day told, – of heart-strings rent and broken, – the weak broken and torn for the profit and convenience of the strong! It needs not to be told; – every day is telling it, – telling it, too, in the ear of One who is not deaf, though he be long silent.

The young man who had spoken for the cause of humanity and God before stood with folded arms, looking on this scene. He turned, and Haley was standing at his side. "My friend," he said, speaking with thick utterance, "how can you, how dare you, carry on a trade like this? Look at those poor creatures! Here I am, rejoicing in my heart that I am going home to my wife and child; and the same bell which is a signal to carry me onward towards them will part this poor man and his wife forever. Depend upon it, God will bring you into judgment for this."

The trader turned away in silence.

"I say, now," said the drover, touching his elbow, "there's differences in parsons, an't there? 'Cussed be

Canaan' don't seem to go down with this 'un, does it?"

Haley gave an uneasy growl.

"And that ar an't the worst on 't," said John; "mabbee it won't go down with the Lord, neither, when ye come to settle with Him, one o' these days, as all on us must, I reckon."

Haley walked reflectively to the other end of the boat.

"If I make pretty handsomely on one or two next gangs," he thought, "I reckon I'll stop off this yer; it's really getting dangerous." And he took out his pocket-book, and began adding over his accounts, – a process which many gentlemen besides Mr. Haley have found a specific for an uneasy conscience.

The boat swept proudly away from the shore, and all went on merrily, as before. Men talked, and loafed, and read, and smoked. Women sewed, and children played, and the boat passed on her way.

One day, when she lay to for a while at a small town in Kentucky, Haley went up into the place on a little matter of business.

Tom, whose fetters did not prevent his taking a moderate circuit, had drawn near the side of the boat, and stood listlessly gazing over the railing. After a time, he saw the trader returning, with an alert step, in company with a colored woman, bearing in her arms a young child. She was dressed quite respectably, and a colored man followed her, bringing along a small trunk. The woman came cheerfully onward, talking, as she came, with the man who bore her trunk, and so passed up the plank into the boat. The bell rung, the steamer whizzed, the engine groaned and coughed, and away swept the boat down the river.

The woman walked forward among the boxes and bales of the lower deck, and, sitting down, busied herself with chirruping to her baby.

Haley made a turn or two about the boat, and then, coming up, seated himself near her, and began saying something to her in an indifferent undertone.

Tom soon noticed a heavy cloud passing over the woman's brow; and that she answered rapidly, and with great vehemence.

"I don't believe it, – I won't believe it!" he heard her say. "You're jist a foolin with me."

"If you won't believe it, look here!" said the man, drawing out a paper; "this yer's the bill of sale, and there's your master's name to it; and I paid down good solid cash for it, too, I can tell you, – so, now!"

"I don't believe Mas'r would cheat me so; it can't be true!" said the woman, with increasing agitation.

"You can ask any of these men here, that can read writing. Here!" he said, to a man that was passing by, "jist read this yer, won't you! This yer gal won't believe me, when I tell her what 't is."

"Why, it's a bill of sale, signed by John Fosdick," said the man, "making over to you the girl Lucy and her child. It's all straight enough, for aught I see."

The woman's passionate exclamations collected a crowd around her, and the trader briefly explained to them the cause of the agitation.

"He told me that I was going down to Louisville, to hire out as cook to the same tavern where my husband works, - that's what Mas'r told me, his own self; and I can't believe he'd lie to me," said the woman.

"But he has sold you, my poor woman, there's no doubt about it," said a good-natured looking man, who had been examining the papers; "he has done it, and no mistake."

"Then it's no account talking," said the woman, suddenly growing quite calm; and, clasping her child tighter in her arms, she sat down on her box, turned her back round, and gazed listlessly into the river.

"Going to take it easy, after all!" said the trader. "Gal's got grit, I see."

The woman looked calm, as the boat went on; and a beautiful soft summer breeze passed like a compassionate spirit over her head, - the gentle breeze, that never inquires whether the brow is dusky or fair that it fans. And she saw sunshine sparkling on the water, in golden ripples, and heard gay voices, full of ease and pleasure, talking around her everywhere; but her heart lay as if a great stone had fallen on it. Her baby raised himself up against her, and stroked her cheeks with his little hands; and, springing up and down, crowing and chatting, seemed determined to arouse her. She strained him suddenly and tightly in her arms, and slowly one tear after another fell on his wondering, unconscious face; and gradually she seemed, and little by little, to grow calmer, and busied herself with tending and nursing him.

The child, a boy of ten months, was uncommonly large and strong of his age, and very vigorous in his limbs. Never, for a moment, still, he kept his mother constantly busy in holding him, and guarding his springing activity.

"That's a fine chap!" said a man, suddenly stopping opposite to him, with his hands in his pockets. "How old is he?"

"Ten months and a half," said the mother.

The man whistled to the boy, and offered him part of a stick of candy, which he eagerly grabbed at, and very soon had it in a baby's general depository, to wit, his mouth.

"Rum fellow!" said the man "Knows what's what!" and he whistled, and walked on. When he had got to the other side of the boat, he came across Haley, who was smoking on top of a pile of boxes.

The stranger produced a match, and lighted a cigar, saying, as he did so,

"Decentish kind o' wench you've got round there, stranger."

"Why, I reckon she *is* tol'able fair," said Haley, blowing the smoke out of his mouth.

"Taking her down south?" said the man.

Haley nodded, and smoked on.

"Plantation hand?" said the man.

"Wal," said Haley, "I'm fillin' out an order for a plantation, and I think I shall put her in. They telled me she was a good cook; and they can use her for that, or set her at the cotton-picking. She's got the right fingers for that; I looked at 'em. Sell well, either way;" and Haley resumed his cigar.

"They won't want the young 'un on the plantation," said the man.

"I shall sell him, first chance I find," said Haley, lighting another cigar.

"S'pose you'd be selling him tol'able cheap," said the stranger, mounting the pile of boxes, and sitting down comfortably.

"Don't know 'bout that," said Haley; "he's a pretty smart young 'un, straight, fat, strong; flesh as hard as a brick!"

"Very true, but then there's the bother and expense of raisin'."

"Nonsense!" said Haley; "they is raised as easy as any kind of critter there is going; they an't a bit more trouble than pups. This yer chap will be running all around, in a month."

"I've got a good place for raisin', and I thought of takin' in a little more stock," said the man. "One cook lost a young 'un last week, - got drownded in a washtub, while she was a hangin' out the clothes, - and I reckon it would be well enough to set her to raisin' this yer."

Haley and the stranger smoked a while in silence, neither seeming willing to broach the test question of the interview. At last the man resumed:

"You wouldn't think of wantin' more than ten dollars for that ar chap, seeing you *must* get him off yer hand, any how?"

Haley shook his head, and spit impressively.

"That won't do, no ways," he said, and began his smoking again.

"Well, stranger, what will you take?"

"Well, now," said Haley, "I *could* raise that ar chap myself, or get him raised; he's oncommon likely and healthy, and he'd fetch a hundred dollars, six months hence; and, in a year or two, he'd bring two hundred, if I had him in the right spot; I shan't take a cent less nor fifty for him now."

"O, stranger! that's rediculous, altogether," said the man.

"Fact!" said Haley, with a decisive nod of his head.

"I'll give thirty for him," said the stranger, "but not a cent more."

"Now, I'll tell ye what I will do," said Haley, spitting again, with renewed decision. "I'll split the difference, and say forty-five; and that's the most I will do."

"Well, agreed!" said the man, after an interval.

"Done!" said Haley. "Where do you land?"

"At Louisville," said the man.

"Louisville," said Haley. "Very fair, we get there about dusk. Chap will be asleep, – all fair, – get him off quietly, and no screaming, – happens beautiful, – I like to do everything quietly, – I hates all kind of agitation and fluster." And so, after a transfer of certain bills had passed from the man's pocket-book to the trader's, he resumed his cigar.

It was a bright, tranquil evening when the boat stopped at the wharf at Louisville. The woman had been sitting with her baby in her arms, now wrapped in a heavy sleep. When she heard the name of the place called out, she hastily laid the child down in a little cradle formed by the hollow among the boxes, first carefully spreading under it her cloak; and then she sprung to the side of the boat, in hopes that, among the various hotel-waiters who thronged the wharf, she might see her husband. In this hope, she pressed forward to the front rails, and, stretching far over them, strained her eyes intently on the moving heads on the shore, and the crowd pressed in between her and the child.

"Now's your time," said Haley, taking the sleeping child up, and handing him to the stranger. "Don't wake him up, and set him to crying, now; it would make a devil of a fuss with the gal." The man took the bundle carefully, and was soon lost in the crowd that went up the wharf.

When the boat, creaking, and groaning, and puffing, had loosed from the wharf, and was beginning slowly to strain herself along, the woman returned to her old seat. The trader was sitting there, - the child was gone!

"Why, why, - where?" she began, in bewildered surprise.

"Lucy," said the trader, "your child's gone; you may as well know it first as last. You see, I know'd you couldn't take him down south; and I got a chance to sell him to a first-rate family, that'll raise him better than you can."

The trader had arrived at that stage of Christian and political perfection which has been recommended by some preachers and politicians of the north, lately, in which he had completely overcome every humane weakness and prejudice. His heart was exactly where yours, sir, and mine could be brought, with proper effort and cultivation. The wild look of anguish and utter despair that the woman cast on him might have disturbed one less practised; but he was used to it. He had seen that same look hundreds of times. You can get used to such things, too, my friend; and it is the great object of recent efforts to make our whole northern community used to them, for the glory of the Union. So the trader only regarded the mortal anguish which he saw working in those dark features, those clenched hands, and suffocating breathings, as necessary incidents of the trade, and merely calculated whether she was going to scream, and get up a commotion on the boat; for, like other supporters of our peculiar institution, he decidedly disliked agitation.

But the woman did not scream. The shot had passed too straight and direct through the heart, for cry or tear.

Dizzily she sat down. Her slack hands fell lifeless by her side. Her eyes looked straight forward, but she saw nothing. All the noise and hum of the boat, the groaning of the machinery, mingled dreamily to her bewildered ear; and the poor, dumb-stricken heart had neither cry not tear to show for its utter misery. She was quite calm.

The trader, who, considering his advantages, was almost as humane as some of our politicians, seemed to feel called on to administer such consolation as the case admitted of.

"I know this yer comes kinder hard, at first, Lucy," said he; "but such a smart, sensible gal as you are, won't give way to it. You see it's *necessary*, and can't be helped!"

"O! don't, Mas'r, don't!" said the woman, with a voice like one that is smothering.

"You're a smart wench, Lucy," he persisted; "I mean to do well by ye, and get ye a nice place down river; and you'll soon get another husband, – such a likely gal as you–"

"O! Mas'r, if you *only* won't talk to me now," said the woman, in a voice of such quick and living anguish that the trader felt that there was something at present in the case beyond his style of operation. He got up, and the woman turned away, and buried her head in her cloak.

The trader walked up and down for a time, and occasionally stopped and looked at her.

"Takes it hard, rather," he soliloquized, "but quiet, tho'; – let her sweat a while; she'll come right, by and by!"

Tom had watched the whole transaction from first to last, and had a perfect understanding of its results. To him, it looked like something unutterably horrible and cruel, because, poor, ignorant black soul! he had not learned to generalize, and to take enlarged views. If he had only been instructed by certain ministers of Christianity, he might have thought better of it, and seen in it an every-day incident of a lawful trade; a trade which is the vital support of an institution which an American divine[8] tells us has *"no evils but such as are inseparable from any other relations in social and domestic life."* But Tom, as we see, being a poor, ignorant fellow, whose reading had been confined entirely to the New Testament, could not comfort and solace himself with views like these. His very soul bled within him for what seemed to him the *wrongs* of the poor suffering thing that lay like a crushed reed on the boxes; the feeling, living, bleeding, yet immortal *thing*, which American state law coolly classes with the bundles, and bales, and boxes, among which she is lying.

Tom drew near, and tried to say something; but she only groaned. Honestly, and with tears running down his own cheeks, he spoke of a heart of love in the skies, of a pitying Jesus, and an eternal home; but the ear was deaf with anguish, and the palsied heart could not feel.

Night came on, – night calm, unmoved, and glorious, shining down with her innumerable and solemn angel eyes, twinkling, beautiful, but silent. There was no speech nor language, no pitying voice or helping hand, from that distant sky. One after another, the voices of business or pleasure died away; all on the boat were sleeping, and the ripples at the prow were plainly heard. Tom stretched himself out on a box, and there, as he lay, he heard, ever and anon, a smothered sob

---

8 Dr. Joel Parker of Philadelphia. Presbyterian clergyman (1799-1873), a friend of the Beecher family. Mrs. Stowe attempted unsuccessfully to have this identifying note removed from the stereotype-plate of the first edition.

or cry from the prostrate creature, – "O! what shall I do? O Lord! O good Lord, do help me!" and so, ever and anon, until the murmur died away in silence.

At midnight, Tom waked, with a sudden start. Something black passed quickly by him to the side of the boat, and he heard a splash in the water. No one else saw or heard anything. He raised his head, – the woman's place was vacant! He got up, and sought about him in vain. The poor bleeding heart was still, at last, and the river rippled and dimpled just as brightly as if it had not closed above it.

Patience! patience! ye whose hearts swell indignant at wrongs like these. Not one throb of anguish, not one tear of the oppressed, is forgotten by the Man of Sorrows, the Lord of Glory. In his patient, generous bosom he bears the anguish of a world. Bear thou, like him, in patience, and labor in love; for sure as he is God, "the year of his redeemed *shall* come."

The trader waked up bright and early, and came out to see to his live stock. It was now his turn to look about in perplexity.

"Where alive is that gal?" he said to Tom.

Tom, who had learned the wisdom of keeping counsel, did not feel called upon to state his observations and suspicions, but said he did not know.

"She surely couldn't have got off in the night at any of the landings, for I was awake, and on the lookout, whenever the boat stopped. I never trust these yer things to other folks."

This speech was addressed to Tom quite confidentially, as if it was something that would be specially interesting to him. Tom made no answer.

The trader searched the boat from stem to stern, among boxes, bales and barrels, around the machinery, by the chimneys, in vain.

"Now, I say, Tom, be fair about this yer," he said, when, after a fruitless search, he came where Tom was standing. "You know something about it, now. Don't tell me, – I know you do. I saw the gal stretched out here about ten o'clock, and ag'in at twelve, and ag'in between one and two; and then at four she was gone, and you was a sleeping right there all the time. Now, you know something, – you can't help it."

"Well, Mas'r," said Tom, "towards morning something brushed by me, and I kinder half woke; and then I hearn a great splash, and then I clare woke up, and the gal was gone. That's all I know on 't."

The trader was not shocked nor amazed; because, as we said before, he was used to a great many things that you are not used to. Even the awful presence of Death struck no solemn chill upon him. He had seen Death many times, – met him in the way of trade, and got acquainted with him, – and he only thought of him as a hard customer, that embarrassed his property operations very unfairly; and so he only swore that the gal was a baggage, and that he was devilish unlucky, and that, if things went on in this way, he should not make a cent on the trip. In short, he seemed to consider himself an ill-used man, decidedly; but there was no help for it, as the woman had escaped into a state which *never will* give up a fugitive, – not even at the demand of the whole glorious Union. The trader, therefore, sat discontentedly down, with his little account-book, and put down the missing body and soul under the head of *losses!*

"He's a shocking creature, isn't he, – this trader? so unfeeling! It's dreadful, really!"

"O, but nobody thinks anything of these traders! They are universally despised, – never received into any decent society."

But who, sir, makes the trader? Who is most to blame? The enlightened, cultivated, intelligent man, who supports the system of which the trader is the inevitable result, or the poor trader himself? You make the public statement that calls for his trade, that debauches and depraves him, till he feels no shame in it; and in what are you better than he?

Are you educated and he ignorant, you high and he low, you refined and he coarse, you talented and he simple?

In the day of a future judgment, these very considerations may make it more tolerable for him than for you.

In concluding these little incidents of lawful trade, we must beg the world not to think that American legislators are entirely destitute of humanity, as might, perhaps, be unfairly inferred from the great efforts made in our national body to protect and perpetuate this species of traffic.

Who does not know how our great men are outdoing themselves, in declaiming against the *foreign* slave-trade. There are a perfect host of Clarksons and Wilberforces[9] risen up among us on that subject, most edifying to hear and behold. Trading negroes from Africa, dear reader, is so horrid! It is not to be thought of! But trading them from Kentucky, – that's quite another thing!

---

9 Thomas Clarkson (1760-1846) and William Wilberforce (1759-1833), English philanthropists and anti-slavery agitators who helped to secure passage of the Emancipation Bill by Parliament in 1833.

Chapter 13

The Quaker Settlement

A quiet scene now rises before us. A large, roomy, neatly-painted kitchen, its yellow floor glossy and smooth, and without a particle of dust; a neat, well-blacked cooking-stove; rows of shining tin, suggestive of unmentionable good things to the appetite; glossy green wood chairs, old and firm; a small flag-bottomed rocking-chair, with a patch-work cushion in it, neatly contrived out of small pieces of different colored woollen goods, and a larger sized one, motherly and old, whose wide arms breathed hospitable invitation, seconded by the solicitation of its feather cushions, - a real comfortable, persuasive old chair, and worth, in the way of honest, homely enjoyment, a dozen of your plush or *brochetelle* drawing-room gentry; and in the chair, gently swaying back and forward, her eyes bent on some fine sewing, sat our fine old friend Eliza. Yes, there she is, paler and thinner than in her Kentucky home, with a world of quiet sorrow lying under the shadow of her long eyelashes, and marking the outline of her gentle mouth! It was plain to see how old and firm the girlish heart was grown under the discipline of heavy sorrow; and when, anon, her large dark eye was raised to follow the gambols of her little Harry, who was sporting, like some tropical butterfly, hither and thither over the floor, she showed a depth of firmness and steady resolve that was never there in her earlier and happier days.

By her side sat a woman with a bright tin pan in her lap, into which she was carefully sorting some dried peaches. She might be fifty-five or sixty; but hers was one of those faces that time seems to touch only to brighten and adorn. The snowy lisse crape cap, made after the strait Quaker pattern, – the plain white muslin handkerchief, lying in placid folds across her bosom, – the drab shawl and dress, – showed at once the community to which she belonged. Her face was round and rosy, with a healthful downy softness, suggestive of a ripe peach. Her hair, partially silvered by age, was parted smoothly back from a high placid forehead, on which time had written no inscription, except peace on earth, good will to men, and beneath shone a large pair of clear, honest, loving brown eyes; you only needed to look straight into them, to feel that you saw to the bottom of a heart as good and true as ever throbbed in woman's bosom. So much has been said and sung of beautiful young girls, why don't somebody wake up to the beauty of old women? If any want to get up an inspiration under this head, we refer them to our good friend Rachel Halliday, just as she sits there in her little rocking-chair. It had a turn for quacking and squeaking, – that chair had, – either from having taken cold in early life, or from some asthmatic affection, or perhaps from nervous derangement; but, as she gently swung backward and forward, the chair kept up a kind of subdued "creechy crawchy," that would have been intolerable in any other chair. But old Simeon Halliday often declared it was as good as any music to him, and the children all avowed that they wouldn't miss of hearing mother's chair for anything in the world. For why? for twenty years or more, nothing but loving words, and gentle moralities, and motherly loving kindness, had come from that chair; – head-aches and heart-aches innumerable had been cured there, – difficulties spiritual and temporal solved there, – all by one good, loving woman, God bless her!

"And so thee still thinks of going to Canada, Eliza?" she said, as she was quietly looking over her peaches.

"Yes, ma'am," said Eliza, firmly. "I must go onward. I dare not stop."

"And what'll thee do, when thee gets there? Thee must think about that, my daughter."

"My daughter" came naturally from the lips of Rachel Halliday; for hers was just the face and form that made "mother" seem the most natural word in the world.

Eliza's hands trembled, and some tears fell on her fine work; but she answered, firmly,

"I shall do – anything I can find. I hope I can find something."

"Thee knows thee can stay here, as long as thee pleases," said Rachel.

"O, thank you," said Eliza, "but" – she pointed to Harry – "I can't sleep nights; I can't rest. Last night I dreamed I saw that man coming into the yard," she said, shuddering.

"Poor child!" said Rachel, wiping her eyes; "but thee mustn't feel so. The Lord hath ordered it so that never hath a fugitive been stolen from our village. I trust thine will not be the first."

The door here opened, and a little short, round, pin-cushiony woman stood at the door, with a cheery, blooming face, like a ripe apple. She was dressed, like Rachel, in sober gray, with the muslin folded neatly across her round, plump little chest.

"Ruth Stedman," said Rachel, coming joyfully forward; "how is thee, Ruth? she said, heartily taking both her hands.

"Nicely," said Ruth, taking off her little drab bonnet, and dusting it with her handkerchief, displaying, as she did so, a round little head, on which the Quaker cap sat with a sort of jaunty air, despite all the stroking and patting of the small fat hands, which were busily applied to arranging it. Certain stray locks of decidedly curly hair, too, had escaped here and there, and had to be coaxed and cajoled into their place again; and then the new comer, who might have been five-and-twenty, turned from the small looking-glass, before which she had been making these arrangements, and looked well pleased, – as most people who looked at her might have been, – for she was decidedly a wholesome, whole-hearted, chirruping little woman, as ever gladdened man's heart withal.

"Ruth, this friend is Eliza Harris; and this is the little boy I told thee of."

"I am glad to see thee, Eliza, – very," said Ruth, shaking hands, as if Eliza were an old friend she had long been expecting; "and this is thy dear boy, – I brought a cake for him," she said, holding out a little heart to the boy, who came up, gazing through his curls, and accepted it shyly.

"Where's thy baby, Ruth?" said Rachel.

"O, he's coming; but thy Mary caught him as I came in, and ran off with him to the barn, to show him to the children."

At this moment, the door opened, and Mary, an honest, rosy-looking girl, with large brown eyes, like her mother's, came in with the baby.

"Ah! ha!" said Rachel, coming up, and taking the great, white, fat fellow in her arms, "how good he looks, and how he does grow!"

"To be sure, he does," said little bustling Ruth, as she took the child, and began taking off a little blue silk hood, and various layers and wrappers of outer garments; and having given a twitch here, and a pull there, and variously adjusted and arranged him, and kissed him heartily, she set him on the floor to collect his thoughts. Baby seemed quite used to this mode of proceeding, for he put his thumb in his mouth (as if it were quite a thing of course), and seemed soon absorbed in his own reflections, while the mother seated herself, and taking out a long stocking of mixed blue and white yarn, began to knit with briskness.

"Mary, thee'd better fill the kettle, hadn't thee?" gently suggested the mother.

Mary took the kettle to the well, and soon reappearing, placed it over the stove, where it was soon purring and steaming, a sort of censer of hospitality and good cheer. The peaches, moreover, in obedience to a few gentle whispers from Rachel, were soon deposited, by the same hand, in a stew-pan over the fire.

Rachel now took down a snowy moulding-board, and, tying on an apron, proceeded quietly to making up some biscuits, first saying to Mary, – "Mary, hadn't thee better tell John to get a chicken ready?" and Mary disappeared accordingly.

"And how is Abigail Peters?" said Rachel, as she went on with her biscuits.

"O, she's better," said Ruth; "I was in, this morning; made the bed, tidied up the house. Leah Hills went in, this afternoon, and baked bread and pies enough to last some days; and I engaged to go back to get her up, this evening."

"I will go in tomorrow, and do any cleaning there may be, and look over the mending," said Rachel.

"Ah! that is well," said Ruth. "I've heard," she added, "that Hannah Stanwood is sick. John was up there, last night, – I must go there tomorrow."

"John can come in here to his meals, if thee needs to stay all day," suggested Rachel.

"Thank thee, Rachel; will see, tomorrow; but, here comes Simeon."

Simeon Halliday, a tall, straight, muscular man, in drab coat and pantaloons, and broad-brimmed hat, now entered.

"How is thee, Ruth?" he said, warmly, as he spread his broad open hand for her little fat palm; "and how is John?"

"O! John is well, and all the rest of our folks," said Ruth, cheerily.

"Any news, father?" said Rachel, as she was putting her biscuits into the oven.

"Peter Stebbins told me that they should be along tonight, with *friends*," said Simeon, significantly, as he was washing his hands at a neat sink, in a little back porch.

"Indeed!" said Rachel, looking thoughtfully, and glancing at Eliza.

"Did thee say thy name was Harris?" said Simeon to Eliza, as he reentered.

Rachel glanced quickly at her husband, as Eliza tremulously answered "yes;" her fears, ever uppermost, suggesting that possibly there might be advertisements out for her.

"Mother!" said Simeon, standing in the porch, and calling Rachel out.

"What does thee want, father?" said Rachel, rubbing her floury hands, as she went into the porch.

"This child's husband is in the settlement, and will be here tonight," said Simeon.

"Now, thee doesn't say that, father?" said Rachel, all her face radiant with joy.

"It's really true. Peter was down yesterday, with the wagon, to the other stand, and there he found an old woman and two men; and one said his name was George Harris; and from what he told of his history, I am certain who he is. He is a bright, likely fellow, too."

"Shall we tell her now?" said Simeon.

"Let's tell Ruth," said Rachel. "Here, Ruth, – come here."

Ruth laid down her knitting-work, and was in the back porch in a moment.

"Ruth, what does thee think?" said Rachel. "Father says Eliza's husband is in the last company, and will be here tonight."

A burst of joy from the little Quakeress interrupted the speech. She gave such a bound from the floor, as she clapped her little hands, that two stray curls fell from under her Quaker cap, and lay brightly on her white neckerchief.

"Hush thee, dear!" said Rachel, gently; "hush, Ruth! Tell us, shall we tell her now?"

"Now! to be sure, – this very minute. Why, now, suppose 't was my John, how should I feel? Do tell her, right off."

"Thee uses thyself only to learn how to love thy neighbor, Ruth," said Simeon, looking, with a beaming face, on Ruth.

"To be sure. Isn't it what we are made for? If I didn't love John and the baby, I should not know how to feel for her. Come, now do tell her, - do!" and she laid her hands persuasively on Rachel's arm. "Take her into thy bed-room, there, and let me fry the chicken while thee does it."

Rachel came out into the kitchen, where Eliza was sewing, and opening the door of a small bed-room, said, gently, "Come in here with me, my daughter; I have news to tell thee."

The blood flushed in Eliza's pale face; she rose, trembling with nervous anxiety, and looked towards her boy.

"No, no," said little Ruth, darting up, and seizing her hands. "Never thee fear; it's good news, Eliza, - go in, go in!" And she gently pushed her to the door which closed after her; and then, turning round, she caught little Harry in her arms, and began kissing him.

"Thee'll see thy father, little one. Does thee know it? Thy father is coming," she said, over and over again, as the boy looked wonderingly at her.

Meanwhile, within the door, another scene was going on. Rachel Halliday drew Eliza toward her, and said, "The Lord hath had mercy on thee, daughter; thy husband hath escaped from the house of bondage."

The blood flushed to Eliza's cheek in a sudden glow, and went back to her heart with as sudden a rush. She sat down, pale and faint.

"Have courage, child," said Rachel, laying her hand on her head. "He is among friends, who will bring him here tonight."

"Tonight!" Eliza repeated, "tonight!" The words lost all meaning to her; her head was dreamy and confused; all was mist for a moment.

When she awoke, she found herself snugly tucked up on the bed, with a blanket over her, and little Ruth rubbing her hands with camphor. She opened her eyes in a state of dreamy, delicious languor, such as one who has long been bearing a heavy load, and now feels it gone, and would rest. The tension of the nerves, which had never ceased a moment since the first hour of her flight, had given way, and a strange feeling of security and rest came over her; and as she lay, with her large, dark eyes open, she followed, as in a quiet dream, the motions of those about her. She saw the door open into the other room; saw the supper-table, with its snowy cloth; heard the dreamy murmur of the singing tea-kettle; saw Ruth tripping backward and forward, with plates of cake and saucers of preserves, and ever and anon stopping to put a cake into Harry's hand, or pat his head, or twine his long curls round her snowy fingers. She saw the ample, motherly form of Rachel, as she ever and anon came to the bedside, and smoothed and arranged something about the bedclothes, and gave a tuck here and there, by way of expressing her good-will; and was conscious of a kind of sunshine beaming down upon her from her large, clear, brown eyes. She saw Ruth's husband come in, – saw her fly up to him, and commence whispering very earnestly, ever and anon, with impressive gesture, pointing her little finger toward the room. She saw her, with the baby in her arms, sitting down to tea; she saw them all at table, and little Harry in a high chair, under the shadow of Rachel's ample wing; there were low murmurs of talk, gentle tinkling of tea-spoons, and musical clatter of cups and saucers, and all mingled in a delightful dream of rest; and Eliza slept, as she had not slept before, since the fearful midnight hour when she had taken her child and fled through the frosty starlight.

She dreamed of a beautiful country, – a land, it seemed to her, of rest, – green shores, pleasant islands, and beautifully glittering water; and there, in a house which kind voices told her was a home, she saw her boy playing, free and happy child. She heard her husband's footsteps; she felt him coming nearer; his arms were around her, his tears falling on her face, and she awoke! It was no dream. The daylight had long faded; her child lay calmly sleeping by her side; a candle was burning dimly on the stand, and her husband was sobbing by her pillow.

The next morning was a cheerful one at the Quaker house. "Mother" was up betimes, and surrounded by busy girls and boys, whom we had scarce time to introduce to our readers yesterday, and who all moved obediently to Rachel's gentle "Thee had better," or more gentle "Hadn't thee better?" in the work of getting breakfast; for a breakfast in the luxurious valleys of Indiana is a thing complicated and multiform, and, like picking up the rose-leaves and trimming the bushes in

Paradise, asking other hands than those of the original mother. While, therefore, John ran to the spring for fresh water, and Simeon the second sifted meal for corn-cakes, and Mary ground coffee, Rachel moved gently, and quietly about, making biscuits, cutting up chicken, and diffusing a sort of sunny radiance over the whole proceeding generally. If there was any danger of friction or collision from the ill-regulated zeal of so many young operators, her gentle "Come! come!" or "I wouldn't, now," was quite sufficient to allay the difficulty. Bards have written of the cestus of Venus, that turned the heads of all the world in successive generations. We had rather, for our part, have the cestus of Rachel Halliday, that kept heads from being turned, and made everything go on harmoniously. We think it is more suited to our modern days, decidedly.

While all other preparations were going on, Simeon the elder stood in his shirt-sleeves before a little looking-glass in the corner, engaged in the anti-patriarchal operation of shaving. Everything went on so sociably, so quietly, so harmoniously, in the great kitchen, – it seemed so pleasant to every one to do just what they were doing, there was such an atmosphere of mutual confidence and good fellowship everywhere, – even the knives and forks had a social clatter as they went on to the table; and the chicken and ham had a cheerful and joyous fizzle in the pan, as if they rather enjoyed being cooked than otherwise; – and when George and Eliza and little Harry came out, they met such a hearty, rejoicing welcome, no wonder it seemed to them like a dream.

At last, they were all seated at breakfast, while Mary stood at the stove, baking griddle-cakes, which, as they gained the true exact golden-brown tint of perfection, were transferred quite handily to the table.

Rachel never looked so truly and benignly happy as at the head of her table. There was so much motherliness and full-heartedness even in the way she passed a plate of cakes or poured a cup of coffee, that it seemed to put a spirit into the food and drink she offered.

It was the first time that ever George had sat down on equal terms at any white man's table; and he sat down, at first, with some constraint and awkwardness; but they all exhaled and went off like fog, in the genial morning rays of this simple, overflowing kindness.

This, indeed, was a home, *home*, a word that George had never yet known a meaning for; and a belief in God, and trust in his providence, began to encircle his heart, as, with a golden cloud of protection and confidence, dark, misanthropic, pining atheistic doubts, and fierce despair, melted away before the light of a living Gospel, breathed in living faces, preached by a thousand unconscious acts of love and good will, which, like the cup of cold water given in the name of a disciple, shall never lose their reward.

"Father, what if thee should get found out again?" said Simeon second, as he buttered his cake.

"I should pay my fine," said Simeon, quietly.

"But what if they put thee in prison?"

"Couldn't thee and mother manage the farm?" said Simeon, smiling.

"Mother can do almost everything," said the boy. "But isn't it a shame to make such laws?"

"Thee mustn't speak evil of thy rulers, Simeon," said his father, gravely. "The Lord only gives us our worldly goods that we may do justice and mercy; if our rulers require a price of us for it, we must deliver it up.

"Well, I hate those old slaveholders!" said the boy, who felt as unchristian as became any modern reformer.

"I am surprised at thee, son," said Simeon; "thy mother never taught thee so. I would do even the same for the slaveholder as for the slave, if the Lord brought him to my door in affliction."

Simeon second blushed scarlet; but his mother only smiled, and said, "Simeon is my good boy; he will grow older, by and by, and then he will be like his father."

"I hope, my good sir, that you are not exposed to any difficulty on our account," said George, anxiously.

"Fear nothing, George, for therefore are we sent into the world. If we would not meet trouble for a good cause, we were not worthy of our name."

"But, for *me*," said George, "I could not bear it."

"Fear not, then, friend George; it is not for thee, but for God and man, we do it," said Simeon. "And now thou must lie by quietly this day, and tonight, at ten o'clock, Phineas Fletcher will carry thee onward to the next stand, – thee and the rest of they company. The pursuers are hard after thee; we must not delay."

"If that is the case, why wait till evening?" said George.

"Thou art safe here by daylight, for every one in the settlement is a Friend, and all are watching. It has been found safer to travel by night."

Chapter 14

Evangeline

The Mississippi! How, as by an enchanted wand, have its scenes been changed, since Chateaubriand wrote his prose-poetic description of it,[10] as a river of mighty, unbroken solitudes, rolling amid undreamed wonders of vegetable and animal existence.

> "A young star! which shone
> O'er life – too sweet an image, for such glass!
> A lovely being, scarcely formed or moulded;
> A rose with all its sweetest leaves yet folded."

But as in an hour, this river of dreams and wild romance has emerged to a reality scarcely less visionary and splendid. What other river of the world bears on its bosom to the ocean the wealth and enterprise of such another country? – a country whose products embrace all between the tropics and the poles! Those turbid waters, hurrying, foaming, tearing along, an apt resemblance of that headlong tide of business which is poured along its wave by a race more vehement and energetic than any the old world ever saw. Ah! would that they did not also bear along a more fearful freight, – the tears of the oppressed, the sighs of the helpless, the bitter prayers of poor, ignorant hearts to an unknown God – unknown, unseen and silent, but who will

10 In Atala; or the Love and Constantcy of Two Savages in the Desert (1801) by Francois Auguste Rene, Vicomte de Chateaubriand (1768-1848).

yet "come out of his place to save all the poor of the earth!"

The slanting light of the setting sun quivers on the sea-like expanse of the river; the shivery canes, and the tall, dark cypress, hung with wreaths of dark, funereal moss, glow in the golden ray, as the heavily-laden steamboat marches onward.

Piled with cotton-bales, from many a plantation, up over deck and sides, till she seems in the distance a square, massive block of gray, she moves heavily onward to the nearing mart. We must look some time among its crowded decks before we shall find again our humble friend Tom. High on the upper deck, in a little nook among the everywhere predominant cotton-bales, at last we may find him.

Partly from confidence inspired by Mr. Shelby's representations, and partly from the remarkably inoffensive and quiet character of the man, Tom had insensibly won his way far into the confidence even of such a man as Haley.

At first he had watched him narrowly through the day, and never allowed him to sleep at night unfettered; but the uncomplaining patience and apparent contentment of Tom's manner led him gradually to discontinue these restraints, and for some time Tom had enjoyed a sort of parole of honor, being permitted to come and go freely where he pleased on the boat.

Ever quiet and obliging, and more than ready to lend a hand in every emergency which occurred among the workmen below, he had won the good opinion of all the hands, and spent many hours in helping them with as hearty a good will as ever he worked on a Kentucky farm.

When there seemed to be nothing for him to do, he would climb to a nook among the cotton-bales of the upper deck, and busy himself in studying over his Bible, – and it is there we see him now.

For a hundred or more miles above New Orleans, the river is higher than the surrounding country, and rolls its tremendous volume between massive levees twenty feet in height. The traveller from the deck of the steamer, as from some floating castle top, overlooks the whole country for miles and miles around. Tom, therefore, had spread out full before him, in plantation after plantation, a map of the life to which he was approaching.

He saw the distant slaves at their toil; he saw afar their villages of huts gleaming out in long rows on many a plantation, distant from the stately mansions and pleasure-grounds of the master; – and as the moving picture passed on, his poor, foolish heart would be turning backward to the Kentucky farm, with its old shadowy beeches, – to the master's house, with its wide, cool halls, and, near by, the little cabin overgrown with the multiflora and bignonia. There he seemed to see familiar faces of comrades who had grown up with him from infancy; he saw his busy wife, bustling in her preparations for his evening meals; he heard the merry laugh of his boys at their play, and the chirrup of the baby at his knee; and then, with a start, all faded, and he saw again the canebrakes and cypresses and gliding plantations, and heard again the creaking and groaning of the machinery, all telling him too plainly that all that phase of life had gone by forever.

In such a case, you write to your wife, and send messages to your children; but Tom could not write, – the mail for him had no existence, and the gulf of separation was unbridged by even a friendly word or signal.

Is it strange, then, that some tears fall on the pages of his Bible, as he lays it on the cotton-bale, and, with patient finger, threading his slow way from word to word, traces out its promises? Having learned late in life, Tom was but a slow reader, and passed on laboriously from verse to verse. Fortunate for him was it that the book he was intent on was one which slow reading cannot injure, – nay, one whose words, like ingots of gold, seem often to need to be weighed separately, that the mind may take in their priceless value. Let us follow him a moment, as, pointing to each word, and pronouncing each half aloud, he reads,

"Let – not – your – heart – be – troubled. In – my – Father's – house – are – many – mansions. I – go – to – prepare – a – place – for – you."

Cicero, when he buried his darling and only daughter, had a heart as full of honest grief as poor Tom's, – perhaps no fuller, for both were only men; – but Cicero could pause over no such sublime words of hope, and look to no such future reunion; and if he *had* seen them, ten to one he would not have believed, – he must fill his head first with a thousand questions of authenticity of manuscript, and correctness of translation. But, to poor Tom, there it lay, just what he needed, so evidently true and divine that the possibility of a question never entered his simple head. It must be true; for, if not true, how could he live?

As for Tom's Bible, though it had no annotations and helps in margin from learned commentators, still it had been embellished with certain way-marks and guide-boards of Tom's own invention, and which helped him more than the most learned expositions could have done. It had been his custom to get the Bible read to him by his master's children, in particular by young Master George; and, as they read, he would designate, by bold, strong marks and dashes, with pen and ink, the passages which more particularly gratified his ear or affected his heart. His Bible was thus marked through, from one end to the other, with a variety of styles and designations; so he could in a moment seize upon his favorite passages, without the labor of spelling out what lay between them; - and while it lay there before him, every passage breathing of some old home scene, and recalling some past enjoyment, his Bible seemed to him all of this life that remained, as well as the promise of a future one.

Among the passengers on the boat was a young gentleman of fortune and family, resident in New Orleans, who bore the name of St. Clare. He had with him a daughter between five and six years of age, together with a lady who seemed to claim relationship to both, and to have the little one especially under her charge.

Tom had often caught glimpses of this little girl, - for she was one of those busy, tripping creatures, that can be no more contained in one place than a sunbeam or a summer breeze, – nor was she one that, once seen, could be easily forgotten.

Her form was the perfection of childish beauty, without its usual chubbiness and squareness of outline. There was about it an undulating and aerial grace, such as one might dream of for some mythic and allegorical being. Her face was remarkable less for its perfect beauty of feature than for a singular and dreamy earnestness of expression, which made the ideal start when they looked at her, and by which the dullest and most literal were impressed, without exactly knowing why. The shape of her head and the turn of her neck and bust was peculiarly noble, and the long golden-brown hair that floated like a cloud around it, the deep spiritual gravity of her violet blue eyes, shaded by heavy fringes of golden brown, – all marked her out from other children, and made every one turn and look after her, as she glided hither and thither on the boat. Nevertheless, the little one was not what you would have called either a grave child or a sad one. On the contrary, an airy and innocent playfulness seemed to flicker like the shadow of summer leaves over her childish face, and around her buoyant figure. She was always in motion, always with a half smile on her rosy mouth, flying hither and thither, with an undulating and cloud-like tread, singing to herself as she moved as in a happy dream. Her father and female guardian were incessantly busy in pursuit of her, – but, when caught, she melted from them again like a summer cloud; and as no word of chiding or reproof ever fell on her ear for whatever she chose to do, she pursued her own way all over the boat. Always dressed in white, she seemed to move like a shadow through all sorts of places, without contracting spot or stain; and there was not a corner or nook, above or below, where those fairy footsteps had not glided, and that visionary golden head, with its deep blue eyes, fleeted along.

The fireman, as he looked up from his sweaty toil, sometimes found those eyes looking wonderingly into the raging depths of the furnace, and fearfully and pityingly at him, as if she thought him in some dreadful danger. Anon the steersman at the wheel paused and smiled, as the picture-like head gleamed through the window of the round house, and in a moment was gone again. A thousand times a day rough voices blessed her, and smiles of unwonted softness stole over hard faces, as she passed; and when she tripped fearlessly over dangerous places, rough, sooty hands were stretched involuntarily out to save her, and smooth her path.

Tom, who had the soft, impressible nature of his kindly race, ever yearning toward the simple and childlike, watched the little creature with daily increasing interest. To him she seemed something almost divine; and whenever her golden head and deep blue eyes peered out upon him from behind some dusky cotton-bale, or looked down upon him over some ridge of packages, he half believed that he saw one of the angels stepped out of his New Testament.

Often and often she walked mournfully round the place where Haley's gang of men and women sat in their chains. She would glide in among them, and look at them with an air of perplexed and sorrowful earnest-ness; and sometimes she would lift their chains with her slender hands, and then sigh woefully, as she glided away. Several times she appeared suddenly among them, with her hands full of candy, nuts, and oranges, which she would distribute joyfully to them, and then be gone again.

Tom watched the little lady a great deal, before he ventured on any overtures towards acquaintanceship. He knew an abundance of simple acts to propitiate and invite the approaches of the little people, and he resolved to play his part right skilfully. He could cut cunning little baskets out of cherry-stones, could make grotesque faces on hickory-nuts, or odd-jumping figures out of elder-pith, and he was a very Pan in the manufacture of whistles of all sizes and sorts. His pockets were full of miscellaneous articles of attraction, which he had hoarded in days of old for his master's children, and which he now produced, with commendable prudence and economy, one by one, as overtures for acquaintance and friendship.

The little one was shy, for all her busy interest in everything going on, and it was not easy to tame her. For a while, she would perch like a canary-bird on some box or package near Tom, while busy in the little arts afore-named, and take from him, with a kind of grave bashfulness, the little articles he offered. But at last they got on quite confidential terms.

"What's little missy's name?" said Tom, at last, when he thought matters were ripe to push such an inquiry.

"Evangeline St. Clare," said the little one, "though papa and everybody else call me Eva. Now, what's your name?"

"My name's Tom; the little chil'en used to call me Uncle Tom, way back thar in Kentuck."

"Then I mean to call you Uncle Tom, because, you see, I like you," said Eva. "So, Uncle Tom, where are you going?"

"I don't know, Miss Eva."

"Don't know?" said Eva.

"No, I am going to be sold to somebody. I don't know who."

"My papa can buy you," said Eva, quickly; "and if he buys you, you will have good times. I mean to ask him, this very day."

"Thank you, my little lady," said Tom.

The boat here stopped at a small landing to take in wood, and Eva, hearing her father's voice, bounded nimbly away. Tom rose up, and went forward to offer his service in wooding, and soon was busy among the hands.

Eva and her father were standing together by the railings to see the boat start from the landing-place, the wheel had made two or three revolutions in the water, when, by some sudden movement, the little one suddenly lost her balance and fell sheer over the side of the boat into the water. Her father, scarce knowing what he did, was plunging in after her, but was held back by some behind him, who saw that more efficient aid had followed his child.

Tom was standing just under her on the lower deck, as she fell. He saw her strike the water, and sink, and was after her in a moment. A broad-chested, strong-armed fellow, it was nothing for him to keep afloat in the water, till, in a moment or two the child rose to the surface, and he caught her in his arms, and, swimming with her to the boat-side, handed her up, all dripping, to the grasp of hundreds of hands, which, as if they had all belonged to one man, were stretched eagerly out to receive her. A few moments more, and her father bore her, dripping and senseless, to the ladies' cabin, where, as is usual in cases of the kind, there ensued a very well-meaning and kind-hearted strife among the female occupants generally, as to who should do the most things to make a disturbance, and to hinder her recovery in every way possible.

It was a sultry, close day, the next day, as the steamer drew near to New Orleans. A general bustle of expectation and preparation was spread through the boat; in the cabin, one and another were gathering their things together, and arranging them, preparatory to going ashore. The steward and chambermaid, and all, were busily engaged in cleaning, furbishing, and arranging the splendid boat, preparatory to a grand entree.

On the lower deck sat our friend Tom, with his arms folded, and anxiously, from time to time, turning his eyes towards a group on the other side of the boat.

There stood the fair Evangeline, a little paler than the day before, but otherwise exhibiting no traces of the accident which had befallen her. A graceful, elegantly-formed young man stood by her, carelessly leaning one elbow on a bale of cotton while a large pocket-book lay open before him. It was quite evident, at a glance, that the gentleman was Eva's father. There was the same noble cast of head, the same large blue eyes, the same golden-brown hair; yet the expression was wholly different. In the large, clear blue eyes, though in form and color exactly similar, there was wanting that misty, dreamy depth of expression; all was clear, bold, and bright, but with a light wholly of this world: the beautifully cut mouth had a proud and somewhat sarcastic expression, while an air of free-and-easy superiority sat not ungracefully in every turn and movement of his fine form. He was listening, with a good-humored, negligent air, half comic, half contemptuous, to Haley, who was very volubly expatiating on the quality of the article for which they were bargaining.

"All the moral and Christian virtues bound in black Morocco, complete!" he said, when Haley had finished. "Well, now, my good fellow, what's the damage, as they say in Kentucky; in short, what's to be paid out for this business? How much are you going to cheat me, now? Out with it!"

"Wal," said Haley, "if I should say thirteen hundred dollars for that ar fellow, I shouldn't but just save myself; I shouldn't, now, re'ly."

"Poor fellow!" said the young man, fixing his keen, mocking blue eye on him; "but I suppose you'd let me have him for that, out of a particular regard for me."

"Well, the young lady here seems to be sot on him, and nat'lly enough."

"O! certainly, there's a call on your benevolence, my friend. Now, as a matter of Christian charity, how cheap could you afford to let him go, to oblige a young lady that's particular sot on him?"

"Wal, now, just think on 't," said the trader; "just look at them limbs, - broad-chested, strong as a horse. Look at his head; them high forrads allays shows calculatin niggers, that'll do any kind o' thing. I've, marked that ar. Now, a nigger of that ar heft and build is worth considerable, just as you may say, for his body, supposin he's stupid; but come to put in his calculatin faculties, and them which I can show he has oncommon, why, of course, it makes him come higher. Why, that ar fellow managed his master's whole farm. He has a strornary talent for business."

"Bad, bad, very bad; knows altogether too much!" said the young man, with the same mocking smile playing about his mouth. "Never will do, in the world. Your smart fellows are always running off, stealing horses, and raising the devil generally. I think you'll have to take off a couple of hundred for his smartness."

"Wal, there might be something in that ar, if it warnt for his character; but I can show recommends from his master and others, to prove he is one of your real pious, – the most humble, prayin, pious crittur ye ever did see. Why, he's been called a preacher in them parts he came from."

"And I might use him for a family chaplain, possibly," added the young man, dryly. "That's quite an idea. Religion is a remarkably scarce article at our house."

"You're joking, now."

"How do you know I am? Didn't you just warrant him for a preacher? Has he been examined by any synod or council? Come, hand over your papers."

If the trader had not been sure, by a certain good-humored twinkle in the large eye, that all this banter was sure, in the long run, to turn out a cash concern, he might have been somewhat out of patience; as it was, he laid down a greasy pocket-book on the cotton-bales, and began anxiously studying over certain papers in it, the young man standing by, the while, looking down on him with an air of careless, easy drollery.

"Papa, do buy him! it's no matter what you pay," whispered Eva, softly, getting up on a package, and putting her arm around her father's neck. "You have money enough, I know. I want him."

"What for, pussy? Are you going to use him for a rattle-box, or a rocking-horse, or what?

"I want to make him happy."

"An original reason, certainly."

Here the trader handed up a certificate, signed by Mr. Shelby, which the young man took with the tips of his long fingers, and glanced over carelessly.

"A gentlemanly hand," he said, "and well spelt, too. Well, now, but I'm not sure, after all, about this religion," said he, the old wicked expression returning to his eye; "the country is almost ruined with pious white people; such pious politicians as we have just before elections, - such pious goings on in all departments of church and state, that a fellow does not know who'll cheat him next. I don't know, either, about religion's being up in the market, just now. I have not looked in the papers lately, to see how it sells. How many hundred dollars, now, do you put on for this religion?"

"You like to be jokin, now," said the trader; "but, then, there's *sense* under all that ar. I know there's differences in religion. Some kinds is mis'rable: there's your meetin pious; there's your singin, roarin pious; them ar an't no account, in black or white; - but these rayly is; and I've seen it in niggers as often as any, your rail softly, quiet, stiddy, honest, pious, that the hull world couldn't tempt 'em to do nothing that they thinks is wrong; and ye see in this letter what Tom's old master says about him."

"Now," said the young man, stooping gravely over his book of bills, "if you can assure me that I really can buy *this* kind of pious, and that it will be set down to my account in the book up above, as something belonging to me, I wouldn't care if I did go a little extra for it. How d'ye say?"

"Wal, raily, I can't do that," said the trader. "I'm a thinkin that every man'll have to hang on his own hook, in them ar quarters."

"Rather hard on a fellow that pays extra on religion, and can't trade with it in the state where he wants it most, an't it, now?" said the young man, who had been making out a roll of bills while he was speaking. "There, count your money, old boy!" he added, as he handed the roll to the trader.

"All right," said Haley, his face beaming with delight; and pulling out an old inkhorn, he proceeded to fill out a bill of sale, which, in a few moments, he handed to the young man.

"I wonder, now, if I was divided up and inventoried," said the latter as he ran over the paper, "how much I might bring. Say so much for the shape of my head, so much for a high forehead, so much for arms, and hands, and legs, and then so much for education, learning, talent, honesty, religion! Bless me! there would be small charge on that last, I'm thinking. But come, Eva," he said; and taking the hand of his daughter, he stepped across the boat, and carelessly putting the tip of his finger under Tom's chin, said, good-humoredly, "Look-up, Tom, and see how you like your new master."

Tom looked up. It was not in nature to look into that gay, young, handsome face, without a feeling of pleasure; and Tom felt the tears start in his eyes as he said, heartily, "God bless you, Mas'r!"

"Well, I hope he will. What's your name? Tom? Quite as likely to do it for your asking as mine, from all accounts. Can you drive horses, Tom?"

"I've been allays used to horses," said Tom. "Mas'r Shelby raised heaps of 'em."

"Well, I think I shall put you in coachy, on condition that you won't be drunk more than once a week, unless in cases of emergency, Tom."

Tom looked surprised, and rather hurt, and said, "I never drink, Mas'r."

"I've heard that story before, Tom; but then we'll see. It will be a special accommodation to all concerned, if you don't. Never mind, my boy," he added, good-humoredly, seeing Tom still looked grave; "I don't doubt you mean to do well."

"I sartin do, Mas'r," said Tom.

"And you shall have good times," said Eva. "Papa is very good to everybody, only he always will laugh at them."

"Papa is much obliged to you for his recommendation," said St. Clare, laughing, as he turned on his heel and walked away.

Chapter 15

Of Tom's New Master, and Various Other Matters

Since the thread of our humble hero's life has now become interwoven with that of higher ones, it is necessary to give some brief introduction to them.

Augustine St. Clare was the son of a wealthy planter of Louisiana. The family had its origin in Canada. Of two brothers, very similar in temperament and character, one had settled on a flourishing farm in Vermont, and the other became an opulent planter in Louisiana. The mother of Augustine was a Huguenot French lady, whose family had emigrated to Louisiana during the days of its early settlement. Augustine and another brother were the only children of their parents. Having inherited from his mother an exceeding delicacy of constitution, he was, at the instance of physicians, during many years of his boyhood, sent to the care of his uncle in Vermont, in order that his constitution might, be strengthened by the cold of a more bracing climate.

In childhood, he was remarkable for an extreme and marked sensitiveness of character, more akin to the softness of woman than the ordinary hardness of his own sex. Time, however, overgrew this softness with the rough bark of manhood, and but few knew how living and fresh it still lay at the core. His talents were of the very first order, although his mind showed a preference always for the ideal and the aesthetic, and there was about him that repugnance to the actual business of life which is the common result of this balance of the faculties. Soon after the completion of his college course, his whole nature was kindled into one intense and passionate effervescence of romantic passion. His hour came, – the hour that comes only once; his star rose in the horizon, – that star that rises so often in vain, to be remembered only as a thing of dreams; and it rose for him in vain. To drop the figure, – he saw and won the love of a high-minded and beautiful woman, in one of the northern states, and they were affianced. He returned south to make arrangements for their marriage, when, most unexpectedly, his letters were returned to him by mail, with a short note from her guardian, stating to him that ere this reached him the lady would be the wife of another. Stung to madness, he vainly hoped, as many another has done, to fling the whole thing from his heart by one desperate effort. Too proud to supplicate or seek explanation, he threw himself at once into a whirl of fashionable society, and in a fortnight from the time of the fatal letter was the accepted lover of the reigning belle of the season; and as soon as arrangements could be made, he became the husband of a fine figure, a pair of bright dark eyes, and a hundred thousand dollars; and, of course, everybody thought him a happy fellow.

The married couple were enjoying their honeymoon, and entertaining a brilliant circle of friends in their splendid villa, near Lake Pontchartrain, when, one day, a letter was brought to him in *that* well-remembered writing. It was handed to him while he was in full tide of gay and successful conversation, in a whole roomfull of company. He turned deadly pale when he saw the writing, but still preserved his composure, and finished the playful warfare of badinage which he was at the moment carrying on with a lady opposite; and, a short time after, was missed from the circle. In his room, alone, he opened and read the letter, now worse than idle and useless to be read. It was from her, giving a long account of a persecution to which she had been exposed by her guardian's family, to lead her to unite herself with their son: and she related how, for a long time, his letters had ceased to arrive; how she had written time and again, till she became weary and doubtful; how her health had failed under her anxieties, and how, at last, she had discovered the whole fraud which had been practised on them both. The letter ended with expressions of hope and thankfulness, and professions of undying affection, which were more bitter than death to the unhappy young man. He wrote to her immediately:

> "I have received yours, – but too late. I believed all I heard. I was desperate. I am married, and all is over. Only forget, – it is all that remains for either of us."

And thus ended the whole romance and ideal of life for Augustine St. Clare. But the *real* remained, – the *real*, like the flat, bare, oozy tide-mud, when the blue sparkling wave, with all its company of gliding boats and white-winged ships, its music of oars and chiming waters, has gone down, and there it lies, flat, slimy, bare, – exceedingly real.

Of course, in a novel, people's hearts break, and they die, and that is the end of it; and in a story this is very convenient. But in real life we do not die when all that makes life bright dies to us. There is a most busy and important round of eating, drinking, dressing, walking, visiting, buying, selling, talking, reading, and all that makes up what is commonly called *living*, yet to be gone through; and this yet remained to Augustine. Had his wife been a whole woman, she might yet have done something - as woman can - to mend the broken threads of life, and weave again into a tissue of brightness. But Marie St. Clare could not even see that they had been broken. As before stated, she consisted of a fine figure, a pair of splendid eyes, and a hundred thousand dollars; and none of these items were precisely the ones to minister to a mind diseased.

When Augustine, pale as death, was found lying on the sofa, and pleaded sudden sick-headache as the cause of his distress, she recommended to him to smell of hartshorn; and when the paleness and headache came on week after week, she only said that she never thought Mr. St. Clare was sickly; but it seems he was very liable to sick-headaches, and that it was a very unfortunate thing for her, because he didn't enjoy going into company with her, and it seemed odd to go so much alone, when they were just married. Augustine was glad in his heart that he had married so undiscerning a woman; but as the glosses and civilities of the honeymoon wore away, he discovered that a beautiful young woman, who has lived all her life to be caressed and waited on, might prove quite a hard mistress in domestic life. Marie never had possessed much capability of affection, or much sensibility, and the little that she had, had been merged into a most intense and unconscious selfishness; a selfishness the more hopeless, from its quiet obtuseness, its utter ignorance of any claims but her own. From her infancy, she had been surrounded with servants, who lived only to study her caprices; the idea that they had either feelings or rights had never dawned upon her, even in distant perspective. Her father, whose only child she had been, had never denied her anything that lay within the compass of human possibility; and when she entered life, beautiful, accomplished, and an heiress, she had, of course, all the eligibles and non-eligibles of the other sex sighing at her feet, and she had no doubt that Augustine was a most fortunate man in having obtained her. It is a great mistake to suppose that a woman with no heart will be an easy creditor in the exchange of affection. There is not on earth a more merciless exactor of love from others than a thoroughly selfish woman; and the more unlovely she grows, the more jealously and scrupulously she exacts love, to the uttermost farthing. When, therefore, St. Clare began to drop off those gallantries and small attentions which flowed at first through the habitude of courtship, he found his sultana no way ready to resign her slave; there were abundance of tears, poutings, and small tempests, there were discontents, pinings, upbraidings. St. Clare was good-natured and self-indulgent, and sought to buy off with presents and flatteries; and when Marie became mother to a beautiful daughter, he really felt awakened, for a time, to something like tenderness.

St. Clare's mother had been a woman of uncommon elevation and purity of character, and he gave to his child his mother's name, fondly fancying that she would prove a reproduction of her image. The thing had been remarked with petulant jealousy by his wife, and she regarded her husband's absorbing devotion to the child with suspicion and dislike; all that was given to her seemed so much taken from herself. From the time of the birth of this child, her health gradually sunk. A life of constant inaction, bodily and mental, – the friction of ceaseless ennui and discontent, united to the ordinary weakness which attended the period of maternity, – in course of a few years changed the blooming young belle into a yellow faded, sickly woman, whose time was divided among a variety of fanciful diseases, and who considered herself, in every sense, the most ill-used and suffering person in existence.

There was no end of her various complaints; but her principal forte appeared to lie in sick-headache, which sometimes would confine her to her room three days out of six. As, of course, all family arrangements fell into the hands of servants, St. Clare found his menage anything but comfortable. His only daughter was exceedingly delicate, and he feared that, with no one to look after her and attend to her, her health and life might yet fall a sacrifice to her mother's inefficiency. He had taken her with him on a tour to Vermont, and had persuaded his cousin, Miss Ophelia St. Clare, to return with him to his southern residence; and they are now returning on this boat, where we have introduced them to our readers.

And now, while the distant domes and spires of New Orleans rise to our view, there is yet time for an introduction to Miss Ophelia.

Whoever has travelled in the New England States will remember, in some cool village, the large farmhouse, with its clean-swept grassy yard, shaded by the dense and massive foliage of the sugar maple; and remember the air of order and stillness, of perpetuity and unchanging repose, that seemed to breathe over the whole place. Nothing lost, or out of order; not a picket loose in the fence, not a particle of litter in the turfy yard, with its clumps of lilac bushes growing up under the windows. Within, he will remember wide, clean rooms, where nothing ever seems to be doing or going to be done, where everything is once and forever rigidly in place, and where all household arrangements move with the punctual exactness of the old clock in the corner. In the family "keeping-room," as it is termed, he will remember the staid, respectable old book-case, with its glass doors, where Rollin's History,[11] Milton's Paradise Lost, Bunyan's Pilgrim's Progress, and Scott's Family Bible,[12] stand side by side in decorous order, with multitudes of other books, equally solemn and respectable. There are no servants in the house, but the lady in the snowy cap, with the spectacles, who sits sewing every afternoon among her daughters, as if nothing ever had been done, or were to be done, – she and her girls, in some long-forgotten fore part of the day, "*did up the work,*" and for the rest of the time, probably, at all hours when you would see them, it is "*done up.*" The old kitchen floor never seems stained or spotted; the tables, the chairs, and the various cooking utensils, never seem deranged or disordered; though three and sometimes four meals a day are got there, though the family washing and

---

11 The Ancient History, ten volumes (1730-1738), by the French historian Charles Rollin (1661-1741).

12 Scott's Family Bible (1788-1792), edited with notes by the English Biblical commentator, Thomas Scott (1747-1821).

ironing is there performed, and though pounds of butter and cheese are in some silent and mysterious manner there brought into existence.

On such a farm, in such a house and family, Miss Ophelia had spent a quiet existence of some forty-five years, when her cousin invited her to visit his southern mansion. The eldest of a large family, she was still considered by her father and mother as one of "the children," and the proposal that she should go to *Orleans* was a most momentous one to the family circle. The old gray-headed father took down Morse's Atlas[13] out of the book-case, and looked out the exact latitude and longitude; and read Flint's Travels in the South and West,[14] to make up his own mind as to the nature of the country.

The good mother inquired, anxiously, "if Orleans wasn't an awful wicked place," saying, "that it seemed to her most equal to going to the Sandwich Islands, or anywhere among the heathen."

It was known at the minister's and at the doctor's, and at Miss Peabody's milliner shop, that Ophelia St. Clare was "talking about" going away down to Orleans with her cousin; and of course the whole village could do no less than help this very important process of *taking*

---

13 The Cerographic Atlas of the United States (1842-1845), by Sidney Edwards Morse (1794-1871), son of the geographer, Jedidiah Morse, and brother of the painter-inventor, Samuel F.B. Morse.

14 Recollections of the Last Ten Years (1826) by Timothy Flint (1780-1840), missionary of Presbyterianism to the trans-Allegheny West.

about the matter. The minister, who inclined strongly to abolitionist views, was quite doubtful whether such a step might not tend somewhat to encourage the southerners in holding on to their slaves; while the doctor, who was a stanch colonizationist, inclined to the opinion that Miss Ophelia ought to go, to show the Orleans people that we don't think hardly of them, after all. He was of opinion, in fact, that southern people needed encouraging. When however, the fact that she had resolved to go was fully before the public mind, she was solemnly invited out to tea by all her friends and neighbors for the space of a fortnight, and her prospects and plans duly canvassed and inquired into. Miss Moseley, who came into the house to help to do the dress-making, acquired daily accessions of importance from the developments with regard to Miss Ophelia's wardrobe which she had been enabled to make. It was credibly ascertained that Squire Sinclare, as his name was commonly contracted in the neighborhood, had counted out fifty dollars, and given them to Miss Ophelia, and told her to buy any clothes she thought best; and that two new silk dresses, and a bonnet, had been sent for from Boston. As to the propriety of this extraordinary outlay, the public mind was divided, - some affirming that it was well enough, all things considered, for once in one's life, and others stoutly affirming that the money had better have been sent to the missionaries; but all parties agreed that there had been no such parasol seen in those parts as had been sent on from New York, and that she had one silk dress that might fairly be trusted to stand alone, whatever might be said of its mistress. There were credible rumors, also, of a hemstitched pocket-handkerchief; and report even went so far as to state that Miss Ophelia had one pocket-handkerchief with lace all around it, – it was even added that it was worked in the corners; but this latter point was never satisfactorily ascertained, and remains, in fact, unsettled to this day.

Miss Ophelia, as you now behold her, stands before you, in a very shining brown linen travelling-dress, tall, square-formed, and angular. Her face was thin, and rather sharp in its outlines; the lips compressed, like those of a person who is in the habit of making up her mind definitely on all subjects; while the keen, dark eyes had a peculiarly searching, advised movement, and travelled over everything, as if they were looking for something to take care of.

All her movements were sharp, decided, and energetic; and, though she was never much of a talker, her words were remarkably direct, and to the purpose, when she did speak.

In her habits, she was a living impersonation of order, method, and exactness. In punctuality, she was as inevitable as a clock, and as inexorable as a railroad engine; and she held in most decided contempt and abomination anything of a contrary character.

The great sin of sins, in her eyes, – the sum of all evils, – was expressed by one very common and important word in her vocabulary – "shiftlessness." Her finale and ultimatum of contempt consisted in a very emphatic pronunciation of the word "shiftless;" and by this she characterized all modes of procedure which had not a direct and inevitable relation to accomplishment of some purpose then definitely had in mind. People who did nothing, or who did not know exactly what they were going to do, or who did not take the most direct way to accomplish what they set their hands to, were objects of her entire contempt, – a contempt shown less frequently by anything she said, than by a kind of stony grimness, as if she scorned to say anything about the matter.

As to mental cultivation, – she had a clear, strong, active mind, was well and thoroughly read in history and the older English classics, and thought with great strength within certain narrow limits. Her theological tenets were all made up, labelled in most positive and distinct forms, and put by, like the bundles in her patch trunk; there were just so many of them, and there were never to be any more. So, also, were her ideas with regard to most matters of practical life, – such as housekeeping in all its branches, and the various political relations of her native village. And, underlying all, deeper than anything else, higher and broader, lay the strongest principle of her being – conscientiousness. Nowhere is conscience so dominant and all-absorbing as with New England women. It is the granite formation, which lies deepest, and rises out, even to the tops of the highest mountains.

Miss Ophelia was the absolute bond-slave of the "*ought*." Once make her certain that the "path of duty," as she commonly phrased it, lay in any given direction, and fire and water could not keep her from it. She would walk straight down into a well, or up to a loaded cannon's mouth, if she were only quite sure that there the path lay. Her standard of right was so high, so all-embracing, so minute, and making so few concessions to human frailty, that, though she strove with heroic ardor to reach it, she never actually did so, and of course was burdened with a constant and often harassing sense of deficiency; - this gave a severe and somewhat gloomy cast to her religious character.

But, how in the world can Miss Ophelia get along with Augustine St. Clare, - gay, easy, unpunctual, unpractical, sceptical, - in short, - walking with impudent and nonchalant freedom over every one of her most cherished habits and opinions?

To tell the truth, then, Miss Ophelia loved him. When a boy, it had been hers to teach him his catechism, mend his clothes, comb his hair, and bring him up generally in the way he should go; and her heart having a warm side to it, Augustine had, as he usually did with most people, monopolized a large share of it for himself, and therefore it was that he succeeded very easily in persuading her that the "path of duty" lay in the direction of New Orleans, and that she must go with him to take care of Eva, and keep everything from going to wreck and ruin during the frequent illnesses of his wife. The idea of a house without anybody to take care of it went to her heart; then she loved the lovely little girl, as few could help doing; and though she regarded Augustine as very much of a heathen, yet she loved him, laughed at his jokes, and forbore with his failings, to an extent which those who knew him thought perfectly incredible. But what more or other is to be known of Miss Ophelia our reader must discover by a personal acquaintance.

There she is, sitting now in her state-room, surrounded by a mixed multitude of little and big carpet-bags, boxes, baskets, each containing some separate responsibility which she is tying, binding up, packing, or fastening, with a face of great earnestness.

"Now, Eva, have you kept count of your things? Of course you haven't, - children never do: there's the spotted carpet-bag and the little blue band-box with your best bonnet, - that's two; then the India rubber satchel is three; and my tape and needle box is four; and my band-box, five; and my collar-box; and that little hair trunk, seven. What have you done with your sunshade? Give it to me, and let me put a paper round it, and tie it to my umbrella with my shade; - there, now."

"Why, aunty, we are only going up home; - what is the use?"

"To keep it nice, child; people must take care of their things, if they ever mean to have anything; and now, Eva, is your thimble put up?"

"Really, aunty, I don't know."

"Well, never mind; I'll look your box over, - thimble, wax, two spools, scissors, knife, tape-needle; all right, - put it in here. What did you ever do, child, when you were coming on with only your papa. I should have thought you'd a lost everything you had."

"Well, aunty, I did lose a great many; and then, when we stopped anywhere, papa would buy some more of whatever it was."

"Mercy on us, child, - what a way!"

"It was a very easy way, aunty," said Eva.

"It's a dreadful shiftless one," said aunty.

"Why, aunty, what'll you do now?" said Eva; "that trunk is too full to be shut down."

"It *must* shut down," said aunty, with the air of a general, as she squeezed the things in, and sprung upon the lid; - still a little gap remained about the mouth of the trunk.

"Get up here, Eva!" said Miss Ophelia, courageously; "what has been done can be done again. This trunk has *got to be* shut and locked - there are no two ways about it."

And the trunk, intimidated, doubtless, by this resolute statement, gave in. The hasp snapped sharply in its hole, and Miss Ophelia turned the key, and pocketed it in triumph.

"Now we're ready. Where's your papa? I think it time this baggage was set out. Do look out, Eva, and see if you see your papa."

"O, yes, he's down the other end of the gentlemen's cabin, eating an orange."

"He can't know how near we are coming," said aunty; "hadn't you better run and speak to him?"

"Papa never is in a hurry about anything," said Eva, "and we haven't come to the landing. Do step on the guards, aunty. Look! there's our house, up that street!"

The boat now began, with heavy groans, like some vast, tired monster, to prepare to push up among the multiplied steamers at the levee. Eva joyously pointed out the various spires, domes, and way-marks, by which she recognized her native city.

"Yes, yes, dear; very fine," said Miss Ophelia. "But mercy on us! the boat has stopped! where is your father?"

And now ensued the usual turmoil of landing - waiters running twenty ways at once - men tugging trunks, carpet-bags, boxes - women anxiously calling to their children, and everybody crowding in a dense mass to the plank towards the landing.

Miss Ophelia seated herself resolutely on the lately vanquished trunk, and marshalling all her goods and chattels in fine military order, seemed resolved to defend them to the last.

"Shall I take your trunk, ma'am?" "Shall I take your baggage?" "Let me 'tend to your baggage, Missis?" "Shan't I carry out these yer, Missis?" rained down upon her unheeded. She sat with grim determination, upright as a darning-needle stuck in a board, holding on her bundle of umbrella and parasols, and replying with a determination that was enough to strike dismay even into a hackman, wondering to Eva, in each interval, "what upon earth her papa could be thinking of; he couldn't have fallen over, now, - but something must have happened;" - and just as she had begun to work herself into a real distress, he came up, with his usually careless motion, and giving Eva a quarter of the orange he was eating, said,

"Well, Cousin Vermont, I suppose you are all ready."

"I've been ready, waiting, nearly an hour," said Miss Ophelia; "I began to be really concerned about you.

"That's a clever fellow, now," said he. "Well, the carriage is waiting, and the crowd are now off, so that one can walk out in a decent and Christian manner, and not be pushed and shoved. Here," he added to a driver who stood behind him, "take these things."

"I'll go and see to his putting them in," said Miss Ophelia.

"O, pshaw, cousin, what's the use?" said St. Clare.

"Well, at any rate, I'll carry this, and this, and this," said Miss Ophelia, singling out three boxes and a small carpet-bag.

"My dear Miss Vermont, positively you mustn't come the Green Mountains over us that way. You must adopt at least a piece of a southern principle, and not walk out under all that load. They'll take you for a waiting-maid; give them to this fellow; he'll put them down as if they were eggs, now."

Miss Ophelia looked despairingly as her cousin took all her treasures from her, and rejoiced to find herself once more in the carriage with them, in a state of preservation.

"Where's Tom?" said Eva.

"O, he's on the outside, Pussy. I'm going to take Tom up to mother for a peace-offering, to make up for that drunken fellow that upset the carriage."

"O, Tom will make a splendid driver, I know," said Eva; "he'll never get drunk."

The carriage stopped in front of an ancient mansion, built in that odd mixture of Spanish and French style, of which there are specimens in some parts of New Orleans. It was built in the Moorish fashion, – a square building enclosing a court-yard, into which the carriage drove through an arched gateway. The court, in the inside, had evidently been arranged to gratify a picturesque and voluptuous ideality. Wide galleries ran all around the four sides, whose Moorish arches, slender pillars, and arabesque ornaments, carried the mind back, as in a dream, to the reign of oriental romance in Spain. In the middle of the court, a fountain threw high its silvery water, falling in a never-ceasing spray into a marble basin, fringed with a deep border of fragrant violets. The water in the fountain, pellucid as crystal, was alive with myriads of gold and silver fishes, twinkling and darting through it like so many living jewels. Around the fountain ran a walk, paved with a mosaic of pebbles, laid in various fanciful patterns; and this, again, was surrounded by turf, smooth as green velvet, while a carriage-drive enclosed the whole. Two large orange-trees, now fragrant with blossoms, threw a delicious shade; and, ranged in a circle round upon the turf, were marble vases of arabesque sculpture, containing the choicest flowering plants of the tropics. Huge pomegranate trees, with their glossy leaves and flame-colored flowers, dark-leaved Arabian jessamines, with their silvery stars, geraniums, luxuriant roses bending beneath their heavy abundance of flowers, golden jessamines, lemon-scented verbenum, all united their bloom and fragrance, while here and there a mystic old aloe, with its strange, massive leaves, sat looking like some old enchanter, sitting in weird grandeur among the more perishable bloom and fragrance around it.

The galleries that surrounded the court were festooned with a curtain of some kind of Moorish stuff, and could be drawn down at pleasure, to exclude the beams of the sun. On the whole, the appearance of the place was luxurious and romantic.

As the carriage drove in, Eva seemed like a bird ready to burst from a cage, with the wild eagerness of her delight.

"O, isn't it beautiful, lovely! my own dear, darling home!" she said to Miss Ophelia. "Isn't it beautiful?"

"'T is a pretty place," said Miss Ophelia, as she alighted; "though it looks rather old and heathenish to me."

Tom got down from the carriage, and looked about with an air of calm, still enjoyment. The negro, it must be remembered, is an exotic of the most gorgeous and superb countries of the world, and he has, deep in his heart, a passion for all that is splendid, rich, and fanciful; a passion which, rudely indulged by an untrained taste, draws on them the ridicule of the colder and more correct white race.

St. Clare, who was in heart a poetical voluptuary, smiled as Miss Ophelia made her remark on his premises, and, turning to Tom, who was standing looking round, his beaming black face perfectly radiant with admiration, he said,

"Tom, my boy, this seems to suit you."

"Yes, Mas'r, it looks about the right thing," said Tom.

All this passed in a moment, while trunks were being hustled off, hackman paid, and while a crowd, of all ages and sizes, - men, women, and children, - came running through the galleries, both above and below to see Mas'r come in. Foremost among them was a highly-dressed young mulatto man, evidently a very *distingue* personage, attired in the ultra extreme of the mode, and gracefully waving a scented cambric handkerchief in his hand.

This personage had been exerting himself, with great alacrity, in driving all the flock of domestics to the other end of the verandah.

"Back! all of you. I am ashamed of you," he said, in a tone of authority. "Would you intrude on Master's domestic relations, in the first hour of his return?"

All looked abashed at this elegant speech, delivered with quite an air, and stood huddled together at a respectful distance, except two stout porters, who came up and began conveying away the baggage.

Owing to Mr. Adolph's systematic arrangements, when St. Clare turned round from paying the hackman, there was nobody in view but Mr. Adolph himself, conspicuous in satin vest, gold guard-chain, and white pants, and bowing with inexpressible grace and suavity.

"Ah, Adolph, is it you?" said his master, offering his hand to him; "how are you, boy?" while Adolph poured forth, with great fluency, an extemporary speech, which he had been preparing, with great care, for a fortnight before.

"Well, well," said St. Clare, passing on, with his usual air of negligent drollery, "that's very well got up, Adolph. See that the baggage is well bestowed. I'll come to the people in a minute;" and, so saying, he led Miss Ophelia to a large parlor that opened on the verandah.

While this had been passing, Eva had flown like a bird, through the porch and parlor, to a little boudoir opening likewise on the verandah.

A tall, dark-eyed, sallow woman, half rose from a couch on which she was reclining.

"Mamma!" said Eva, in a sort of a rapture, throwing herself on her neck, and embracing her over and over again.

"That'll do, – take care, child, – don't, you make my head ache," said the mother, after she had languidly kissed her.

St. Clare came in, embraced his wife in true, orthodox, husbandly fashion, and then presented to her his cousin. Marie lifted her large eyes on her cousin with an air of some curiosity, and received her with languid politeness. A crowd of servants now pressed to the entry door, and among them a middle-aged mulatto woman, of very respectable appearance, stood foremost, in a tremor of expectation and joy, at the door.

"O, there's Mammy!" said Eva, as she flew across the room; and, throwing herself into her arms, she kissed her repeatedly.

This woman did not tell her that she made her head ache, but, on the contrary, she hugged her, and laughed, and cried, till her sanity was a thing to be doubted of; and when released from her, Eva flew from one to another, shaking hands and kissing, in a way that Miss Ophelia afterwards declared fairly turned her stomach.

"Well!" said Miss Ophelia, "you southern children can do something that *I* couldn't."

"What, now, pray?" said St. Clare.

"Well, I want to be kind to everybody, and I wouldn't have anything hurt; but as to kissing–"

"Niggers," said St. Clare, "that you're not up to, – hey?"

"Yes, that's it. How can she?"

St. Clare laughed, as he went into the passage. "Halloa, here, what's to pay out here? Here, you all – Mammy, Jimmy, Polly, Sukey – glad to see Mas'r?" he said, as he went shaking hands from one to another. "Look out for the babies!" he added, as he stumbled over a sooty little urchin, who was crawling upon all fours. "If I step upon anybody, let 'em mention it."

There was an abundance of laughing and blessing Mas'r, as St. Clare distributed small pieces of change among them.

"Come, now, take yourselves off, like good boys and girls," he said; and the whole assemblage, dark and light, disappeared through a door into a large verandah, followed by Eva, who carried a large satchel, which she had been filling with apples, nuts, candy, ribbons, laces, and toys of every description, during her whole homeward journey.

As St. Clare turned to go back his eye fell upon Tom, who was standing uneasily, shifting from one foot to the other, while Adolph stood negligently leaning against the banisters, examining Tom through an opera-glass, with an air that would have done credit to any dandy living.

"Puh! you puppy," said his master, striking down the opera glass; "is that the way you treat your company? Seems to me, Dolph," he added, laying his finger on the elegant figured satin vest that Adolph was sporting, "seems to me that's *my* vest."

"O! Master, this vest all stained with wine; of course, a gentleman in Master's standing never wears a vest like this. I understood I was to take it. It does for a poor nigger-fellow, like me."

And Adolph tossed his head, and passed his fingers through his scented hair, with a grace.

"So, that's it, is it?" said St. Clare, carelessly. "Well, here, I'm going to show this Tom to his mistress, and then you take him to the kitchen; and mind you don't put on any of your airs to him. He's worth two such puppies as you."

"Master always will have his joke," said Adolph, laughing. "I'm delighted to see Master in such spirits."

"Here, Tom," said St. Clare, beckoning.

Tom entered the room. He looked wistfully on the velvet carpets, and the before unimagined splendors of mirrors, pictures, statues, and curtains, and, like the Queen of Sheba before Solomon, there was no more spirit in him. He looked afraid even to set his feet down.

"See here, Marie," said St. Clare to his wife, "I've bought you a coachman, at last, to order. I tell you, he's a regular hearse for blackness and sobriety, and will drive you like a funeral, if you want. Open your eyes, now, and look at him. Now, don't say I never think about you when I'm gone."

Marie opened her eyes, and fixed them on Tom, without rising.

"I know he'll get drunk," she said.

"No, he's warranted a pious and sober article."

"Well, I hope he may turn out well," said the lady; "it's more than I expect, though."

"Dolph," said St. Clare, "show Tom down stairs; and, mind yourself," he added; "remember what I told you."

Adolph tripped gracefully forward, and Tom, with lumbering tread, went after.

"He's a perfect behemoth!" said Marie.

"Come, now, Marie," said St. Clare, seating himself on a stool beside her sofa, "be gracious, and say something pretty to a fellow."

"You've been gone a fortnight beyond the time," said the lady, pouting.

"Well, you know I wrote you the reason."

"Such a short, cold letter!" said the lady.

"Dear me! the mail was just going, and it had to be that or nothing."

"That's just the way, always," said the lady; "always something to make your journeys long, and letters short."

"See here, now," he added, drawing an elegant velvet case out of his pocket, and opening it, "here's a present I got for you in New York."

It was a daguerreotype, clear and soft as an engraving, representing Eva and her father sitting hand in hand.

Marie looked at it with a dissatisfied air.

"What made you sit in such an awkward position?" she said.

"Well, the position may be a matter of opinion; but what do you think of the likeness?"

"If you don't think anything of my opinion in one case, I suppose you wouldn't in another," said the lady, shutting the daguerreotype.

"Hang the woman!" said St. Clare, mentally; but aloud he added, "Come, now, Marie, what do you think of the likeness? Don't be nonsensical, now."

"It's very inconsiderate of you, St. Clare," said the lady, "to insist on my talking and looking at things. You know I've been lying all day with the sick-headache; and there's been such a tumult made ever since you came, I'm half dead."

"You're subject to the sick-headache, ma'am!" said Miss Ophelia, suddenly rising from the depths of the large arm-chair, where she had sat quietly, taking an inventory of the furniture, and calculating its expense.

"Yes, I'm a perfect martyr to it," said the lady.

"Juniper-berry tea is good for sick-headache," said Miss Ophelia; "at least, Auguste, Deacon Abraham Perry's wife, used to say so; and she was a great nurse."

"I'll have the first juniper-berries that get ripe in our garden by the lake brought in for that special purpose," said St. Clare, gravely pulling the bell as he did so; "meanwhile, cousin, you must be wanting to retire to your apartment, and refresh yourself a little, after your journey. Dolph," he added, "tell Mammy to come here." The decent mulatto woman whom Eva had caressed so rapturously soon entered; she was dressed neatly, with a high red and yellow turban on her head, the recent gift of Eva, and which the child had been arranging on her head. "Mammy," said St. Clare, "I put this lady under your care; she is tired, and wants rest; take her to her chamber, and be sure she is made comfortable," and Miss Ophelia disappeared in the rear of Mammy.

Chapter 16

Tom's Mistress and Her Opinions

"And now, Marie," said St. Clare, "your golden days are dawning. Here is our practical, business-like New England cousin, who will take the whole budget of cares off your shoulders, and give you time to refresh yourself, and grow young and handsome. The ceremony of delivering the keys had better come off forthwith."

This remark was made at the breakfast-table, a few mornings after Miss Ophelia had arrived.

"I'm sure she's welcome," said Marie, leaning her head languidly on her hand. "I think she'll find one thing, if she does, and that is, that it's we mistresses that are the slaves, down here."

"O, certainly, she will discover that, and a world of wholesome truths besides, no doubt," said St. Clare.

"Talk about our keeping slaves, as if we did it for our *convenience*," said Marie. "I'm sure, if we consulted *that*, we might let them all go at once."

Evangeline fixed her large, serious eyes on her mother's face, with an earnest and perplexed expression, and said, simply, "What do you keep them for, mamma?"

"I don't know, I'm sure, except for a plague; they are the plague of my life. I believe that more of my ill health is caused by them than by any one thing; and ours, I know, are the very worst that ever anybody was plagued with."

"O, come, Marie, you've got the blues, this morning," said St. Clare. "You know 't isn't so. There's Mammy, the best creature living, – what could you do without her?"

"Mammy is the best I ever knew," said Marie; "and yet Mammy, now, is selfish – dreadfully selfish; it's the fault of the whole race."

"Selfishness *is* a dreadful fault," said St. Clare, gravely.

"Well, now, there's Mammy," said Marie, "I think it's selfish of her to sleep so sound nights; she knows I need little attentions almost every hour, when my worst turns are on, and yet she's so hard to wake. I absolutely am worse, this very morning, for the efforts I had to make to wake her last night."

"Hasn't she sat up with you a good many nights, lately, mamma?" said Eva.

"How should you know that?" said Marie, sharply; "she's been complaining, I suppose."

"She didn't complain; she only told me what bad nights you'd had, – so many in succession."

"Why don't you let Jane or Rosa take her place, a night or two," said St. Clare, "and let her rest?"

"How can you propose it?" said Marie. "St. Clare, you really are inconsiderate. So nervous as I am, the least breath disturbs me; and a strange hand about me would drive me absolutely frantic. If Mammy felt the interest in me she ought to, she'd wake easier, - of course, she would. I've heard of people who had such devoted servants, but it never was *my* luck;" and Marie sighed.

Miss Ophelia had listened to this conversation with an air of shrewd, observant gravity; and she still kept her lips tightly compressed, as if determined fully to ascertain her longitude and position, before she committed herself.

"Now, Mammy has a *sort* of goodness," said Marie; "she's smooth and respectful, but she's selfish at heart. Now, she never will be done fidgeting and worrying about that husband of hers. You see, when I was married and came to live here, of course, I had to bring her with me, and her husband my father couldn't spare. He was a blacksmith, and, of course, very necessary; and I thought and said, at the time, that Mammy and he had better give each other up, as it wasn't likely to be convenient for them ever to live together again. I wish, now, I'd insisted on it, and married Mammy to somebody else; but I was foolish and indulgent, and didn't want to insist. I told Mammy, at the time, that she mustn't ever expect to see him more than once or twice in her life again, for the air of father's place doesn't agree with my health, and I can't go there; and I advised her to take up with somebody else; but no - she wouldn't. Mammy has a kind of obstinacy about her, in spots, that everybody don't see as I do."

"Has she children?" said Miss Ophelia.

"Yes; she has two."

"I suppose she feels the separation from them?"

"Well, of course, I couldn't bring them. They were little dirty things – I couldn't have them about; and, besides, they took up too much of her time; but I believe that Mammy has always kept up a sort of sulkiness about this. She won't marry anybody else; and I do believe, now, though she knows how necessary she is to me, and how feeble my health is, she would go back to her husband tomorrow, if she only could. I *do*, indeed," said Marie; "they are just so selfish, now, the best of them."

"It's distressing to reflect upon," said St. Clare, dryly.

Miss Ophelia looked keenly at him, and saw the flush of mortification and repressed vexation, and the sarcastic curl of the lip, as he spoke.

"Now, Mammy has always been a pet with me," said Marie. "I wish some of your northern servants could look at her closets of dresses, – silks and muslins, and one real linen cambric, she has hanging there. I've worked sometimes whole afternoons, trimming her caps, and getting her ready to go to a party. As to abuse, she don't know what it is. She never was whipped more than once or twice in her whole life. She has her strong coffee or her tea every day, with white sugar in it. It's abominable, to be sure; but St. Clare will have high life below-stairs, and they every one of them live just as they please. The fact is, our servants are over-indulged. I suppose it is partly our fault that they are selfish, and act like spoiled children; but I've talked to St. Clare till I am tired."

"And I, too," said St. Clare, taking up the morning paper.

Eva, the beautiful Eva, had stood listening to her mother, with that expression of deep and mystic earnestness which was peculiar to her. She walked softly round to her mother's chair, and put her arms round her neck.

"Well, Eva, what now?" said Marie.

"Mamma, couldn't I take care of you one night - just one? I know I shouldn't make you nervous, and I shouldn't sleep. I often lie awake nights, thinking–"

"O, nonsense, child - nonsense!" said Marie; "you are such a strange child!"

"But may I, mamma? I think," she said, timidly, "that Mammy isn't well. She told me her head ached all the time, lately."

"O, that's just one of Mammy's fidgets! Mammy is just like all the rest of them - makes such a fuss about every little headache or finger-ache; it'll never do to encourage it - never! I'm principled about this matter," said she, turning to Miss Ophelia; "you'll find the necessity of it. If you encourage servants in giving way to every little disagreeable feeling, and complaining of every little ailment, you'll have your hands full. I never complain myself – nobody knows what I endure. I feel it a duty to bear it quietly, and I do."

Miss Ophelia's round eyes expressed an undisguised amazement at this peroration, which struck St. Clare as so supremely ludicrous, that he burst into a loud laugh.

"St. Clare always laughs when I make the least allusion to my ill health," said Marie, with the voice of a suffering martyr. "I only hope the day won't come when he'll remember it!" and Marie put her handkerchief to her eyes.

Of course, there was rather a foolish silence. Finally, St. Clare got up, looked at his watch, and said he had an engagement down street. Eva tripped away after him, and Miss Ophelia and Marie remained at the table alone.

"Now, that's just like St. Clare!" said the latter, withdrawing her handkerchief with somewhat of a spirited flourish when the criminal to be affected by it was no longer in sight. "He never realizes, never can, never will, what I suffer, and have, for years. If I was one of the complaining sort, or ever made any fuss about my ailments, there would be some reason for it. Men do get tired, naturally, of a complaining wife. But I've kept things to myself, and borne, and borne, till St. Clare has got in the way of thinking I can bear anything."

Miss Ophelia did not exactly know what she was expected to answer to this.

While she was thinking what to say, Marie gradually wiped away her tears, and smoothed her plumage in a general sort of way, as a dove might be supposed to make toilet after a shower, and began a housewifely chat with Miss Ophelia, concerning cupboards, closets, linen-presses, storerooms, and other matters, of which the latter was, by common understanding, to assume the direction, - giving her so many cautious directions and charges, that a head less systematic and business-like than Miss Ophelia's would have been utterly dizzied and confounded.

"And now," said Marie, "I believe I've told you everything; so that, when my next sick turn comes on, you'll be able to go forward entirely, without consulting me; - only about Eva, - she requires watching."

"She seems to be a good child, very," said Miss Ophelia; "I never saw a better child."

"Eva's peculiar," said her mother, "very. There are things about her so singular; she isn't like me, now, a particle;" and Marie sighed, as if this was a truly melancholy consideration.

Miss Ophelia in her own heart said, "I hope she isn't," but had prudence enough to keep it down.

"Eva always was disposed to be with servants; and I think that well enough with some children.

Now, I always played with father's little negroes – it never did me any harm. But Eva somehow always seems to put herself on an equality with every creature that comes near her. It's a strange thing about the child. I never have been able to break her of it. St. Clare, I believe, encourages her in it. The fact is, St. Clare indulges every creature under this roof but his own wife."

Again Miss Ophelia sat in blank silence.

"Now, there's no way with servants," said Marie, "but to *put them down*, and keep them down. It was always natural to me, from a child. Eva is enough to spoil a whole house-full. What she will do when she comes to keep house herself, I'm sure I don't know. I hold to being *kind* to servants – I always am; but you must make 'em *know their place*. Eva never does; there's no getting into the child's head the first beginning of an idea what a servant's place is! You heard her offering to take care of me nights, to let Mammy sleep! That's just a specimen of the way the child would be doing all the time, if she was left to herself."

"Why," said Miss Ophelia, bluntly, "I suppose you think your servants are human creatures, and ought to have some rest when they are tired."

"Certainly, of course. I'm very particular in letting them have everything that comes convenient, – anything that doesn't put one at all out of the way, you know. Mammy can make up her sleep, some time or other; there's no difficulty about that. She's the sleepiest concern that ever I saw; sewing, standing, or sitting, that creature will go to sleep, and sleep anywhere and everywhere. No danger but Mammy gets sleep enough. But this treating servants as if they were exotic flowers, or china vases, is really ridiculous," said Marie, as she plunged languidly into the depths of a voluminous and pillowy lounge, and drew towards her an elegant cut-glass vinaigrette.

"You see," she continued, in a faint and lady-like voice, like the last dying breath of an Arabian jessamine, or something equally ethereal, "you see, Cousin Ophelia, I don't often speak of myself. It isn't my *habit*; 't isn't agreeable to me. In fact, I haven't strength to do it. But there are points where St. Clare and I differ. St. Clare never understood me, never appreciated me. I think it lies at the root of all my ill health. St. Clare means well, I am bound to believe; but men are constitutionally selfish and inconsiderate to woman. That, at least, is my impression."

Miss Ophelia, who had not a small share of the genuine New England caution, and a very particular horror of being drawn into family difficulties, now began to foresee something of this kind impending; so, composing her face into a grim neutrality, and drawing out of her pocket about a yard and a quarter of stocking, which she kept as a specific against what Dr. Watts asserts to be a personal habit of Satan when people have idle hands, she proceeded to knit most energetically, shutting her lips together in a way that said, as plain as words could, "You needn't try to make me speak. I don't want anything to do with your affairs," – in fact, she looked about as sympathizing as a stone lion. But Marie didn't care for that. She had got somebody to talk to, and she felt it her duty to talk, and that was enough; and reinforcing herself by smelling again at her vinaigrette, she went on.

"You see, I brought my own property and servants into the connection, when I married St. Clare, and I am legally entitled to manage them my own way. St. Clare had his fortune and his servants, and I'm well enough content he should manage them his way; but St. Clare will be interfering. He has wild, extravagant notions about things, particularly about the treatment of servants. He really does act as if he set his servants before me, and before himself, too; for he lets them make him all sorts of trouble, and never lifts a finger. Now, about some things, St. Clare is really frightful - he frightens me - good-natured as he looks, in general. Now, he has set down his foot that, come what will, there shall not be a blow struck in this house, except what he or I strike; and he does it in a way that I really dare not cross him. Well, you may see what that leads to; for St. Clare wouldn't raise his hand, if every one of them walked over him, and I - you see how cruel it would be to require me to make the exertion. Now, you know these servants are nothing but grown-up children."

"I don't know anything about it, and I thank the Lord that I don't!" said Miss Ophelia, shortly.

"Well, but you will have to know something, and know it to your cost, if you stay here. You don't know what a provoking, stupid, careless, unreasonable, childish, ungrateful set of wretches they are."

Marie seemed wonderfully supported, always, when she got upon this topic; and she now opened her eyes, and seemed quite to forget her languor.

"You don't know, and you can't, the daily, hourly trials that beset a housekeeper from them, everywhere and every way. But it's no use to complain to St. Clare. He talks the strangest stuff. He says we have made them what they are, and ought to bear with them. He says their faults are all owing to us, and that it would be cruel to make the fault and punish it too. He says we shouldn't do any better, in their place; just as if one could reason from them to us, you know."

"Don't you believe that the Lord made them of one blood with us?" said Miss Ophelia, shortly.

"No, indeed not I! A pretty story, truly! They are a degraded race."

"Don't you think they've got immortal souls?" said Miss Ophelia, with increasing indignation.

"O, well," said Marie, yawning, "that, of course – nobody doubts that. But as to putting them on any sort of equality with us, you know, as if we could be compared, why, it's impossible! Now, St. Clare really has talked to me as if keeping Mammy from her husband was like keeping me from mine. There's no comparing in this way. Mammy couldn't have the feelings that I should. It's a different thing altogether, – of course, it is, – and yet St. Clare pretends not to see it. And just as if Mammy could love her little dirty babies as I love Eva! Yet

St. Clare once really and soberly tried to persuade me that it was my duty, with my weak health, and all I suffer, to let Mammy go back, and take somebody else in her place. That was a little too much even for *me* to bear. I don't often show my feelings, I make it a principle to endure everything in silence; it's a wife's hard lot, and I bear it. But I did break out, that time; so that he has never alluded to the subject since. But I know by his looks, and little things that he says, that he thinks so as much as ever; and it's so trying, so provoking!"

Miss Ophelia looked very much as if she was afraid she should say something; but she rattled away with her needles in a way that had volumes of meaning in it, if Marie could only have understood it.

"So, you just see," she continued, "what you've got to manage. A household without any rule; where servants have it all their own way, do what they please, and have what they please, except so far as I, with my feeble health, have kept up government. I keep my cowhide about, and sometimes I do lay it on; but the exertion is always too much for me. If St. Clare would only have this thing done as others do–"

"And how's that?"

"Why, send them to the calaboose, or some of the other places to be flogged. That's the only way. If I wasn't such a poor, feeble piece, I believe I should manage with twice the energy that St. Clare does."

"And how does St. Clare contrive to manage?" said Miss Ophelia. "You say he never strikes a blow."

"Well, men have a more commanding way, you know; it is easier for them; besides, if you ever looked full in his eye, it's peculiar, - that eye, - and if he speaks decidedly, there's a kind of flash. I'm afraid of it, myself; and the servants know they must mind. I couldn't do as much by a regular storm and scolding as St. Clare can by one turn of his eye, if once he is in earnest. O, there's no trouble about St. Clare; that's the reason he's no more feeling for me. But you'll find, when you come to manage, that there's no getting along without severity, - they are so bad, so deceitful, so lazy".

"The old tune," said St. Clare, sauntering in. "What an awful account these wicked creatures will have to settle, at last, especially for being lazy! You see, cousin," said he, as he stretched himself at full length on a lounge opposite to Marie, "it's wholly inexcusable in them, in the light of the example that Marie and I set them, - this laziness."

"Come, now, St. Clare, you are too bad!" said Marie.

"Am I, now? Why, I thought I was talking good, quite remarkably for me. I try to enforce your remarks, Marie, always."

"You know you meant no such thing, St. Clare," said Marie.

"O, I must have been mistaken, then. Thank you, my dear, for setting me right."

"You do really try to be provoking," said Marie.

"O, come, Marie, the day is growing warm, and I have just had a long quarrel with Dolph, which has fatigued me excessively; so, pray be agreeable, now, and let a fellow repose in the light of your smile."

"What's the matter about Dolph?" said Marie. "That fellow's impudence has been growing to a point that is perfectly intolerable to me. I only wish I had the undisputed management of him a while. I'd bring him down!"

"What you say, my dear, is marked with your usual acuteness and good sense," said St. Clare. "As to Dolph, the case is this: that he has so long been engaged in imitating my graces and perfections, that he has, at last, really mistaken himself for his master; and I have been obliged to give him a little insight into his mistake."

"How?" said Marie.

"Why, I was obliged to let him understand explicitly that I preferred to keep *some* of my clothes for my own personal wearing; also, I put his magnificence upon an allowance of cologne-water, and actually was so cruel as to restrict him to one dozen of my cambric handkerchiefs. Dolph was particularly huffy about it, and I had to talk to him like a father, to bring him round."

"O! St. Clare, when will you learn how to treat your servants? It's abominable, the way you indulge them!" said Marie.

"Why, after all, what's the harm of the poor dog's wanting to be like his master; and if I haven't brought him up any better than to find his chief good in cologne and cambric handkerchiefs, why shouldn't I give them to him?"

"And why haven't you brought him up better?" said Miss Ophelia, with blunt determination.

"Too much trouble, – laziness, cousin, laziness, – which ruins more souls than you can shake a stick at. If it weren't for laziness, I should have been a perfect angel, myself. I'm inclined to think that laziness is what your old Dr. Botherem, up in Vermont, used to call the 'essence of moral evil.' It's an awful consideration, certainly."

"I think you slaveholders have an awful responsibility upon you," said Miss Ophelia. "I wouldn't have it, for a thousand worlds. You ought to educate your slaves, and treat them like reasonable creatures, – like immortal creatures, that you've got to stand before the bar of God with. That's my mind," said the good lady, breaking suddenly out with a tide of zeal that had been gaining strength in her mind all the morning.

"O! come, come," said St. Clare, getting up quickly; "what do you know about us?" And he sat down to the piano, and rattled a lively piece of music. St. Clare had a decided genius for music. His touch was brilliant and firm, and his fingers flew over the keys with a rapid and bird-like motion, airy, and yet decided. He played piece after piece, like a man who is trying to play himself into a good humor. After pushing the music aside, he rose up, and said, gayly, "Well, now, cousin, you've given us a good talk and done your duty; on the whole, I think the better of you for it. I make no manner of doubt that you threw a very diamond of truth at me, though you see it hit me so directly in the face that it wasn't exactly appreciated, at first."

"For my part, I don't see any use in such sort of talk," said Marie. "I'm sure, if anybody does more for servants than we do, I'd like to know who; and it don't do 'em a bit good, - not a particle, - they get worse and worse. As to talking to them, or anything like that, I'm sure I have talked till I was tired and hoarse, telling them their duty, and all that; and I'm sure they can go to church when they like, though they don't understand a word of the sermon, more than so many pigs, - so it isn't of any great use for them to go, as I see; but they do go, and so they have every chance; but, as I said before, they are a degraded race, and always will be, and there isn't any help for them; you can't make anything of them, if you try. You see, Cousin Ophelia, I've tried, and you haven't; I was born and bred among them, and I know."

Miss Ophelia thought she had said enough, and therefore sat silent. St. Clare whistled a tune.

"St. Clare, I wish you wouldn't whistle," said Marie; "it makes my head worse."

"I won't," said St. Clare. "Is there anything else you wouldn't wish me to do?"

"I wish you *would* have some kind of sympathy for my trials; you never have any feeling for me."

"My dear accusing angel!" said St. Clare.

"It's provoking to be talked to in that way."

"Then, how will you be talked to? I'll talk to order, – any way you'll mention, – only to give satisfaction."

A gay laugh from the court rang through the silken curtains of the verandah. St. Clare stepped out, and lifting up the curtain, laughed too.

"What is it?" said Miss Ophelia, coming to the railing.

There sat Tom, on a little mossy seat in the court, every one of his button-holes stuck full of cape jessamines, and Eva, gayly laughing, was hanging a wreath of roses round his neck; and then she sat down on his knee, like a chip-sparrow, still laughing.

"O, Tom, you look so funny!"

Tom had a sober, benevolent smile, and seemed, in his quiet way, to be enjoying the fun quite as much as his little mistress. He lifted his eyes, when he saw his master, with a half-deprecating, apologetic air.

"How can you let her?" said Miss Ophelia.

"Why not?" said St. Clare.

"Why, I don't know, it seems so dreadful!"

"You would think no harm in a child's caressing a large dog, even if he was black; but a creature that can think, and reason, and feel, and is immortal, you shudder at; confess it, cousin. I know the feeling among some of you northerners well enough. Not that there is a particle of virtue in our not having it; but custom with us does what Christianity ought to do, – obliterates the feeling of personal prejudice. I have often noticed, in my travels north, how much stronger this was with you than with us. You loathe them as you would a snake or a toad, yet you are indignant at their wrongs. You would not have them abused; but you don't want to have anything to do with them yourselves. You would send them to Africa, out of your sight and smell, and then send a missionary or two to do up all the self-denial of elevating them compendiously. Isn't that it?"

"Well, cousin," said Miss Ophelia, thoughtfully, "there may be some truth in this."

"What would the poor and lowly do, without children?" said St. Clare, leaning on the railing, and watching Eva, as she tripped off, leading Tom with her. "Your little child is your only true democrat. Tom, now is a hero to Eva; his stories are wonders in her eyes, his songs and Methodist hymns are better than an opera, and the traps and little bits of trash in his pocket a mine of jewels, and he the most wonderful Tom that ever wore a black skin. This is one of the roses of Eden that the Lord has dropped down expressly for the poor and lowly, who get few enough of any other kind."

"It's strange, cousin," said Miss Ophelia, "one might almost think you were a *professor*, to hear you talk."

"A professor?" said St. Clare.

"Yes; a professor of religion."

"Not at all; not a professor, as your town-folks have it; and, what is worse, I'm afraid, not a *practiser*, either."

"What makes you talk so, then?"

"Nothing is easier than talking," said St. Clare. "I believe Shakespeare makes somebody say, 'I could sooner show twenty what were good to be done, than be one of the twenty to follow my own showing.'[15] Nothing like division of labor. My forte lies in talking, and yours, cousin, lies in doing."

In Tom's external situation, at this time, there was, as the world says, nothing to complain of Little Eva's fancy for him - the instinctive gratitude and loveliness of a noble nature - had led her to petition her father that he might be her especial attendant, whenever she needed the escort of a servant, in her walks or rides; and Tom had general orders to let everything else go, and attend to Miss Eva whenever she wanted him, - orders which our readers may fancy were far from disagreeable to him. He was kept well dressed, for St. Clare was fastidiously particular on this point. His stable services were merely a sinecure, and consisted simply in a daily care and inspection, and directing an under-servant in his duties; for Marie St. Clare declared that she could not have any smell of the horses about him when he came near her, and that he must positively not be put to any service that would make him un-

---

15 The Merchant of Venice, Act 1, scene 2, lines 17-18.

pleasant to her, as her nervous system was entirely inadequate to any trial of that nature; one snuff of anything disagreeable being, according to her account, quite sufficient to close the scene, and put an end to all her earthly trials at once. Tom, therefore, in his well-brushed broadcloth suit, smooth beaver, glossy boots, faultless wristbands and collar, with his grave, good-natured black face, looked respectable enough to be a Bishop of Carthage, as men of his color were, in other ages.

Then, too, he was in a beautiful place, a consideration to which his sensitive race was never indifferent; and he did enjoy with a quiet joy the birds, the flowers, the fountains, the perfume, and light and beauty of the court, the silken hangings, and pictures, and lustres, and statuettes, and gilding, that made the parlors within a kind of Aladdin's palace to him.

If ever Africa shall show an elevated and cultivated race, - and come it must, some time, her turn to figure in the great drama of human improvement. - life will awake there with a gorgeousness and splendor of which our cold western tribes faintly have conceived. In that far-off mystic land of gold, and gems, and spices, and waving palms, and wondrous flowers, and miraculous fertility, will awake new forms of art, new styles of splendor; and the negro race, no longer despised and trodden down, will, perhaps, show forth some of the latest and most magnificent revelations of human life. Certainly they will, in their gentleness, their lowly docility of heart, their aptitude to repose on a superior mind and rest on a higher power, their childlike simplicity of affection, and facility of forgiveness. In all these they will exhibit the highest form of the peculiarly *Christian life*, and, perhaps, as God chasteneth whom he loveth, he hath chosen poor Africa in the furnace of affliction, to make her the highest and noblest in that kingdom which he will set up, when every other kingdom has been tried, and failed; for the first shall be last, and the last first.

Was this what Marie St. Clare was thinking of, as she stood, gorgeously dressed, on the verandah, on Sunday morning, clasping a diamond bracelet on her slender wrist? Most likely it was. Or, if it wasn't that, it was something else; for Marie patronized good things, and she was going now, in full force, - diamonds, silk, and lace, and jewels, and all, - to a fashionable church, to be very religious. Marie always made a point to be very pious on Sundays. There she stood, so slender, so elegant, so airy and undulating in all her motions, her lace scarf enveloping her like a mist. She looked a graceful creature, and she felt very good and very elegant indeed. Miss Ophelia stood at her side, a perfect contrast. It was not that she had not as handsome a silk dress and shawl, and as fine a pocket-handkerchief; but stiffness and squareness, and bolt-uprightness, enveloped her with as indefinite yet appreciable a presence as did grace her elegant neighbor; not the grace of God, however, - that is quite another thing!

"Where's Eva?" said Marie.

"The child stopped on the stairs, to say something to Mammy."

And what was Eva saying to Mammy on the stairs? Listen, reader, and you will hear, though Marie does not.

"Dear Mammy, I know your head is aching dreadfully."

"Lord bless you, Miss Eva! my head allers aches lately. You don't need to worry."

"Well, I'm glad you're going out; and here," – and the little girl threw her arms around her, – "Mammy, you shall take my vinaigrette."

"What! your beautiful gold thing, thar, with them diamonds! Lor, Miss, 't wouldn't be proper, no ways."

"Why not? You need it, and I don't. Mamma always uses it for headache, and it'll make you feel better. No, you shall take it, to please me, now."

"Do hear the darlin talk!" said Mammy, as Eva thrust it into her bosom, and kissing her, ran down stairs to her mother.

"What were you stopping for?"

"I was just stopping to give Mammy my vinaigrette, to take to church with her."

"Eva" said Marie, stamping impatiently, – "your gold vinaigrette to *Mammy!* When will you learn what's *proper*? Go right and take it back this moment!"

Eva looked downcast and aggrieved, and turned slowly.

"I say, Marie, let the child alone; she shall do as she pleases," said St. Clare.

"St. Clare, how will she ever get along in the world?" said Marie.

"The Lord knows," said St. Clare, "but she'll get along in heaven better than you or I."

"O, papa, don't," said Eva, softly touching his elbow; "it troubles mother."

"Well, cousin, are you ready to go to meeting?" said Miss Ophelia, turning square about on St. Clare.

"I'm not going, thank you."

"I do wish St. Clare ever would go to church," said Marie; "but he hasn't a particle of religion about him. It really isn't respectable."

"I know it," said St. Clare. "You ladies go to church to learn how to get along in the world, I suppose, and your piety sheds respectability on us. If I did go at all, I would go where Mammy goes; there's something to keep a fellow awake there, at least."

"What! those shouting Methodists? Horrible!" said Marie.

"Anything but the dead sea of your respectable churches, Marie. Positively, it's too much to ask of a man. Eva, do you like to go? Come, stay at home and play with me."

"Thank you, papa; but I'd rather go to church."

"Isn't it dreadful tiresome?" said St. Clare.

"I think it is tiresome, some," said Eva, "and I am sleepy, too, but I try to keep awake."

"What do you go for, then?"

"Why, you know, papa," she said, in a whisper, "cousin told me that God wants to have us; and he gives us everything, you know; and it isn't much to do it, if he wants us to. It isn't so very tiresome after all."

"You sweet, little obliging soul!" said St. Clare, kissing her; "go along, that's a good girl, and pray for me."

"Certainly, I always do," said the child, as she sprang after her mother into the carriage.

St. Clare stood on the steps and kissed his hand to her, as the carriage drove away; large tears were in his eyes.

"O, Evangeline! rightly named," he said; "hath not God made thee an evangel to me?"

So he felt a moment; and then he smoked a cigar, and read the Picayune, and forgot his little gospel. Was he much unlike other folks?

"You see, Evangeline," said her mother, "it's always right and proper to be kind to servants, but it isn't proper to treat them *just* as we would our relations, or people in our own class of life. Now, if Mammy was sick, you wouldn't want to put her in your own bed."

"I should feel just like it, mamma," said Eva, "because then it would be handier to take care of her, and because, you know, my bed is better than hers."

Marie was in utter despair at the entire want of moral perception evinced in this reply.

"What can I do to make this child understand me?" she said.

"Nothing," said Miss Ophelia, significantly.

Eva looked sorry and disconcerted for a moment; but children, luckily, do not keep to one impression long, and in a few moments she was merrily laughing at various things which she saw from the coach-windows, as it rattled along.

***

"Well, ladies," said St. Clare, as they were comfortably seated at the dinner-table, "and what was the bill of fare at church today?"

"O, Dr. G– preached a splendid sermon," said Marie. "It was just such a sermon as you ought to hear; it expressed all my views exactly."

"It must have been very improving," said St. Clare. "The subject must have been an extensive one."

"Well, I mean all my views about society, and such things," said Marie. "The text was, 'He hath made everything beautiful in its season;' and he showed how all the orders and distinctions in society came from God; and that it was so appropriate, you know, and beautiful, that some should be high and some low, and that some were born to rule and some to serve, and all that, you know; and he applied it so well to all this ridiculous fuss that is made about slavery, and he proved distinctly that the Bible was on our side, and supported all our institutions so convincingly. I only wish you'd heard him."

"O, I didn't need it," said St. Clare. "I can learn what does me as much good as that from the Picayune, any time, and smoke a cigar besides; which I can't do, you know, in a church."

"Why," said Miss Ophelia, "don't you believe in these views?"

"Who, – I? You know I'm such a graceless dog that these religious aspects of such subjects don't edify me much. If I was to say anything on this slavery matter, I would say out, fair and square, 'We're in for it; we've got 'em, and mean to keep 'em, – it's for our convenience and our interest;' for that's the long and short of it, – that's just the whole of what all this sanctified stuff amounts to, after all; and I think that it will be intelligible to everybody, everywhere."

"I do think, Augustine, you are so irreverent!" said Marie. "I think it's shocking to hear you talk."

"Shocking! it's the truth. This religious talk on such matters, – why don't they carry it a little further, and show the beauty, in its season, of a fellow's taking a glass too much, and sitting a little too late over his cards, and various providential arrangements of that sort, which are pretty frequent among us young men; – we'd like to hear that those are right and godly, too."

"Well," said Miss Ophelia, "do you think slavery right or wrong?"

"I'm not going to have any of your horrid New England directness, cousin," said St. Clare, gayly. "If I answer that question, I know you'll be at me with half a dozen others, each one harder than the last; and I'm not a going to define my position. I am one of the sort that lives by throwing stones at other people's glass houses, but I never mean to put up one for them to stone."

"That's just the way he's always talking," said Marie; "you can't get any satisfaction out of him. I believe it's just because he don't like religion, that he's always running out in this way he's been doing."

"Religion!" said St. Clare, in a tone that made both ladies look at him. "Religion! Is what you hear at church, religion? Is that which can bend and turn, and descend and ascend, to fit every crooked phase of selfish, worldly society, religion? Is that religion which is less scrupulous, less generous, less just, less considerate for man, than even my own ungodly, worldly, blinded nature? No! When I look for a religion, I must look for something above me, and not something beneath."

"Then you don't believe that the Bible justifies slavery," said Miss Ophelia.

"The Bible was my *mother's* book," said St. Clare. "By it she lived and died, and I would be very sorry to think it did. I'd as soon desire to have it proved that my mother could drink brandy, chew tobacco, and swear, by way of satisfying me that I did right in doing the same. It wouldn't make me at all more satisfied with these things in myself, and it would take from me the comfort of respecting her; and it really is a comfort, in this world, to have anything one can respect. In short, you see," said he, suddenly resuming his gay tone, "all I want is that different things be kept in different boxes. The whole frame-work of society, both in Europe and America, is made up of various things which will not stand the scrutiny of any very ideal standard of morality. It's pretty generally understood that men don't aspire after the absolute right, but only to do about as well as the rest of the world. Now, when any one speaks up, like a man, and says slavery is necessary to us, we can't get along without it, we should be beggared if we give it up, and, of course, we mean to hold on to it, – this is strong, clear, well-defined language; it has the respectability of truth to it; and, if we may judge by their practice, the majority of the world will bear us out in it. But when he begins to put on a long face, and snuffle, and quote Scripture, I incline to think he isn't much better than he should be."

"You are very uncharitable," said Marie.

"Well," said St. Clare, "suppose that something should bring down the price of cotton once and forever, and make the whole slave property a drug in the market, don't you think we should soon have another version of the Scripture doctrine? What a flood of light would pour into the church, all at once, and how immediately it would be discovered that everything in the Bible and reason went the other way!"

"Well, at any rate," said Marie, as she reclined herself on a lounge, "I'm thankful I'm born where slavery exists; and I believe it's right, – indeed, I feel it must be; and, at any rate, I'm sure I couldn't get along without it."

"I say, what do you think, Pussy?" said her father to Eva, who came in at this moment, with a flower in her hand.

"What about, papa?"

"Why, which do you like the best, – to live as they do at your uncle's, up in Vermont, or to have a house-full of servants, as we do?"

"O, of course, our way is the pleasantest," said Eva.

"Why so?" said St. Clare, stroking her head.

"Why, it makes so many more round you to love, you know," said Eva, looking up earnestly.

"Now, that's just like Eva," said Marie; "just one of her odd speeches."

"Is it an odd speech, papa?" said Eva, whisperingly, as she got upon his knee.

"Rather, as this world goes, Pussy," said St. Clare. "But where has my little Eva been, all dinner-time?"

"O, I've been up in Tom's room, hearing him sing, and Aunt Dinah gave me my dinner."

"Hearing Tom sing, hey?"

"O, yes! he sings such beautiful things about the New Jerusalem, and bright angels, and the land of Canaan."

"I dare say; it's better than the opera, isn't it?"

"Yes, and he's going to teach them to me."

"Singing lessons, hey? – you *are* coming on."

"Yes, he sings for me, and I read to him in my Bible; and he explains what it means, you know."

"On my word," said Marie, laughing, "that is the latest joke of the season."

"Tom isn't a bad hand, now, at explaining Scripture, I'll dare swear," said St. Clare. "Tom has a natural genius for religion. I wanted the horses out early, this morning, and I stole up to Tom's cubiculum there, over the stables, and there I heard him holding a meeting by himself; and, in fact, I haven't heard anything quite so savory as Tom's prayer, this some time. He put in for me, with a zeal that was quite apostolic."

"Perhaps he guessed you were listening. I've heard of that trick before."

"If he did, he wasn't very polite; for he gave the Lord his opinion of me, pretty freely. Tom seemed to think there was decidedly room for improvement in me, and seemed very earnest that I should be converted."

"I hope you'll lay it to heart," said Miss Ophelia.

"I suppose you are much of the same opinion," said St. Clare. "Well, we shall see, – shan't we, Eva?"

Chapter 17

The Freeman's Defence

There was a gentle bustle at the Quaker house, as the afternoon drew to a close. Rachel Halliday moved quietly to and fro, collecting from her household stores such needments as could be arranged in the smallest compass, for the wanderers who were to go forth that night. The afternoon shadows stretched eastward, and the round red sun stood thoughtfully on the horizon, and his beams shone yellow and calm into the little bed-room where George and his wife were sitting. He was sitting with his child on his knee, and his wife's hand in his. Both looked thoughtful and serious and traces of tears were on their cheeks.

"Yes, Eliza," said George, "I know all you say is true. You are a good child, - a great deal better than I am; and I will try to do as you say. I'll try to act worthy of a free man. I'll try to feel like a Christian. God Almighty knows that I've meant to do well, - tried hard to do well, - when everything has been against me; and now I'll forget all the past, and put away every hard and bitter feeling, and read my Bible, and learn to be a good man."

"And when we get to Canada," said Eliza, "I can help you. I can do dress-making very well; and I understand fine washing and ironing; and between us we can find something to live on."

"Yes, Eliza, so long as we have each other and our boy. O! Eliza, if these people only knew what a blessing it is for a man to feel that his wife and child belong to *him*! I've often wondered to see men that could call their wives and children *their own* fretting and worrying about anything else. Why, I feel rich and strong, though we have nothing but our bare hands. I feel as if I could scarcely ask God for any more. Yes, though I've worked hard every day, till I am twenty-five years old, and have not a cent of money, nor a roof to cover me, nor a spot of land to call my own, yet, if they will only let me alone now, I will be satisfied, - thankful; I will work, and send back the money for you and my boy. As to my old master, he has been paid five times over for all he ever spent for me. I don't owe him anything."

"But yet we are not quite out of danger," said Eliza; "we are not yet in Canada."

"True," said George, "but it seems as if I smelt the free air, and it makes me strong."

At this moment, voices were heard in the outer apartment, in earnest conversation, and very soon a rap was heard on the door. Eliza started and opened it.

Simeon Halliday was there, and with him a Quaker brother, whom he introduced as Phineas Fletcher. Phineas was tall and lathy, red-haired, with an expression of great acuteness and shrewdness in his face. He had not the placid, quiet, unworldly air of Simeon Halliday; on the contrary, a particularly wide-awake and *au fait* appearance, like a man who rather prides himself on knowing what he is about, and keeping a bright lookout ahead; peculiarities which sorted rather oddly with his broad brim and formal phraseology.

"Our friend Phineas hath discovered something of importance to the interests of thee and thy party, George," said Simeon; "it were well for thee to hear it."

"That I have," said Phineas, "and it shows the use of a man's always sleeping with one ear open, in certain places, as I've always said. Last night I stopped at a little lone tavern, back on the road. Thee remembers the place, Simeon, where we sold some apples, last year, to that fat woman, with the great ear-rings. Well, I was tired with hard driving; and, after my supper I stretched myself down on a pile of bags in the corner, and pulled a buffalo over me, to wait till my bed was ready; and what does I do, but get fast asleep."

"With one ear open, Phineas?" said Simeon, quietly.

"No; I slept, ears and all, for an hour or two, for I was pretty well tired; but when I came to myself a little, I found that there were some men in the room, sitting round a table, drinking and talking; and I thought, before I made much muster, I'd just see what they were up to, especially as I heard them say something about the Quakers. 'So,' says one, 'they are up in the Quaker settlement, no doubt,' says he. Then I listened with both ears, and I found that they were talking about this very party. So I lay and heard them lay off all their plans. This young man, they said, was to be sent back to Kentucky, to his master, who was going to make an example of him, to keep all niggers from running away; and his wife two of them were going to run down to New Orleans to sell, on their own account, and they calculated to get sixteen or eighteen hundred dollars for her; and the child, they said, was going to a trader, who had bought him; and then there was the boy, Jim, and his mother, they were to go back to their masters in Kentucky. They said that there were two constables, in a town a little piece ahead, who would go in with 'em to get 'em taken up, and the young woman was to be taken before a judge; and one of the fellows, who is small and smooth-spoken, was to swear to her for his property, and get her delivered over to him to take south. They've got a right notion of the track we are going tonight; and they'll be down after us, six or eight strong. So now, what's to be done?"

The group that stood in various attitudes, after this communication, were worthy of a painter. Rachel Halliday, who had taken her hands out of a batch of biscuit, to hear the news, stood with them upraised and floury, and with a face of the deepest concern. Simeon looked profoundly thoughtful; Eliza had thrown her arms around her husband, and was looking up to him. George stood with clenched hands and glowing eyes, and looking as any other man might look, whose wife was to be sold at auction, and son sent to a trader, all under the shelter of a Christian nation's laws.

"What *shall* we do, George?" said Eliza faintly.

"I know what *I* shall do," said George, as he stepped into the little room, and began examining pistols.

"Ay, ay," said Phineas, nodding his head to Simeon; "thou seest, Simeon, how it will work."

"I see," said Simeon, sighing; "I pray it come not to that."

"I don't want to involve any one with or for me," said George. "If you will lend me your vehicle and direct me, I will drive alone to the next stand. Jim is a giant in strength, and brave as death and despair, and so am I."

"Ah, well, friend," said Phineas, "but thee'll need a driver, for all that. Thee's quite welcome to do all the fighting, thee knows; but I know a thing or two about the road, that thee doesn't."

"But I don't want to involve you," said George.

"Involve," said Phineas, with a curious and keen expression of face, "When thee does involve me, please to let me know."

"Phineas is a wise and skilful man," said Simeon. "Thee does well, George, to abide by his judgment; and," he added, laying his hand kindly on George's shoulder, and pointing to the pistols, "be not over hasty with these, - young blood is hot."

"I will attack no man," said George. "All I ask of this country is to be let alone, and I will go out peaceably; but," - he paused, and his brow darkened and his face worked, - "I've had a sister sold in that New Orleans market. I know what they are sold for; and am I going to stand by and see them take my wife and sell her, when God has given me a pair of strong arms to defend her? No; God help me! I'll fight to the last breath, before they shall take my wife and son. Can you blame me?"

"Mortal man cannot blame thee, George. Flesh and blood could not do otherwise," said Simeon. "Woe unto the world because of offences, but woe unto them through whom the offence cometh."

"Would not even you, sir, do the same, in my place?"

"I pray that I be not tried," said Simeon; "the flesh is weak."

"I think my flesh would be pretty tolerable strong, in such a case," said Phineas, stretching out a pair of arms like the sails of a windmill. "I an't sure, friend George, that I shouldn't hold a fellow for thee, if thee had any accounts to settle with him."

"If man should *ever* resist evil," said Simeon, "then George should feel free to do it now: but the leaders of our people taught a more excellent way; for the wrath of man worketh not the righteousness of God; but it goes sorely against the corrupt will of man, and none can receive it save they to whom it is given. Let us pray the Lord that we be not tempted."

"And so *I* do," said Phineas; "but if we are tempted too much – why, let them look out, that's all."

"It's quite plain thee wasn't born a Friend," said Simeon, smiling. "The old nature hath its way in thee pretty strong as yet."

To tell the truth, Phineas had been a hearty, two-fisted backwoodsman, a vigorous hunter, and a dead shot at a buck; but, having wooed a pretty Quakeress, had been moved by the power of her charms to join the society in his neighborhood; and though he was an honest, sober, and efficient member, and nothing particular could be alleged against him, yet the more spiritual among them could not but discern an exceeding lack of savor in his developments.

"Friend Phineas will ever have ways of his own," said Rachel Halliday, smiling; "but we all think that his heart is in the right place, after all."

"Well," said George, "isn't it best that we hasten our flight?"

"I got up at four o'clock, and came on with all speed, full two or three hours ahead of them, if they start at the time they planned. It isn't safe to start till dark, at any rate; for there are some evil persons in the villages ahead, that might be disposed to meddle with us, if they saw our wagon, and that would delay us more than the waiting; but in two hours I think we may venture. I will go over to Michael Cross, and engage him to come behind on his swift nag, and keep a bright lookout on the road, and warn us if any company of men come on. Michael keeps a horse that can soon get ahead of most other horses; and he could shoot ahead and let us know, if there were any danger. I am going out now to warn Jim and the old woman to be in readiness, and to see about the horse. We have a pretty fair start, and stand a good chance to get to the stand before they can come up with us. So, have good courage, friend George; this isn't the first ugly scrape that I've been in with thy people," said Phineas, as he closed the door.

"Phineas is pretty shrewd," said Simeon. "He will do the best that can be done for thee, George."

"All I am sorry for," said George, "is the risk to you."

"Thee'll much oblige us, friend George, to say no more about that. What we do we are conscience bound to do; we can do no other way. And now, mother," said he, turning to Rachel, "hurry thy preparations for these friends, for we must not send them away fasting."

And while Rachel and her children were busy making corn-cake, and cooking ham and chicken, and hurrying on the *et ceteras* of the evening meal, George and his wife sat in their little room, with their arms folded about each other, in such talk as husband and wife have when they know that a few hours may part them forever.

"Eliza," said George, "people that have friends, and houses, and lands, and money, and all those things *can't* love as we do, who have nothing but each other. Till I knew you, Eliza, no creature had loved me, but my poor, heart-broken mother and sister. I saw poor Emily that morning the trader carried her off. She came to the corner where I was lying asleep, and said, 'Poor George, your last friend is going. What will become of you, poor boy?' And I got up and threw my arms round her, and cried and sobbed, and she cried too; and those were the last kind words I got for ten long years; and my heart all withered up, and felt as dry as ashes, till I met you. And your loving me, – why, it was almost like raising one from the dead! I've been a new man ever since! And now, Eliza, I'll give my last drop of blood, but they *shall not* take you from me. Whoever gets you must walk over my dead body."

"O, Lord, have mercy!" said Eliza, sobbing. "If he will only let us get out of this country together, that is all we ask."

"Is God on their side?" said George, speaking less to his wife than pouring out his own bitter thoughts. "Does he see all they do? Why does he let such things happen? And they tell us that the Bible is on their side; certainly all the power is. They are rich, and healthy, and happy; they are members of churches, expecting to go to heaven; and they get along so easy in the world, and have it all their own way; and poor, honest, faithful Christians, - Christians as good or better than they, - are lying in the very dust under their feet. They buy 'em and sell 'em, and make trade of their heart's blood, and groans and tears, - and God *lets* them."

"Friend George," said Simeon, from the kitchen, "listen to this Psalm; it may do thee good."

George drew his seat near the door, and Eliza, wiping her tears, came forward also to listen, while Simeon read as follows:

> "But as for me, my feet were almost gone; my steps had well-nigh slipped. For I was envious of the foolish, when I saw the prosperity of the wicked. They are not in trouble like other men, neither are they plagued like other men. There-

> fore, pride compasseth them as a chain; violence covereth them as a garment. Their eyes stand out with fatness; they have more than heart could wish. They are corrupt, and speak wickedly concerning oppression; they speak loftily. Therefore his people return, and the waters of a full cup are wrung out to them, and they say, How doth God know? and is there knowledge in the Most High?"

"Is not that the way thee feels, George?"

"It is so indeed," said George, – "as well as I could have written it myself."

"Then, hear," said Simeon:

> "When I thought to know this, it was too painful for me until I went unto the sanctuary of God. Then understood I their end. Surely thou didst set them in slippery places, thou castedst them down to destruction. As a dream when one awaketh, so, oh Lord, when thou awakest, thou shalt despise their image. Nevertheless I am continually with thee; thou hast holden me by my right hand. Thou shalt guide me by thy counsel, and afterwards receive me to glory. It is good for me to draw near unto God. I have put my trust in the Lord God."[16]

---

16 Ps. 73, "The End of the Wicked contrasted with that of the Righteous."

The words of holy trust, breathed by the friendly old man, stole like sacred music over the harassed and chafed spirit of George; and after he ceased, he sat with a gentle and subdued expression on his fine features.

"If this world were all, George," said Simeon, "thee might, indeed, ask where is the Lord? But it is often those who have least of all in this life whom he chooseth for the kingdom. Put thy trust in him and, no matter what befalls thee here, he will make all right hereafter."

If these words had been spoken by some easy, self-indulgent exhorter, from whose mouth they might have come merely as pious and rhetorical flourish, proper to be used to people in distress, perhaps they might not have had much effect; but coming from one who daily and calmly risked fine and imprisonment for the cause of God and man, they had a weight that could not but be felt, and both the poor, desolate fugitives found calmness and strength breathing into them from it.

And now Rachel took Eliza's hand kindly, and led the way to the supper-table. As they were sitting down, a light tap sounded at the door, and Ruth entered.

"I just ran in," she said, "with these little stockings for the boy, – three pair, nice, warm woollen ones. It will be so cold, thee knows, in Canada. Does thee keep up good courage, Eliza?" she added, tripping round to Eliza's side of the table, and shaking her warmly by the hand, and slipping a seed-cake into Harry's hand. "I brought a little parcel of these for him," she said, tugging at her pocket to get out the package. "Children, thee knows, will always be eating."

"O, thank you; you are too kind," said Eliza.

"Come, Ruth, sit down to supper," said Rachel.

"I couldn't, any way. I left John with the baby, and some biscuits in the oven; and I can't stay a moment, else John will burn up all the biscuits, and give the baby all the sugar in the bowl. That's the way he does," said the little Quakeress, laughing. "So, good-by, Eliza; good-by, George; the Lord grant thee a safe journey;" and, with a few tripping steps, Ruth was out of the apartment.

A little while after supper, a large covered-wagon drew up before the door; the night was clear starlight; and Phineas jumped briskly down from his seat to arrange his passengers. George walked out of the door, with his child on one arm and his wife on the other. His step was firm, his face settled and resolute. Rachel and Simeon came out after them.

"You get out, a moment," said Phineas to those inside, "and let me fix the back of the wagon, there, for the women-folks and the boy."

"Here are the two buffaloes," said Rachel. "Make the seats as comfortable as may be; it's hard riding all night."

Jim came out first, and carefully assisted out his old mother, who clung to his arm, and looked anxiously about, as if she expected the pursuer every moment.

"Jim, are your pistols all in order?" said George, in a low, firm voice.

"Yes, indeed," said Jim.

"And you've no doubt what you shall do, if they come?"

"I rather think I haven't," said Jim, throwing open his broad chest, and taking a deep breath. "Do you think I'll let them get mother again?"

During this brief colloquy, Eliza had been taking her leave of her kind friend, Rachel, and was handed into the carriage by Simeon, and, creeping into the back part with her boy, sat down among the buffalo-skins. The old woman was next handed in and seated and George and Jim placed on a rough board seat front of them, and Phineas mounted in front.

"Farewell, my friends," said Simeon, from without.

"God bless you!" answered all from within.

And the wagon drove off, rattling and jolting over the frozen road.

There was no opportunity for conversation, on account of the roughness of the way and the noise of the wheels. The vehicle, therefore, rumbled on, through long, dark stretches of woodland, – over wide dreary plains, – up hills, and down valleys, – and on, on, on they jogged, hour after hour. The child soon fell asleep, and lay heavily in his mother's lap. The poor, frightened old woman at last forgot her fears; and, even Eliza, as the night waned, found all her anxieties insufficient to keep her eyes from closing. Phineas seemed, on the whole, the briskest of the company, and beguiled his long drive with whistling certain very unquaker-like songs, as he went on.

But about three o'clock George's ear caught the hasty and decided click of a horse's hoof coming behind them at some distance and jogged Phineas by the elbow. Phineas pulled up his horses, and listened.

"That must be Michael," he said; "I think I know the sound of his gallop;" and he rose up and stretched his head anxiously back over the road.

A man riding in hot haste was now dimly descried at the top of a distant hill.

"There he is, I do believe!" said Phineas. George and Jim both sprang out of the wagon before they knew what they were doing. All stood intensely silent, with their faces turned towards the expected messenger. On he came. Now he went down into a valley, where they could not see him; but they heard the sharp, hasty tramp, rising nearer and nearer; at last they saw him emerge on the top of an eminence, within hail.

"Yes, that's Michael!" said Phineas; and, raising his voice, "Halloa, there, Michael!"

"Phineas! is that thee?"

"Yes; what news – they coming?"

"Right on behind, eight or ten of them, hot with brandy, swearing and foaming like so many wolves."

And, just as he spoke, a breeze brought the faint sound of galloping horsemen towards them.

"In with you, – quick, boys, *in!*" said Phineas. "If you must fight, wait till I get you a piece ahead." And, with the word, both jumped in, and Phineas lashed the horses to a run, the horseman keeping close beside them. The wagon rattled, jumped, almost flew, over the frozen ground; but plainer, and still plainer, came the noise of pursuing horsemen behind. The women heard it, and, looking anxiously out, saw, far in the rear, on the brow of a distant hill, a party of men looming up against the red-streaked sky of early dawn. Another hill, and their pursuers had evidently caught sight of their wagon, whose white cloth-covered top made it conspicuous at some distance, and a loud yell of brutal triumph came forward on the wind. Eliza sickened, and strained her child closer to her bosom; the old woman prayed and groaned, and George and Jim clenched their pistols with the grasp of despair. The pursuers gained on them fast; the carriage made a sudden turn, and brought them near a ledge of a steep overhanging rock, that rose in an isolated ridge or clump in a large lot, which was, all around it, quite clear and smooth. This isolated pile, or range of rocks, rose up black and heavy against the brightening sky, and seemed to promise shelter and concealment. It was a place well known to Phineas, who had been familiar with the spot in his hunting days; and it was to gain this point he had been racing his horses.

"Now for it!" said he, suddenly checking his horses, and springing from his seat to the ground. "Out with you, in a twinkling, every one, and up into these rocks with me. Michael, thee tie thy horse to the wagon, and drive ahead to Amariah's and get him and his boys to come back and talk to these fellows."

In a twinkling they were all out of the carriage.

"There," said Phineas, catching up Harry, "you, each of you, see to the women; and run, *now* if you ever *did* run!"

They needed no exhortation. Quicker than we can say it, the whole party were over the fence, making with all speed for the rocks, while Michael, throwing himself from his horse, and fastening the bridle to the wagon, began driving it rapidly away.

"Come ahead," said Phineas, as they reached the rocks, and saw in the mingled starlight and dawn, the traces of a rude but plainly marked foot-path leading up among them; "this is one of our old hunting-dens. Come up!"

Phineas went before, springing up the rocks like a goat, with the boy in his arms. Jim came second, bearing his trembling old mother over his shoulder, and George and Eliza brought up the rear. The party of horsemen came up to the fence, and, with mingled shouts and oaths, were dismounting, to prepare to follow them. A few moments' scrambling brought them to the top of the ledge; the path then passed between a narrow defile, where only one could walk at a time, till suddenly they came to a rift or chasm more than a yard in breadth, and beyond which lay a pile of rocks, separate from the rest of the ledge, standing full thirty feet high, with its sides steep and perpendicular as those of a castle. Phineas easily leaped the chasm, and sat down the boy on a smooth, flat platform of crisp white moss, that covered the top of the rock.

"Over with you!" he called; "spring, now, once, for your lives!" said he, as one after another sprang across. Several fragments of loose stone formed a kind of breast-work, which sheltered their position from the observation of those below.

"Well, here we all are," said Phineas, peeping over the stone breast-work to watch the assailants, who were coming tumultuously up under the rocks. "Let 'em get us, if they can. Whoever comes here has to walk single file between those two rocks, in fair range of your pistols, boys, d'ye see?"

"I do see," said George! "and now, as this matter is ours, let us take all the risk, and do all the fighting."

"Thee's quite welcome to do the fighting, George," said Phineas, chewing some checkerberry-leaves as he spoke; "but I may have the fun of looking on, I suppose. But see, these fellows are kinder debating down there, and looking up, like hens when they are going to fly up on to the roost. Hadn't thee better give 'em a word of advice, before they come up, just to tell 'em handsomely they'll be shot if they do?"

The party beneath, now more apparent in the light of the dawn, consisted of our old acquaintances, Tom Loker and Marks, with two constables, and a posse consisting of such rowdies at the last tavern as could be engaged by a little brandy to go and help the fun of trapping a set of niggers.

"Well, Tom, yer coons are farly treed," said one.

"Yes, I see 'em go up right here," said Tom; "and here's a path. I'm for going right up. They can't jump down in a hurry, and it won't take long to ferret 'em out."

"But, Tom, they might fire at us from behind the rocks," said Marks. "That would be ugly, you know."

"Ugh!" said Tom, with a sneer. "Always for saving your skin, Marks! No danger! niggers are too plaguy scared!"

"I don't know why I *shouldn't* save my skin," said Marks. "It's the best I've got; and niggers *do* fight like the devil, sometimes."

At this moment, George appeared on the top of a rock above them, and, speaking in a calm, clear voice, said,

"Gentlemen, who are you, down there, and what do you want?"

"We want a party of runaway niggers," said Tom Loker. "One George Harris, and Eliza Harris, and their son, and Jim Selden, and an old woman. We've got the officers, here, and a warrant to take 'em; and we're going to have 'em, too. D'ye hear? An't you George Harris, that belongs to Mr. Harris, of Shelby county, Kentucky?"

"I am George Harris. A Mr. Harris, of Kentucky, did call me his property. But now I'm a free man, standing on God's free soil; and my wife and my child I claim as mine. Jim and his mother are here. We have arms to defend ourselves, and we mean to do it. You can come up, if you like; but the first one of you that comes within the range of our bullets is a dead man, and the next, and the next; and so on till the last."

"O, come! come!" said a short, puffy man, stepping forward, and blowing his nose as he did so. "Young man, this an't no kind of talk at all for you. You see, we're officers of justice. We've got the law on our side, and the power, and so forth; so you'd better give up peaceably, you see; for you'll certainly have to give up, at last."

"I know very well that you've got the law on your side, and the power," said George, bitterly. "You mean to take my wife to sell in New Orleans, and put my boy like a calf in a trader's pen, and send Jim's old mother to the brute that whipped and abused her before, because he couldn't abuse her son. You want to send Jim and me back to be whipped and tortured, and ground down under the heels of them that you call masters; and your laws *will* bear you out in it, - more shame for you and them! But you haven't got us. We don't own your laws; we don't own your country; we stand here as free, under God's sky, as you are; and, by the great God that made us, we'll fight for our liberty till we die."

George stood out in fair sight, on the top of the rock, as he made his declaration of independence; the glow of dawn gave a flush to his swarthy cheek, and bitter indignation and despair gave fire to his dark eye; and, as if appealing from man to the justice of God, he raised his hand to heaven as he spoke.

If it had been only a Hungarian youth, now bravely defending in some mountain fastness the retreat of fugitives escaping from Austria into America, this would have been sublime heroism; but as it was a youth of African descent, defending the retreat of fugitives through America into Canada, of course we are too well instructed and patriotic to see any heroism in it; and if any of our readers do, they must do it on their own private responsibility. When despairing Hungarian fugitives make their way, against all the search-warrants and authorities of their lawful government, to America, press and political cabinet ring with applause and welcome. When despairing African fugitives do the same thing, – it is – what *is* it?

Be it as it may, it is certain that the attitude, eye, voice, manner, of the speaker for a moment struck the party below to silence. There is something in boldness and determination that for a time hushes even the rudest nature. Marks was the only one who remained wholly untouched. He was deliberately cocking his pistol, and, in the momentary silence that followed George's speech, he fired at him.

"Ye see ye get jist as much for him dead as alive in Kentucky," he said coolly, as he wiped his pistol on his coat-sleeve.

George sprang backward, – Eliza uttered a shriek, – the ball had passed close to his hair, had nearly grazed the cheek of his wife, and struck in the tree above.

"It's nothing, Eliza," said George, quickly.

"Thee'd better keep out of sight, with thy speechifying," said Phineas; "they're mean scamps."

"Now, Jim," said George, "look that your pistols are all right, and watch that pass with me. The first man that shows himself I fire at; you take the second, and so on. It won't do, you know, to waste two shots on one."

"But what if you don't hit?"

"I *shall* hit," said George, coolly.

"Good! now, there's stuff in that fellow," muttered Phineas, between his teeth.

The party below, after Marks had fired, stood, for a moment, rather undecided.

"I think you must have hit some on 'em," said one of the men. "I heard a squeal!"

"I'm going right up for one," said Tom. "I never was afraid of niggers, and I an't going to be now. Who goes after?" he said, springing up the rocks.

George heard the words distinctly. He drew up his pistol, examined it, pointed it towards that point in the defile where the first man would appear.

One of the most courageous of the party followed Tom, and, the way being thus made, the whole party began pushing up the rock, – the hindermost pushing the front ones faster than they would have gone of themselves. On they came, and in a moment the burly form of Tom appeared in sight, almost at the verge of the chasm.

George fired, – the shot entered his side, – but, though wounded, he would not retreat, but, with a yell like that of a mad bull, he was leaping right across the chasm into the party.

"Friend," said Phineas, suddenly stepping to the front, and meeting him with a push from his long arms, "thee isn't wanted here."

Down he fell into the chasm, crackling down among trees, bushes, logs, loose stones, till he lay bruised and groaning thirty feet below. The fall might have killed him, had it not been broken and moderated by his clothes catching in the branches of a large tree; but he came down with some force, however, – more than was at all agreeable or convenient.

"Lord help us, they are perfect devils!" said Marks, heading the retreat down the rocks with much more of a will than he had joined the ascent, while all the party came tumbling precipitately after him, – the fat constable, in particular, blowing and puffing in a very energetic manner.

"I say, fellers," said Marks, "you jist go round and pick up Tom, there, while I run and get on to my horse to go back for help, – that's you;" and, without minding the hootings and jeers of his company, Marks was as good as his word, and was soon seen galloping away.

"Was ever such a sneaking varmint?" said one of the men; "to come on his business, and he clear out and leave us this yer way!"

"Well, we must pick up that feller," said another. "Cuss me if I much care whether he is dead or alive."

The men, led by the groans of Tom, scrambled and crackled through stumps, logs and bushes, to where that hero lay groaning and swearing with alternate vehemence.

"Ye keep it agoing pretty loud, Tom," said one. "Ye much hurt?"

"Don't know. Get me up, can't ye? Blast that infernal Quaker! If it hadn't been for him, I'd a pitched some on 'em down here, to see how they liked it."

With much labor and groaning, the fallen hero was assisted to rise; and, with one holding him up under each shoulder, they got him as far as the horses.

"If you could only get me a mile back to that ar tavern. Give me a handkerchief or something, to stuff into this place, and stop this infernal bleeding."

George looked over the rocks, and saw them trying to lift the burly form of Tom into the saddle. After two or three ineffectual attempts, he reeled, and fell heavily to the ground.

"O, I hope he isn't killed!" said Eliza, who, with all the party, stood watching the proceeding.

"Why not?" said Phineas; "serves him right."

"Because after death comes the judgment," said Eliza.

"Yes," said the old woman, who had been groaning and praying, in her Methodist fashion, during all the encounter, "it's an awful case for the poor crittur's soul."

"On my word, they're leaving him, I do believe," said Phineas.

It was true; for after some appearance of irresolution and consultation, the whole party got on their horses and rode away. When they were quite out of sight, Phineas began to bestir himself.

"Well, we must go down and walk a piece," he said. "I told Michael to go forward and bring help, and be along back here with the wagon; but we shall have to walk a piece along the road, I reckon, to meet them. The Lord grant he be along soon! It's early in the day; there won't be much travel afoot yet a while; we an't much more than two miles from our stopping-place. If the road hadn't been so rough last night, we could have outrun 'em entirely."

As the party neared the fence, they discovered in the distance, along the road, their own wagon coming back, accompanied by some men on horseback.

"Well, now, there's Michael, and Stephen and Amariah," exclaimed Phineas, joyfully. "Now we *are* made - as safe as if we'd got there."

"Well, do stop, then," said Eliza, "and do something for that poor man; he's groaning dreadfully."

"It would be no more than Christian," said George; "let's take him up and carry him on."

"And doctor him up among the Quakers!" said Phineas; "pretty well, that! Well, I don't care if we do. Here, let's have a look at him;" and Phineas, who in the course of his hunting and backwoods life had acquired some rude experience of surgery, kneeled down by the wounded man, and began a careful examination of his condition.

"Marks," said Tom, feebly, "is that you, Marks?"

"No; I reckon 'tan't friend," said Phineas. "Much Marks cares for thee, if his own skin's safe. He's off, long ago."

"I believe I'm done for," said Tom. "The cussed sneaking dog, to leave me to die alone! My poor old mother always told me 't would be so."

"La sakes! jist hear the poor crittur. He's got a mammy, now," said the old negress. "I can't help kinder pityin' on him."

"Softly, softly; don't thee snap and snarl, friend," said Phineas, as Tom winced and pushed his hand away. "Thee has no chance, unless I stop the bleeding." And Phineas busied himself with making some off-hand surgical arrangements with his own pocket-handkerchief, and such as could be mustered in the company.

"You pushed me down there," said Tom, faintly.

"Well if I hadn't thee would have pushed us down, thee sees," said Phineas, as he stooped to apply his bandage. "There, there, – let me fix this bandage. We mean well to thee; we bear no malice. Thee shall be taken to a house where they'll nurse thee first rate, well as thy own mother could."

Tom groaned, and shut his eyes. In men of his class, vigor and resolution are entirely a physical matter, and ooze out with the flowing of the blood; and the gigantic fellow really looked piteous in his helplessness.

The other party now came up. The seats were taken out of the wagon. The buffalo-skins, doubled in fours, were spread all along one side, and four men, with great difficulty, lifted the heavy form of Tom into it. Before he was gotten in, he fainted entirely. The old negress, in the abundance of her compassion, sat down on the bottom, and took his head in her lap. Eliza, George and Jim, bestowed themselves, as well as they could, in the remaining space and the whole party set forward.

"What do you think of him?" said George, who sat by Phineas in front.

"Well it's only a pretty deep flesh-wound; but, then, tumbling and scratching down that place didn't help him much. It has bled pretty freely, – pretty much drained him out, courage and all, – but he'll get over it, and may be learn a thing or two by it."

"I'm glad to hear you say so," said George. "It would always be a heavy thought to me, if I'd caused his death, even in a just cause."

"Yes," said Phineas, "killing is an ugly operation, any way they'll fix it, - man or beast. I've seen a buck that was shot down and a dying, look that way on a feller with his eye, that it reely most made a feller feel wicked for killing on him; and human creatures is a more serious consideration yet, bein', as thy wife says, that the judgment comes to 'em after death. So I don't know as our people's notions on these matters is too strict; and, considerin' how I was raised, I fell in with them pretty considerably."

"What shall you do with this poor fellow?" said George.

"O, carry him along to Amariah's. There's old Grandmam Stephens there, - Dorcas, they call her, - she's most an amazin' nurse. She takes to nursing real natural, and an't never better suited than when she gets a sick body to tend. We may reckon on turning him over to her for a fortnight or so."

A ride of about an hour more brought the party to a neat farmhouse, where the weary travellers were received to an abundant breakfast. Tom Loker was soon carefully deposited in a much cleaner and softer bed than he had, ever been in the habit of occupying. His wound was carefully dressed and bandaged, and he lay languidly opening and shutting his eyes on the white window-curtains and gently-gliding figures of his sick room, like a weary child. And here, for the present, we shall take our leave of one party.

Chapter 18

Miss Ophelia's Experiences and Opinions

Our friend Tom, in his own simple musings, often compared his more fortunate lot, in the bondage into which he was cast, with that of Joseph in Egypt; and, in fact, as time went on, and he developed more and more under the eye of his master, the strength of the parallel increased.

St. Clare was indolent and careless of money. Hitherto the providing and marketing had been principally done by Adolph, who was, to the full, as careless and extravagant as his master; and, between them both, they had carried on the dispersing process with great alacrity. Accustomed, for many years, to regard his master's property as his own care, Tom saw, with an uneasiness he could scarcely repress, the wasteful expenditure of the establishment; and, in the quiet, indirect way which his class often acquire, would sometimes make his own suggestions.

St. Clare at first employed him occasionally; but, struck with his soundness of mind and good business capacity, he confided in him more and more, till gradually all the marketing and providing for the family were intrusted to him.

"No, no, Adolph," he said, one day, as Adolph was deprecating the passing of power out of his hands; "let Tom alone. You only understand what you want; Tom understands cost and come to; and there may be some end to money, bye and bye if we don't let somebody do that."

Trusted to an unlimited extent by a careless master, who handed him a bill without looking at it, and pocketed the change without counting it, Tom had every facility and temptation to dishonesty; and nothing but an impregnable simplicity of nature, strengthened by Christian faith, could have kept him from it. But, to that nature, the very unbounded trust reposed in him was bond and seal for the most scrupulous accuracy.

With Adolph the case had been different. Thoughtless and self-indulgent, and unrestrained by a master who found it easier to indulge than to regulate, he had fallen into an absolute confusion as to *meum tuum* with regard to himself and his master, which sometimes troubled even St. Clare. His own good sense taught him that such a training of his servants was unjust and dangerous. A sort of chronic remorse went with him everywhere, although not strong enough to make any decided change in his course; and this very remorse reacted again into indulgence. He passed lightly over the most serious faults, because he told himself that, if he had done his part, his dependents had not fallen into them.

Tom regarded his gay, airy, handsome young master with an odd mixture of fealty, reverence, and fatherly solicitude. That he never read the Bible; never went to church; that he jested and made free with any and every thing that came in the way of his wit; that he spent his Sunday evenings at the opera or theatre;

that he went to wine parties, and clubs, and suppers, oftener than was at all expedient, – were all things that Tom could see as plainly as anybody, and on which he based a conviction that "Mas'r wasn't a Christian;" – a conviction, however, which he would have been very slow to express to any one else, but on which he founded many prayers, in his own simple fashion, when he was by himself in his little dormitory. Not that Tom had not his own way of speaking his mind occasionally, with something of the tact often observable in his class; as, for example, the very day after the Sabbath we have described, St. Clare was invited out to a convivial party of choice spirits, and was helped home, between one and two o'clock at night, in a condition when the physical had decidedly attained the upper hand of the intellectual. Tom and Adolph assisted to get him composed for the night, the latter in high spirits, evidently regarding the matter as a good joke, and laughing heartily at the rusticity of Tom's horror, who really was simple enough to lie awake most of the rest of the night, praying for his young master.

"Well, Tom, what are you waiting for?" said St. Clare, the next day, as he sat in his library, in dressing-gown and slippers. St. Clare had just been entrusting Tom with some money, and various commissions. "Isn't all right there, Tom?" he added, as Tom still stood waiting.

"I'm 'fraid not, Mas'r," said Tom, with a grave face.

St. Clare laid down his paper, and set down his coffee-cup, and looked at Tom.

"Why Tom, what's the case? You look as solemn as a coffin."

"I feel very bad, Mas'r. I allays have thought that Mas'r would be good to everybody."

"Well, Tom, haven't I been? Come, now, what do you want? There's something you haven't got, I suppose, and this is the preface."

"Mas'r allays been good to me. I haven't nothing to complain of on that head. But there is one that Mas'r isn't good to."

"Why, Tom, what's got into you? Speak out; what do you mean?"

"Last night, between one and two, I thought so. I studied upon the matter then. Mas'r isn't good to *himself*."

Tom said this with his back to his master, and his hand on the door-knob. St. Clare felt his face flush crimson, but he laughed.

"O, that's all, is it?" he said, gayly.

"All!" said Tom, turning suddenly round and falling on his knees. "O, my dear young Mas'r; I'm 'fraid it will be *loss of all – all* – body and soul. The good Book says, 'it biteth like a serpent and stingeth like an adder!' my dear Mas'r!"

Tom's voice choked, and the tears ran down his cheeks.

"You poor, silly fool!" said St. Clare, with tears in his own eyes. "Get up, Tom. I'm not worth crying over."

But Tom wouldn't rise, and looked imploring.

"Well, I won't go to any more of their cursed nonsense, Tom," said St. Clare; "on my honor, I won't. I don't know why I haven't stopped long ago. I've always despised *it*, and myself for it, – so now, Tom, wipe up your eyes, and go about your errands. Come, come," he added, "no blessings. I'm not so wonderfully good, now," he said, as he gently pushed Tom to the door. "There, I'll pledge my honor to you, Tom, you don't see me so again," he said; and Tom went off, wiping his eyes, with great satisfaction.

"I'll keep my faith with him, too," said St. Clare, as he closed the door.

And St. Clare did so, – for gross sensualism, in any form, was not the peculiar temptation of his nature.

But, all this time, who shall detail the tribulations manifold of our friend Miss Ophelia, who had begun the labors of a Southern housekeeper?

There is all the difference in the world in the servants of Southern establishments, according to the character and capacity of the mistresses who have brought them up.

South as well as north, there are women who have an extraordinary talent for command, and tact in educating. Such are enabled, with apparent ease, and without severity, to subject to their will, and bring into harmonious and systematic order, the various members of their small estate, – to regulate their peculiarities, and so balance and compensate the deficiencies of one by the excess of another, as to produce a harmonious and orderly system.

Such a housekeeper was Mrs. Shelby, whom we have already described; and such our readers may remember to have met with. If they are not common at the South, it is because they are not common in the world. They are to be found there as often as anywhere; and, when existing, find in that peculiar state of society a brilliant opportunity to exhibit their domestic talent.

Such a housekeeper Marie St. Clare was not, nor her mother before her. Indolent and childish, unsystematic and improvident, it was not to be expected that servants trained under her care should not be so likewise; and she had very justly described to Miss Ophelia the state of confusion she would find in the family, though she had not ascribed it to the proper cause.

The first morning of her regency, Miss Ophelia was up at four o'clock; and having attended to all the adjustments of her own chamber, as she had done ever since she came there, to the great amazement of the chambermaid, she prepared for a vigorous onslaught on the cupboards and closets of the establishment of which she had the keys.

The store-room, the linen-presses, the china-closet, the kitchen and cellar, that day, all went under an awful review. Hidden things of darkness were brought to light to an extent that alarmed all the principalities and powers of kitchen and chamber, and caused many wonderings and murmurings about "dese yer northern ladies" from the domestic cabinet.

Old Dinah, the head cook, and principal of all rule and authority in the kitchen department, was filled with wrath at what she considered an invasion of privilege. No feudal baron in Magna Charta times could have more thoroughly resented some incursion of the crown.

Dinah was a character in her own way, and it would be injustice to her memory not to give the reader a little idea of her. She was a native and essential cook, as much as Aunt Chloe, - cooking being an indigenous talent of the African race; but Chloe was a trained and methodical one, who moved in an orderly domestic harness, while Dinah was a self-taught genius, and, like geniuses in general, was positive, opinionated and erratic, to the last degree.

Like a certain class of modern philosophers, Dinah perfectly scorned logic and reason in every shape, and always took refuge in intuitive certainty; and here she was perfectly impregnable. No possible amount of talent, or authority, or explanation, could ever make her believe that any other way was better than her own, or that the course she had pursued in the smallest matter could be in the least modified. This had been a conceded point with her old mistress, Marie's mother; and "Miss Marie," as Dinah always called her young mistress, even after her marriage, found it easier to submit than contend; and so Dinah had ruled supreme. This was the easier, in that she was perfect mistress of that diplomatic art which unites the utmost subservience of manner with the utmost inflexibility as to measure.

Dinah was mistress of the whole art and mystery of excuse-making, in all its branches. Indeed, it was an axiom with her that the cook can do no wrong; and a cook in a Southern kitchen finds abundance of heads and shoulders on which to lay off every sin and frailty, so as to maintain her own immaculateness entire. If any part of the dinner was a failure, there were fifty indisputably good reasons for it; and it was the fault undeniably of fifty other people, whom Dinah berated with unsparing zeal.

But it was very seldom that there was any failure in Dinah's last results. Though her mode of doing everything was peculiarly meandering and circuitous, and without any sort of calculation as to time and place, - though her kitchen generally looked as if it had been arranged by a hurricane blowing through it, and she had about as many places for each cooking utensil as there were days in the year, - yet, if one would have patience to wait her own good time, up would come her dinner in perfect order, and in a style of preparation with which an epicure could find no fault.

It was now the season of incipient preparation for dinner. Dinah, who required large intervals of reflection and repose, and was studious of ease in all her arrangements, was seated on the kitchen floor, smoking a short, stumpy pipe, to which she was much addicted, and which she always kindled up, as a sort of censer, whenever she felt the need of an inspiration in her arrangements. It was Dinah's mode of invoking the domestic Muses.

Seated around her were various members of that rising race with which a Southern household abounds, engaged in shelling peas, peeling potatoes, picking pin-feathers out of fowls, and other preparatory arrangements, - Dinah every once in a while interrupting her meditations to give a poke, or a rap on the head, to some of the young operators, with the pudding-stick that lay by her side. In fact, Dinah ruled over the woolly heads of the younger members with a rod of iron, and seemed to consider them born for no earthly purpose but to "save her steps," as she phrased it. It was the spirit of the system under which she had grown up, and she carried it out to its full extent.

Miss Ophelia, after passing on her reformatory tour through all the other parts of the establishment, now entered the kitchen. Dinah had heard, from various sources, what was going on, and resolved to stand on defensive and conservative ground, - mentally determined to oppose and ignore every new measure, without any actual observable contest.

The kitchen was a large brick-floored apartment, with a great old-fashioned fireplace stretching along one side of it, - an arrangement which St. Clare had vainly tried to persuade Dinah to exchange for the convenience of a modern cookstove. Not she. No Puseyite,[17] or conservative of

---

17 Edward Bouverie Pusey (1800-1882), champion of the orthodoxy of revealed religion, defender of the Oxford

any school, was ever more inflexibly attached to time-honored inconveniences than Dinah.

When St. Clare had first returned from the north, impressed with the system and order of his uncle's kitchen arrangements, he had largely provided his own with an array of cupboards, drawers, and various apparatus, to induce systematic regulation, under the sanguine illusion that it would be of any possible assistance to Dinah in her arrangements. He might as well have provided them for a squirrel or a magpie. The more drawers and closets there were, the more hiding-holes could Dinah make for the accommodation of old rags, hair-combs, old shoes, ribbons, cast-off artificial flowers, and other articles of *vertu*, wherein her soul delighted.

When Miss Ophelia entered the kitchen Dinah did not rise, but smoked on in sublime tranquillity, regarding her movements obliquely out of the corner of her eye, but apparently intent only on the operations around her.

Miss Ophelia commenced opening a set of drawers.

"What is this drawer for, Dinah?" she said.

"It's handy for most anything, Missis," said Dinah. So it appeared to be. From the variety it contained, Miss Ophelia pulled out first a fine damask table-cloth

---

movement, and Regius professor of Hebrew and Canon of Christ Church, Oxford.

stained with blood, having evidently been used to envelop some raw meat.

"What's this, Dinah? You don't wrap up meat in your mistress' best table-cloths?"

"O Lor, Missis, no; the towels was all a missin' - so I jest did it. I laid out to wash that a, - that's why I put it thar."

"Shif'less!" said Miss Ophelia to herself, proceeding to tumble over the drawer, where she found a nutmeg-grater and two or three nutmegs, a Methodist hymn-book, a couple of soiled Madras handkerchiefs, some yarn and knitting-work, a paper of tobacco and a pipe, a few crackers, one or two gilded china-saucers with some pomade in them, one or two thin old shoes, a piece of flannel carefully pinned up enclosing some small white onions, several damask table-napkins, some coarse crash towels, some twine and darning-needles, and several broken papers, from which sundry sweet herbs were sifting into the drawer.

"Where do you keep your nutmegs, Dinah?" said Miss Ophelia, with the air of one who prayed for patience.

"Most anywhar, Missis; there's some in that cracked tea-cup, up there, and there's some over in that ar cupboard."

"Here are some in the grater," said Miss Ophelia, holding them up.

"Laws, yes, I put 'em there this morning, - I likes to keep my things handy," said Dinah. "You, Jake! what are you stopping for! You'll cotch it! Be still, thar!" she added, with a dive of her stick at the criminal.

"What's this?" said Miss Ophelia, holding up the saucer of pomade.

"Laws, it's my har *grease*; – I put it thar to have it handy."

"Do you use your mistress' best saucers for that?"

"Law! it was cause I was driv, and in sich a hurry; – I was gwine to change it this very day."

"Here are two damask table-napkins."

"Them table-napkins I put thar, to get 'em washed out, some day."

"Don't you have some place here on purpose for things to be washed?"

"Well, Mas'r St. Clare got dat ar chest, he said, for dat; but I likes to mix up biscuit and hev my things on it some days, and then it an't handy a liftin' up the lid."

"Why don't you mix your biscuits on the pastry-table, there?"

"Law, Missis, it gets sot so full of dishes, and one thing and another, der an't no room, noway–"

"But you should *wash* your dishes, and clear them away."

"Wash my dishes!" said Dinah, in a high key, as her wrath began to rise over her habitual respect of manner; "what does ladies know 'bout work, I want to know? When 'd Mas'r ever get his dinner, if I vas to spend all my time a washin' and a puttin' up dishes? Miss Marie never telled me so, nohow."

"Well, here are these onions."

"Laws, yes!" said Dinah; "thar *is* whar I put 'em, now. I couldn't 'member. Them 's particular onions I was a savin' for dis yer very stew. I'd forgot they was in dat ar old flannel."

Miss Ophelia lifted out the sifting papers of sweet herbs.

"I wish Missis wouldn't touch dem ar. I likes to keep my things where I knows whar to go to 'em," said Dinah, rather decidedly.

"But you don't want these holes in the papers."

"Them 's handy for siftin' on 't out," said Dinah.

"But you see it spills all over the drawer."

"Laws, yes! if Missis will go a tumblin' things all up so, it will. Missis has spilt lots dat ar way," said Dinah, coming uneasily to the drawers. "If Missis only will go up stars till my clarin' up time comes, I'll have everything right; but I can't do nothin' when ladies is round, a henderin'. You, Sam, don't you gib the baby dat ar sugar-bowl! I'll crack ye over, if ye don't mind!"

"I'm going through the kitchen, and going to put everything in order, *once*, Dinah; and then I'll expect you to *keep* it so."

"Lor, now! Miss Phelia; dat ar an't no way for ladies to do. I never did see ladies doin' no sich; my old Missis nor Miss Marie never did, and I don't see no kinder need on 't;" and Dinah stalked indignantly about, while Miss Ophelia piled and sorted dishes, emptied dozens of scattering bowls of sugar into one receptacle, sorted napkins, table-cloths, and towels, for washing; washing, wiping, and arranging with her own hands, and with a speed and alacrity which perfectly amazed Dinah.

"Lor now! if dat ar de way dem northern ladies do, dey an't ladies, nohow," she said to some of her satellites, when at a safe hearing distance. "I has things as straight as anybody, when my clarin' up times comes; but I don't want ladies round, a henderin', and getting my things all where I can't find 'em."

To do Dinah justice, she had, at irregular periods, paroxyms of reformation and arrangement, which she called "clarin' up times," when she would begin with great zeal, and turn every drawer and closet wrong side outward, on to the floor or tables, and make the ordinary confusion seven-fold more confounded. Then she would light her pipe, and leisurely go over her arrangements, looking things over, and discoursing upon them; making all the young fry scour most vigorously on the tin things, and keeping up for several hours a most energetic state of confusion, which she would explain to the satisfaction of all inquirers, by the remark that she was a "clarin' up." "She couldn't hev things a gwine on so as they had been, and she was gwine to make these yer young ones keep better order;" for Dinah herself, somehow, indulged the illusion that she, herself, was the soul of order, and it was only the *young uns*, and the everybody else in the house, that were the cause of anything that fell short of perfection in this respect. When all the tins were scoured, and the tables scrubbed snowy white, and everything that could offend tucked out of sight in holes and corners, Dinah would dress herself up in a smart dress, clean apron, and high, brilliant Madras turban, and tell all marauding "young uns" to keep out of the kitchen, for she was gwine to have things kept nice. Indeed, these periodic seasons were often an inconvenience to the whole household; for Dinah would contract such an immoderate attachment to her scoured tin, as to insist upon it that it shouldn't be used again for any possible purpose, - at least, till the ardor of the "clarin' up" period abated.

Miss Ophelia, in a few days, thoroughly reformed every department of the house to a systematic pattern; but her labors in all departments that depended on the cooperation of servants were like those of Sisyphus or the Danaides. In despair, she one day appealed to St. Clare.

"There is no such thing as getting anything like a system in this family!"

"To be sure, there isn't," said St. Clare.

"Such shiftless management, such waste, such confusion, I never saw!"

"I dare say you didn't."

"You would not take it so coolly, if you were housekeeper."

"My dear cousin, you may as well understand, once for all, that we masters are divided into two classes, oppressors and oppressed. We who are good-natured and hate severity make up our minds to a good deal of inconvenience. If we *will keep* a shambling, loose, untaught set in the community, for our convenience, why, we must take the consequence. Some rare cases I have seen, of persons, who, by a peculiar tact, can produce order and system without severity; but I'm not one of them, – and so I made up my mind, long ago, to let things go just as they do. I will not have the poor devils thrashed and cut to pieces, and they know it, – and, of course, they know the staff is in their own hands."

"But to have no time, no place, no order, – all going on in this shiftless way!"

"My dear Vermont, you natives up by the North Pole set an extravagant value on time! What on earth is the use of time to a fellow who has twice as much of it as he knows what to do with? As to order and system, where there is nothing to be done but to lounge on the sofa and read, an hour sooner or later in breakfast or dinner isn't of much account. Now, there's Dinah gets you a capital dinner, – soup, ragout, roast fowl, dessert, ice-creams and all, – and she creates it all out of chaos and old night down there, in that kitchen. I think it really sublime, the way she manages. But, Heaven bless us! if we are to go down there, and view all the smoking and squatting about, and hurryscurryation of the preparatory process, we should never eat more! My good cousin, absolve yourself from that! It's more than a Catholic penance, and does no more good. You'll only lose your own temper, and utterly confound Dinah. Let her go her own way."

"But, Augustine, you don't know how I found things."

"Don't I? Don't I know that the rolling-pin is under her bed, and the nutmeg-grater in her pocket with her tobacco, – that there are sixty-five different sugar-bowls, one in every hole in the house, – that she washes dishes with a dinner-napkin one day, and with a fragment of an old petticoat the next? But the upshot is, she gets up glorious dinners, makes superb coffee; and you must judge her as warriors and statesmen are judged, *by her success*."

"But the waste, – the expense!"

"O, well! Lock everything you can, and keep the key. Give out by driblets, and never inquire for odds and ends, – it isn't best."

"That troubles me, Augustine. I can't help feeling as if these servants were not *strictly honest*. Are you sure they can be relied on?"

Augustine laughed immoderately at the grave and anxious face with which Miss Ophelia propounded the question.

"O, cousin, that's too good, – *honest!* – as if that's a thing to be expected! Honest! – why, of course, they arn't. Why should they be? What upon earth is to make them so?"

"Why don't you instruct?"

"Instruct! O, fiddlestick! What instructing do you think I should do? I look like it! As to Marie, she has spirit enough, to be sure, to kill off a whole plantation, if I'd let her manage; but she wouldn't get the cheatery out of them."

"Are there no honest ones?"

"Well, now and then one, whom Nature makes so impracticably simple, truthful and faithful, that the worst possible influence can't destroy it. But, you see, from the mother's breast the colored child feels and sees that there are none but underhand ways open to it. It can get along no other way with its parents, its mistress, its young master and missie play-fellows. Cunning and deception become necessary, inevitable habits. It isn't fair to expect anything else of him. He ought not to be punished for it. As to honesty, the slave is kept in that dependent, semi-childish state, that there is no making him realize the rights of property, or feel that his master's goods are not his own, if he can get them. For my part, I don't see how they *can* be honest. Such a fellow as Tom, here, is, – is a moral miracle!"

"And what becomes of their souls?" said Miss Ophelia.

"That isn't my affair, as I know of," said St. Clare; "I am only dealing in facts of the present life. The fact is, that the whole race are pretty generally understood to be turned over to the devil, for our benefit, in this world, however it may turn out in another!"

"This is perfectly horrible!" said Miss Ophelia; "you ought to be ashamed of yourselves!"

"I don't know as I am. We are in pretty good company, for all that," said St. Clare, "as people in the broad road generally are. Look at the high and the low, all the world over, and it's the same story, – the lower class used up, body, soul and spirit, for the good of the upper. It is so in England; it is so everywhere; and yet all Christendom stands aghast, with virtuous indignation, because we do the thing in a little different shape from what they do it."

"It isn't so in Vermont."

"Ah, well, in New England, and in the free States, you have the better of us, I grant. But there's the bell; so, Cousin, let us for a while lay aside our sectional prejudices, and come out to dinner."

As Miss Ophelia was in the kitchen in the latter part of the afternoon, some of the sable children called out, "La, sakes! thar's Prue a coming, grunting along like she allers does."

A tall, bony colored woman now entered the kitchen, bearing on her head a basket of rusks and hot rolls.

"Ho, Prue! you've come," said Dinah.

Prue had a peculiar scowling expression of countenance, and a sullen, grumbling voice. She set down her basket, squatted herself down, and resting her elbows on her knees said,

"O Lord! I wish't I 's dead!"

"Why do you wish you were dead?" said Miss Ophelia.

"I'd be out o' my misery," said the woman, gruffly, without taking her eyes from the floor.

"What need you getting drunk, then, and cutting up, Prue?" said a spruce quadroon chambermaid, dangling, as she spoke, a pair of coral ear-drops.

The woman looked at her with a sour surly glance.

"Maybe you'll come to it, one of these yer days. I'd be glad to see you, I would; then you'll be glad of a drop, like me, to forget your misery."

"Come, Prue," said Dinah, "let's look at your rusks. Here's Missis will pay for them."

Miss Ophelia took out a couple of dozen.

"Thar's some tickets in that ar old cracked jug on the top shelf," said Dinah. "You, Jake, climb up and get it down."

"Tickets, – what are they for?" said Miss Ophelia.

"We buy tickets of her Mas'r, and she gives us bread for 'em."

"And they counts my money and tickets, when I gets home, to see if I 's got the change; and if I han't, they half kills me."

"And serves you right," said Jane, the pert chamber-maid, "if you will take their money to get drunk on. That's what she does, Missis."

"And that's what I *will* do, – I can't live no other ways, – drink and forget my misery."

"You are very wicked and very foolish," said Miss Ophelia, "to steal your master's money to make yourself a brute with."

"It's mighty likely, Missis; but I will do it, – yes, I will. O Lord! I wish I 's dead, I do, – I wish I 's dead, and out of my misery!" and slowly and stiffly the old creature rose, and got her basket on her head again; but before she went out, she looked at the quadroon girt, who still stood playing with her ear-drops.

"Ye think ye're mighty fine with them ar, a frolickin' and a tossin' your head, and a lookin' down on everybody. Well, never mind, – you may live to be a poor, old, cut-up crittur, like me. Hope to the Lord ye will, I do; then see if ye won't drink, – drink, – drink, – yerself into torment; and sarve ye right, too – ugh!" and, with a malignant howl, the woman left the room.

"Disgusting old beast!" said Adolph, who was getting his master's shaving-water. "If I was her master, I'd cut her up worse than she is."

"Ye couldn't do that ar, no ways," said Dinah. "Her back's a far sight now, – she can't never get a dress together over it."

"I think such low creatures ought not to be allowed to go round to genteel families," said Miss Jane. "What do you think, Mr. St. Clare?" she said, coquettishly tossing her head at Adolph.

It must be observed that, among other appropriations from his master's stock, Adolph was in the habit of adopting his name and address; and that the style under which he moved, among the colored circles of New Orleans, was that of *Mr. St. Clare*.

"I'm certainly of your opinion, Miss Benoir," said Adolph.

Benoir was the name of Marie St. Clare's family, and Jane was one of her servants.

"Pray, Miss Benoir, may I be allowed to ask if those drops are for the ball, tomorrow night? They are certainly bewitching!"

"I wonder, now, Mr. St. Clare, what the impudence of you men will come to!" said Jane, tossing her pretty head 'til the ear-drops twinkled again. "I shan't dance with you for a whole evening, if you go to asking me any more questions."

"O, you couldn't be so cruel, now! I was just dying to know whether you would appear in your pink tarletane," said Adolph.

"What is it?" said Rosa, a bright, piquant little quadroon who came skipping down stairs at this moment.

"Why, Mr. St. Clare's so impudent!"

"On my honor," said Adolph, "I'll leave it to Miss Rosa now."

"I know he's always a saucy creature," said Rosa, poising herself on one of her little feet, and looking maliciously at Adolph. "He's always getting me so angry with him."

"O! ladies, ladies, you will certainly break my heart, between you," said Adolph. "I shall be found dead in my bed, some morning, and you'll have it to answer for."

"Do hear the horrid creature talk!" said both ladies, laughing immoderately.

"Come, – clar out, you! I can't have you cluttering up the kitchen," said Dinah; "in my way, foolin' round here."

"Aunt Dinah's glum, because she can't go to the ball," said Rosa.

"Don't want none o' your light-colored balls," said Dinah; "cuttin' round, makin' b'lieve you 's white folks. Arter all, you 's niggers, much as I am."

"Aunt Dinah greases her wool stiff, every day, to make it lie straight," said Jane.

"And it will be wool, after all," said Rosa, maliciously shaking down her long, silky curls.

"Well, in the Lord's sight, an't wool as good as bar, any time?" said Dinah. "I'd like to have Missis say which is worth the most, - a couple such as you, or one like me. Get out wid ye, ye trumpery, - I won't have ye round!"

Here the conversation was interrupted in a two-fold manner. St. Clare's voice was heard at the head of the stairs, asking Adolph if he meant to stay all night with his shaving-water; and Miss Ophelia, coming out of the dining-room, said,

"Jane and Rosa, what are you wasting your time for, here? Go in and attend to your muslins."

Our friend Tom, who had been in the kitchen during the conversation with the old rusk-woman, had followed her out into the street. He saw her go on, giving every once in a while a suppressed groan. At last she set her basket down on a doorstep, and began arranging the old, faded shawl which covered her shoulders.

"I'll carry your basket a piece," said Tom, compassionately.

"Why should ye?" said the woman. "I don't want no help."

"You seem to be sick, or in trouble, or somethin'," said Tom.

"I an't sick," said the woman, shortly.

"I wish," said Tom, looking at her earnestly, – "I wish I could persuade you to leave off drinking. Don't you know it will be the ruin of ye, body and soul?"

"I knows I'm gwine to torment," said the woman, sullenly. "Ye don't need to tell me that ar. I 's ugly, I 's wicked, – I 's gwine straight to torment. O, Lord! I wish I 's thar!"

Tom shuddered at these frightful words, spoken with a sullen, impassioned earnestness.

"O, Lord have mercy on ye! poor crittur. Han't ye never heard of Jesus Christ?"

"Jesus Christ, – who's he?"

"Why, he's *the Lord*," said Tom.

"I think I've hearn tell o' the Lord, and the judgment and torment. I've heard o' that."

"But didn't anybody ever tell you of the Lord Jesus, that loved us poor sinners, and died for us?"

"Don't know nothin' 'bout that," said the woman; "nobody han't never loved me, since my old man died."

"Where was you raised?" said Tom.

"Up in Kentuck. A man kept me to breed chil'en for market, and sold 'em as fast as they got big enough; last of all, he sold me to a speculator, and my Mas'r got me o' him."

"What set you into this bad way of drinkin'?"

"To get shet o' my misery. I had one child after I come here; and I thought then I'd have one to raise, cause Mas'r wasn't a speculator. It was de peartest little thing! and Missis she seemed to think a heap on 't, at first; it never cried, - it was likely and fat. But Missis tuck sick, and I tended her; and I tuck the fever, and my milk all left me, and the child it pined to skin and bone, and Missis wouldn't buy milk for it. She wouldn't hear to me, when I telled her I hadn't milk. She said she knowed I could feed it on what other folks eat; and the child kinder pined, and cried, and cried, and cried, day and night, and got all gone to skin and bones, and Missis got sot agin it and she said 't wan't nothin' but crossness. She wished it was dead, she said; and she wouldn't let me have it o' nights, cause, she said, it kept me awake, and made me good for nothing. She made me sleep in her room; and I had to put it away off in a little kind o' garret, and thar it cried itself to death, one night. It did; and I tuck to drinkin', to keep its crying out of my ears! I did, - and I will drink! I will, if I do go to torment for it! Mas'r says I shall go to torment, and I tell him I've got thar now!"

"O, ye poor crittur!" said Tom, "han't nobody never telled ye how the Lord Jesus loved ye, and died for ye? Han't they telled ye that he'll help ye, and ye can go to heaven, and have rest, at last?"

"I looks like gwine to heaven," said the woman; "an't thar where white folks is gwine? S'pose they'd have me thar? I'd rather go to torment, and get away from Mas'r and Missis. I had *so*," she said, as with her usual groan, she got her basket on her head, and walked sullenly away.

Tom turned, and walked sorrowfully back to the house. In the court he met little Eva, – a crown of tuberoses on her head, and her eyes radiant with delight.

"O, Tom! here you are. I'm glad I've found you. Papa says you may get out the ponies, and take me in my little new carriage," she said, catching his hand. "But what's the matter Tom? – you look sober."

"I feel bad, Miss Eva," said Tom, sorrowfully. "But I'll get the horses for you."

"But do tell me, Tom, what is the matter. I saw you talking to cross old Prue."

Tom, in simple, earnest phrase, told Eva the woman's history. She did not exclaim or wonder, or weep, as other children do. Her cheeks grew pale, and a deep, earnest shadow passed over her eyes. She laid both hands on her bosom, and sighed heavily.

Chapter 19

Miss Ophelia's Experiences and Opinions Continued

"Tom, you needn't get me the horses. I don't want to go," she said.

"Why not, Miss Eva?"

"These things sink into my heart, Tom," said Eva, – "they sink into my heart," she repeated, earnestly. "I don't want to go;" and she turned from Tom, and went into the house.

A few days after, another woman came, in old Prue's place, to bring the rusks; Miss Ophelia was in the kitchen.

"Lor!" said Dinah, "what's got Prue?"

"Prue isn't coming any more," said the woman, mysteriously.

"Why not?" said Dinah, "she an't dead, is she?"

"We doesn't exactly know. She's down cellar," said the woman, glancing at Miss Ophelia.

After Miss Ophelia had taken the rusks, Dinah followed the woman to the door.

"What *has* got Prue, any how?" she said.

The woman seemed desirous, yet reluctant, to speak, and answered, in low, mysterious tone.

"Well, you mustn't tell nobody, Prue, she got drunk agin, - and they had her down cellar, - and thar they left her all day, - and I hearn 'em saying that the *flies had got to her,* - and *she's dead*!"

Dinah held up her hands, and, turning, saw close by her side the spirit-like form of Evangeline, her large, mystic eyes dilated with horror, and every drop of blood driven from her lips and cheeks.

"Lor bless us! Miss Eva's gwine to faint away! What go us all, to let her har such talk? Her pa'll be rail mad."

"I shan't faint, Dinah," said the child, firmly; "and why shouldn't I hear it? It an't so much for me to hear it, as for poor Prue to suffer it."

"*Lor sakes*! it isn't for sweet, delicate young ladies, like you, - these yer stories isn't; it's enough to kill 'em!"

Eva sighed again, and walked up stairs with a slow and melancholy step.

Miss Ophelia anxiously inquired the woman's story. Dinah gave a very garrulous version of it, to which Tom added the particulars which he had drawn from her that morning.

"An abominable business, - perfectly horrible!" she exclaimed, as she entered the room where St. Clare lay reading his paper.

"Pray, what iniquity has turned up now?" said he.

"What now? why, those folks have whipped Prue to death!" said Miss Ophelia, going on, with great strength of detail, into the story, and enlarging on its most shocking particulars.

"I thought it would come to that, some time," said St. Clare, going on with his paper.

"Thought so! – an't you going to *do* anything about it?" said Miss Ophelia. "Haven't you got any *select-men*, or anybody, to interfere and look after such matters?"

"It's commonly supposed that the *property* interest is a sufficient guard in these cases. If people choose to ruin their own possessions, I don't know what's to be done. It seems the poor creature was a thief and a drunkard; and so there won't be much hope to get up sympathy for her."

"It is perfectly outrageous, – it is horrid, Augustine! It will certainly bring down vengeance upon you."

"My dear cousin, I didn't do it, and I can't help it; I would, if I could. If low-minded, brutal people will act like themselves, what am I to do? they have absolute control; they are irresponsible despots. There would be no use in interfering; there is no law that amounts to anything practically, for such a case. The best we can do is to shut our eyes and ears, and let it alone. It's the only resource left us."

"How can you shut your eyes and ears? How can you let such things alone?"

"My dear child, what do you expect? Here is a whole class, - debased, uneducated, indolent, provoking, - put, without any sort of terms or conditions, entirely into the hands of such people as the majority in our world are; people who have neither consideration nor self-control, who haven't even an enlightened regard to their own interest, - for that's the case with the largest half of mankind. Of course, in a community so organized, what can a man of honorable and humane feelings do, but shut his eyes all he can, and harden his heart? I can't buy every poor wretch I see. I can't turn knight-errant, and undertake to redress every individual case of wrong in such a city as this. The most I can do is to try and keep out of the way of it."

St. Clare's fine countenance was for a moment overcast; he said,

"Come, cousin, don't stand there looking like one of the Fates; you've only seen a peep through the curtain, - a specimen of what is going on, the world over, in some shape or other. If we are to be prying and spying into all the dismals of life, we should have no heart to anything. 'T is like looking too close into the details of Dinah's kitchen;" and St. Clare lay back on the sofa, and busied himself with his paper.

Miss Ophelia sat down, and pulled out her knitting-work, and sat there grim with indignation. She knit and knit, but while she mused the fire burned; at last she broke out – "I tell you, Augustine, I can't get over things so, if you can. It's a perfect abomination for you to defend such a system, – that's *my* mind!"

"What now?" said St. Clare, looking up. "At it again, hey?"

"I say it's perfectly abominable for you to defend such a system!" said Miss Ophelia, with increasing warmth.

"*I* defend it, my dear lady? Who ever said I did defend it?" said St. Clare.

"Of course, you defend it, – you all do, – all you Southerners. What do you have slaves for, if you don't?"

"Are you such a sweet innocent as to suppose nobody in this world ever does what they don't think is right? Don't you, or didn't you ever, do anything that you did not think quite right?"

"If I do, I repent of it, I hope," said Miss Ophelia, rattling her needles with energy.

"So do I," said St. Clare, peeling his orange; "I'm repenting of it all the time."

"What do you keep on doing it for?"

"Didn't you ever keep on doing wrong, after you'd repented, my good cousin?"

"Well, only when I've been very much tempted," said Miss Ophelia.

"Well, I'm very much tempted," said St. Clare; "that's just my difficulty."

"But I always resolve I won't and I try to break off."

"Well, I have been resolving I won't, off and on, these ten years," said St. Clare; "but I haven't, some how, got clear. Have you got clear of all your sins, cousin?"

"Cousin Augustine," said Miss Ophelia, seriously, and laying down her knitting-work, "I suppose I deserve that you should reprove my short-comings. I know all you say is true enough; nobody else feels them more than I do; but it does seem to me, after all, there is some difference between me and you. It seems to me I would cut off my right hand sooner than keep on, from day to day, doing what I thought was wrong. But, then, my conduct is so inconsistent with my profession, I don't wonder you reprove me."

"O, now, cousin," said Augustine, sitting down on the floor, and laying his head back in her lap, "don't take on so awfully serious! You know what a good-for-nothing, saucy boy I always was. I love to poke you up, – that's all, – just to see you get earnest. I do think you are desperately, distressingly good; it tires me to death to think of it."

"But this is a serious subject, my boy, Auguste," said Miss Ophelia, laying her hand on his forehead.

"Dismally so," said he; "and I – well, I never want to talk seriously in hot weather. What with mosquitos and all, a fellow can't get himself up to any very sublime moral flights; and I believe," said St. Clare, suddenly rousing himself up, "there's a theory, now! I understand now why northern nations are always more virtuous than southern ones, – I see into that whole subject."

"O, Augustine, you are a sad rattle-brain!"

"Am I? Well, so I am, I suppose; but for once I will be serious, now; but you must hand me that basket of oranges; – you see, you'll have to 'stay me with flagons and comfort me with apples,' if I'm going to make this effort. Now," said Augustine, drawing the basket up, "I'll begin: When, in the course of human events, it becomes necessary for a fellow to hold two or three dozen of his fellow-worms in captivity, a decent regard to the opinions of society requires–"

"I don't see that you are growing more serious," said Miss Ophelia.

"Wait, – I'm coming on, – you'll hear. The short of the matter is, cousin," said he, his handsome face suddenly settling into an earnest and serious expression, "on this abstract question of slavery there can, as I think, be but one opinion. Planters, who have money to make by it, – clergymen, who have planters to please, – politicians, who want to rule by it, – may warp and bend language and ethics to a degree that shall astonish the world at their ingenuity; they can press nature and the Bible, and nobody knows what else, into the service; but, after all, neither they nor the world believe in it one particle the more. It comes from the devil, that's the short of it; – and, to my mind, it's a pretty respectable specimen of what he can do in his own line."

Miss Ophelia stopped her knitting, and looked surprised, and St. Clare, apparently enjoying her astonishment, went on.

"You seem to wonder; but if you will get me fairly at it, I'll make a clean breast of it. This cursed business, accursed of God and man, what is it? Strip it of all its ornament, run it down to the root and nucleus of the whole, and what is it? Why, because my brother Quashy is ignorant and weak, and I am intelligent and strong, – because I know how, and *can* do it, – therefore, I may steal all he has, keep it, and give him only such and so much as suits my fancy. Whatever is too hard, too dirty, too disagreeable, for me, I may set Quashy to doing. Because I don't like work, Quashy shall work. Because the sun burns me, Quashy shall stay in the sun. Quashy shall earn the money, and I will spend it. Quashy shall lie down in every puddle, that I may walk over dry-shod. Quashy shall do my will, and not his, all the days of his mortal life, and have such chance of getting to heaven, at last, as I find convenient. This I take to be about what slavery *is*. I defy anybody on earth to read our slave-code, as it stands in our law-books, and make anything else of it. Talk of the *abuses* of slavery! Humbug! The *thing itself* is the essence of all abuse! And the only reason why the land don't sink under it, like Sodom and Gomorrah, is because it is *used* in a way infinitely better than it is. For pity's sake, for shame's sake, because we are men born of women, and not savage beasts, many of us do not, and dare not, – we would *scorn* to use the full power which our savage laws put into our hands. And he who goes the furthest, and does the worst, only uses within limits the power that the law gives him."

St. Clare had started up, and, as his manner was when excited, was walking, with hurried steps, up and down the floor. His fine face, classic as that of a Greek statue, seemed actually to burn with the fervor of his feelings. His large blue eyes flashed, and he gestured with an unconscious eagerness. Miss Ophelia had never seen him in this mood before, and she sat perfectly silent.

"I declare to you," said he, suddenly stopping before his cousin "(It's no sort of use to talk or to feel on this subject), but I declare to you, there have been times when I have thought, if the whole country would sink, and hide all this injustice and misery from the light, I would willingly sink with it. When I have been travelling up and down on our boats, or about on my collecting tours, and reflected that every brutal, disgusting, mean, low-lived fellow I met, was allowed by our laws to become absolute despot of as many men, women and children, as he could cheat, steal, or gamble money enough to buy, – when I have seen such men in actual ownership of helpless children, of young girls and women, – I have been ready to curse my country, to curse the human race!"

"Augustine! Augustine!" said Miss Ophelia, "I'm sure you've said enough. I never, in my life, heard anything like this, even at the North."

"At the North!" said St. Clare, with a sudden change of expression, and resuming something of his habitual careless tone. "Pooh! your northern folks are cold-blooded; you are cool in everything! You can't begin to curse up hill and down as we can, when we get fairly at it."

"Well, but the question is," said Miss Ophelia.

"O, yes, to be sure, the *question is*, – and a deuce of a question it is! How came *you* in this state of sin and misery? Well, I shall answer in the good old words you used to teach me, Sundays. I came so by ordinary generation. My servants were my father's, and, what is more, my mother's; and now they are mine, they and their increase, which bids fair to be a pretty considerable item. My father, you know, came first from New England; and he was just such another man as your father, – a regular old Roman, – upright, energetic, noble-minded, with an iron will. Your father settled down in New England, to rule over rocks and stones, and to force an existence out of Nature; and mine settled in Louisiana, to rule over men and women, and force existence out of them. My mother," said St. Clare, getting up and walking to a picture at the end of the room, and gazing upward with a face fervent with veneration, "*she was divine!* Don't look at me so! – you know what I mean! She probably was of mortal birth; but, as far as ever I could observe, there was no trace of any human weakness or error about her; and everybody that lives to remember her, whether bond or free, servant, acquaintance, relation, all say the same. Why, cousin, that mother has been all that has stood between me and utter unbelief for years. She was a direct embodiment and personification of the New Testament, – a living fact, to be accounted for, and to be accounted for in no other way than by its truth. O, mother! mother!" said St. Clare, clasping his hands, in a sort of transport; and then suddenly checking himself, he came back, and seating himself on an ottoman, he went on:

(Continued in the next Volume)

Books For ALL Kinds of Readers

At ReadHowYouWant we understand that one size does not fit all types of readers. Our innovative, patent pending technology allows us to design new formats to make reading easier and more enjoyable for you. This helps improve your speed of reading and your comprehension. Our EasyRead printed books have been optimized to improve word recognition, ease eye tracking by adjusting word and line spacing as well as minimizing hyphenation. Our EasyRead SuperLarge editions have been developed to make reading easier and more accessible for vision-impaired readers. We offer Braille and DAISY formats of our books and all popular E-Book formats.

We are continually introducing new formats based upon research and reader preferences. Visit our web-site to see all of our formats and learn how you can Personalize our books for yourself or as gifts. Sign up to Become A RHYW Registered Reader.

www.readhowyouwant.com

Printed in Great Britain by
Amazon.co.uk, Ltd.,
Marston Gate.